Time slowed as Venduss watched them gallop closer. Bright magic sparkled over every inch of their silvery armor. Sparks leapt at the crash of hoofbeats. The officer in the lead raised the visor of his helmet and Venduss recognized the intense gaze of Montenegro himself. He was shouting something inaudible in the chaos. He waved his shield arm as if warning Venduss of danger.

When the sorcerers began their assault on the smoke cauldron, Venduss realized his error in timing. Like molasses were his movements as he scrambled over the pipes and levers of the war machine, while torrents of lightning and flaming stones smashed into the heavy iron. Hard sounds cracked the air. Geysers of smoke and fire rocketed from gaps where seams burst their rivets. Then the wave of charging knights rammed their lances into the machine. Enchanted tips punctured the boiler in a neat row, drawing a scream from the twisting metal as internal pressure ripped it apart. . . .

A line of mounted knights
had begun a second charge.

ULTIMA™

THE TECHNOCRAT WAR

BOOK II OF III
MASQUERADE

AUSTEN ANDREWS

POCKET BOOKS

New York   London   Toronto   Sydney   Singapore

This book is a work of fiction. Names, characters, places, and incidents are products of the author's imagination or are used fictitiously. Any resemblance to actual events or locales or persons, living or dead, is entirely coincidental.

An *Original* Publication of POCKET BOOKS

POCKET BOOKS, a division of Simon & Schuster, Inc.
1230 Avenue of the Americas, New York, NY 10020

Copyright © 2002 by Electronic Arts

ISBN: 0-7434-0380-0

First Pocket Books printing January 2002

10 9 8 7 6 5 4 3 2 1

POCKET and colophon are registered trademarks of Simon & Schuster, Inc.

For information regarding special discounts for bulk purchases, please contact Simon & Schuster Special Sales at 1-800-456-6798 or business@simonandschuster.com

Front cover illustration by Jerry Vanderstelt

Printed in the U.S.A.

for the team

ACKNOWLEDGMENTS

Sosaria, as it appears in *The Technocrat War*, is the synthesis of many extraordinary talents. Armand de Orive, Andy Hoyos, Starr Long, Damion Schubert and the entire team on the Origin project deserve credit for dreaming the world in which I am privileged to write.

Thanks also go out to the Ultima Online team at Origin Systems, who picked up the ball and ran with it. And of course we owe everything to the "Lost King" himself, who flapped his wings in Texas and sent hurricanes around the world.

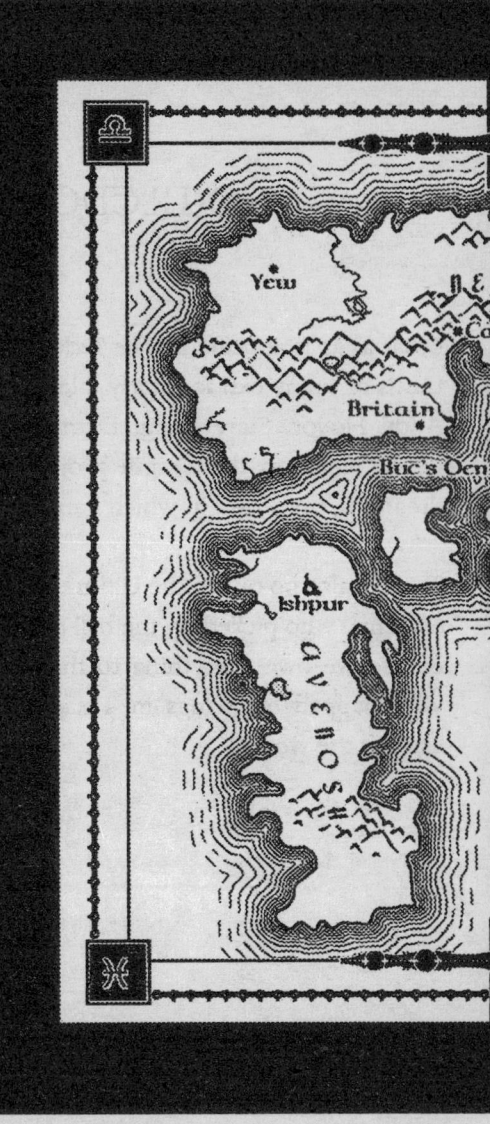

CHAPTER
1

The Viper of Levanto

U nder a lavish, tropical starscape, the
knight Montenegro stood motionless among the ramshackle boardwalks of Port Levanto. A windblown cloak
swathed him in black wool, allowing only glimpses of the
steel armor he wore underneath. His hand rested on the hilt
of his sword. His eyes blended into the darkness of midnight.

The buccaneer town was a boneyard of driftwood and
dead ships and stooped palm trees. Cracked, rickety houses
slouched against the grit of the ocean wind. Mounds of sand
and splashes of moonlight glazed the port with a wan, skeletal pallor. The surf rolled and slobbered at the shore.
Unclean scents and sounds gathered in leeward hollows,
where things that washed up from the sea lurked or rotted,
unmolested by the town's inhabitants. A consortium of
rangy cats stalked the gloom.

Starry candle flames gleamed in a scattering of windows.
The restless, rancid air flustered with tiny noises, like the
sounds of distant revelry or of swift, muffled murders.

Montenegro's back was to the harbor, where the dark

water reflected the lanterns of many tall ships. Furtive silhouettes creaked past him on the boardwalk, but the knight paid them little heed. His gaze was fixed on the dilapidated hall in front of him. The sign over the door pictured two tumbling dice. The clamor of a casino spilled out from unshuttered windows.

A figure appeared beside him. The brown-skinned man wore a full coat in the buccaneer style and a plumed hat on his head. He smelled of exotic spices. A long feline shape lounged across his shoulders.

Montenegro murmured, "Is it done?"

The sailor nodded. "You're sure he's in there?"

The knight glanced at the door of the casino. A tiny geometric symbol had been carved into the top corner. "I am absolutely sure."

The sailor fingered his cat's ears. "Good, 'cause I want this to go quick. My crew and I are dead men if we haven't set sail inside of an hour."

"Don't worry, Bawdewyn. I don't intend to tarry." He turned a somber glance on the man. "Relax, Captain. You serve the Virtue of Justice tonight. And if that is not currency enough for your troubled soul, your pardons and letters of marque are waiting for you at Vesper."

"I trust your word, Montenegro. I only hope I'm alive to collect them, hey?"

Montenegro twitched a momentary grin. "To die with Honor is to die with glory. The end is not unwelcome if you walk the path of Virtue. Don't you agree?"

Bawdewyn grimaced. "That's something you don't hear much on this island. And yeah, I do agree. Now shut up and let's do this. Annis is anxious to get to sea."

The oversize cat rumbled at its name.

The knight's grin vanished. He flexed the fingers of his sword hand. His metal gauntlet clicked at the motion. "Right. Move your people in."

The door to the casino rasped in complaint as Montenegro pulled it open. A tumble of pipe smoke spilled out. His nose wrinkled at the miasma of odors, of sweat and stale tobacco and cheap liquor. The room was warm with haze and body heat. Then the cool sea wind rushed past him and into the gambling hall, swirling his cloak and flickering lamps and candles. Thirty disheveled men and women looked up from their cards and coins. At the sight of Montenegro, they fell silent. In the corner, a one-eyed musician nudged his lute into a wooden chest, where it might evade harm.

Montenegro scanned the room. The man he sought was not difficult to find. In the far corner, at a table near an open window, sat the largest person in the hall. Scarves fluttered across his loose, exotic clothing. The Juka's skin was the color of kelp. His long face was cold and rugged. The squat horns on his brow had been shaved to a fine point. His tiny eyes glinted like a knife.

Around his neck he wore a silver pendant, in the shape of a wriggling snake.

Montenegro's gut churned at the sight. His mouth was dry as he growled, "I seek the Viper of Levanto. I am here for Justice."

The Juka opened a chilling smile. "Montenegro! It's about time you tracked me down again. But you came without a platoon of knights? Not even a sorcerer to back you up?"

"I have Truth on my side," said Montenegro, "and this." From his scabbard he withdrew a black longsword. The blade rang like a faraway bell. Its steel gleamed like obsidian.

The room tensed. "You know this sword and you know why I've brought it. Make your peace with whatever power you serve. I shall meet you outside or I shall tear down this casino around you. I give you that choice, Pikas of Logosia."

A younger, smaller human was sitting at the table beside the Juka. His blond hair and white silk clothes were unusually clean compared to his fellow patrons. With unflinching ease the man interjected, "Sir Gabriel Montenegro, isn't it? My name is Mister Chase. I am a representative of the guild that runs this island." He bowed his head cordially. "You must have eliminated my guards outside, or you would not be standing in that doorway. That distresses me."

The knight smiled. "Captain Bawdewyn gave your henchmen the night off."

Chase squinted. "Bawdewyn and his crew did that?"

Behind Montenegro, the tall buccaneer stepped into the casino. In the glow of the room his wildcat Annis raised her spotted hackles. "Believe it," said the sailor. "I can show you proof, but there are ladies present."

The blond man leaned back in his chair. "I see. Interesting. Then you have subscribed to your own death, Captain. But that is a matter for another day. Pikas, I believe you must go with this knight."

The Juka chuckled and furrowed his brow. "No, I don't. He can't touch me here. I answer to no one but Anzo, just like you, Chase. Why are you humoring him?"

Montenegro stepped closer. "Because I'm here to avenge the murder of Lord Valente, one year ago tonight."

"An assassination," Mister Chase added, "which you undertook before Anzo hired you as his enforcer, Pikas. Since you killed Valente without guild sanction, I'm afraid we can't help you. Do try to face the consequences with

4

some dignity." He nodded to Montenegro. "I wondered if you would play this hand, sir. Your cunning does credit to your courage."

The knight snorted. "I don't want your praise. I want him."

"He is yours, if you can take him."

Pikas glowered at Chase. "You know I'm not a man you want to upset."

The blond human nodded briefly. "I have accounted for that, of course." A soft *clack* leapt through the air. In Chase's grip rested a hand weapon consisting of levers and springs. Montenegro recognized it as a Technocrat bolt-thrower. The point of a crossbow quarrel jutted from the tip, aimed at the Juka's face. "Please conclude your business with this knight. If you are still alive afterward, you and I can review our working relationship, mmm?"

In a burst of motion Pikas kicked over the table and leapt for the window.

Montenegro was charging forward even before he registered what had occurred. The force of the Juka's movement had knocked Chase backward over his chair. As Montenegro sprang across the fallen table, he passed through a ribbon of blood slung by Pikas's quickly drawn blade. From the corner of his eye the knight spotted the Technocrat bolt-thrower tumbling through the air. Chase's severed fist still clung to the unfired weapon.

Montenegro thrust his sword at Pikas. The black steel hurtled forward like a war hound on a leash. The Jukan assassin had perched in the open window, facing out; with a snarl he somersaulted backward and over Montenegro's strike. He landed in a handstand and flipped toward the center of the room.

The knight's black sword slammed against the window frame. Brittle wood snapped and splintered. Outside the window he saw a formation of sailors brandishing spears: Bawdewyn's crewmen, deployed to keep Pikas from escaping. Pikemen surrounded the building, securing every window and door. Montenegro flashed them an approving look before he wheeled to face the casino again.

The gambling hall was in chaos. Loose coins and cards spilled across the boardwalk floor. Sweaty patrons clambered into corners and behind tables. Their cries resounded in the cramped space. Captain Bawdewyn warned them back with a wave of his scoop-hilted cutlass.

Montenegro saw Pikas dart for the farthest window, halting at a wall of speartips outside. The assassin cursed and jumped atop a bar made of old shipping crates, which groaned under his weight. His glare was that of a caged predator.

The knight stroked the air with his ebon sword. "The famous Viper of Levanto fears a single knight! But every warrior knows that assassins drink the finest vintage of cowardice."

Pikas bared his teeth. A scimitar glinted in his grasp. "Drop that hellish blade and I'll drink the wine straight from your veins!"

The knight smirked and shook his head. "I have no control over the sword's enchantment. Starfell wants to avenge Lord Valente almost as much as I do. I'm afraid neither it nor I shall listen to reason in this matter."

The assassin leapt like an attacking animal. Something in his off hand spat flames. Montenegro swung the longsword named Starfell to smash the fiery object out of the air. It was a crystal lantern, which shattered and set its fuel ablaze. The knight was drenched with flames. Then the Juka's whirling kick bashed him in the chest. Montenegro flew backward. Rickety boards cracked when he slammed against the wall.

He dared to glance down. Burning oil licked his hip and his leg. An instant later he whirled Starfell in the path of Pikas's oncoming scimitar. The assassin's loose scarves swam in a dazzling flurry. Montenegro rang out a sequence of five parries in the span of a single breath. He slashed a riposte. They traded cuts and blocks, pounding the hall with a harsh metallic clamor. Then he felt an overextension. He had time only to wince.

Pikas hacked at a seam in the plate armor under Montenegro's arm. The blow felt like a hammer. He knew the artery was severed. Spikes of pain lanced the knight's torso. He heard himself growl as he threw a punch into the assassin's gut, then followed with a snap kick that shoved the Juka away.

The spray of blood from Montenegro's wound doused the sputtering flames on his leg.

He ground his teeth. "That was your one shot, murderer. You had best hope it's fatal." Ignoring the cold horror of the cut, he pushed his weight into another charge.

Pikas sprang backward in a tumbling dodge. Montenegro carved the air with elaborate strokes as the assassin ducked and contorted. The Juka's scimitar crashed against the knight's armor in several places. Montenegro barely felt the blows. Fury drove him onward. When Pikas kicked off the wall to leap away from a strike, the knight lashed out with such vigor that Starfell plowed through the weathered boards in a cascade of splinters, then chopped into a support post. One corner of the casino roof lurched down several feet.

The huddled onlookers protested as roof slates shattered around them. Bawdewyn hunched under the wide brim of his hat.

Montenegro flung back his swirling cape and extended a long, quick thrust. Pikas blocked it, but had no answer for the knight's return stroke. Starfell caught the assassin's abdomen, peeled open the leather armor under his shirt and sliced a groove in the Juka's flesh. Montenegro closed with a pirouette and jammed his swordpoint into Pikas's gut.

The world exploded. Montenegro felt himself falling on his back. He tasted blood and realized that the assassin had kicked or punched him. Pain knifed through his face. His jaw had been crushed.

Staggering, Pikas clutched one hand to a savaged belly as he raised his scimitar for a blow Montenegro could not avoid. Then the Juka howled and fell abruptly to his knees. A crossbow quarrel jutted from his neck.

In the corner stood Mister Chase, holding the bolt-thrower in his single hand. A frightened woman was bandaging his sundered wrist. Chase's white silk clothes were stained crimson.

"I am sorry if I upset you, Pikas," said the young man, his face agleam with sweat.

The Juka hissed as he jumped straight up and scrambled across a ceiling beam.

Montenegro kicked his legs to stand. His head pounded like a drum. For an instant he was blind, yet he wheeled Starfell overhead in the Juka's direction. The sword connected with the wooden rafter and sheared it in half. Just as Montenegro's eyesight returned, the roof of the decrepit gambling hall collapsed.

The casino patrons shrieked and clamored. With a grunt

Montenegro tossed away the heavy debris that covered him. He was now standing outside, in the midst of a matchstick pile of broken wood and slate shingles. Fires started to smolder around him.

A few dozen of Bawdewyn's crewmen were scrambling around the boardwalk. Montenegro opened his mouth to shout a command, but his shattered jaw mangled the words. With a snarl he fished a glass vial from a bag at his waist. Painfully he slurped the tangy contents. Warm pressure pulsed through his flesh. In seconds the healing potion stitched together his jawbone and relieved the frosty ache from the wound under his arm. Strength returned to his limbs.

"Which way?" he bellowed to Captain Bawdewyn, just as he saw the answer for himself. A string of corpses marked the path where sailors had intercepted the fleeing assassin. Montenegro followed bloody footprints to an open trapdoor underneath the boardwalk, through which Pikas had ducked.

A small, geometric symbol was carved on a plank beside the opening. As the knight peered into the rancid gloom, Bawdewyn leaned over him. His overcoat was calico with dirt and sand from the casino roof. "I see your accomplice won't let him get away," he muttered with an irate edge.

Montenegro braced himself to confront the stench heaving up from the trapdoor. He brushed his thumb over the carved symbol. "She is the only reason I found him here."

"I hope she can do more than just track the man, 'cause I can't help you anymore. The lads from the *Blackjack* and the *Scarlet Lady* are headed this way and they ain't coming to play cards. I'm pulling back to my ship before any more of my people die. You want to come, too?"

"Not when I'm this close. Didn't you notice? Chase's bolt was poisoned. This ends tonight."

The buccaneer slapped Montenegro on the shoulder, then stood and cradled his wildcat in one arm. "You just remember what they say about cornered animals, hey? If I don't see you tonight, I'll see you in Vesper. Go with Virtue, Sir Gabriel."

Montenegro nodded, though he did not turn away from the trapdoor. Instead, he sucked in a deep breath and jumped down the hole, into a blackness as rotten as it was opaque.

His boots sank into a vile sludge that burped rancid smells at the disturbance. The cool mud came almost to his knees. Though he could see nothing in the dark, Montenegro knew he was standing in a bog that spanned the breadth of Port Levanto's boardwalks, like a foul shadow. The muck was a foamy stew of sewage, decomposing fish, stagnant water and whatever garbage and corpses the sea regurgitated onto the shore. Sickly waves slurped the filth not far from where Montenegro had landed. As his eyes adjusted to the gloom, he could almost make out the spumy breakers.

Something was moving among them.

"The pirosohmoi are skittish tonight," said a voice from farther ashore. Montenegro lunged to the side and searched for a glimpse of Pikas. He had not brought a torch with him, as it would have given the assassin a clear target; but he wished now for a light to fling in the direction of his enemy.

He crouched and squinted. Seeing nothing, he answered, "Pirosohmoi don't come on land or I would have left you to them."

"Who says they don't? You haven't met the tribe that lives in these waters. They'll crawl through this muck to get their hands on you. Nasty creatures. They even have shamans."

Montenegro could not pinpoint the Juka's voice. It

seemed to roll through the blackness like the soft thunder of waves. He shook his head, flinched at the sour air. "I have heard the legends. But you're not a man of words, Pikas. This conversation reveals your weakness. Has Chase's poison turned your body to lead?"

A snort rang out. "Britannian poisons. They don't deserve to be called that. Come to Logosia and I'll show you what real poisons do."

The knight stepped away from the water. Something underfoot grabbed his ankle. He tensed, then freed his boot from the clinging muck. "Don't try to bluff. If you had the strength to kill me, I'd be dead right now."

"Nah, I'm just waiting for a friend."

Montenegro strained his ears for any revealing sound. Somewhere ahead, he imagined cautious footsteps. "I think you lost your only friend in the casino. You're a walking corpse at the Den now."

"I was finished with Anzo anyway. I got a better offer."

Then the darkness tore apart in a fiery blaze. Montenegro arched aside as a pillar of flame roared at him. He sprawled in the calf-deep slime and choked when it slopped over his face. Muck steamed from the heat.

The flame vanished in a twist of smoke.

Twenty yards away, within a globe of unearthly red light, stood a corpulent man wearing a long robe. His thick beard was braided into multiple strands. Atop his head perched a wide-brimmed hat, decorated with a horse's tail. A satchel draped over his shoulder. A smoking staff in his hand radiated the magical light.

His eyes seethed like hot metal.

From the darkness Pikas called out, "You missed him, Grynholt! I told you, he's not as slow as the other knights."

The sorcerer barked, "Shut your frog hole! I know how to do my job."

"I'm not good at long waits, petalskin."

Montenegro grimaced as he labored to sneak through the filth. He had not anticipated Pikas allying with a spellcaster. All evidence had suggested that the Logosian was afraid of sorcery. Montenegro quickly reconsidered his tactics. Though this Grynholt appeared to be a skilled fire mage, the knight had in his career defeated wizards whose mastery was renowned. He knew he could still win. Unfortunately, it might be a lot more painful than he had expected.

The chill slime tugged at his legs again. This time he could not seem to pull free. When his knee exploded with pain he knew a pirosohmo had crawled ashore and clawed him with some jagged weapon. Despite himself he cried out in pain, then sliced the dark air with Starfell. The magic blade split a scaly, unseen arm. The merman bleated an inhuman shriek and let go. Its fins slapped the mud as it squirmed back to the waterline.

Then a scarlet light enveloped Montenegro. In a flash his steel armor glowed hot. His soggy cloak threw off steam and smoke. Where his skin touched metal it screamed burning agony. He bellowed fiercely and whirled to face Grynholt, whose sorcery gushed from his fingertips in roiling, smoky streams.

"Enough!" barked the knight as he slogged forward, despite his tortured flesh. He was a glowing spectre plunging through the murk. But his knee failed where the pirosohmo had cut him. He dropped onto all fours. His earlier healing potion had not entirely repaired the damage he had sustained in the casino. Now he was fast losing his grip on consciousness. Quickly he plunged beneath the cold, wet muck and snatched a heartbeat's respite from the pain. Then he gathered his legs under him and rose to try again.

His armor abruptly cooled when fierce white light crackled underneath the boardwalk. A silhouette in a rippling skirt stood tall among the high crossbeams, ejecting a bolt of lightning from a stout metal device. In a curl of smoke the woman blasted Grynholt, whose spells wavered as he shouted a surprised curse. After several seconds the burly wizard fell. Then the bright lightning was gone, and so was the woman.

Montenegro felt a smile cross his face. He pushed forward in the direction of Grynholt's toppled, glowing staff.

"Dammit, sister!" snapped Pikas from the gloom. "You're wearing a miner's monocle, aren't you? I'm going to enjoy killing you for it!"

Then the wizard's light blinked out. The pit under the boardwalks slumped into coal darkness once more.

Quiet settled heavily, but for the surf lapping the mud with its frothy tongue. Montenegro knelt and caught his breath. His skin continued to burn from its wounds. He mashed shut his eyes and tried to subsume the pain.

Something brushed against his cheek. He shot upright and whipped Starfell to a guard position. Then he paused. A small hand had caressed him.

A nearby whisper shushed him. "They're gone. You need to leave, too. The pirates will come down here soon."

Montenegro heaved a tired sigh, then hissed at a streak of pain under his chestplate. "I would berate you for not helping sooner, Raveka, but I don't feel I can criticize your timing."

The woman's voice answered, "You cannot, of course. I

had limited fuel for my static scourge. I believe I employed it judiciously."

"So you did. Who the hell was that fire mage?"

"I don't know, but he saved Pikas's skin. You were right. Pikas was bluffing. Between your blows and Mister Chase's poison, he was in agony. It took all his strength to haul that barrel of a wizard out of here."

"You could see them in this murk?"

"I'm wearing a miner's monocle. It is another of Blackthorn's devices, which your sorcerers find more foul than this bog."

He clenched his gauntleted fist. "Then why didn't you follow them? Pikas is nearly down!"

"Pikas had an excellent escape route. Besides, I would not want to rob you of the killing stroke, hey?"

Montenegro pursed his lips. From the tone of Raveka's words, he knew that she had a logical reason. He also knew that she would not divulge it. But he trusted her decision, despite his disappointment.

He opened his hand and reached through the darkness. "As long as you're able to see in the dark, help me out of this pit."

"Captain Bawdewyn's got a bath and a healer on board the *Menagerie*. Seek your solace there. Hurry and you might catch him."

"A Technocrat's compassion, cold and functional as a machine. But you have two halves, Sister Raveka, a Technocrat and a Britannian woman. There's more of New Britannia in your blood than you want to believe. You should come back to Cove with me."

Her smile was audible. "You might be surprised what I want to believe, Gabriel Montenegro."

The knight considered a grin. "And what now for you? Will you pick up the trail of the Viper again tomorrow?"

"I do have other business besides plotting your revenge. The Juka Clans are invading my lands. It is time I returned home for a while."

"New Britannia is allied with the Clans. I would be unhappy to hear that you harmed any of my people."

A warm fingertip pressed against his lips. "Hush, or the pirates will hear."

Montenegro eased Starfell forward. The point nudged against what he presumed was her chest. "I could take you with me by force. I'd be a hero in the Senate if I captured a Technocrat spy."

She laughed. The motion shook the tip of the sword. *"Beza rhem,"* she murmured. Then she vanished, a shadow in the dark.

He lifted Starfell unseen before his face. His voice lowered to a sonorous pitch. "And so the pursuit of Justice continues, my lord." He spoke to the memory of Lord Valente, the noble leader of the House of the Lion whom Pikas had slain a year earlier. Montenegro owed much to the murdered nobleman. Valente had championed him when the rest of New Britannia clamored to throw him into prison. The knight could do no less than to wield Starfell, Valente's enchanted sword, on the path of the Virtue of Justice. He would slay the assassin or die from the effort.

Generations ago the Lost King had defined the eight Virtues as ethical beacons for the people of Britannia: Honor, Justice, Sacrifice, Compassion, Humility, Honesty, Spirituality and Valor. In the eighty-eight years since the Cataclysm tore the world apart, the Virtues had assumed even greater importance. Montenegro's grandfather, the legendary Sir Lazaro, had achieved the highest degree of respect for his adherence to those ideals. But the Cataclysm took his life, even as it did the Lost King himself. Sir Gabriel Montenegro intended to recapture the glory of his honored name. The Virtues showed the only path to that destiny, a fact that Lord Valente's murder had revealed to him.

Presently Sister Raveka was the greatest benefactor of his enlightenment. Indeed, it was she who had enabled Pikas to assassinate Valente in the first place, but in the time since the deed she had worked with Montenegro in secret to hunt down the renegade Logosian. The knight's instincts told him she was sincere in her quest for atonement. He wanted to believe his instincts. So he applied the Virtue of Compassion to her case.

He was, after all, the last person to deny someone a chance for redemption. Besides, there would be time enough for Raveka's punishment once Pikas was dead.

He found the ladder and climbed up to the trapdoor. Fresh air was nectar on his tongue. As he stumbled past the flaming cinders of the gambling hall, bystanders and angry pirates avoided the man whose cloak and hood were caked with filth. A bank of dinghies was moored to a low pier. He took one and began to row in the direction of the barquentine *Menagerie,* which was gently gliding out to sea. Other tall ships were unfurling their great sails, in preparation for pursuit.

On the ramshackle boardwalks of Port Levanto, a one-eyed musician sat on a post plucking his lute, while tall flames capered to the lively tune.

The lurch of the sea made constellations sway in the dark skies of early morning. Montenegro steadied himself on the baroque frame of a large window that dominated the ship's cabin. The narrow bedroom displayed rich appointments of silk and gold and lush tapestry, crowding every inch of space. Clove incense tinged the humid air. The rolling creak of the *Menagerie* sounded like a chorus of wooden frogs.

The knight stared at two lights blinking in the distance.

Captain Bawdewyn reclined in a velvet chair, his tall boots propped on a desk. A ledger lay open under the half-furled rolltop. The wildcat Annis stretched across the hutch and stared with enormous eyes at a tawny dog under the sailor's chair. Bawdewyn leaned down to pinch one of the dog's pointed ears. The animal squealed and nipped back.

The captain grimaced. "Come away from that window, Montenegro. You're making Kiye skittish."

"Then you shouldn't keep feral pets."

"They ain't feral. Feral is like an alleycat. Annis here is an ocelot and Kiye is a coyote. They're *wild* animals."

Montenegro rolled his eyes. "Ah, the subtleties of nondo-mestication. It's truly a shame you're leaving piracy, you know. You have a gift for civilized barbarity."

"Ha! I've had enough of Anzo's barbarity, I can tell you that. 'Pirate King,' my hind-end. He's nothing but a very enterprising extortionist." The sailor waved a long-fingered hand. "Now come sit down. Those galleons ain't gonna catch us. Square-riggers can't make half our speed sailing into the wind. Pour yourself some rum and relax."

"I don't drink."

Bawdewyn pinched his eyebrows together. "Sit down anyway. You and me have got to talk about something."

The knight darkened his expression as he turned away from the window. "What's on your mind, Captain?"

"That Technocrat woman you deal with."

"What about her?"

"She's using you as a pawn."

Montenegro eased into an intricately carved chair. "Of course she is."

"I can tell by your face, she's trying to seduce you."

"Undoubtedly."

"And you're walking right into her net? Why? Did you forget she's on the enemy's side?"

"Your concern is touching, but I know exactly what I am getting into. Right now she and I want the same thing. Pikas of Enclave. On that score I can trust her without reservation. Can you say the same about your fellow buccaneers?"

The captain spat a derisive sound as he poured rum into a mug. "That was a cheap shot."

"No, it wasn't. Trust is a precious thing, Captain. It's an essential component of Spirituality—trust in the Virtues and in yourself. It's not something I often make light of."

"Okay, you want to talk about trusting that Technocrat? I've got another question and you won't want to answer it."

"I'm listening."

"If this woman is so good at what she does, how come you've cornered the Viper three times in the past year and never taken him down? Her traps don't seem to close quick enough."

The knight frowned. "Because Pikas is good at what *he* does. You saw him. It's like trying to catch a fish with your bare hands."

"Yeah. Or maybe this Technocrat ain't as trustworthy as you think she is."

He paused before saying, "You're wrong. Time will prove that. See if you can refrain from talking about her in the

18

meantime, Captain Bawdewyn. I agreed to this arrangement because I was led to believe I could rely on your discretion."

The captain swallowed a tongue of liquor. "Don't get like that. I walk with Honor, the same as you. I just don't want to see a decent fellow stick his head in a noose."

Montenegro steepled his fingers. "She plays her cards and I shall play mine. When it's over we'll see which one trumps the other."

"Uh-huh. But I say you should stick to training with those war masters from Jukaran. You can trust them. Leave the Logosians in Logosia."

"You can't trust all Jukan masters. Believe me." The knight smirked. "In point of fact, I might visit Logosia myself soon. I've got fifty knights who would break down their stalls for a chance to fight the Technocrat army toe-to-toe. I'm thinking of taking them to Garron as a strike force."

"I thought you said you lost your command."

"I did. We won't be sanctioned by the Senate. Rather call us mercenaries whose fee is paid in glory and experience."

"And if you're successful, maybe General Nathaniel will give you a real command, hey?"

Montenegro smiled. "I'll have more knowledge of Black-thorn's war machines than any other New Britannian."

The captain raised his eyebrows. "And let me guess—your Technocrat lady is going back to Logosia, too, ain't she?"

The knight glanced away for a fraction of a second.

Bawdewyn opened a wide grin and chanted:

Gabriel was a fearsome rapscallion,
Wild and free as a Ravenmoor stallion
Hitched up his reins to a fair maiden's skirt
And lived out his life dragging plows through the dirt!

His laugh shook the timbers of the cabin. Then he raised his mug to the languid wildcat. "You and me are going to be privateers, Annis! Here's to the yoke of legitimacy." He tipped back the remainder of his rum, then blew a sharp breath at the ocelot. She squinted and flattened her ears.

The knight played an ironic smile over his lips, but it did not look entirely natural.

CHAPTER
2

Battle at Enclave

The Logosian port of Enclave lay in a precise, geometric arrangement, like the chassis of a huge machine. Each stone wall and smokestack and metal paving slab answered some specific purpose to the design of the settlement. The buildings were stark, angular; constructed for maximum integrity. Copper pipes negotiated perfect arcs to join the structures together. The streets were planes of granite and steel. Drawbridge piers kissed the pearl-grey sea. Though decades of soot and dust patterned every surface, Enclave remained a sleek example of meticulous Technocrat engineering.

So mathematical was the execution of the town that the trenchant Logosian winds, when blowing through at a certain angle, conjured several octaves of pure metallic resonance in a chorus that sang to the ocean.

Thulann of Garron listened to that luxurious drone from a low balcony inside the town. The notes rang deep in her chest. They felt plaintive, dolorous, like the wail of an abandoned hound. She scanned the barren streets. Indeed, Enclave was empty of its human and Jukan builders. The

Technocrats had fled west from an invading Garronite army. Thulann's people now occupied the town, staked along its borders.

She imagined that the buildings knew, in some inanimate way, that their masters were gone.

Though the Jukan Clans had controlled Enclave for more than a month, Thulann had not yet grown accustomed to the stolid architecture of the Technocrats. The shapes and angles were too calculated. The buildings were bereft of ornamentation. They did not lack in detail, but rather the mechanical necessities—rivets and girders, scaffolds and pipes—defined their character. Though the style admitted to Jukan and human origins, it was as if the Technocrats had surrendered all heritage to the aesthetic of the Machine, the strange, cold philosophy at the center of their religion.

The notion offended Thulann. Her people had a proud, assertive culture. The chieftains of Garron stood tall and brazen. Their achievements had come through sweat and strong hands. Even Thulann herself, whose life was spent mastering the sober discipline of the Way, could not imagine dissociating herself from the glory she had achieved.

She wondered what sort of people the Logosians were, these Juka and humans, intermingled under a dark technocracy. How could they live so disconnected from history and passion and the rich, organic world? Did they dream of gears and numbers at night?

There was only one explanation. The Logosians had been misguided by their mad leader, Blackthorn, whom they called the Techno-Prophet. As the armies of Garron took bloody control of each new Technocrat territory, Thulann consoled herself that her people were curtailing Blackthorn's twisted philosophy.

The Juka laid down the hood of her cloak. The chill of late winter unsettled her ghostly white braids. Her jade-colored skin was wrinkled with age, the muscles of her face and body taut from a lifetime of strenuous pursuits. She wore light Jukan armor under a belted cloak, in the manner of Garronite soldiers. A long, subtly curved broadsword snugged against her back.

She watched with dread as a shroud of black smoke crawled over the western edge of the town. The opaque cloud patiently, irresistibly swallowed buildings made of granite and copper and dull, grey metals. From the depths of the smoke came strobes of light and dense, thunderous sounds. The ground shivered, pulsated. Thulann tightened her grip on the balcony railing.

The Technocrats had returned this morning. They meant to reclaim this settlement. The smoke was a harbinger of their mechanical advance. Thulann wondered what new steam-gorged terrors they had brought to accomplish that goal.

She turned away from the darkening scene and stepped inside the blocky, two-story building. The room within was fashioned of metal plates and oversize rivets. Cabinets of steel and glass clung to the walls, holding shelf after shelf of books and scrolls. A pale glow frosted the library from a hissing light fixture overhead. The colors of Thulann's garb seemed inverted in the alchemic illumination.

She grimaced. Wrinkles sprayed across her face. "Toria! The ground shakes with Blackthorn's footsteps. You had best finish picking that lock before someone shows up with a key."

"Are they that close, Mistress?"

"The sun cannot resist nightfall, and Warlord Pakahm's troops cannot resist the Technocrats. Until Bahrok arrives with reinforcements we cannot hope to keep this town. And Bahrok has still not been sighted."

A small shape crouched in a corner before an armored cabinet. Nimble hands manipulated the lock. "Dammit! Why did they have to attack today, of all days?"

Thulann grimaced and gave no answer.

"It's almost open, Mistress." A *clack* shot into the air and the cabinet door swung open. A pile of scrolls rested within.

Toria rose to her feet. The human girl brushed sweat and russet curls from her face. Her leather armor creaked, but only slightly. As she slipped her tools into a pouch she murmured, "You were right, Mistress. There were four incendiary traps on that door. Whatever these scrolls are, the Technocrats would have rather burned them than surrender them. They're safe for the taking now, though. The traps were all on the door, not the shelf."

"I shall discern that for myself."

Toria frowned. "Two years in your instruction and you still don't trust my skills?"

"Your talent for lockpicking surpasses even my own. But remember, child, that the greatest swordsmen are certain to die of a stab wound. Now stand back and let an old woman have a look."

Thulann touched her fingertips to the cabinet door, nudging it open a bit farther. At that moment flames leapt into the room with a gurgling roar.

Through an interior door plunged a man whose body gushed with fire. Quickly he dove to the ground and rolled, muffling the blaze to a grey smoke. For an instant he crouched in a heap, coughing wetly.

"Venduss!" shouted Toria as she rushed to the young Juka's side.

The warrior retched and waved her off. His armor and clothes were more damaged than his flesh. Frantically he rasped, "Four on my tail!"

Thulann was already at the open door. She cleared her thoughts with a quick, internal mantra, one she had repeated daily for most of her sixty-six years. The disciplines of a Way Master, of course, were most suited for combat. Her limbs felt loose. Her breaths came in short, easy bursts. She knew she would have to take down the enemy quickly lest the noise of battle attract more.

The library was smoky from Venduss's clothes. She lurked in the haze as four Logosian silhouettes rushed through the door. Without a sound she sprang into their midst, dropped to the ground and twirled. Her legsweep knocked all four off their feet. One of them cradled a flame belcher in his arms. She kicked the steel-jawed weapon loose, then whisked her longsword from its scabbard. A quick stroke laid open the man's throat. Her blade flashed in the smoke, swatting away three strikes before she impaled a second Technocrat in the chest.

Toria appeared at her mistress's side, drawing a short blade. The teenager lunged at a Logosian soldier twice her size, who was regaining his feet. They exchanged parries. Sparks popped from the Technocrat's static-charged sword. Several of Toria's cuts drew blood from the soldier's thighs, but he struck her hard on the shoulder. An electric snap bit through her leather armor. She slammed back into the metal wall. The Technocrat stamped his armored boot on her stomach, pinning her upright, and shoved his static sword at her heart.

Thulann hacked the man's spine between the shoulder blades. He did not complete his thrust. A heartbeat later a thrown knife sprouted from his face. The Technocrat dropped to the ground, revealing the burnt Venduss unsheathing a second knife.

The remaining Logosian bolted out the door. Thulann knelt to allow Venduss a clear target. The young warrior's dagger fluttered over her head and stuck in the back of the Logosian's neck. Venduss somersaulted beside the man and finished him with a pair of brutal kicks.

The Way Master helped Toria to her feet. "He drew out your cross parry. I told you the day would come when you would regret that weakness."

"Thank you, Mistress." The human touched the seared gash in her armor and winced.

"Though you should not have needed to parry at all, if Venduss had led the enemy away, as I instructed him, instead of toward us."

Toria widened her large eyes and wheeled to look out the doorway. "Venduss! Are you hurt? Take my healing potion—"

Thulann touched her injured shoulder. "Use it yourself, child. He is singed, but just as hale and foolish as he has been since birth."

"I had no choice but to come up here, teacher!" protested the young warrior as he dashed back into the room. "They came up through the floor. I was cut off from the doors and windows. I had nowhere else to go."

Thulann ground her teeth. "A dreadnought tunneled in under the building?"

Venduss nodded. "With more than a dozen soldiers. Your prediction came true. They must know we are in here. Right now they are searching the rooms downstairs, but we do not have much time. Are these the scrolls we are after?"

She shook her head. "Leave them. We do not yet know if

they are safe." Frustration built inside her chest and emerged as a growl in her throat. "Dammit! Who told them we were so close to getting these documents?"

"Who cares?" said Venduss. "Toria, quickly, search the cabinet for traps before that dreadnought comes up here!"

Thulann stepped in front of the open cabinet. "No. If we set off a trap in haste, the scrolls will be destroyed. Better that we leave them to the enemy and try again later."

"But teacher—!"

"Listen!" shouted Toria, pointing to the open door. From farther inside the metal building came the grumble and clank of heavy machinery.

Thulann took a deep breath and frowned. "That is the trumpet to retreat, my children. The balcony should make a serviceable exit, I think, unless you want to stay here and let the dreadnought join this debate. I suspect he will bring it to a decisive end."

The late morning sun threw short, heavy shadows onto the roof of a nearby building. Thulann, Venduss and Toria hid in the shade of chimneys and ductwork as they monitored the occupation of the Technocrat library. The Logosians had secured every entrance. To unsuspecting eyes, however, nothing would seem amiss.

Thulann was impressed by the operation. "This was well-planned. No one will know they are in there. Our people are all fighting at the edges of town."

Gulping a second healing potion, Venduss squinted. "I do not understand. If they meant to recapture a few documents, why are they bothering to secure the whole library? Why not take the scrolls and tunnel back behind their own lines?"

"Perhaps they value the entire library. The Technocrats

are not like us, Venduss. They do not sing all of their traditions. Logosians must write down their lore or there is a danger they will forget it."

"But they know that we escaped, that we will bring back troops. Their devotion to lore cannot be that strong."

"Their strength lies in their army. They gamble that we cannot afford to summon men away from the front."

Toria pulled her mass of red curls back into a foxtail. "The scrolls in that cabinet weren't lore, were they, Mistress? They were some kind of diagrams."

Thulann closed her eyes, then nodded. "That is so, child. That library once belonged to the Order of Engineers. Those diagrams are construction plans, what the Technocrats call 'schematics,' for a war machine."

Venduss raised his eyebrows. "So that is what we have been searching for all this time. What kind of machine is it?"

"I wish I could tell you, but that is a mystery even to most Logosians. We know only that the Engineers have devoted great resources to building it in secret, so it must be a device of considerable power. They call it 'Braun's Needle' for Lector Braun, the head of the Order." She peeked over a metal duct at the distant wall of heavy, black smoke. It obscured the western half of the town, but did not advance any closer. Its acrid smell drifted past on a breeze. "Much was sacrificed to locate those diagrams. Many spies were killed or injured. We must not lose them again."

Toria sighed gravely. "Then let's go in there and try it one more time."

Venduss snorted. "With that dreadnought standing watch? Great Mother, we might as well try to steal Blackthorn's crown! Do not be a dullard, Toria."

The girl looked away.

Thulann nodded. "You are correct. We have to lure the dreadnought out of the library first. But it will not budge without proper motivation. I suggest a frontal assault."

The younger Juka stifled a laugh. "The three of us? Perhaps the dreadnought will simply surrender out of fear."

"Perhaps I should send you alone, nursling," grunted the Way Master, "as a cure for your insolence. I mean that we must attack with enough soldiers to force the dreadnought to come out and defend the building. Once the creature leaves the library, we can slip in and fetch away our prize."

Venduss nibbled on his lower lip. "It would take twenty men, at least. Do you think Warlord Pakahm would part with them? He is undermanned already, and there is no sign of Bahrok's reinforcements."

"I shall not ask that of Pakahm," said Thulann, "and I would rather duel the dreadnought myself than to have Bahrok meddle in this. No, I want soldiers of a more exotic persuasion, if they can be convinced to answer the call."

Toria's green eyes brightened. "You're talking about Montenegro and his knights!"

"They have harried this column of Logosians for more than a week, studying the Technocrat war machines. They are certainly fighting beside Pakahm by now."

"But teacher, how shall we contact them? And more to the point, why would Montenegro agree to help us?"

"I am told Montenegro came to Logosia specifically to learn about the Technocrats' war engines. He will help us if he knows about the diagrams. As for finding him, Venduss, you will have ample time to devise a plan on your way to the battlefront. Surely it cannot be difficult to spot fifty Britannian knights on horseback?"

The warrior frowned, glancing at the smoky battlefield.

"It would be easier if the Technocrats had not smirched the air. But I shall find the humans by smell if I must. Toria, come with me. Be quick about it!"

The girl looked incredulous at his tone.

Thulann glanced at Toria's reaction and interjected, "She will stay here. We must be ready to steal inside if the dreadnought moves out of the library. Hurry now, suckling! And remember, speak to no one except Montenegro about the diagrams. Not even to Warlord Pakahm. I fear some of our soldiers listen with Logosian ears."

Venduss nodded, glanced over Toria's crouching form, then scuttled to the edge of the rooftop and vanished.

Thulann exhaled some tension as she arranged herself in a cross-legged position. Toria sat back against a metal pipe, one leg stretched out. The redhead conspicuously avoided Thulann's eyes.

The Way Master murmured, "Venduss is thirsty for command, do you not think?"

Toria shrugged.

"Sometimes the bite of a young serpent is the most dangerous. It has not yet learned to regulate its venom." Thulann began a mental regimen to relax her old muscles. On steady breaths she muttered, "Never forget that Venduss is the Shirron's son. You must allow him the opportunity to explore that power."

"I'm getting tired of that serpent's tongue, Mistress."

"I know you are, child. But you must remain strong. It is a difficult role we have chosen, you with Venduss and I with his father. Fortune is cruel to a chieftain's concubine."

Toria gaped. "Concubine! No wonder you don't trust my skills, if that's all you think of me!" She rolled to her knees and spun her back to the Way Master.

The old Juka frowned. "I think of you as a traveler, who must learn to keep pace in fair weather as well as foul. Hardship fatigues, but courtship decapitates. Relish the freedom of youth, child. On the path ahead lurk difficult times—intrigues, separations, even political marriages. When they come you shall long for that young serpent who cannot control his passions." When she realized the human was not going to respond, she added, "And I also think of you as a young woman I am proud to have as a student and servant. And as long as you are both of those things, do me the kindness of watching the library while I meditate. It has been a frustrating morning. I shall need to regain my strength if Sir Gabriel Montenegro is going to share it with us. He is to my patience what lightning is to a very tall tree."

Venduss stepped between wounded Jukan soldiers as he neared the wall of bitter smoke. Dozens of maimed troops crowded the streets just outside the battleground. Their cries scrabbled between the town's reverberant buildings. Physicians moved among the injured, dispensing bandages, potions and flashes of healing magic taught to them by New Britannian sorcerers. Yet for each clansman they restored, many new ones were laid down. Those with healthy legs dragged the others away from the advancing smoke.

Venduss shut out the screams of torment. They were only distractions from the true course of the battle.

These Juka warriors were commanded by Warlord Pakahm, the chieftain of Clan Athul. The troops were the finest of his clansmen. Venduss knew he was witnessing the heroic devastation of Athul's fighting strength, as they battled to hold the port town long enough for Warlord Bahrok and his massive army to arrive.

The defeat was taking place inside the roiling murk. Generated by Technocrat boilers, the thick, ashy haze smeared the air like soot on a glass window. The sounds coming from within chilled the young warrior's blood.

Clan Athul was being slaughtered to the grotesque music of Technocrat machines. Venduss entered the stinging, black cloud and felt the song shudder his bones.

A concert of steam whistles harmonized like crass, breathy flutes. The tones directed the movement of Logosian units by a code that Garron had not yet unraveled. Using this system the Technocrat formations sacrificed little effectiveness in the acrid gloom, while the clansmen struggled to organize in the dark. The technique was sufficient to compensate for the superior skills of individual Garronite warriors.

Underlying the whistles' keening was a syncopation of levers and gears—the innards of the Technocrat war machines—clanking and clattering with dizzy complexity across the entire breadth of the battlefield. The air was thick with the grumble of heavy wheels and the dragon hiss of steam engines. Terrible weapons of fire and lightning barked and growled and roared. And driving the mad symphony was the temblor beat of gigantic drums, booming out the unearthly pulse of a crawling, mechanical behemoth that devoured the town of Enclave and every defender who stood in the way.

The young warrior coughed as he adjusted to the smoke. It burned his eyes and made them water, increasing the lack of visibility. He relied on his pointed ears for guidance. From ahead came the familiar din of melee. He plunged in that direction, into a throng of Jukan soldiers with spears and shields. In the gloom they were hale, dauntless silhouettes. Their armor was resplendent with curves and tapers. Their rallying cries recalled generations of proud warrior tradition. He could make out banners where the smoke cleared in the wake of a breeze. The flags stood tall, even when darkness clamped around them.

The troops on this street were converging around several portable barricades. Crews shoved the rolling walls into place while infantrymen fought back the Logosian footsoldiers. Then Venduss saw the reason for the barriers. Though it was only a towering shadow in the haze, a war engine rumbled forward from the Technocrat ranks on heavy, spiked wheels. The armored turret loomed twenty feet above the ground. From its high, barbed cupola struck lashes of electrical fury, carving through the Garronite forces like many-fingered claws. The archers of Clan Athul deluged the structure with a hurricane of bolts and arrows, but only the portable barricades stopped the lumbering advance of the machine. And so the spearmen of each army clashed, butchering one another for the sake of another foot of ground.

Venduss's chest swelled with exhilaration. This was the purpose of Jukan strength, the vindication of a clan's warrior spirit: to fight with skill and honor and courage. Though the battle for Enclave would surely devastate this fearless army, he was proud that Athul was an ally of his own clan. When the hour came for Venduss to take his father's place as chieftain of Clan Kumar, he would remember with honor this terrible day.

But for the moment he resolved not to embroil himself in the melee. His mission was urgent. So he turned northward, parallel to the line of defense, and left the war engine behind. As he trotted between buildings he heard the crack of wood and metal breaking—the barricades had suddenly been crushed. He knew the war engine could not have destroyed the barriers. Only Blackthorn's juggernauts possessed such strength and maneuverability.

Venduss grated his teeth as he pressed on, denying his hunger to return and join the fray. Of all the Techno-Prophet's mechanical abominations, juggernauts and dreadnoughts and their steel-enhanced ilk were the most terrible. They were the mating of men and war engines, or perhaps they were slaves bound physically to the controls of a machine. They possessed tremendous might, a battery of technological weapons and an unshakable loyalty to their leader at Logos. The thought of them made Venduss's hand ache for a sword. Though dreadnoughts were lethal to any but a large force of soldiers, Venduss and Thulann had once defeated a juggernaut between them. The experience made him crave more encounters.

But he forced himself away from the battle. He had to find Montenegro before the Logosians reached the library, or many Jukan deaths and many months of Thulann's work would have been in vain. Onward he pushed through the dense, roiling smoke, hardening his ears against the cries and shrieks of the clansmen of Athul, whose barricades had been shattered. He did not like to hear them. Screams tarnished the luster of glorious death.

Thulann sat motionless with her eyes closed, infusing her body with calm, measured breaths. She took inventory of the aches that flared in her joints and spine. As her body grew older, she found that its memory was sharpening. A throb in her shoulder recalled the swordstroke that saved Toria in the library. Her knees remembered the leap from the balcony. Cramps in her limbs defined an array of combat maneuvers. At sixty-six years of age Thulann's veteran body forgot nothing anymore, but kept a chronicle of increasingly trivial actions. When she meditated, a hundred recollections trilled inside her flesh.

Not many years ago she had taken the pain as a cue for retirement. The dusk years of a Way Master were a time for teaching the young. Rituals prepared the flesh for its demise. But even while she took Venduss as a full-time student, politics denied her a proper resignation. The Shirron Turlogan, head of the Jukan Clans, who was Venduss's father and her own lord and lover, would not allow her to fade into the shadows. He needed her experience as a spy and a leader to face the coming war with the Technocrats. He had all but forced her bodily to continue working.

For that, she was more grateful than she could have imagined. It awakened forgotten joy to brandish weapons and wits against such a mighty opponent. Her spirit felt like a wheel turning inside her. Faster and faster it spun now, as the forces of Garron pressed into enemy territory. Every offensive maneuver met with unexpected success. At this pace the Technocrats must surely surrender and relinquish their hold on the disputed borderlands. Only then would Thulann retire. Only when Turlogan's glory was complete would she enter the haven of old age.

Until then, each day brought a regimen of trance and meditation to ease the damage to her weathered body. She had to be diligent to keep up with her two companions, who had not lived forty years between them. Yet Thulann knew she was up to the task. Her seasoned will outmatched their youthful energy. It was they who must heel to her gait.

During her meditation, the Way Master's senses were attuned to Toria's quiet sounds. When the girl shifted her weight and stuttered a breath, Thulann opened one eye.

At the edge of the rooftop, the young human was staring at the library with a furrowed brow. "Mistress? Someone new is in there."

Thulann unfolded from her meditation and knelt beside Toria. Through the window of the library they watched a strange figure moving about. He was a bald, skeletal man in a tailored black robe. Thulann recognized the raiment of a Technocrat of the Order of Theorists. He was engaged in animated conversation with a hard-edged shadow that she presumed was the dreadnought itself.

Then the Theorist stepped directly to the window. For a moment Thulann thought he would catch her eyes. A tingle of excitement shot through her. But the man simply opened the glass panes, thrust out his hairless head and peered at the overcast sky. Then he held one arm into the air.

In his palm rested a small, disc-shaped device. The Theorist flipped a lever with his thumb. A series of bat-wing vanes popped out along the disc's perimeter. With a metallic squeak it leapt from his hand and spun wildly into the air. High above the rooftops it flew, becoming a speck against the feathery cloud cover. Then it pulsed out a sequence of quick, colorful flashes. When the lights ended, the device could no longer be seen.

Toria glanced at the Way Master. "Some kind of signal?"

"Undoubtedly. Though it was not bright enough to penetrate the Logosians' smoke cloud. Someone is watching and not from the battlefront." Thulann gazed at the Theorist until he stepped away from the window. Then she collected herself to rise. "I am going to shadow that man. They are doing more down there than just occupying the building. I do not want it to jeopardize our goal."

"What should I do?"

"Stay here, keep watching and hope that Venduss does not take long. If that signal was designed to summon more troops—or, Great Mother forbid, more dreadnoughts—then Montenegro and his knights might be coming here to meet their own extinction."

Venduss proceeded through the cloying smoke, searching for Montenegro and his men. Passing soldiers confirmed that the New Britannian knights were engaged in the day's conflict, though none of them knew where. The young warrior continued north through the haze until he left behind the metal streets of Enclave. He reasoned that a cavalry unit would fight in the open ground outside of town.

A bloodied officer confirmed the theory. The old, haggard soldier pointed west, to territory held by the Technocrats. Rumor suggested that the human knights were traversing the tree-spiked landscape astride their tall, nimble mounts, harrying the Logosian column with swift charges. The officer spoke as if recounting a legend. Only two years had passed since Garron allied with the New Britannians. Besides Montenegro's knights, no more than a few dozen of the soft-skinned strangers had visited the continent, mostly healers instructing clan physicians in the curative arts of Water Magic. Their sorcerous talents and exotic ways still gave wonder to the rare Juka who met them. The clans felt great relief that, unlike the Technocrats, these humans were their allies.

Venduss had more experience with New Britannians than did most of his people. Toria had served Thulann for two years. Hardly a day passed in which Venduss did not marvel at the girl's pale beauty or test the boundaries of her peculiar culture. He suspected he had seen, in Toria and others, the best and worst of humanity. They continued to be a wonder to him.

He could see the wonder in Toria's sea-green eyes, as well, when she looked back.

He snuck through the enemy lines to find Montenegro, somewhere beyond. Smoke provided him ample cover. For good measure he shoved his blade into a Technocrat's gut and took the weeping man's cloak. A steady tension informed the Juka's movements as he crept among the Logosian ranks. The clanking, whistling chorus of war machines made him flinch. The ground throbbed from the hammer of giant drums. His senses grew untrustworthy. Before he knew it he had walked within a yard of a juggernaut. The creature stank of soot and hot grease. When it rolled past on toothed wheels he wanted to stop and compose himself, but he dared take no suspicious actions. Instead he plunged deeper into the gloom, seeking any trace of the New Britannians.

His ears gave him hope. Amid the thrum and clangor he picked out a noise distinctive to the northern humans: the hoofbeats of the athletic mounts they called horses. He hurried in that direction, approaching the perimeter of the Technocrat army. Then the sound was gone. He knelt and took stock of his situation.

The opaque cloud was thicker here. He soon realized why. Not many yards away moved an enormous, wheeled device. He could only see glimpses of it in the murk, but it consisted of a round iron boiler that seethed from red coals underneath. Huge bellows animated the flames. A viscous, gurgling sound shook the machine's heavy rivets, lengthening into a ghastly moan as it rose up some kind of high vertical member. Venduss could not tell if it was a pipe or flue or some more complex apparatus. At the summit was an indistinct opening. It gave the impression of a pitcher or a gaping mouth. Smoke vomited out in heavy, billowing gouts and was dispersed by the windmill blades of an enormous fan. Black-robed Technocrat engineers operated the contraption by wheels and levers. Several ranks of human and Jukan soldiers marched around it, protecting one of the many smoke cauldrons that were so vital to the success of their assault.

Kneeling in the spiny grass, Venduss channeled all of his will to resist a fit of coughing. The scalding heat of the war machine grew uncomfortable as it lumbered closer.

Abruptly through the gloom darted a new troop of Logosians. They whirled their weapons and shields as if in the midst of a retreat. Their arrival inspired the cauldron's guards to brandish their own polearms. The huge machine groaned and squealed as ponderous brakes halted its forward movement. One of the engineers blew a strident steam whistle. The soldiers formed into a bristling defensive array. An expectant lull seemed to amplify the roar of the boiler.

Then a wall of flashing silver exploded from the murk. A volley of lances sprang into view, long shafts crackling with brilliant sorcery. A flood of knights in glittering armor leapt through the air atop steel-clapped horses, slamming into the enemy phalanx and shattering the dense formation. From horseback the helmeted warriors tore a swath through the Technocrats, strewing pitiless blows from swords and maces, hammers and morningstars. Their strapping chargers reared and whinnied in white-eyed fury.

The engineers on board the cauldron swiveled ballistas to bear on the glittering attackers. The Technocrats churned giant cranks and arrows streamed out in brutal, unending waves. Several knights were peppered out of their saddles.

But from behind the New Britannian line emerged a rank of heavy crossbowmen, visible in silhouette, who scoured the exterior of the iron machine.

Then different shadows replaced the archers, wearing robes and hoods and lifting staves and wands into the air. The sorcerers from New Britannia erupted with light. Across the battleground cascaded an inferno of dazzling spells, resolving into fire and ice and stone and crystal, lashing the air with screaming sounds and stirring the haze with swooping gusts of wind. Curtains of flame ripped through the enemy. The ground softened to mud and engulfed Logosian boots.

Venduss recognized the tight integration of wizardry and melee fighting. The knights, their weapons and even their horses glimmered with magical enhancements. The warriors' maneuvers anticipated the sorcery. Not even the mathematical Technocrats were so efficient with their machines. This was why the New Britannians made formidable allies and why Logos so feared the alliance.

The young Juka could stand by no longer. He whisked out his blade and crept toward the fray. At the last moment he remembered to doff the Technocrat robe he was wearing.

A sound froze him in place. Heavy steel clanked many yards behind him. The stench of burned grease invaded his nostrils. His flesh crawled. Juggernauts were coming, a great many of them. Perhaps an entire platoon.

In the din of battle he had no hope of warning the New Britannians. His eyes darted for a solution. He found it atop the smoke cauldron itself. A quick shout drew the attention of a pikeman, who thrust out a spear as Venduss charged. The young warrior dodged the point, then grabbed the end of the polearm and jumped. His momentum flung him high. He used the haft of the spear to propel himself over the heads of the Technocrat troops and onto the hard, black surface of the war machine.

The heat of the boiler struck him like a fist, but he shrugged it off and climbed. His goal was the main arbalest, mounted atop the iron tank just under the windmill blades of the fan. An engineer appeared in front of him, lunging with a buzzing dagger. The Juka's blade rent through flesh and thin armor in rapid strokes, toppling the man to the ground. Then Venduss sprang behind the arbalest and pivoted it to face the oncoming juggernauts.

At least ten or fifteen hulking shapes loomed in the haze. Spirals of flame danced in their jagged claws. Venduss let out a war cry and shoved the crank of the arbalest, which chattered and shook as a fountain of arrows sprayed the juggernaut company. His aim was poor but that did not matter. His purpose was to catch the New Britannians' attention. He glanced at them to gauge his success.

A line of mounted knights had begun a second lance charge. Time slowed as he watched them gallop closer. Bright magic sparkled over every inch of their silvery armor. Sparks leapt at the crash of hoofbeats. The officer in the lead raised the visor of his helmet and Venduss recognized the intense gaze of Montenegro himself. He was shouting something inaudible in the chaos. He waved his shield arm as if warning Venduss of danger.

When the sorcerers began their assault on the smoke cauldron, Venduss realized his error in timing. Like molasses were his movements as he scrambled over the pipes and levers of the war machine, while torrents of lightning and flaming stones smashed into the heavy iron. Hard sounds cracked the air. Geysers of smoke and fire rocketed from gaps where seams burst their rivets. Then the wave of charging knights rammed their lances into the machine. Enchanted tips punctured the boiler in a neat row, drawing a scream from the twisting metal as internal pressure ripped it apart.

Venduss felt the cauldron explode as he threw himself from the top of the boiler. The blast hurled him over the knights. He watched the New Britannians vanish under a sheet of burning fluid even as he felt its searing embrace himself. Then he plummeted into the thick of the smoke. He landed hard and rolled. His own voice howled, unbidden, when the boiling liquid seemed to claw the flesh from his bones.

On hands and knees he raked the muddy ground. Without warning Thulann's voice filled his head, droning the chants of the Way which she had taught him for as long as he could remember. Thulann's voice chanted and the pain receded. He drove his knees until his feet caught the earth and he staggered forward in the fog of trance.

Some mighty spell engaged behind him, coloring the acrid smoke bright white.

Then he was lifted off his feet by a pair of gauntlets. He found himself slung over the pommel of a saddle, galloping away from the wreckage of the smoke cauldron. All around him were the heads and tails of tasseled Britannian steeds and the flashes of polished armor. When the company hurtled out of the Technocrat cloud, Venduss could not believe his eyes. None of the knights looked injured, not even Montenegro, whose face he saw from below as he peered up at his rescuer. Montenegro did not return the look, but kept his eyes forward until the thunderstorm of horses and riders had put more than a mile behind them.

Finally the company of knights halted on a low hilltop, in a grove of thorny trees, to survey their work. In the distance stretched the outskirts of Enclave, still shrouded in smoke; though now a portion of the Logosian army lay exposed. War engines and low-hovering airbarges looked black under the brightening sky. Venduss noticed a dearth of Logosian infantry units. Already a division of ridgeback-mounted Athul cavalry were closing in on the uncovered Technocrat flank, swarming around a platoon of juggernauts.

As he examined the battlefield, Venduss's internal chant faltered. The pain of his injuries spiked through him once more. He crawled off Montenegro's ebony horse and clutched his own torso, choking down the screams that rose from inside. Behind him a strong voice called out: "Badralghazi, erase his wounds."

The Juka was startled that, though they had not spoken for two years, Montenegro's voice still gave him both resentment and inspiration. But the thought vanished under a deluge of healing magic, which saturated his ravaged flesh with complex, exquisite relief.

Then the sensation dwindled and strength returned to his limbs. He turned an astonished look upon the dismounting Montenegro. "I saw you bathed in fire! How are you still alive?"

The knight motioned with his head to the tired healer who had restored the Juka. "Badralghazi here is the finest water mage in New Britannia. Our attack was built around his power to keep us from dying. I owe him several lifetimes of gratitude."

Venduss stood tall, stretching his back. "And I owe my life to you, Montenegro."

"I do seem to make a habit of rescuing you, don't I? And

yet you have done the same for me in the past. Think no more of it." He looked over the Juka's stout frame. "But you're a man now, not the boy who wanted to kill me all that time ago. I'm almost pleased to see you, Venduss of Garron."

The Juka pursed his lips. "Your greetings are as warm as ever."

"You take me wrong. I am happy to see you, yet I judge by the worry lines carved into your brow that your old teacher still hangs over your shoulder, like a vulture. This was no chance meeting, was it? And where Thulann appears, some unreasonable demand will soon be made of me. So come out with it, then. What does Thulann want?"

Venduss smirked before he could stop himself. He explained the situation at the library. Montenegro listened with a deepening grimace, until the Juka told him about the schematics for the war machine called Braun's Needle. Then the knight's eyes glinted like the steel of his armor.

He let out a dark chuckle. "Thulann is as persuasive as ever. Aziz! Evanthe! Come here. Valor calls us back to the fray." As several knights approached, Montenegro laid a hand on the Juka's shoulder. "Take us to this library, then, Venduss. Thulann has invited me, so she must be prepared for the reunion. It is past time she and I got reacquainted."

Venduss said nothing, but watched as the human gathered his officers and meted out brusque commands. The mounted knights and spellcasters attended him without hesitation. It seemed to Venduss that Montenegro's demeanor was remarkably lighter than it had been on the New Britannian continent two years earlier. Clearly the challenge of command brought vitality to the grim human. His troops responded to their leader's animation.

The young Juka resisted a smile. The time would come, soon, for his own command. As great as this human's accomplishments had been, they would seem meager beside Venduss's deeds. Clan Kumar would one day be his army. Even the legendary Warlord Bahrok would fear him then. The thought of it lent volume to Venduss's order: "Montenegro! Hurry your people! I do not want to keep my teacher waiting."

The dark-haired knight turned a bemused look upon him. "You've grown teeth in that mouth of yours! I suggest you keep them under your lips. But given that I am also impatient for this reunion, I shall heed your suggestion. If you would be so kind as to lead the way, I shall see if I can inspire my knights to keep up with you."

CHAPTER
3

The Warlord's Schemes

$\mathcal{A}$ cluster of iron pipes thrust out of the exterior of the library, not far from a second-floor window. Thulann clung to them with her thighs and stretched her torso parallel, so that she could only be seen from very select angles. She drew a long dagger. The polished blade reflected her green, wrinkled face. She tilted the knife to peek through the window without revealing herself.

Inside the library were the people she expected to see: several Logosian soldiers, both Juka and human, and the Technocrat who had sent up the flying signal. The latter was a tall, raw-boned human, with a meticulous demeanor and a ghoulish pallor. Thulann could see the veins under his bald, white scalp. He seemed agitated as he paced before the open doors of the cabinet that contained the valuable schematics.

Beside the cabinet waited the enormous dreadnought. Its metallic bulk filled the corner of the room. The creature's armored mechanics hissed and whirred as it hovered a foot above the floor. Its half-organic physique suggested the shapeless flesh of a human being, crushed and stretched to fit the inhuman geometry of a war engine. Long, many-jointed arms were tipped with drills and scoops for digging. Soulless eyes watched the Technocrat as he stalked the perimeter of the library.

Whatever was happening, it was clear to Thulann that the Theorist was not happy.

At that moment a figure appeared on the street below. Thulann adjusted her perch, making sure she was out of sight. The person was wrapped in a long cloak but wore the helmet of a Jukan officer. The huge Garronite was a walking mountain. Though Thulann squinted, she could not make out the face. Her suspicion, however, sent a chill through her. When the stranger ambled uncontested through the front door, she decided it was time to get closer.

She slipped to the ground and crept through a window. The front room of the library was a wide antechamber, busy with chairs and tables and the ubiquitous Logosian pipework. The center of the floor had been split open from below. The dreadnought's earthen tunnel, partially collapsed, yawned underneath.

Like an arrow she shot behind a chair, then crouched and listened.

The antechamber grew tense as the Logosian soldiers faced the cloaked man. No weapons were drawn, but hands waited at the ready. Then footsteps echoed from the large staircase. A gaunt, black-robed spectre strode down into the room. "Thank you for being prompt," said the Technocrat in a tone like cold wind.

When the cloaked stranger answered, Thulann winced.

"Turn up a lantern in here! You know I despise these cloak and dagger meetings. I should skewer you for this, Brother Rictor." The baritone voice belonged to Warlord Bahrok. Though the Jukan officer was a hero in Garron, Thulann was well versed in his secret intrigues. The chieftain of Clan Varang took no action that did not further his aim to become the Shirron himself; and the war with the Technocrats had offered him a bounty of opportunities.

Thulann had suspected that Bahrok employed spies among the Logosians. His meeting with this Technocrat confirmed the evidence she had gathered. Nor could she begrudge him his stratagems. But his appearance at this moment could not be a coincidence. And where were Bahrok's reinforcements, which Clan Athul so desperately needed?

The Technocrat named Brother Rictor brushed off the warlord's threat with an elaborate gesture. "There is no time for debate today. One of the diagrams has been taken. Is this some kind of trick?"

The large warrior grunted. "Not on my part. Are you sure it was stolen? Maybe it was missing the whole time."

"I cannot be more certain. The locks were picked and the traps were disabled. They were intact and engaged when the Engineers left this place a month ago. Somewhere there is a Garronite with possession of my property."

Thulann bit down a spike of anger in her throat. So Bahrok knew about the schematics as well. He must have been the one who tipped off these Logosians. Had he also given them permission to use deadly force against Thulann?

The warlord snorted. "Listen to your own words, Rictor. You say they took one diagram. Why only one? A Garron clansman would not have the knowledge to be so selective. He would have taken the lot and let a Technocrat sort them out." He pinched his brow. "You had best look to your Order of Engineers for an answer. They must have learned about our bargain and sent someone here to steal a critical document. As you have said, they guard their secrets zealously."

The Theorist clasped his palms together and frowned. "Perhaps you are right. Or perhaps you know more than you are telling me."

"Do not even consider accusing me of treachery. You are only a messenger, human. My bargain is with your employer. He may judge my actions, but not you. Now, I have yet to receive my payment for allowing you to come here at all. Give me the deployment plans. My patience is ended."

Brother Rictor paused for a moment, then reached his long fingers into a pocket. From it he withdrew a fold of parchment, which he handed to the Juka. "I shall make my report when I return to Logos. We shall see what judgment is passed."

"Look to your Engineers," Bahrok repeated as he glanced over the folded message. "Logosians wallow in treachery. I do not dirty my hands with it."

Frowning in the shadows, Thulann wondered if the warlord's ego made him truly believe that statement, or if he was simply lying.

When they met on the rooftop, Montenegro was startled by the delight in Toria's eyes. He imagined the girl might throw her arms around him, though she settled for clasping his steel-encased hands. Two years had transformed the young minstrel into a fetching woman. Her pale, freckled face bore the dignity—and the weight—of hard experience in a foreign land. The extra lines suited her.

He grinned and kept her hands. "Toria, let me hear that beautiful voice of yours."

Her smile was sheer excitement. "You're still something to see, hey? Like a silver ghost in that plate mail."

The knight chuckled. "You haven't seen Britannian armor in two years, have you? I can tell by your homesick eyes. I'm surprised you're still lurking around this carcass of a continent."

She blinked and chuckled, but made no reply.

Venduss pushed between them. "Do not delay us, Toria. Montenegro's knights are waiting not far from here. Where is Thulann? What is the situation?"

The girl recounted the incident with the Technocrat's signal. "And a Jukan officer just went in there. I couldn't see who it was. I was about to go look, to make sure Mistress is okay, but I saw the two of you coming."

Montenegro looked down at the blocky building. "A clansman, eh? I suppose I shouldn't be surprised. Wherever Thulann of Garron is, there must be subterfuge."

"Enough," growled Venduss. "I am going down there. Wait for my signal to summon your troops."

The knight shook his head. "You've got five minutes to contact Thulann. If I don't hear from you, we're moving in. Be prepared to get the schematics."

"You are an impatient man, Montenegro."

"I shall be an old man before Thulann concludes her intrigues. She is a spy. I am a warrior. We define patience differently."

The Juka frowned, then turned to go.

"Venduss," added Montenegro, "the day will come when you must decide what you are. Spy or warrior? What does your honor demand?"

The youth did not look back. "My destiny has never been in question," he grumbled, then slipped over the edge of the roofline.

The knight chuckled and glanced at Toria. "I wager you a senator's codpiece that he doesn't remain Thulann's student very much longer."

The girl sighed and laid her head on his armored shoulder. "Let's just get this over with, hey? I'd love a chance to ride a real horse again. Do you mind if I borrow yours?"

Montenegro smiled. "Toria, promise me a song and I'll let you ride him over the sea and all the way back home."

In the antechamber of the library, Thulann watched from hiding as a Logosian soldier handed Brother Rictor the schematics to Braun's Needle. Warlord Bahrok looked on with indifference.

Thulann's fists tightened. Her prize was vanishing fast. Steeling herself, she rose from behind the chair and stepped into the pale glow of a buzzing Technocrat lamp. "I should prefer it if those documents did not leave this building." Immediately the soldiers in the room converged. She made no move to defend herself, though she marked each Logosian and calculated moves to take them down.

Before the soldiers reached her, Bahrok held up a hand. "Stop! Leave her be! I wondered if you would turn up, Thulann. It is fortunate that you are here."

"Fortunate for you, of course, since it was I who found the schematics." She moved closer to Bahrok and Brother Rictor. The soldiers aimed blades and bolt-throwers at her. She warned them off with a disdainful glower. "Too much was sacrificed to obtain those diagrams. I cannot let you give them back to Blackthorn."

Bahrok waved a hand. "Do not interfere with my business. You and your spies did well to find the schematics, when even Brother Rictor's people could not. You have my gratitude. Now, tell me where the missing scroll is."

She stopped a few feet in front of the warlord. "What is written on that fold of parchment, that is worth the cost of those schematics?"

The huge warrior grumbled. "Very well, if it shall make this go faster, Brother Rictor has given me the plans for Technocrat troop deployments. I shall devise our next attack based upon them. This parchment will grant us another victory and probably save the lives of hundreds of Garronite soldiers in the bargain. Will that satisfy your wounded pride?"

She flinched. With effort she murmured, "Yes, I suppose it will. Damn you. I see now why you have such success on the battlefield. You sacrifice your allies to get it."

"Each of us does what he must to gain victory. Be content with your contribution."

"And Warlord Pakahm? How much shall he sacrifice before your reinforcements arrive?"

Bahrok drew his face taut. Thulann could swear he was laboring not to smile. "My army shall march as soon as I return to them, so let us waste no more time. Where is the missing scroll, Thulann?"

"I did not take any scrolls."

"What about your people? Venduss? The human girl?"

"We did not touch the diagrams. I had not yet determined if they were safe to remove from the cabinet."

"She's lying," said Brother Rictor. His sneer furrowed the sides of his hooked nose. "She has my document."

The soldiers tensed, their weapons ready to fly. Thulann worked out an escape route in her mind.

Bahrok shook his head. "Thulann does not lie, except by

omission. On your honor, Way Master, tell me you know nothing about the missing document."

Thulann watched Rictor as she answered, "On my honor, I know nothing about it."

"I am satisfied," said Bahrok.

The Technocrat grimaced. "I am not. Let's see how sincere she really is." In his upraised fingers appeared a long, steel dart. The tip gleamed with a sap-like gel. "I have the antidote to this poison. I shall trade it for the scroll." He cocked his wrist to fling the dart. Thulann prepared to dodge as Bahrok threw up his hands in protest; but a metallic *snap* caused the Theorist to leap backward.

The poison dart in his hand was sheared in half. Beside him stood Venduss with sword drawn. The young warrior whisked his blade under Brother Rictor's chin and hissed, "There is no antidote to my steel, Technocrat!"

Thulann's heart warmed, though she knew it was a dangerous time to indulge in such feelings.

Warlord Bahrok yelled at the Logosian soldiers to stay back, then glared at Venduss. "Sheath your weapon! This is not a battle!"

Thulann murmured, "Brother Rictor would have it so."

The Technocrat swallowed, his throat nudging the razor edge of Venduss's sword. "Do you hear that sound, Juka? The dreadnought is coming. You had best leave your mark on the world before it arrives, eh?"

A clanking noise grew louder, echoing from the staircase. Thulann felt a chill of urgency. "Put away your sword, Venduss. This battle we cannot win."

The youth narrowed his eyes. "Can we not? I hear another sound that suggests we can."

From outside the library came the rumble of dozens of

hoofbeats. Only New Britannian horses produced that noise. Thulann tried not to laugh, but failed.

The frustrated Bahrok let out a growl. "The human knights! This has gone too far."

Brother Rictor furrowed his brow. "The dreadnought shall disperse them."

Bahrok grunted, "Montenegro's troops are a match for your monster. Put away your poisons, Rictor. Everyone lower your weapons. I have made my transaction and I intend to leave this place before that dreadnought gets here. I may conduct business with Technocrats, but not with your grotesque machines."

Venduss gazed at Thulann with pleading eyes. With regret, she motioned for him to put down his sword. He complied, though he returned her a look of disappointment.

She hardened her own expression. This was no time to compromise her dignity. Though Bahrok had used her in his schemes, she might yet turn the situation to her own advantage. But for today, all that remained was to graciously step aside.

Venduss had no such restraint. He whirled suddenly and kicked a nearby table, smashing it into several pieces. He expressed his frustration with enough vigor to satisfy both himself and Thulann.

Astride his tall charger, Montenegro inspected the formation of his knights as they surrounded the library. Dismounted and prepared to attack, they created a glittering circle of steel. Their excitement was audible, in the fidget of their armor and the timbre of their whispers. Montenegro felt it, as well. Though they had wandered Logosia for seven months, this was only their third opportunity to battle a dreadnought. They were eager to try some new ideas.

As he completed his circuit of the building, he saw the front door opening. Archers and spellcasters prepared to fire. But when three familiar figures emerged, Montenegro wondered if the battle was already over.

As the knight trotted his black warhorse to the entrance, Warlord Bahrok of Clan Varang locked eyes with him. Montenegro could see that the Juka chieftain was not thinking friendly thoughts. He returned the sentiment. Next came Venduss, looking furious, and then Thulann of Garron. The Way Master was wearing that insufferably dignified expression that chafed Montenegro like a burr.

He lifted the visor of his helmet and called out, "Have we missed the action, Bahrok, or am I here to fight you?"

The warlord bared his teeth. "You know I would give much for that opportunity, human! Yet this is not the time. Collect your soldiers. There is nothing to do here."

"You might be mistaken," said Montenegro as he glanced at the doorway. A figure watched from within. The white-skinned, black-robed Technocrat looked like the very spectre of death. Montenegro glanced at Thulann. "I am here at your behest, not Bahrok's. What do you say, old woman?"

"We have settled this matter," replied the Way Master, "though I extend you my warmest thanks for answering my call. I am at your service in return."

The knight stilled his horse, which had begun to prance at the approach of Warlord Bahrok. "The only service I require is for you to show me the schematics that Venduss told me about. That was the real bait to lure me here, as you well know."

The aged Juka frowned. "Well do I know that, yet I must

disappoint you. Warlord Bahrok has employed those documents for other purposes. They are no longer available."

Montenegro grinned, glancing away. "How did I expect anything less? I am a fool whose memory is too short. Well, the Virtue of Humility does not permit me to complain. If you Juka will please move aside, my troops and I shall console ourselves by killing the dreadnought inside that building."

Bahrok stood in front of him. "The dreadnought has already tunneled away. I told you, there is nothing to do here. Besides, you and your troops have much to prepare for now."

"Oh? What do we have to prepare for?"

"Leaving."

Montenegro chuckled. "I think we'll stay until the battle is finished."

The warlord did not flinch. "I do not mean leaving Enclave. I mean leaving this continent and returning to New Britannia."

The knight lost his smirk. "You're going to have to explain that remark."

"Your knights have been pestering the Logosians for too long now. It is inconvenient for me. I am trying to conduct a war for Garron. It does not help when a band of bloodthirsty humans randomly provokes the enemy. You are a thorn in my side, Montenegro. That is why you are going to leave."

"I see. I shall take it under advisement, then. I'll let you know in a few months what my decision is."

The warlord snatched the reins of Montenegro's horse. The knight reached for his sword, but held himself in check. The other New Britannians tensed.

The two men glared at each other. Bahrok muttered, "This is not a contest, human. I have the authority to make this demand."

"What authority is that?"

"An army of ten thousand at my command."

Montenegro leaned closer. "Oh? Do you have lightning throwers and smoke cauldrons, too? Maybe even a dreadnought? Don't threaten me, Bahrok. We don't fear you any more than we fear the Technocrats."

"That is not the point," Thulann interjected. "Bahrok has the support of the clans. If he commands it, they will shun you. You cannot survive in Logosia on your own."

The knight sneered. "After all this time, you still underestimate human resolve? I had taken you for a wise woman."

"I would never impugn your skills or your Virtues. You may not believe it, but you are something of an inspiration to my kind. Inspiration, however, does not put livestock over your fires or fresh water in your casks. You cannot continue your campaign without the support of the people of Jukaran. Bahrok can take that from you."

Montenegro turned a grimace on the burly warlord. "Surely you would not demean yourself with such a cowardly plot."

Bahrok grinned. "If you prefer, we can negotiate on the battlefield. My army awaits the signal to march on this city. You have my permission to meet them ahead of the Logosians."

Montenegro glanced at his fellow humans, who began to grow agitated. He calmed them with a shake of his head. "Bahrok, I truly believe that you would undertake such a pointless exercise just to satisfy your bloated ego. Count yourself fortunate that I do not play games with the lives of my troops, nor with my allies' troops." Then he turned to Thulann. "It seems I am forced to accept your assessment of Bahrok's treachery. And if that is the case, I shall require your services after all."

"Name the favor and I shall grant it."

"Meet me in Garron. I want to speak to the Shirron. A just authority will not support this insult."

She nodded. "I look forward to returning to Garron as well. These Technocrat settlements have all the charm of a cold dagger. I shall present you to the Shirron, Montenegro, on the condition that you do not resist Bahrok in the meantime. We shall never defeat Blackthorn if we turn our blades upon each other."

"Agreed," said the knight, though it nearly lodged in his throat.

Bahrok lifted a finger. "The Shirron will not contradict me. Your people will be escorted to the coast. See to it that ships are there to take them home. Do not despair, Montenegro. Surely they must long to rejoin their families. And you as well, eh? Do you not have a cousin at home?"

In one stroke Montenegro snatched Starfell from its scabbard and held the black point at the warlord's face. An instant later the street clattered with sound as the other knights drew their weapons. Bahrok stood at the center of a ring of sharp metal.

"Do not mock the memory of Damario," Montenegro snarled, anger tightening his voice.

Bahrok, however, had not even blinked. Instead, he opened up a toothy smile. "You have my apologies. I shall leave you to your preparations." Brusquely he pushed his way through the crowd of knights. They kept their weapons unsheathed until the large Juka was out of sight.

For an instant Montenegro considered pursuing the overbearing warlord. Both of them dreamed of the luxury of a duel. But Montenegro did not dare to strike down Bahrok in this land, any more than Bahrok could strike him down in New Britannia two years ago. Wars and alliances made grudges difficult to satisfy.

Instead, he rammed Starfell back into its sheath and gazed at Thulann. His tone had a furious growl. "How can you stand by and watch this? You seem at ease with the fact that Bahrok stole your schematics! Do you have some magic victory up your sleeve?"

"Sorcery is not a game for Way Masters. My only magic is perseverance. The schematics will surface again. I shall find them."

He hissed. "Sometimes I envy your serenity, Thulann! I could never be so comfortable with defeat. Instruct me, then. How does the Way advise a man who's been stabbed in the back?"

The old Juka narrowed her eyes. "It shall be several hours before Bahrok's reinforcements arrive. That means you have several hours left to engage the Technocrats. Take advantage of the time. If it helps, you can imagine the warlord's face on every Logosian you slay."

Montenegro stirred his warhorse to leave. To the Way Master he said, "By the Virtues, you always find a way to surprise me! You plucked that thought straight from my mind. Aziz! Evanthe! Get everyone onto horseback! Let's see if we can find another platoon of juggernauts. This time we're not going to spare them a standup fight." A swell of anger rose in his chest. He indulged it by rearing his tall, black charger. "I look forward to the gloomy faces of the juggernauts. Say what you will about Blackthorn's automatons, Thulann, but at least they're not as devious as a Garronite!"

The Hall of the Shirron was a garden of hard granite. Its chambers and corridors echoed haunting sounds among lofty vaults and sharp, chiseled corners. The doorways and windows asserted the severe designs of the Juka Clans. Every detail reflected the cold beauty of a proud warrior race. The gloom of night lent a stoic calm to the atmosphere.

In a long meeting room, three figures gathered around a table of polished marble. Thulann of Garron sat quietly at one end. She wore the dark, textured robes of a Way Master. Beside her was the Shirron Turlogan himself, more than a head taller and built like a fighter. His chieftain's clothes were lavish with traditional embroidery, sparkling golden in the flicker of several lanterns. His skin was the color of emeralds.

Across from the two Juka sat Sir Gabriel Montenegro. His chair was pushed back from the table. He gripped the heavy marble edge. Dressed in his traveling armor, he gave the appearance that he was ready to leave at any moment. With a sour expression he leaned closer to the lamp beside him. "Let me put this in the simplest terms. Bahrok has escorted my knights to Jamark. My people shall set sail for New Britannia in a matter of days, unless you send a messenger to stop them. I am asking you to intervene, Shirron."

The old Jukan chieftain shook his bald head. "Perhaps it is better that you return to New Britannia. Your government is preparing for war, after all. Our own war masters are in your homeland now, training your soldiers."

"I studied with your war masters myself. If I thought that was a worthwhile pursuit, I wouldn't have left home."

The long-fingered Turlogan spread his hands on the table. "I wish I had better news to give you, but Bahrok is adamant. He wants you gone. I cannot afford to fight him over this. Battles with the warlord are costly to me. I must select them judiciously."

"You are the head of the Juka Clans. Won't they obey if you tell them to disregard Bahrok's prejudice?"

"Some clans would obey me. Others would obey Bahrok. He has been consolidating his power for many years. His victories on the battlefield have earned him a great deal of respect."

"Victories like the one at Enclave? Bahrok could have fortified the town a day before the Technocrats arrived, yet he deliberately waited for Clan Athul to be decimated first. Tell me, Athul was one of your own allies, wasn't it?"

The Shirron sighed. "Warlord Pakahm's bravery shall never be forgotten among my people."

Montenegro snorted. "Bahrok rides you like a steed, Shirron."

The Juka tilted down his head, aiming his short horns in the knight's direction. "Do not endeavor to provoke me, Montenegro. I am aware of Bahrok's plots. I can handle him when he truly challenges me. Until then I shall use my own discretion when it comes to choosing my battles."

Montenegro glanced at the Way Master sitting beside Turlogan. "And what is your opinion, Thulann? Don't you have some pithy advice to offer? You know this is unjust. Stop sitting there while the knife twists in my back!"

The old woman clasped her fingers together. "I fear I can offer you little except an apology. I have advised the Shirron to take this course of action. If you feel a knife turning, Montenegro, it is my hand on the hilt."

He pounded his fist on the table and bolted out of his seat. "What? After I came to your aid?"

"It is a disgraceful situation, but one into which Bahrok forces us. We must not form a rift between the clans. To divide our people now would mean defeat at the hands of Blackthorn. This matter is not worthy of the risk." She sighed. "I know our politics must seem brutal to you. You come from a nation that is mercifully united. You are blessed and I envy you for it."

Montenegro grimaced. "Then you're telling me that I have no recourse? I must leave this land simply because Bahrok commands it?"

Turlogan leaned forward. "You are here because I granted you license. In the name of diplomacy I must now rescind it. Have courage. I am certain your people shall return to our country soon. The time will come for us to join forces and strike down Blackthorn once and for all."

The knight shoved aside his chair with a brusque motion. "And who shall strike down Warlord Bahrok? I begin to get my enemies confused." He stalked toward the tall exit, then paused. With a bow he added, "Good evening to you, Shirron Turlogan. And to you, Way Master Thulann. I'm going home now. May your Great Mother save you from your own kind."

He wandered through the granite corridors of the Shirron's Hall, dark thoughts clouding his head. His blood boiled. Starfell beckoned his grasp. He almost reached for the sword, but snarled and punched a wall instead. A needle of pain shot through his hand. He cursed and walked on.

Despite their claims of honor, the Juka shamed themselves with their infighting. He marveled that Bahrok conjured victory from such discord, even with the aid of Logosian traitors. The thought tightened his fists. Montenegro would love to skewer Thulann for her actions, but his fiercest wish at that moment was for Bahrok to appear. He no longer feared the repercussions of a duel. For too long he had ignored the warlord's offenses. Disrespect and betrayal was his reward.

Yet Bahrok was away with his army. Montenegro could not hope to reach him in less than a few days. And in momentary flashes of calm, the knight understood that the warlord, while infuriating, was not the source of his pain. Bahrok simply aggravated an existing concern.

Montenegro dreaded what awaited him when he sailed home. His blemished past lurked there, and the uncertainty of his future.

In Logosia, Montenegro was a military leader. In New Britannia he had no such authority. Bahrok's interference had cut in half the experience he hoped to gain by fighting the Technocrats. He would still present his arguments to General Nathaniel for his own command, but he was unsure now of his chances for success. The possibility of rebuff carved a hollow place inside him.

He stepped outdoors into the thin mountaintop air. The night wind of late winter bore a razor's edge. The cloudy sky of Garron hung low overhead, faintly illumed by the crimson glow of a nearby lava pit.

Montenegro's black warhorse was tethered near the front entrance of the Shirron's Hall. He patted the beast on the rump, then sent away a Jukan guard who stood nearby.

He found himself reluctant to climb into the saddle. He could not shake the urge to ride to Bahrok's army and express his displeasure with whistling steel. Such bloodshed would be detrimental to his career, but glorious to his soul.

Without warning a voice met his ears, low and smoky and pleasant:

Of all the winds o'er sea and foam,
The warmest is the one blowing home.

From a shadow emerged Toria. Dressed in a Garronite robe she was a petite, exotic vision.

He discovered a smile on his lips. "Are you here to make sure I am leaving? It seems everyone else wants me gone."

She clutched a large bag to her chest. "That's not why I've come."

He glanced at the sack. "You're joining me?"

She swallowed and looked down. After a pause she murmured, "No. I have to stay. I can't leave—I can't leave Thulann." She turned her lips into a smile and caught his eyes again. "I brought you something. But you have to keep it a secret."

He furrowed his brow as he accepted the bag. "That is a stipulation I have grown to distrust. What is it?" From the sack he withdrew a long scroll. Unfurling a corner he saw a mass of thin lines, arranged in geometric patterns. Quickly he dropped the scroll into the sack again. "This is the missing—"

"—something I brought from Enclave. I took it when Thulann was not watching. I didn't mean to keep it from her, but if I tell her about it now she'll be honor bound to give it to Bahrok. She gave her word to him."

"Honor can be ruthless. That is the lesson of my lamentable life." He slipped the scroll into his saddlebag and buckled it firmly. "Very well, I won't tell Thulann. What do you want me to do with it?"

"Whatever you were going to do if you had gotten it at Enclave. Study it. Give it to the Royal Senate. I don't care. You don't deserve what's happened to you. I figure this might help."

He smiled again, with unexpected warmth. "Of all the hearts in this desolate land, the only good one belongs to a thief."

She giggled. "No one's called me that since I left the Den."

"Toria, you should come back to New Britannia. You're not at home here. I'm going to sail out of Ruhn, if you want to join me."

"I thought your knights were leaving from Jamark?"

"I intend to arrive in Britain before they do, to debrief General Nathaniel. If you're interested, I'm hoping to engage Captain Bawdewyn of the *Menagerie,* who should be in Ruhn about now. I am positive he would take you as a passenger. He claims to remember the tavern songs you performed as a child."

Her face brightened. "Bawdewyn the Beast! That rake! I played with his animals when I was growing up. How is he?"

"Free and successful. He's a privateer now. He makes his living chasing pirates and nosy Technocrat ships away from the Vesper coast."

"Give him my love," she smiled. "I wish I could come with you, but I have to stay with Thulann."

Montenegro could see that the Way Master was not the one who kept her here. He did not press the issue. "As you like. Do me a favor then, if you will. Send a message to Sir Aziz in Jamark. Tell him we shall meet again in Britain. I have done my best, but we cannot protect a henhouse if the chickens turn on each other." He took the girl's hand and laid a kiss upon it. "Thank you, Toria. Take care of yourself. You are a beacon of Compassion. Remember, the Virtues serve you just as well in this place as they do in more wholesome lands. Perhaps even more so." He leapt onto his horse. The saddle creaked under him. "Farewell, little thief!"

As he rode away toward the gates of Garron, his eyes sparkled. In the darkness the Virtues lit the path once again. He considered what he might do, upon his return to New Britannia, with the schematics in his saddlebag. General Nathaniel would appreciate such a gift. Because of Toria's kindness, his fortunes might just have changed for the better.

CHAPTER
4

Flight from Garron

"Good evening to you, Shirron Turlogan," grumbled Montenegro with a bow. "And to you, Way Master Thulann. I'm going home now. May your Great Mother save you from your own kind."

As the raven-haired knight stormed out the door, a pair of eyes watched him from the shadows of a distant corner. The lurker was wrapped in a mask and cloak woven in the colors of the granite wall. In the gloom of night, the spy was invisible.

Sister Raveka sensed a tug inside her stomach. In a visceral way she felt the urge to follow Montenegro. Months had passed since she last heard his rich voice. Its tone reminded her of the thrum of waves on the New Britannian shore. She did not want to stop hearing it. Yet she could not leave her hiding place. Thulann of Garron remained in the room. The Way Master would sense any movement and if Raveka was discovered, the best she could hope for would be a quick death.

Besides, the Technocrat had come here to spy on the Shirron. Now that Montenegro had gone, she hoped the discussion might turn candid. So Sister Raveka remained motionless and watched the two elderly Juka as they rose from the table and paced the room slowly, side by side.

Thulann, who had said little to the knight, spoke more easily now. "Montenegro was in a generous mood. He only insulted you once and he never offered to duel me to the death. Fighting the Technocrats has improved his disposition."

The tall Shirron Turlogan chuckled. "I can see why he and Bahrok want to kill each other. They both have a talent for making enemies."

"Montenegro's worst enemy is the mirror. He cannot look at himself without seeing his famous grandfather, Sir Lazaro. He measures himself short of a legend. Every setback is an affront to his name."

"I sympathize with him," said Turlogan. "My deeds are compared to both my father and my mother. Heritage is a daily burden."

Thulann stepped into the Shirron's arms and leaned against his muscular chest. "I served your mother for ten years. She burdened me with enough duties to tire a pteranx. It is a marvel I was not a hunchback by the time she died. But your burden does not come from the past, my love. It comes from the future. Montenegro is correct, after all. Every day Bahrok abuses us more brazenly. Never again do I want to turn my back on an ally, like I did tonight. We must apply the brakes or Bahrok's wheels shall crush us."

Turlogan stroked the back of her neck, unraveling a long, white braid. "I know the way. I have simply been reluctant to pursue it. Bahrok's victories are intoxicating, you see, after the Technocrats defeated us for so long. But this strategy of his makes me unhappy. I certainly do not approve of our clan's allies taking the brunt of the casualties. And I dislike relying upon Logosian traitors for our battle plans."

Listening from the shadows, Sister Raveka agreed with that statement. The Technocrats did not approve of traitors, either. The Lectors of Logos were desperate to know who was betraying them. Raveka hoped one of these two Garronites might enlighten her.

Thulann nodded. "Then tell me, how do you plan to rein him in?"

"By taking charge of the war personally. The time has come to invade Logosia in earnest. That means calling the New Britannians to my side. A hundred sorcerers and a thousand knights will round out our army quite nicely, would you not say?"

The Technocrat widened her eyes. This was the caliber of information she sought tonight, yet the thought of it was like a nightmare. If Montenegro's successes were any indication, the New Britannian forces matched all too well against the Logosians.

At that moment she knew she had to return to Logos. Her master, Lector Gaff, must learn this news without delay.

Thulann looked up into the Shirron's face. "That is a serious step. Do you think the Royal Senate will agree to come?"

"Of course they will. They have spent the last two years building ships to transport their army here. They hunger to stick a lance into Blackthorn. Remember, they believe it was he who caused the Great Cataclysm."

She rested her brow against his shoulder. "And when the New Britannians arrive on our shores, the clans will rally behind you for the push to Logos. And Bahrok will have no choice but to follow. That is your plan?"

"That is the largest part of it. You seem uncertain?"

"I confess, full invasion is not a comfortable idea for me. This is supposed to be a dispute over border territories."

"The Technocrats turned it into a war when they attacked Garron two years ago. I know the suffering troubles you, my dear, but do not become reticent. The Technocrats answer only to defeat. When summer dawns I shall march on Akar. It is the linchpin to a southern invasion and the first step on the road to Logos itself. Tonight I shall compose a message to the Royal Senate, inviting their forces to join ours. Would you care to help me?"

Thulann sighed. "No. I must confer with Dhayin tonight. I need to instruct our spies in Logos to watch for the schematics for Braun's Needle. Whenever they appear, I shall know with which Technocrat Bahrok has struck a bargain."

As she eavesdropped, Raveka squinted. Schematics for Braun's Needle? She knew of the project, but the particulars were kept secret. Had Thulann found something at Enclave?

The Juka stopped pacing. Turlogan bent down to kiss the Way Master's hair. "There is a role for you in my plan, as well."

She closed her eyes. "Yes?"

"Marry me, Thulann."

She nudged an elbow into his rib. "Stop it, old man."

"It is not idle fancy this time. I need you at my side."

Thulann turned her cheek against his chest. She seemed to be listening to his heartbeat. "I serve you best in the field, not as a wife mired in the administration of a household. That road is very worn, Turlogan, and badly maintained. Let us not walk it again."

"Am I not your Shirron? I command you to marry me."

"I am too old to intimidate. Save your commands and

your weddings for the young. They will give you better sport."

Turlogan chuckled. "Will they? Perhaps you are right. I must have a conversation with Venduss soon about marriage. We shall see what sport he provides."

"He believes he is ready to do what it takes to become a leader. But I do not think he will welcome a political marriage." She blinked, as if shaking off a memory. "I shall miss the annoyance of teaching him. I fear I have not sufficiently prepared him."

"Venduss has always made me proud," said the Shirron, "brash though he can be. He will do what is right. You have taught him well."

Thulann said nothing more, but pressed closer to her giant lover. They held one another in silence.

Raveka's mind was not silent, however. Every second weighed upon her as she longed for the open doorway. Her heart pounded in anticipation of a quick flight to Logos. Her trained Mathematician's memory had captured every word of the Jukas' conversation. She had the unsettling notion that it was an epitaph for Logos.

A mental chant of geometric proofs calmed her nerves. By the time she finished, the Juka had wandered from the room. Without hesitation she slipped out of the meeting chamber, through a high window and into the rust-and-stone city of Garron.

The back room of the alehouse smelled of yeast and tannin. Sister Raveka knelt in a shadowy corner as she buckled into her grey Mathematician's robe. Carefully she checked the straps of her equipment. Then she took a satchel of food from the burly tavernkeeper who assisted her.

"Do you need me to escort you to your carriole?" asked the Juka, a battle-scarred man with a tall war hammer at his side.

Raveka shook her head. "I want you to watch the Shirron's Hall for messengers. By morning Turlogan will send that letter to New Britannia. We must ensure that it does not reach the Royal Senate."

The Juka turned a pointed ear toward the front room. "Someone has come in. Keep quiet." He adjusted his apron, hoisted the war hammer across his shoulders and walked out of sight. Raveka eased a spring slinger into her palm. A knuckle-size ball of iron nestled in the weapon's firing chamber.

From the front room came the clash of weapons. Raveka darted to the door, to see the tavernkeeper swinging his war hammer. His opponent cartwheeled to the side, then drew blood with a quick swordstroke. A dusty moonbeam from a window revealed the intruder's face.

Raveka's chest tightened. Way Master Thulann had found her. Though the tavernkeeper was a skilled veteran and a loyal ally, he could only win her a few moments to escape. She cocked her spring slinger and dashed out the back door.

A lanky silhouette waited in the cloud-dappled moonlight of the alley. Venduss pointed two gleaming short swords at Raveka's chest. "Mathematician," growled the young Juka, "your only logical choice is to surrender to me."

She crouched and fired her weapon. A powerful spring hurled the iron ball into Venduss's chest. It smashed against his light armor. He snarled and staggered back.

Raveka flipped a catch on her high leather boots. As Venduss charged forward again she kicked her heels into the rocky ground. Pressure plates activated in her soles. From her hollow heels thrust tightly-coiled springs, propelling her into an exaggerated leap. She hurtled over the Juka's head. Her target was a pipe jutting out from the roof of the next building. She grabbed it, swung her legs over the edge and scrambled onto the rooftop.

Her shoulder exploded with fiery pain. The spring slinger toppled from her grip. She saw a dagger buried to the hilt next to her collarbone, just inches from the flesh of her neck.

A small figure rose from the gloom of the rooftop. Raveka recognized the shape of Toria, the minstrel from Buccaneer's Den. The diminutive human brandished a static-charged sword, which she must have taken from a Logosian soldier at Enclave. The blade threw sparks as the girl cleaved the air, driving Raveka back to the edge of the roof.

The Technocrat grimaced. These teenagers were stalling her until Thulann arrived. Raveka could not wait that long. With a grunt she plucked the dagger out of her shoulder. Venduss was scurrying up the same pipe she had employed. She flung the dagger at the Juka. It jammed into his arm. He cursed and swayed precariously.

Then Raveka reached into her sleeve. To one forearm was strapped a heavy device. She drew back a latch. From a spindle unreeled a long, thin chain that puddled at her feet. Rapidly she pirouetted, lashing the chain through the air like a whip. It smashed against the oncoming Toria. When the chain whip drew taut, small razors snapped out like fangs along its length. Raveka jerked the whip and the razors dragged along the minstrel's flesh, shredding her Garronite blouse and soaking it with blood. The girl screamed and leapt backward.

Sister Raveka sprinted across the roof, reeling in the chain whip. Another dagger sailed over her shoulder, missing by less than a hand's breadth. She paused at the far edge. The streets were empty from here to the Garron Arena, where her carriole was hidden. Moonlight through the clouds gave her a labyrinth of shadows in which to vanish. A few seconds' head start was all she required.

Footsteps approached. Toria and Venduss were closing in. Raveka fished into a pocket for the ammunition to her discarded spring slinger. Two dozen iron spheres clattered across the edge of the roof. Then she cranked down her spring boots for another assisted leap. When her pursuers were only yards away, Raveka jammed her heels against the ground and jumped high into the air. As she dropped to street level inside a cluster of deep shadows, she saw the two teenagers stumbling over her slinger balls.

She left them behind as she navigated the shadows of the stone city. Her injured shoulder burned, though not unbearably. The gravelly earth chittered underfoot more than she wanted, but just then haste was as important as stealth. Thulann of Garron must have spotted her leaving the Hall of the Shirron. The Way Master probably knew that Raveka had overheard them. And the old woman would surely kill a Technocrat spy before allowing information about the invasion of Logos to reach Blackthorn's ears. Raveka shivered at the thought. Besides Warlord Bahrok and perhaps Pikas of Enclave, she knew of no deadlier swordsman than Thulann of Garron. The crafty old Juka would not be stopped by the same tricks as her young companions. So the Mathematician resolved not to give Thulann a chance to catch up.

Minutes later she reached the tall pillars of the Garron Arena. The long building was topped with high, metal gratings like openwork canopies. Through a grid of moonshadows slipped the grey-robed Technocrat along the smooth exterior walls. On the opposite side of the building she ducked into a shaded recess. In the darkness she found her carriole. The flying machine was untouched where she had left it at sundown, draped with a thin black cloth to deter curious eyes. Raveka threw off the cloth and turned a valve wheel. The steam engine began to heat and chug to life. Tiny fires rippled within.

A tangy smell filled the air. Raveka wrinkled her nose at the silvery fluid dribbling from a vent on the side of the saddle-shaped vehicle.

From the darkness a voice murmured, "I am not conversant in the workings of these contraptions, but I do know that they cannot fly if the levitant has been emptied from their tanks. So unless you are concealing wings under that robe, I propose that you surrender to me now."

Raveka watched Thulann of Garron step into the light. The Juka wore the dark, layered robes of a Way Master. She blocked the exit from the niche. The long edge of her sword glinted like a steel thread.

The Technocrat unreeled her chain whip. The links clicked as they pooled on the ground. With shallow breaths she grumbled, "You're too late. Three messengers have already departed for Logos. Blackthorn will know about the invasion before the sun sets tomorrow."

"You are a gifted liar," said the Way Master, "yet I know that you have spoken to no one except the tavernkeeper. He most certainly will not be going to Logos just yet. The evening has not agreed with him."

Raveka frowned. "He is an honorable man. Treat him with dignity."

"I shall do so. And you shall receive similar treatment, Mathematician, unless I am forced to hamstring you. There is an unavoidable degree of indignity in that."

"Do not trouble yourself," said the Technocrat, then lashed out with her whip. The Way Master blocked the attack and captured the end of the chain around the base of her sword. Raveka had counted on the maneuver. She tossed the whip handle at the Juka, twirling it to form large, razor-toothed coils. For an instant Thulann wrestled with the gangly weapon. Raveka used the time to jump atop the carriole, kick a long lever and grip the controls tightly.

The carriole groaned and lurched upward. Raveka shoved a control lever as far forward as it would go. Inside the machine's levitant tanks, copper propellers churned with increasing speed. The Way Master had drained most of the levitant, but Raveka knew that enough remained in the pump valves to lift her out of the city and probably out of the mountains. Then she would be forced to land. The trip to Logos would be perilous on foot, but far less so than fighting Thulann of Garron.

Raveka felt a wash of relief as the carriole rocketed out of the niche and soared high above the Arena. The thin mountain air wafted her robes with a pleasant chill. She steered south, toward her homeland.

The vehicle tilted abruptly. Raveka looked down. The chain whip was caught around an exhaust pipe from the steam engine. Way Master Thulann clung to the other end, slowly climbing up.

The Technocrat could barely hear for the pounding of her heart. She conjured equations in her mind, to steady her nerves. Then she reached into a bag hanging from the side of the vehicle. A weighty device unbalanced her until she braced it on the pommel of the carriole.

The pneumatic bolt thrower was fully loaded. She switched on its steam chamber and aimed it at Thulann.

Raveka yelped. Impossibly the Way Master had climbed just inches from her. The Technocrat yanked the firing handle and fought the bolt-thrower as it bucked and thundered. Steel missiles thudded into the Juka's stomach, one after another. The old woman held with both hands onto the chain whip, resisting the violence of the impacts.

Though the breath was hammered from her lungs, Thulann of Garron managed to scream. Ropes of blood dangled from her lips. Yet the Juka did not fall. Her eyes blazed with fury. She managed to get her fist around the hilt of her sword.

The pneumatic bolt-thrower let out a brutal *clang*, then fell silent. The mechanism had jammed. Thulann sucked down a breath, then hissed as she drew back her sword to strike.

Quickly Raveka adjusted the pitch of the vehicle, angling upward as steeply as possible. The bolt-thrower toppled away. Thulann held on. The city of Garron became a cluster of light and dark specks below. Icy clouds stung them. Raveka knew the quick ascent would expend her levitant that much faster, but she calculated that this was her only chance for survival. Thulann could not drive the carriole. Killing Raveka would be suicide for the Juka.

And so the Technocrat was more amazed than horrified when she felt the Way Master's sword thrust into her abdomen. Talons of pain raked through her body. The wind lifted her from the saddle of the carriole and gently tumbled her end-over-end.

She slammed to an abrupt halt. Something clawed her armpits. Thulann had wrapped the chain whip around Raveka's chest and dropped her. She was now hanging underneath the flying machine. Above her, the Way Master mounted the saddle and threw several levers. The carriole balanced itself, then turned around and clumsily descended toward Garron.

Raveka realized the Juka was calling out to her: "My commendations to your Engineers! I only watched you for thirty seconds and already I feel comfortable enough to steer this clockwork dragon." Then the old woman broke into a fit of savage coughing. She plucked the steel bolts from her stomach. Raveka counted nine gory arrows as they fell past.

The Juka retrieved a crystal vial from her Way Master's garments. She drank the healing potion with obvious relief. Raveka disliked sorcery, but the frosty ache of her stomach wound made her crave the warm kiss of healing magic. She contented herself with ramming a scrap of torn leather into the bloody puncture.

The freezing air penetrated her flesh. She recited geometric proofs to chase away the pain. When she realized she could no longer feel her limbs, she opened her eyes to gauge her position.

They were still soaring over the mountains, but Garron was nowhere to be seen. Raveka guessed that they were heading north. Apparently Thulann had not mastered the controls after all. The carriole had overshot the city. Soon they would clear the mountain range and fly above the forest of tower trees beyond.

Then they would run out of levitant and fall from the sky. Raveka doubted that Thulann could make the descent survivable.

The carriole lost altitude as the craggy foothills gave way to gigantic trees. The massive, twisting limbs rushed past just a few yards under Raveka's feet. Clouds of screeching fleshwings boiled out of the forest canopy, disturbed by the carriole's passing. The treetops swayed and tossed like a restless sea. The atmosphere grew warm; spring came earlier to the lowlands than it did to lofty Garron.

Then the tower trees grew less dense. The terrain looked familiar. Raveka realized that Thulann was steering toward the north road between Garron and Ruhn, where help might find them.

When they dropped below the height of the tree line, the Way Master attempted to guide the carriole between the giant trunks. Their descent, though rapid, was slower than Raveka had anticipated. The old woman had some feel for the controls, thankfully.

The Technocrat decided not to find out if Thulann could land successfully. Summoning her last scraps of strength, she lifted her numb legs, found the cranks of her spring boots and ratcheted the mechanisms until they were fully cocked.

The carriole sped downward at a low angle. The ground streaked past at twice the velocity of a galloping horse. At a height of twenty feet Raveka unhooked the chain whip from around her chest.

Her sense of gravity vanished. The world somersaulted. She caught her bearings at the last instant and pointed her feet earthward as the ground raced at her.

The earth hit like a hammer. The spring boots activated but Raveka barely felt them. A flash of furious pain gripped her, squeezing out her breath and her strength. Her body screamed with agony. She imagined she was rolling. Then she lay in a sparkling, torturous cloud of blackness. She could neither move nor see. Every ounce of her will was required to avoid crying out.

Tall, sharp-edged grass rustled around her. Through the hard soil she felt the thump of many footsteps. She realized they were animal sounds. Her eyes struggled open painfully. In a moonlit grove of trees she saw a herd of rhythmalope trotting in her direction. The bull-size creatures jogged on two squat legs. The air resounded with their guttural barks. No doubt they had been frightened by the crash of the carriole.

Raveka wondered if Thulann was dead. She knew she would perish herself if the rhythmalopes trampled her. She forced her body to move, fighting broken bones to crawl to the base of the nearest tower tree.

The rhythmalopes pounded the earth as they lumbered past. Their musky scent mingled with the taste of her own blood. When their clamor ebbed into the distance, Raveka savored the tender whisper of wind through the trees. Her heartbeat began to steady itself.

Her consciousness dimmed.

A sonorous voice rumbled in her head, reciting the litanies of the Machine. Some sleeping memory had been awakened by her pain. Then she recognized the chants of the Techno-Prophet himself.

A solemn feeling overtook her. She had met Blackthorn two years earlier, when she brought a New Britannian archmage to Logos. The sorcerer and the Techno-Prophet engaged in a terrible battle. Blackthorn had soothed Raveka that day with his perfect chants. She would never forget his cold, reassuring voice. Hearing it was the greatest honor of her life. It was no accident that he came to her again now, in a moment of extreme trial.

Another noise intruded. Raveka wakened herself from the trance. She heard steps in the darkness. The staggering footfalls of an injured person.

Thulann of Garron had survived. Perhaps she had drunk another healing potion. Perhaps she was simply unkillable. Raveka did not want to know. The old Juka was coming closer. The Technocrat dragged herself into the shadows to get away. She could not shake the feeling that destiny was hounding her, that there was no escaping the Way Master. Yet the Techno-Prophet still chanted in Raveka's memory, urging her to keep moving. Tenacious enemies were nothing more than elements in a formula. Shattered bones were an equation to be solved. Sister Raveka was part of the Machine, a component that would continue to function as long as life remained in her body.

She stumbled with a broken leg along the path trampled by the rhythmalope herd. Their lingering stench and chaotic footprints would help to conceal her tracks. The creatures were heading in the direction of the road. Raveka did not know if that was the wisest path for her to take, but she saw no credible alternative. With luck, perhaps the Way Master would find the road herself and head back to the mountains. The thought drove the Technocrat onward.

After an eternity the trees parted. A wide road slashed through the forest, illuminated by two cloud-striped moons. Raveka dropped facedown into a patch of tall grass. Her body felt ragged and feverish. The pain had dulled to a steady, deafening throb.

Her cheek lay against the prickly grass. She inhaled the raspy scent. Her heart knocked swiftly under fractured ribs.

Hoofbeats patted the earth nearby.

Hoofbeats?

The voice in her head murmured, "Look what fell out of the heavens." Yet it was not Blackthorn speaking to her but another voice, one whose tone reminded her of the thrum of ocean waves on the New Britannian shore. She opened her eyes to see Gabriel Montenegro kneeling over her. His giant, black horse panted behind him.

Her lips parted to speak, but she was unsure if any words came out.

Something exquisite filled her mouth. Her body seemed to vanish in the tingling spell of a liquid poured down her throat. The sensation was overwhelming. She allowed it to consume her, vaguely aware that she was being lifted off the ground. Then her thoughts swirled away, replaced by the deep, yawning succor of oblivion.

When she was a little girl, Raveka lived with her father and mother inside a tall, stone windmill. The wide, whirling blades drove a huge pump that sucked water from underground. The water filled giant copper tanks in the basement. Raveka had always marveled at the intricate gears and pipes. They were her playground, and the shape of her earliest memories.

The wind pump rose from the parched earth of a vast, dry lake bed. A single road stretched across the cracked wasteland. Travelers would use the place as a roadhouse, an oasis in the desert terrain. Raveka learned much about the behavior of humans and Juka from the parade of visitors through their home. Her mother often remarked that the girl was too perceptive for her own good.

Raveka's father spent his time maintaining the huge machine. The pump might have been his sworn enemy, for every day they battled amid much cursing and clamor.

Raveka had learned not to interfere. The man was trenchant when his mood soured. Yet some of her fondest memories involved her father's strong hands, creased with oil, piquant with the scent of sweat and grease. At the end of the day she always felt safe knowing that he would be there to keep the wind blades turning.

And so the rains of spring were a bittersweet time. For several weeks the sky was clogged with thunderclouds. Steady rains filled the lake bed to the depth of Raveka's knees. The road became impassable and the wind pump unusable. During this period her father would travel north to the city of Junction, in the shadow of mighty Logos, to find extra work and to buy replacement parts. These were strange, magical days for Raveka, when the world grew black and stormy and she huddled with her mother among the stillness of unmoving machinery.

The rains had fallen for more than a week on the afternoon she found the rusted lock. The metal door was underground, in a damp corner, painted with vertical stripes from a constant trickle of water. Raveka had always known about it, but a padlock had kept her from investigating. To all appearances, the door had not been opened during her lifetime.

On that day she discovered that the lock had rusted away. It fell apart in her hands. She wiped the orange mess on her shirt, made certain that her mother was not around, and then labored to open the ancient, corroded door. A bitter, mildewy odor assaulted her.

Inside she found a treasure.

The storage room was full of moldering crates. Within them lay cups and plates, utensils, tools, water-smeared books and parchments, small articles of furniture, weapons of primitive construction. The objects had an exotic, even alien demeanor, bursting with ornate designs, frivolous in their carven excess. Raveka spent hours examining each fantastical piece.

They were, of course, possessions brought to this land from Britannia itself. Raveka's mother explained in hushed tones how the girl's great grandmother had fled with her husband to the shores of Logosia, aboard one of Lord Blackthorn's ships, after the Great Cataclysm cracked the world. They had been a wealthy family, she a rich lady and he a prosperous knight. But after Blackthorn embraced the wonders of the Machine, all remnants of the past became forbidden. Lector Exedur, the first of Blackthorn's Chosen, decreed that old possessions must be destroyed. The Machine rejected all vestiges of the primitive.

Raveka's artifacts were contraband. Her mother declared that they must be burned, lest they be found by the authorities. But Raveka would not have it. She insisted that they could keep the treasure secret. In the end they agreed not to destroy the objects until the rains ended. But Raveka's father must not learn of the discovery. He maintained the wind pump by license from the Technocrats, and could well lose everything if such a disgrace were known. Raveka reluctantly agreed.

And so while the rains fell, she filled her days and nights with fantasies of her ancestors. She imagined what might have been if her forebears had not left Britannia. Her father would have ridden a tall charger and she would be a lady herself, swaddled with indulgent clothes, surrounded by the lush, florid landscape of the Lost King's realm. To indulge her daydreams she decorated the pump tower with silver and brass and mildewed tapestry. The quiet machinery sparkled with aged opulence.

When the rain clouds fractured and the storms began to falter, Raveka's mother announced that the time had come to burn the artifacts. Raveka screamed her protests. Though her mother attempted to calm her, the precocious girl answered every reassurance with the cry, "I want to be a Britannian lady! I want to be a Britannian lady!"

Yet Sister Raveka did not remember the words being quite so painful on her lips. She murmured them again. Her mouth burned. Her throat felt stony.

A voice answered, "If that is a proposal, we shall need to discuss your dowry."

She opened her eyes. The world lurched around her. She was wrapped in a blanket, lying on the saddle of a warhorse as it thundered down the road from Garron. The haze of predawn drenched the tower trees in watery blue light.

Her back pressed against something warm. Strong hands embraced her from behind. The black, muscular horse surged forward with powerful strides, cleaving through the cool morning air.

She wet her crackled lips and rasped, "Where are we going?"

"Ruhn," said Montenegro.

Another memory bubbled up, of Thulann and Turlogan. The Juka Clans were going to invade Logosia in the summer. She had to take the news to Lector Gaff. "I must go south. Turn around."

"I can't do that."

"Then stop here. I shall travel on foot."

"That would not be wise. Thulann of Garron is following us. You're safe with me, as long as we keep ahead of her. On your own you wouldn't make it farther south than the Shirron's prison, and that is assuming Thulann does not kill you outright."

She stirred. Her injured body stung with every movement. A throbbing fever still gripped her flesh. She began to shiver. "Please give me another healing draught."

"I am saving my last one for Humbolt here." He patted his steed's tossing neck. "He'll need it if we are to ride to Ruhn without camping."

"I cannot go to the coast."

"But you shall go. Sleep now. Thulann could catch up to us in the city. You might need your strength to get away, though I daresay your talent for escaping is surpassed only by the Viper of Levanto himself."

She closed her heavy eyelids. "Why are you helping me, Gabriel?"

"There are eight Virtues. I leave it to your judgment, Raveka, to determine which one I serve today."

The Technocrat smiled, though the action drew blood from her lips.

At the end of the rainy season, Raveka's father had returned from Junction a week early. He brought with him a Technocrat from Logos to inspect the old wind pump. The stoic man wore the raiment of the Order of Mathematicians. His name was Brother Gaff.

When they arrived, Raveka's mother had not yet destroyed the Britannian artifacts. The two men entered the pump tower and found it strewn with lavish decorations. Her father roared with anger. Brother Gaff simply questioned each member of the family with a brusque, icy demeanor. He oversaw the incineration of every forbidden artifact. Then he returned to Logos, to bring the case before a judge.

Not many weeks later, Gaff reappeared with more Technocrats. The judge had rendered the expected punishment. Raveka's parents were removed from the wind pump and commanded to work in a mine somewhere to the northwest. Raveka herself was destined for Logos, where the Order of Mathematicians would harvest her promising, if undisciplined, intelligence.

Raveka's soul screamed on the last day she saw her mother and father. Her anger fell upon the man named Brother Gaff, the long-boned Technocrat who challenged her with his disapproving gaze. She intended to challenge him back. No amount of coercion would transform her into a Mathematician. Nothing could make her forget that she was the great granddaughter of a Britannian noblewoman. Though the Order might force her to bury her past, like rains in the dry lake bed it would remain underground, waiting to be brought to the surface again.

Raveka woke to the memory of the wind blades creaking steadily in the hot Logosian breeze. But the sound was more immediate than a fading dream. She blinked. Her eyesight resolved upon a strange, wooden room. The walls curved oddly and were decorated with silk and gold in lavish detail. A New Britannian tapestry covered what must be a window. The air smelled of cloves and salt.

She lay on a narrow bed in a pool of lush furs. Her body still ached. Her head swam in rhythm with the sound of creaking wood.

This was a ship. She was resting in an officer's cabin. And she was not alone.

In front of a rolltop desk sat Gabriel Montenegro. His ebony curls were wet and tousled. His face was haggard with fatigue. Around him on the desktop were stacks of nautical charts, yet the scroll he held up to a lantern contained far more precise designs. Raveka squinted to make out the details.

The document was a schematic from the Order of Engineers. She did not recognize the machine it depicted, though clearly a master had designed it. From this distance she imagined it might have been inked by Lector Braun himself. Was this one of the schematics for Braun's Needle that Thulann had discovered at Enclave?

Whatever it was, Montenegro had no business examining it. She considered rising, until she realized she was undressed beneath the fur blankets. She glanced around the cabin for her clothes.

Her eyes met the gaze of a spotted animal stretched across the hutch of the desk. She recognized Annis, Captain Bawdewyn's tamed ocelot. She had encountered the beast a year earlier, when she and Montenegro had tracked Pikas to Port Levanto.

The languid wildcat moaned a canorous growl. Montenegro lifted his head, then furled the scroll into a leather tube and slipped it inside a sack.

He did not turn to face her. "I apologize for not waking you, but I enjoyed the sight of you lying there. You remind me of a statue I once saw at Empath Abbey. Perhaps my chivalry was compromised, but since I bathed and bandaged you I thought you might forgive me."

She clutched the furs to her chest as she sat up. Her bruised spine complained. "You are . . . indelicate for a knight."

"I have been called far worse."

"Where are we?"

"On board the *Menagerie*, in the harbor at Ruhn. We sail with the evening tide."

"And Thulann of Garron?"

"If she is in the city, she has not seen fit to call."

Raveka exhaled from relief. "Would you care to give me my clothes, then?"

"I have been looking forward to it." Still facing away from her, he pointed to a tall, narrow wardrobe. She gathered the furs around herself and tried to stand. Her legs and feet were sore, but she felt no broken bones. The healing potions must have restored them. Balanced on the swaying deck, she opened the wardrobe. Inside was a slender, green dress of New Britannian style. The velvet was exquisitely brocaded.

Raveka thumbed the soft fabric. "Where are my raiments?"

"I sank them in the bay. I doubt the Jukan washerwomen would agree to clean them. Besides, Captain Bawdewyn had that gown in his stores and I knew you would want to try it on."

She lifted the dress from its hooks and held it against herself. "You do not serve the Virtue of Humility, if you are arrogant enough to presume what I want."

"I am probably arrogant," he murmured, "but fever makes you talk in your sleep, 'Lady' Raveka."

She felt herself blush. "Leave the room while I dress."

"Riona Lynch was never so modest."

"Riona was a disguise. You know nothing of Sister Raveka."

He rose and looked at her. His dark gaze did not stray from her face. "Your eyes tell me everything about you. It is a trait all women desire, except those who possess it." Then he took the sack holding the Technocrat scroll and stepped through the cabin door. The spotted wildcat bounded after him.

Quickly she dropped the dress and furs and searched the cluttered room. She found no trace of her equipment or weaponry, though one of the desk drawers yielded a curved dagger. A jeweled brooch from the wardrobe had a clasp which might double as a lockpick. She gathered these into a scarf around her waist and threw back the tapestry that covered the window.

The sun was low in the afternoon sky. The ship was anchored a quarter mile from the Jukan port of Ruhn. She could swim to shore in a matter of minutes, steal some local garments and make for Logos at nightfall.

She felt rested enough for the journey. Her fever persisted but her injuries were mostly gone. In the hubbub of the docks she might even elude Thulann of Garron, if the Way Master had followed her this far.

Though her fingers wrapped around the window latch, she did not open it.

The green dress lay draped across the furs on the bed. She glanced over its fine details. The laces were woven with golden strands. The embroidery depicted entwined animals. It was classic New Britannian garishness.

She lifted the dress and held it against her skin. The fit looked close. With a chuckle she untied the scarf from her waist, slackened the laces of the gown and stepped into it.

As if by instinct her body assumed the posture of a Britannian lady.

The wardrobe contained no shoes, but she did not mind. On bare feet she walked out of the cabin and up the steps to the main deck. The wooden surface was cool and soggy. The ocean wind swathed her in the warmth of budding spring. Bawdewyn's coyote, Kiye, snuffled at her ankles.

The human sailors, ragged and sweaty, halted their work

to stare at her. She smiled back. She recognized these men. They were pirates, or had been at one time, and would have cheered and whistled if the courtesan Riona Lynch had materialized among them. Yet now they fell silent. Some of them removed their hats. To them, she now appeared as a noblewoman. It was a dubious compliment from such a shabby audience, yet the feeling was marvelous.

One of them approached her from behind. She tensed, but the hand that touched her shoulder had a familiar gentleness. She laid her palm over Montenegro's fingers before she had a chance to consider the gesture.

He drew beside her. They leaned against the softly pitching bulwark, facing the shoreline. The tall knight squeezed her shoulder and muttered, "Thulann might see you on deck. She has a buzzard's eyes."

She smirked. "You'll protect me, won't you?"

"Indeed I shall, if you agree to my conditions."

"How mysterious! Please do elaborate."

"There is no mystery. Come with me to Cove. You'll be safe at my estate. The eagles should be nesting by now. It is a magnificent sight."

"You want to intrigue me with birds?"

"You would be quite a sight among them."

She chuckled. "And I take it you're eager to resume the search for Pikas, since Bahrok has thrown you out of Logosia."

He narrowed his eyes. "Do not poke at recent wounds. I am liable to flinch. Yes, in time I shall skewer Pikas's heart, but that is not the reason for my invitation."

She watched his face. "Then explain it to me."

He turned his hand over, brushing callused knuckles against her bare neck. His gaze was steady. "There is no mystery."

She smiled and looked away. "I see. You do not want to be alone while you lick your wounds."

"Precisely. And neither do you."

A sigh escaped her lips. She closed her eyelids. "You're right. I don't." She tilted her head, pressing a cheek against the back of his large hand. "I'm tired and sore, Gabriel. Which cabin is yours?"

He paused. "The one below the captain's."

"Join me there in ten minutes, if you care to." With some effort she peered into his eyes. They were as captivatingly grey as she remembered. Then she padded to the steps that led belowdecks.

Montenegro was berthed in what appeared to be the mate's quarters. The cabin was almost as large as the captain's, though not half as opulent. Components of plate armor were stacked on the bunk. Satchels and saddlebags were piled in the corner. Without delay she rummaged through his belongings until she found the leather tube that contained the schematics. The cap had been waxed shut to make it waterproof. That suited her needs.

She peeled off the New Britannian dress and arranged it carefully beside Montenegro's armor. The scarf was knotted around her thigh, holding the brooch and dagger. She held fast to the scroll tube as she pushed open the window. The heaving waterline was less than ten feet below. She braced a foot on the sill.

The cabin door scraped open. She whirled around. A small figure stepped in, no higher than her knee. The creature was a species of bird, standing on two legs and craning its long, muscular neck. She had heard of ostards, which served as riding beasts to the Meer. This must have been a young hatchling. It watched her with stern, curious eyes.

She grinned and pressed a finger to her lips. *"Beza rhem,"* she whispered, then drew her dagger and carved on the window frame the mathematical symbol for that name. The little bird observed with care as she climbed outside and dove into the satiny waves. The chilly water shocked her bare, feverish skin. The sensation was exhilarating.

Onshore, pilfering clothes proved simple enough. She made certain to wrap a hood over her head. Her black hair would not stand out among the Juka but her ivory-pale skin certainly would, not to mention her human face, which bore a nose where the Juka had none.

Disguised by a cowl, she crept between two stone buildings and popped open the scroll tube. Something slender floated out. It was an eagle's feather, brown and sleek.

The only document inside the tube was a note that read, *I borrowed this from the captain's hat. I should be most obliged if you return it to me at your earliest opportunity. Consider it an invitation. Gabriel.*

She could not resist laughing as she twirled the feather in her fingers. It snapped the air as it spun, like the blades of a wind pump.

The *Menagerie* was a tall, proud apparition among the smaller Jukan ships in the harbor. Its triangular sails filled with color as if the sunset were an ocean breeze. From the docks Raveka watched it move northward, cutting through the spry, silvery waves.

Another figure stood on the boardwalk nearby. The Technocrat blanched when she saw the person's face. Thulann of Garron had arrived. The old Way Master stared out at the receding barquentine. Her expression was dour.

Sister Raveka realized that the Juka did not see her. In the most disinterested manner she could calculate, the Mathematician turned away from the harbor and walked off the docks. When she was nearly out of sight, she dared to glance behind.

Thulann had not moved. The Way Master seemed rooted by indignation, casting a dark glower across the water to Montenegro's ship. Even if Raveka had been wearing her Technocrat's robes, the old woman would probably not have noticed.

The Technocrat had learned not to question good luck. She quickened her pace away from the shoreline, looking for a ridgeback to take her south. One hour's head start ought to be enough to evade the Way Master, but Sister Raveka preferred a greater margin. The trip to Logos would be very long. She craved the opportunity to sleep along the way with both eyes closed.

CHAPTER
5

The Pact of Four

Springtime arrived in the city of Britain on the wings of returning swallows. Belfries blackened with tiny bodies and stiletto tails, swarming like noisy, writhing smoke. As if awakened by the cacophony, plant life erupted across the surrounding meadows and forests. Animals ventured from their winter dens and signaled the return of the hunt. Warm winds soared from the eastern desert to stir up capricious weather. The people of the capital celebrated with festivals of fire.

Montenegro knew that he was viewing his homeland with prejudice, but after half a year in the desolate tracts of Logosia, New Britannia looked like paradise to him. The grassy hillsides and rocky streams were glorious in their meandering ease. Even the sky was the proper shade of blue.

Presently he was trotting on his warhorse down a tree-lined roadway under a golden, late morning sun. The terrain about him was immaculate even for Britain, as it comprised the grounds of the estate of General Nathaniel. The general was the highest ranking officer in the Britannian army. His regal white manor stood like a pearly sculpture at the far end of the lane.

The black warhorse snorted and halted abruptly, kicking up a plume of dust. Montenegro looked ahead. A short, simian figure darted across the road in front of him. Its back was stooped and its long arms pounded the dirt like extra legs. It wore a shirt of primitive leather armor. In close pursuit were a handful of soldiers with spears and halberds.

The knight laughed. Apparently this year would be difficult for landowners trying to keep the goblins away. He reminded himself to monitor the problem when he returned to his own lands outside Cove, though he did not know when that might happen. If today's enterprise went smoothly, he might not visit his family home for some time.

He nudged the stallion forward. Large saddlebags jingled as the warhorse resumed its gait. Montenegro smiled. The bags contained only a fraction of the booty he had taken from the Technocrats, yet even this small collection would astonish the general. The knight had occupied the trip home in collaboration with the *Menagerie*'s tinker, working to repair and operate as many of the bizarre Logosian devices as they could. In more than a few cases they succeeded.

The jewel of the booty, however, was the scroll that Toria had given him at Garron. Montenegro, Bawdewyn and the tinker were unable to determine what the schematics depicted, but the information they did glean was shocking. Braun's Needle was an enormous war machine, larger than several galleons. It was designed to travel both by sea and by air. The weapon on board was mysterious in its operation, though the sheer size of it caused Montenegro to fear its power in battle. He trusted that more technical eyes could interpret the diagrams to find some weakness in the machine, in case the New Britannian military had to face it, or perhaps even to discover a means to build one for themselves.

In any event he knew that the scroll, the mechanical devices and his own experiences on the battlefields of Logosia would be excellent bargaining points for a real command again. General Nathaniel would have no choice but to grant him a hearing with the other high officers. He resolved not to leave until he had secured that promise.

When he clopped in front of the two-story manor house, a barrel-chested soldier greeted him with a smile. Montenegro dismounted and clutched the man's arm. "Sergeant Matthias! The general still has you chained to his front door, I see."

The soldier chortled. "He throws me a scrap of meat sometimes. Welcome back, sir! I didn't know you were in the city."

"I have made sure no one knows. I want to surprise the general."

"Well, you can't surprise him just now. He mustn't be disturbed."

"Nonsense. He'll want to play with the toys I have brought him."

"He has another visitor."

"Does he? I see no expensive carriages waiting, nor footmen pitching dice in the corner. Whoever it is cannot be noble, and no less a person than a noble will suffice to delay me today."

The soldier chuckled. "I'd show you to a parlor to wait, sir, but I know you too well. The moment you were out of my sight, you'd go looking for him."

Montenegro dropped the reins into the guard's hand.

"Who says I would wait? Besides, I already know where he is. I can see the curtains drawn open in the trophy parlor." He pointed to a second-floor balcony.

Sergeant Matthias stood his ground. "If you can fly, maybe you can join him, but I can't let you through this door, sir."

The knight grinned and knelt underneath the balcony. He clicked the latch of a device strapped to his boot. "As you like it, Sergeant." When he rammed his heel into the ground, Sister Raveka's spring mechanism propelled him into the air. He twisted unexpectedly in mid-leap, but managed to grab the railing and keep from falling back to the ground.

He climbed over the banister and waved to the flabber-gasted soldier. "Keep an eye on my things, would you, Matthias? I'll be down for them momentarily. You have a goblin problem and I do not want anything to walk away."

The door of the balcony was unlocked. The parlor beyond was a museum of taxidermy, its walls crowded with the mounted extremities of Britannia's diverse fauna. Montenegro had visited this room many times before. He always found the stuffed troll head distasteful, though the gazer pelt was handsomely iridescent and the dragon skull above the mantel commanded the room as majestically as ever.

Two men were seated before the unlit fireplace. Both of them turned in their chairs and regarded Montenegro with confusion. General Nathaniel was a strapping officer who appeared much younger than he was. His trim beard had not greyed and his waist-length hair was knotted into two braids, in the manner of less aged men. He wore a casual tunic and boots. When he recognized the intruder, the general wrinkled his face into a frown.

"By Honor and Humility, how did you get in here, Montenegro?"

But the knight did not acknowledge General Nathaniel's words. His eyes were transfixed on the second man. The fellow's clothes resembled those of a western merchant, though Montenegro knew this was no Britannian tradesman. The man's gaunt frame, bald head and white, ghastly flesh were unmistakable.

This was the Technocrat who Montenegro had seen in Enclave, peeking out from the library where the dreadnought had been. He was the Logosian traitor to whom Bahrok had given Thulann's schematics. Montenegro recalled the man looking like the spectre of death.

The knight squeezed his fists. A feeling rushed through him that he had somehow been outmaneuvered. He thought of the scroll in his saddlebag and wished he had not let it from his sight.

The Technocrat's pale eyes saw the recognition in Montenegro's face. He returned a stony gaze.

General Nathaniel glanced between the two men. Then he stood in front of Montenegro, presenting a disapproving stare. "What do you mean by creeping in like that? You're not supposed to be here."

"Have I surprised you, General? That's odd. I thought this Technocrat would have informed you that my knights and I had sailed home."

The officer hesitated before patting Montenegro's shoulder. His voice lowered. "This is not the time for explanations."

The knight grumbled, "Perhaps you need to save your explanation for Lord Gideon, sir. I have plans to make an appointment with him after I leave your company."

Nathaniel narrowed his eyes. "In fact, his lordship was to be my guest for dinner tonight, as well as High Admiral Duarte. But I have an unexpected visitor today, as you can see, so I had to postpone. However, you are welcome to join me tonight, Sir Gabriel. It will give us the opportunity to address the questions that you cannot ask right now."

Montenegro examined the bald Technocrat. Except for his ghoulish pallor, the man's disguise was unsettlingly convincing. Montenegro muttered, "I shall be delighted to come, sir. I'm interested to see what he has told you. And I have a few stories of my own to relate."

"Good. I'll have a place set for you, then. And please, don't mention this to anyone until we speak again."

"General, I am unsure whom I would trust enough to tell." He gave the Technocrat a suspicious nod, then bowed to the officer in military fashion. "Look for me at nightfall."

As Montenegro walked from the trophy room, General Nathaniel halted him. "Sir Gabriel, would you be good enough to send Sergeant Matthias up? Thank you."

"Sir, my intrusion was not due to any negligence of his. The sergeant is a good man."

The general made no answer. Montenegro simply nodded, then navigated the marble corridors and exited the manor through the main doors. On the front drive, Matthias still held the reins of the knight's warhorse. Montenegro told him of the general's summons, adding, "Has anyone touched my saddlebags?"

"Of course not, sir. No one has been here but me."

"Excellent. Thank you."

As the knight climbed atop his steed, Matthias waved and entered the manor through the ornate front doors. When the soldier was out of sight, Montenegro unbuckled a saddlebag and slipped his hand inside. The scroll was still there. He glanced at the doors and blew a sigh of relief, then urged the warhorse on.

On a nearby hilltop a pack of guards trudged into view. One of them carried the corpse of a goblin slung over his shoulder. The soldiers were laughing as they mimed the killing blows with their steel-tipped polearms. Dark blood smeared the keen edges, glistening in the lively sun of the newborn springtime.

Though he tried to remain inconspicuous in the city, Montenegro drew a small audience as he walked the cobble-stone lanes of Britain. The townsfolk recognized him even in his black, unadorned tunic. He became a spectacle in the lunchtime glare. Mostly children dogged his steps, asking him to recount his adventures fighting Blackthorn. They spoke as if he had personally clashed swords with the legendary tyrant. When he realized they would not be chased away by angry looks, Montenegro resigned himself to the entourage and quickened his steps. His destination was not far.

The Blue Boar Tavern was a stack of grey, vine-threaded stones. Like most buildings that survived the Cataclysm, it was strewn with cracks that had been bandaged with wooden transoms. Many stone blocks were fractured or missing. The walls of the place reminded Montenegro of an old codger's snaggletooth grin. Even the ancient signboard was weathered with lines like wrinkled flesh. The yeasty breath of the common room was a greeting from an old friend.

Montenegro's youthful entourage stopped at the entrance, though they peeked into the noisy tavern. The patrons lifted their goblets with a cheer as the knight stepped inside. He smiled back and scanned the room. Then he picked his way between the crowded chairs and tables. Welcoming hands slapped him on the back. Along the far wall he dropped into a seat at a thick, round table. When the patrons started to gather he tossed a pouch full of coins to the barmaid and shouted, "Drinks for the house! On the condition that I am given a little peace."

The taverngoers cheered again and obliged him.

He entwined his fingers, rested his elbows on the knife-scarred surface and gazed at the other man occupying the table. "I thought I might find you here. I'll buy your next drink, as well, though I expect no peace from your energetic voice."

The fellow wore a tangle of ill-fitting clothes, as if he did not entirely grasp the workings of city fashion. His hair was a burst of sunshine blond. His tanned face looked sullen. "I fear that peace is a luxury in which I shall never indulge. The world has become my cage, you see, and like a captive animal I am doomed to pace back and forth, always moving and yet never advancing beyond the cold iron bars. I am a chained bear, Montenegro, baited with sharp-toothed dogs."

The knight accepted a cup of water from the barmaid. It tasted gloriously cold. He leaned back in his chair and propped a boot on the table. "Fairfax, I have rarely seen you in so gloomy a state. Only one sort of dog bites a man like you so cruelly, and that is the bitch. Am I right?"

Fairfax the Ranger dragged fingers through his yellow hair. "That is the very truth. It is a bewilderment to me, Montenegro. You would think, would you not, that the fortunes of a warrior with my charm and propriety might burgeon in the company of as many maidens as this confounded city provides. And yet at every turn I am met with scorn and feminine rancor. I tell you, something poisons the city air. Perhaps women were not meant to be herded so closely together in the same pen."

The knight swallowed a cool mouthful of water. "Surely at least one woman has resigned her attentions to you?"

"One? My tally has reached five simultaneously! And yet when I am nearly sated by the sweetmeats of success, these gingerbread city girls inevitably cross paths with one another. Then the bakery closes, my friend, and the ovens grow very, very cold." He slurped the foam from the bottom of his goblet. "But fie upon inconstant women! Not one is as faithful as a good bottle of Trinsic port. And in honor of your homecoming I propose that you and I divide the contents of just such a bottle, while you tell me how you divided Lord Blackthorn from his entrails."

Montenegro chuckled. "You know I don't drink, Fairfax, nor could you afford a bottle of Trinsic if I did. Yet I shall buy one for you, provided that you agree to undertake a pair of favors for me in return."

"If they require me to leave the walls of this henhouse called Britain, I shall gladly perform both favors for a single bottle."

"One of the favors will take you out of town, though not far. I need you to assist me in an appointment this evening."

"Pleasure or business?"

"Business. Wear your good armor."

The ranger held his goblet to the barmaid, who topped it off. With a grin he toasted the knight. "At last, a feat of daring again! I shall be glad for the chance to stick a blade in the enemy, as a change from my present altercations. And the second favor?"

"Bring along your better half, Jatha the Meer. I may have need of you both."

Fairfax lost his smile. "We may have trouble separating him from his own affairs. He has been studying ruthlessly with Mistress Aurora. I doubt he has seen daylight in over a month." He nibbled the froth of his beer. "It's for his sake alone that I remain in this wench-infested capital, you know, while troops of rangers are sharpening their spears on troll bones in the north. You have heard, I assume, that the troll king is raiding villages around the Serpentspine foothills?"

Montenegro nodded. "I wonder if he is still upset over our expedition to his domain a few years back. He did lose four sons that day."

"That would probably raise my dander, as well," nodded the ranger. "Luckily I am not aware of any sons that have issued from my own escapades. As to Jatha, I shall direct my rather unreliable charm to coaxing him from the company of Mistress Aurora. What shall I tell him is the reason for our adventure?"

"Intrigue, of course."

"Ah, the chief export of Britain."

The knight snorted. "Lately we have been importing it from abroad."

Fairfax laughed. "You are well aware, of course, that Jatha and I do not indulge in the profligacy of political schemes. We keep our motivations simple and pure. Yet I may just convince him that helping a friend is as pure a motive as any man could require. And perhaps that bottle of Trinsic port will be sweet to his tongue, if my words are not sweet to his mulish ears."

Montenegro grinned. "You're lucky that I trust you enough to pay for the wine beforehand. But if you arrive tonight and I find more of it on your breath than in the bottle, you shall indeed wish you were facing the troll king instead of me."

"The implication! I'm shocked at you, Montenegro. Jatha and I are always discreet in our dissolution. It is what separates us from baser species."

"Truly, you are a paragon of civilization. Now drink up. It's time to leave. We have preparations to make."

The ranger abandoned his nearly full goblet as he rose from his seat. "Drink up? Alas, the charm of the Blue Boar alehouse is the house, not the ale. To leave a cup unfinished might insult the brewer, but to drink it in haste would insult my mouth. I choose the less personal of two evils."

"Unless the beer has improved since I gave up alcohol, I cannot fault you for that."

Fairfax pursed his lips. "Women are inconstant. The Blue Boar Tavern is as unchanging as the very heavens."

Outside the front door the cluster of children had not dispersed. The two men found themselves in the midst of a squall of high-pitched voices. Yet Fairfax seemed to take pleasure in teasing the urchins and their attention soon focused upon the amiable ranger. That alone, thought Montenegro, was worth the cost of Trinsic port. He decided their first stop would be the wine seller, and from there, a few, more exotic vendors. He did not know what strategy General Nathaniel might take in dealing with him, but on a tactical level, even the highest officer in the land did not intimidate Montenegro. He would be prepared for any action, political or otherwise.

General Nathaniel's dining hall was a trove of silver and gold. The engraved dinnerware was polished to a faultless glow. The tables and chairs were ornate with precious metals. Even the chandelier flashed in its own candlelight. Much of the decor was centuries old, brought back by Nathaniel from a dragon's lair deep in the crags of the Serpentspine. The rest had been commissioned using the dragon's treasure. To commemorate the monster's generosity, a painting of the fearsome reptile dominated the head of the hall.

It was common knowledge, however, that the general was not himself prone to displays of wealth. Rather his wife, Lady Annabel, made a career of transforming the spoils of his campaigns into lavish domestic tableaus. The general indulged her expensive requests. Montenegro might have regarded the arrangement as ostentatious, except that Lady Annabel herself was the very portrait of noble elegance. The middle-aged gentlewoman was courteous, handsome and erudite. Her company was always a delight.

When dinner was finished Montenegro, General Nathaniel and Lady Annabel talked over dessert. The lady neglected her cream cake as she motioned to the knight with her spoon. "Please, Sir Gabriel, help me clarify a few terms. Of course Blackthorn is the ruler of Logosia. But who exactly is 'Blackthorn's Chosen?' And what are these 'Lectors' I have heard about? Are they religious leaders?"

Montenegro absently picked at his food. "The philosophy of the Machine is not a religion, my lady, but a secular form of spirituality, in the same manner as our own Virtues. However, the Technocrats are just as zealous as a religious cult. And they are the ruling class of Logos. Now, there are three divisions within Technocrat society. They are the Orders of Engineers, Mathematicians and Theorists. Each order has a Lector at its head. Blackthorn is the Techno-Prophet, the master of all three orders. They consider him to be something of a demigod. Yet he does not directly handle the daily affairs of state. Instead he names one of the Lectors as his representative, who assumes the title of Blackthorn's Chosen and acts on the Techno-Prophet's behalf."

Lady Annabel lifted her eyebrows. "How opportune for that Lector."

"Indeed. Currently the Chosen is a man named Lector Sartorius of the Theorists. Some Garronites believe that he is the actual ruler of Logosia. They think that Blackthorn has become a recluse, or even a madman, after so many years on his mechanical throne. I cannot say whether or not that's true, but I do know that the Chosen acts with Blackthorn's own authority. He speaks with a demigod's voice. The real Tyrant of Logos, my lady, may actually be Lector Sartorius himself."

She chuckled. "They sound much like the Royal Senate— a room full of children and no guardian."

The knight smirked. "That is an apt characterization. Remember, the Technocrats are not many generations removed from New Britannia. They are us, stripped of our traditions and Virtues. As a culture they are like children, playing with a new toy."

General Nathaniel sipped from a glass of scarlet liqueur. "I wish Montenegro had brought along some of his captured machines this evening. If they are half as amazing as the ones I have seen in the past, they would truly astonish you, my dear. The Technocrat government might be rotten with Blackthorn's corruption, but their engineering skills are unparalleled."

Lady Annabel smiled with a glint of challenge in her eye. "You know my thoughts on that subject, Nathaniel. Clockwork creations can be splendid, I grant you, but I disagree with using alchemy to enhance them, as the Technocrats do. It is an irresponsible use of magic. Sorcery should be controlled by trained masters, not thoughtless machines in the hands of the uninitiated."

"And yet, my dear, you would put an enchanted sword in the fist of a simple warrior?"

"Magic swords are an ancient tradition. Wizards give them to warriors because by and large, warriors only use them to kill each other. That is an acceptable loss, from a wizard's perspective."

The general chuckled. "You must forgive Annabel. She was trained in water magery before we married. The House of the Griffin still taints her opinions."

"I agree with her in some cases," said the knight, "and so would you, sir, if you met a dreadnought face-to-face. Blackthorn has created some undeniable abominations. Yet I have seen fountains of fire in his public squares that would stun you with their beauty, my lady."

"Beauty exists in many forms," replied Lady Annabel, "and not all of them are Virtuous." She glanced at the painting of the dragon, its scales glittering. Then she opened a warm smile. "But let's not allow Nathaniel to drag us into a debate. I canceled quite an affair tonight in deference to his urgent business, and so I shall leave you gentlemen to conduct it." She rose and bowed her head to Montenegro. "It's a joy to see you back safe and sound, Sir Gabriel. Please let us arrange for a more proper reception soon. Nathaniel, shall I summon your mysterious guests now?"

"Please do, my darling, to the trophy room. And have a bottle of brandy sent up."

A small blaze crackled in the fireplace of the trophy parlor. The dragon skull above the mantel watched Montenegro and the general with eyes that fluttered shadows. The two men leaned back in velvet chairs. General Nathaniel swirled a glass of brandy and commented, "Annabel is very fond of you. It's pleasing to see a smile on her lips again. Lately her mood has been somber."

The knight was not drinking. "Does she know the nature of your guest?"

"She suspects more than she'll admit. But I oblige her business and she obliges mine. Ours is a deferential marriage."

Montenegro darkened his eyes. "I met with Lord Gideon this afternoon."

The general shot him a look of alarm. "What did you tell him?"

"Nothing, as we agreed. I simply invited him to have dinner at my estate in two weeks' time. But I'm telling you about it up front, so you understand that I walk with Honesty. So should you, sir." He captured Nathaniel's eyes with a heavy gaze. "General, I need to know why that Technocrat is here."

For a moment the long-braided officer examined the glass in his hand. Then he emitted a sigh. "I confess, Montenegro, that you have brought considerable worry upon me. True, it's my fault that you were able to barge in on us this afternoon. I grew inattentive with my security. Nevertheless I am in a nasty bind. I have an agreement, you see, to keep this affair confidential."

The knight frowned. "Trust me, sir, that I understand how inconvenient such a pledge can be. But there may be a solution to satisfy us both."

"What do you have in mind?"

"You betray no confidences if I am part of them. Let me into your scheme."

Nathaniel gave a soft chuckle, then caught his eye. "That, I cannot do."

"Can't you? Then perhaps you would prefer to have this conversation with Lord Gideon. I'm sure he will find it most engaging. But of course, this affair must be kept secret from him, right? Otherwise you would not have canceled your dinner tonight. What plot do you have in motion that you cannot divulge to the House of the Lion? Is it insubordination or something worse?"

The general shot him a piercing glower. "Don't try to strongarm me, Sir Gabriel! We're not enemies and you would be wise to keep it so." He dragged his hand over his face. "Let us conduct ourselves as gentlemen here. You're right, Lord Gideon does not know, and must not. But please, before we continue, tell me what interest you have in this. Intrigue is not in your nature."

Montenegro leaned forward. His face grew warm as he stared at Nathaniel. "Let me tell you about my nature, sir. I am a soldier. What I want is very simple. I want victory on the battlefield. But my Logosian campaign was cut short because of Warlord Bahrok's intrigues. I lost a cache of valuable schematics because Bahrok handed them over to the very Technocrat you have been dealing with. Now I return home to find that these intrigues have taken root here, as well. And I get the uncomfortable feeling that they are going to steal even more victories from me. I cannot ignore the situation any longer, General! The Virtue of Justice demands my action. If these schemes intrude upon me, I will intrude back. That is the crux of it."

Nathaniel swallowed a sip of brandy. "I sympathize with you. Before I became a general I often felt the same way." He sighed. "I can't let you into this affair. But if you pledge not to discuss it with anyone else, I'll do my best to make sure that it does not interfere with your own business."

"That's not good enough, General."

"Oh? What more do you need?"

"Tell me what you're up to. I need to recognize trouble if it comes my way."

The officer grumbled. "You probably do deserve an explanation, though I shall regret it. Very well. I'll tell you something of my secret, as long as I have your promise of silence."

Montenegro paused for a deep breath. "One more thing, General, in exchange for my discretion."

"More! You are hungry tonight, Sir Gabriel. What more?"

"I want my own command again."

The general stroked his beard. "Hmmm. I should have known you would say that. But I'm afraid that is not a simple task. Many officers still consider you to be too headstrong for command. Admiral Duarte would surely fight it." He rolled a thought behind his eyes. "Your experience against the Logosians will help tremendously. When the other knights arrive, I'll collect their testimonials. You say you've brought back a sizable haul of Technocrat machines? Give them to me and I can use them to grease the wheels."

"Done," said Montenegro, though he resolved not to include the schematics for Braun's Needle. He would not see Nathaniel hand it over to the Technocrat.

"Very well. I am not a sorcerer, but I'll try to dig up a command position for you. Do we have a bargain, then?"

The knight grunted. "We have a bargain. I shall keep your secret."

Nathaniel pointed a finger at him. "Despite what your enemies say, I know you to be a Virtuous man. I rely upon you not to make me regret this."

"Men of Honor should never have regrets."

The old officer chuckled. "The world is more cruel than that, yet we must forge ahead nonetheless."

Montenegro flinched as the door squeaked open. A tall figure glided into the parlor. The white-skinned Technocrat still wore the Britannian merchant's costume, though it could not conceal his mechanical demeanor. His mannerisms were fastidious as he bowed.

Nathaniel motioned to the Technocrat. "Montenegro, allow me to introduce Brother Rictor of Logos, of the Order of Theorists. Rictor, of course you know Sir Gabriel Montenegro of Cove, whose exploits in your native land you have related to me in such detail."

The Technocrat bowed again. "Your successes against my people have been most amazing, good sir, if extremely inconvenient to my own work. Yet it is a pleasure to meet you. I am glad we are introduced in a New Britannian sitting room rather than a Logosian battlefield."

Montenegro grimaced. The Technocrat's entrance had been too well timed. He must have been eavesdropping, waiting for Montenegro and the general to strike a deal. The knight did not appreciate being spied upon. He narrowed his eyes and murmured, "Tell me, do you have some kind of clockwork listening device, or did you simply place a glass against the door?"

Brother Rictor grinned. "I used a glass."

Another voice emerged from the open doorway: "Rictor's schemes are baroque, but his methods are very direct. You'll get used to his brand of deviousness."

The speaker was quite small. She wore a scant, kidskin tunic; spotted fur covered the rest of her slight frame. Her tall Meer ears shot up from a whorl of tawny hair. A web of straps fastened weapons to her body, including a crystal dagger hanging at her belly and a staff secured to her back. Montenegro thought he saw movement in a pouch belted to her thigh.

General Nathaniel smiled and said, "Ah, and this is Shavade of Arjun. Like Rictor, she is an agent of the Pact of Four, and a fetching one at that."

The Meer shoved aside a candlestick and sprang with ease onto a marble-topped side table. She hugged her knees to her chest and smirked at the general. "Stick to business, Nathaniel. Flattery can get you killed."

"Shavade's methods are somewhat direct, as well," remarked the bald Technocrat.

Montenegro squinted. "The Meer are part of this? I think it's time you explained this 'Pact of Four,' General. It appears to be much larger than I imagined."

"That is almost certainly true." Nathaniel poured brandy for Shavade and Brother Rictor, and then stretched his legs before the fire. "As I said, Shavade and Brother Rictor are merely our agents. The Pact of Four consists of officials from the four civilized governments. I am the representative from New Britannia. Warlord Bahrok represents the Juka Clans, as you must have guessed. We also have members from Logosia and from Avenosh, both highly placed, though I do not know their identities."

"Interesting. Shirron Turlogan is not aware of your pact, is he? Neither is Lord Gideon, though he is supposed to oversee all military affairs. And you don't even know two of your counterparts. Why is this arrangement so clandestine?"

"It is a delicate affair. If the wrong parties discover us, all of our work shall be for nothing."

Brother Rictor steepled his fingers and explained, "The

Pact of Four is not an arrangement between governments. Governments are fickle and cannot be trusted. The pact is between individuals within the power structure of each nation. Honorable individuals can be trusted, as the theory goes, within an acceptable tolerance."

"And they can be punished if they betray us," added Shavade, sitting cross-legged on the side table.

The general rose from his chair and leaned a forearm against the mantelpiece. His brandy glass sparkled from the modest fire. "Look at our situation, Montenegro. Garron is clashing with Logos and we cannot prevent our own involvement. This war will be costly to everyone. There is nothing we can do to stop it. But we can work to produce a positive outcome. There is no reason why every side shouldn't profit from the sacrifices we're making."

Montenegro smiled without mirth. "Profit? I always thought that wars should be about Virtue."

Nathaniel frowned at him. "Don't be disingenuous. You're not that naive. Wars are about the redistribution of wealth and power. Nothing more."

The knight stared back. "Keep talking, please, General."

"The Meer representative conceived of the pact. He knows that even though his government is neutral, the Meer have a stake in its outcome. So he contacted each of us secretly. By negotiating through our agents," he motioned to Shavade and the Technocrat, "we decided that if we cannot prevent the war, we can at least direct it."

The Technocrat sipped his brandy with a precise motion. "I have been transacting with Warlord Bahrok to strengthen the Garronite advances into Logosia. When the time is right, you New Britannians will provide reinforcements. By giving the Juka Clans an overwhelming advantage, we hope to conclude the war much sooner and with far less destruction."

Montenegro squinted at Brother Rictor. "I don't understand. How does this benefit the Technocrats?"

"Blackthorn has absolute power in my government. The pact member from Logos does not think the Techno-Prophet will ever surrender. But a clear defeat will force his hand and end the fighting. You must understand, we Technocrats did not want this war. Natural resources are scarce in our lands. We were simply digging for ore in the mountains when the Juka Clans attacked us. But Blackthorn and the Shirron decided to make a large-scale conflict out of it. Now we are committed."

"We can help each other once the war is over," added General Nathaniel. "When we've resolved our differences, the Technocrats can teach us about their technology, we can sell them raw materials and the Juka Clans can keep their mountains. Everyone profits."

The knight cocked his head. "It sounds very reasonable, sir, except for one thing. Why have a war at all? Why not spare the lives of all those soldiers and negotiate these terms right now?"

Shavade laughed and slid her legs over the lip of the table. "You're a warrior, Montenegro! You should know that no one is going to back down once their weapons are drawn. Everyone is thirsty for blood."

Nathaniel rubbed his temple. "I would not put it quite so bluntly, but she's essentially correct. The House of the Griffin despises what Blackthorn stands for. They're clamoring for war. Blackthorn is a zealot. The Juka Clans are belligerent by nature. These forces have already been set loose and they cannot be penned up again."

Montenegro stood, crossed his arms and paced before a wall of mounted stag heads. He began with a deep breath. "I confess, your 'Pact of Four' sounds like a noble undertaking. But at the risk of sounding disrespectful, General, allow me to speculate another motive behind it. Your Technocrat ally wants to subvert Blackthorn's power. If this plan succeeds, he might be in a position to overthrow Blackthorn entirely. That would be worth his own army's defeat, would it not?"

Brother Rictor furrowed his large brow. "That is a monstrous charge."

The knight shrugged. "And yet you do not seem scandalized by it. Meanwhile in Garron, Warlord Bahrok uses this opportunity to strengthen his position among the clans. I've seen his treachery myself. It is no mystery that he wants to be Shirron one day. And you, General, keep this pact a secret from Lord Gideon. Is it coincidence that a war victory would guarantee you to replace him as lord of the House of the Lion?" He glanced up at several rows of antlers on the wall. "The Pact of Four will certainly redistribute wealth and power. I must question, however, the selflessness of your intentions."

The Meer warrior slithered off the table and leaned against the doorjamb. She chuckled. "I warned you we shouldn't tell him too much. He may be a knight, but he's sharp as obsidian."

General Nathaniel frowned at her. "I am aware that Montenegro is shrewd. I also know that he is honorable. We've told you what you want to know, Sir Gabriel. Now you must abide by your vow of silence."

Montenegro shook his head. "No."

Brother Rictor cracked a smirk. "You see? People put too much trust in promises."

"I keep my oaths, Technocrat, but let me refresh your memory. I agreed to remain quiet as long as the general does his best to get my command back. That is my stake in this affair and the price of my discretion. Listen, I don't care if your pact is self-serving. If it wins us the war, I wish you luck. I just don't want you interfering with my own plans, as you did in Logosia. Do not stand in my way again."

Shavade grinned, her large eyes flashing. "By my ancestors, I like this human. He's a fighter to the bone."

"And quite self-serving in his own right," added Rictor.

Nathaniel set his brandy glass on the mantel. "You know my word is good, Montenegro. There is no cause for suspicion. Let us shake hands and seal the bargain."

The knight stared at the general's outstretched hand. After a long pause, he clasped the officer's palm. "Very well, General. Thank you for being honest with me."

Somehow the feeling was not as reassuring as Montenegro had hoped it would be.

A jungle of constellations glittered in the sky, yet the twin moons crouched wanly near the horizon. The night hung black and heavy, despite the torches that lined the front drive of the manor. Gravel crunched underfoot as Montenegro walked out the main doors. He took the reins of his warhorse from Sergeant Matthias. The hefty soldier behaved more formally than was his custom. The knight almost apologized to him, but thought better of it.

As he trotted off the grounds of the general's estate, Montenegro's horse whinnied and reared. A tiny white glow appeared before him. It brightened until Montenegro made out two figures blocking the road.

Shavade and Brother Rictor stepped to either side of the

horse. Montenegro watched them but did not move. The Technocrat held up a Logosian static lantern, which derived its light from a strong, continuous spark. Over the buzz of the lamp Rictor murmured, "I am pleased that we caught you before you departed. Shavade and I have some business that needs not involve the general."

The knight grumbled, "It has been a trying day. I would like to reach my townhouse before midnight. Make it fast."

Brother Rictor stared with eyes the color of ice. In the pale glow his bald head looked ghostly. "I believe you know what interests me. The schematics from Enclave. What did Thulann of Garron tell you about them?"

Montenegro scanned the gaunt man's body. He saw no weapons, though the petite Shavade was armed enough for three warriors. He shrugged. "Only that they had something to do with a machine called 'Braun's Needle.' Why, have you come to give them to me? It would be an act of true generosity."

Shavade let out a bantam laugh. "Rictor, generous! And I'm a Terathan queen."

"In truth, I thought you might be generous to me," replied the Technocrat. "Be honest. Did Thulann tell you what happened to the missing scroll?"

"She said she knew nothing about it."

"Are you certain? She did not give it to you, perhaps?"

"On my honor, she did not."

Brother Rictor grinned. "I have never been a very trusting man. You will not mind, will you, if Shavade and I accompany you back to your townhouse, so I can verify that you're telling the truth?"

"I do not think that will be necessary. Good evening to you both."

The Meer warrior thrust her staff in front of the warhorse's snout. The beast huffed and stepped back a pace. "Rictor's only being polite. We don't really care about your permission. You said it yourself, Montenegro: If you intrude on our business, we'll intrude on yours. We're coming with you."

The knight growled, "I do not suggest that you pursue this any further. General Nathaniel will disapprove and I might get perturbed."

The Technocrat lifted his chin. "I think you are unclear on an important point, good sir, which you should keep in mind. We have indulged the general tonight out of respect for local customs. But it is highly inconvenient, to Shavade, myself and the rest of the Pact, that you know what you know. It would not be a chore for us to dispose of you tonight. Rather it would be a great relief. General Nathaniel might get angry, but everyone has bad days."

Montenegro shook his head. "I believe that's enough out of you." In a flash he whisked Starfell from its sheath and split the Meer's staff in two. A second stroke forced her to somersault backward with surprising agility. His warhorse bashed a flank against Brother Rictor, toppling the lanky man to the road. The static lantern threw light across a fountain of dust.

Abruptly a cascade of flickers swarmed from the nearby darkness. The light coalesced around Shavade's ankles, which immediately sank into a foot of mud that had not been there before. The mud instantly hardened. She spat a curse in her native language.

A shadow streaked from the opposite side of the road, falling atop Brother Rictor. The lantern revealed Fairfax the Ranger pressing a knee into the Technocrat's chest and a sword against his belly. The warrior muttered, "I want you to be as still as death."

Rictor complied.

Montenegro dropped from his saddle and approached the trapped Shavade. In one hand she held a crystal sword, in the other a parrying fork. Though her ankles were immobilized she moved with the litheness of a reared serpent. The knight kept out of her reach. He pointed his dark-bladed sword. "Put your weapons at your feet or I shall kill you."

She hurled the dagger-like fork. Montenegro ducked to the side and thrust his sword. The Meer parried it with a curl of her crystal blade and returned a lightning riposte. They exchanged cuts and blocks for a moment until, to the knight's surprise, she sprang into the air and kicked. His throat burst with pain as he fell onto his back. The petite warrior flipped overhead and came down lunging her sword at his chest.

He tumbled underneath her blow, spun to his feet and nicked her forearms with a swift arc of his blade. She snarled and leapt again.

Then the world vanished in a bright light and a snap of thunder.

When Montenegro's eyesight returned, Shavade lay before him on the ground, unmoving. A twist of smoke rose from her scorched back. Out of the darkness emerged a taller Meer figure, dressed in the robes of an Avenosh sorcerer. He panted from exertion.

"I apologize if I interrupted a personal engagement," said Jatha of Ishpur, "but I didn't want your fine doublet to get ruined with blood and punctures."

The knight brushed himself off as he rose. "Most considerate of you. She caught me off guard. Why did the mud soften so quickly?"

"Again, I apologize. I have been distracted of late. I brought too little of a particular reagent, so I cast the enchantment with a shorter duration than normal. What's most impressive is that she recognized that the spell was weakened." He funneled warm light from his hand, illuminating Shavade's unconscious form. "As I thought. Warrior caste. Probably an elite Hunter. Some of them train to fight wizards. You've got hold of a dangerous little vixen here, Montenegro. Lucky you brought your hounds along."

They dragged her into the light of the lantern, where Fairfax kept Brother Rictor pinned. Montenegro knelt beside the indignant Technocrat. "Well, my friend, it has been a very enlightening evening. I would be remiss to leave without informing you of this simple fact: If I see you or your associate again, and you're not in the company of the good general, I am going to kill you. It shall not be a chore. It shall be a great relief."

The Technocrat's stare was unnervingly calm. "I doubt you will see us next time, Montenegro."

A plume of dust exploded around them. The knight whirled to witness Shavade leaping off the ground. From the pouch strapped to her thigh she withdrew a strange weapon. It appeared to be a fist-size insect bound to a wooden handle. She aimed it at Jatha and a volley of yellow spines riddled the wizard's torso. He yelped and doubled over.

Montenegro slashed her chest with Starfell. Blood streamed across her tunic. She shrieked and threw a barrage of quick punches, many of which landed on the knight. He snarled and sliced at her arms. A spinning kick thudded into his stomach. He tumbled backward again.

From the corner of his eye he glimpsed Fairfax. Though the ranger kept the Technocrat pinned, his attention was locked upon Shavade's whirlwind form. His mouth hung open in wonder.

Brother Rictor thrust a razor at his gut. Its edge gleamed with a sap-like substance.

Montenegro cried out, but not in time. The razor engaged a mechanical hum, chewed through the ranger's studded armor and drew a spray of blood. Fairfax stiffened and fell away from the Technocrat.

A spotted blur plucked Rictor from the ground and hauled him several yards away. Shavade bared her teeth at Montenegro, then held a rod of black crystal above her head. A shower of light engulfed the pair. When the light faded, they were gone.

The knight rushed to Fairfax's side. Rictor's poison was devastating his body. Every muscle tightened brutally. His flesh drew taut and began to crack; his face was already unrecognizable. Montenegro snatched a vial from his pocket and emptied the contents into the ranger's foaming mouth. When the antidote took effect, the ranger's body returned to normal. Montenegro sighed with relief.

Fairfax coughed and stared wide-eyed at the scintillating night sky.

Montenegro patted his chest. "I suppose you're glad now that I dragged you to buy that potion this afternoon. Thulann warned me that Technocrat was a poisoner."

The ranger licked his parched lips and rasped, "Who was she?"

"The Meer? Her name is Shavade of Arjun."

He smiled and whispered, "Shavade."

"You're drunk, aren't you? I warned you, Fairfax."

He shook his head. His eyes reflected the stars. "I'm not drunk. I'm . . . intoxicated."

Montenegro rolled his eyes and attended to Jatha, who was crouched on the road, painfully removing the spines from his torso. "She had a Stinger," he explained, "a Living Weapon. The warrior caste breeds them."

"So that was a famous Living Weapon. The venom must have stunned you. You don't look well."

The wizard glanced at the spot where the pact agents had vanished. His expression was agitated. "It's not the venom. It's that crystal rod she had. Such a thing should not exist."

Montenegro helped the Meer to his feet. "I never know what to think when a wizard claims that something 'should not exist.' "

"I mean it is forbidden. That crystal was enchanted with spells that are supposed to be locked away in Ishpur. By the Ar'Kannor, the Matriarchs themselves guard that knowledge! Where did she get it? Who is she working for?"

The knight stroked his warhorse, which continued to stomp nervously. "I do not know exactly who she works for, nor could I tell you if I did. It is a long story, which I have pledged not to relate."

With startling quickness Jatha grabbed the knight's collar. "Montenegro, if you ever felt indebted to my friendship, now is the time to repay it. I have to learn where she acquired that rod."

He clutched the wizard's forearm. "If it's that important, I shall try to find out for you. Perhaps the general knows."

"Do what you can, Montenegro, I beg you. No matter what it takes, I must find that Hunter."

From the ground Fairfax called out, "So must I, my friends! Sleep shall elude me until that golden day. Paradise wears spots, my lads, though I would never have dreamt it! I fear the only remedy is drink, which is waiting for us in my saddlebag next to Montenegro's mysterious scroll. Though the finest Trinsic port is naught but vinegar in the presence of such a nectarean dram as overwhelmed my senses tonight. Hey! Dammit! Did the poison make my hair fall out?"

"Shut up, Fairfax," hissed Jatha.

Montenegro felt his mood sinking with Jatha's. Even in New Britannia, the Land of Virtue, he was forced to connive to protect his interests. He felt as if he were being somehow tested. And yet, though intrigue might taste bitter, his honor would remain intact if he conducted himself according to the ethics of the Lost King. If a knight must employ schemes as well as swords, he must do so unflinchingly. Let no enemy stand when the battle is finished.

CHAPTER
6

CREVASSE

The metal chamber drummed with the clank of heavy machinery. Riveted walls enclosed the interior of a tall cylinder, like a giant steel canister. A bolt of electricity crackled between two spheres on the ceiling. Bluish light stormed the chamber.

Sister Raveka stood within folds of hot steam. Sweat flooded her skin under a Mathematician's grey robe. She hoped that the perspiration would not mar the geometric symbols painted on her face and neck. She felt uneasy enough already.

She was perched on a small, iron platform twenty feet above the floor. Many Technocrats peered up at her through heavy gouts of steam. On the curved walls, at the same height as herself, hung three shadowed balconies. In the center of each gaping hollow sat a grim figure, swathed in black raiment and covered with mathematical tattoos on every inch of their skin.

The three Lectors of Logos regarded her with dour silence.

Then a deep voice half-whispered from the nearest balcony: "Remember, do not speak directly to the ambassador unless she addresses you first. Now relax your mind. You are the sum of your training, Sister Raveka."

She straightened her posture and nodded to the silhouette of Lector Gaff. Her small platform jerked forward. The steam cloud intensified as a telescoping arm hoisted her to the center of the cylindrical audience chamber, where her platform connected to a larger one holding two exotic figures.

One of them sat in a tall, wide chair hewn from an enormous crystal. The Meer Matriarch had brought the sparkling throne from Ishpur. It was a marvel of craftsmanship, with facets so precise that even the Order of Engineers was impressed. Sitting on the throne's silk cushion, the aged Matriarch herself was the embodiment of cultured aloofness. She wore a gown of filmy, layered veils that twinkled with gemstones. Her marbled grey fur was immaculate. She exuded haughty disinterest.

Raveka concealed her apprehension. The old woman made her nervous. The Mystic caste controlled Meer society and the Matriarchs ruled the Mystics, which placed Ambassador Adhayah near the pinnacle of Avenosh government. As with all Mystics of her rank, the ambassador was also a magician of untold skill. Raveka had learned to distrust such power. It could lead to mental instability. She had seen the terrible consequences when she brought the mad Master Gregorio from New Britannia two years before, to meet with the Techno-Prophet. Many buildings in Logos still bore the scars from their nightmarish battle.

Silently she chanted, *I am the sum of my training. I am a component of the Machine.*

A second Meer accompanied the Matriarch. He was a

younger man with exaggerated ears and a frame more stout than Raveka associated with his race. He likewise wore the gown of a high-ranking Mystic, though wide belts on his waist and arms gave him a less aristocratic appearance. He paced the width of the larger platform.

Raveka bowed to the man. He flattened his ears and returned the gesture.

From a shadow-strewn balcony, one of the Lectors amplified his voice through a curved speaking horn. His tone was characteristically emotionless. "Chamberlain Kavah, you are aware that Lector Gaff of the Mathematicians serves as our spymaster. Sister Raveka is one of his operatives who has worked within the Hall of the Shirron. Please beseech the ambassador to attend as the Sister recounts a dark piece of information from Garron."

The Meer chamberlain bowed once more. "The Venerable Mother Adhayah appreciates this opportunity, Lector Sartorius. Pray begin, Sister Raveka."

After a brief introduction, she repeated word for word the conversation between Turlogan and Thulann. The audience of Technocrats shuffled in wordless dismay when she revealed the Shirron's plan to invade Logosia in the summer, with the New Britannians at his side. When her report was complete, Raveka folded her hands and bowed. She felt the muscles of her chest relax when her platform separated from the two Meer and returned to the side of Lector Gaff. Her mentor gave her a conservative nod.

Lector Sartorius's voice boomed from his speaking horn. "Chamberlain Kavah, the ambassador knows the present state of this war. The Juka Clans have defied the odds and matched us at every turn. The addition of the New Britannian army will ensure our downfall. Therefore we entreat the ambassador to reconsider our offer of alliance. The influence of Ishpur can balance the equation of power on this continent and bring an end to this destructive conflict. Thousands of lives pivot on the ambassador's decision."

The two Meer conferred in whispers. When they separated again, Raveka could not read the Matriarch's expression. Kavah, however, bowed in the time-honored fashion of diplomatic apology.

"Lector Sartorius, Your Excellencies, the ambassador conveys her sadness at your impending losses in this war. She reiterates her offer to ease your burden by instructing your people in the healing arts of water magic. She stresses, of course, that the same offer has been accepted by Garron. Yet the government of Avenosh holds fast to its neutrality in this affair. We cannot participate in a conflict that does not directly involve us. To do so would violate our deepest convictions against political violence." He cleared his throat and added, "Dame Adhayah also asks me to convey that if this is the sole reason for her invitation today, she elects to forgo any debate and will now take her leave."

The shadowy form of Lector Sartorius betrayed no disappointment. "That is the extent of our business with the ambassador this afternoon. Offer her our gratitude for attending."

Chamberlain Kavah bowed in turn to each grim Lector, then tugged on a floor-mounted lever. The Meer's platform chirped a metallic squeal and retracted on hydraulic beams into an opening in the wall. Billows of steam engulfed them. A massive door clanged shut. The Matriarch had never once stirred.

Raveka welcomed the old Mystic's departure. She even dared to indulge in a sigh.

Lector Braun of the Engineers cleared his throat. His speaking horn rang with a bell-like hum. "Thus ends our hope of external aid. But there exists another answer to our predicament. My factories have at last finished construction of the Needle. Though you have both expressed doubt over its effectiveness, nevertheless it may well encompass our only hope for survival. I suggest that we deploy it as soon as logistics allow."

Lector Gaff nodded. "My calculations point to diplomacy as our most favorable course of action. Lector Sartorius, however, claims that the Theorists have exhausted all such avenues. And so at this juncture we must engage every resource available. The Needle, as we all know, represents an inordinate fraction of our resources. Lector Braun, how do you propose to use the weapon?"

"Our greatest threat proceeds from New Britannia. If they come to the aid of Garron, we are lost. Therefore I believe that we should send the Needle to New Britannia to destroy their fleet of ships. If they cannot transport their army to our shores, they cannot pose a significant threat."

"An excellent strategy," said Gaff. "Lector Sartorius, I request that you present this plan to the Techno-Prophet. It is best if he authorizes such a bold attack personally."

Sartorius peered over his entwined fingers. "I shall consult my advisors. If they concur with Lector Braun's wisdom, then I shall speak to the Techno-Prophet. But I agree that time is short. Return to your Orders and examine every option. This audience is adjourned."

Hissing engines drew steel shutters across each balcony in turn. When the Lectors had departed, Sister Raveka stepped through a doorway and squeezed down a shoulder-width passage. When she was out of sight of the meeting chamber, she pressed her brow to the wall. The cool metal felt refreshing against her sweat-drenched skin. It was a sliver of comfort for her aching head.

A picture stuck in her mind. Pillars of fire leapt above the cityscape of Britain. Airships loomed in the sapphire-blue sky. Juggernauts and smoke cauldrons rumbled through the winding streets. The forests echoed drums.

The earth turned red from the blood of fallen knights.

She chased away the thought by mentally chanting mathematical formulae. The ritual had become an hourly task since Thulann of Garron had nearly killed her, a week before. The old Way Master had brought her closer to despair than she had ever come. Sister Raveka now appreciated the lure of Entropy upon a mind weakened by hardship and emotion.

She lifted her chin and allowed the silent chant to consume her. *Discipline is courage,* she reminded herself. Slowly she regained cognizance of every movement of her body. When she continued down the dim, narrow corridor she was restored to a stoic vision of control, expressing no more emotion than the steel gears and levers that clanged behind the bolted metal walls.

A sunrise drizzle painted the stone city of Garron with a glassy sheen. Stippled with raindrops, Thulann knelt atop a short pedestal inside the Garron Arena. She watched the center of the muddy field as Venduss wrestled three sparring partners. The boys wore only tight breeches and long braids. Their jade skin was caked with wet, clinging sand. Cuts and bruises covered their bodies.

Venduss was performing well, even when all three of his opponents engaged him at once. His techniques of evasion had improved. Thulann could not remember the last time Venduss had practiced with such vigor.

The anger in his eyes seemed to spur him to greater achievements.

A pair of cloaked shapes approached the Way Master from the entrance to the arena floor. They draped wide cowls over their heads in the New Britannian fashion, even though they were Jukan clansmen. Thulann almost smiled.

The tallest of them kept his eyes upon Venduss. "My son fights fiercely this morning. It pleases me how you motivate him, my dear."

Thulann glanced up at the Shirron. "I nearly threatened him with inversion drills, though that was my sour mood at play. After losing that spy to Montenegro, I am in a humor for strenuous training. But it was not I who put the fire in his belly. That was your doing. He did not even sleep last night."

"I suppose I cannot blame him for being upset. It must have come as a surprise. But Warlord Savan and I have already made the arrangements. Tekmhat is on her way to the city. I believe she will make Venduss an excellent wife."

"The boy maintains the notion that marriage is the evolution of romance." She smirked at Turlogan. "It is a childish conceit, of course."

He laughed. "Perhaps folly runs in his blood. In any case, the sooner we seal the union with Clan Eryem, the easier it will be to plan the invasion. Savan has agreed to lend his armorers to us. That could well make our clan's army the equal of Clan Varang. That ought to chafe Bahrok. But look, I did not come out into the rain to discuss politics. I have brought Dhayin to see you. He has news that you will find quite interesting."

Thulann bowed to the second man. "Good morning, Dhayin. Have we received word from our spies in Logos?"

Dhayin had a warrior's body and a statesman's face. Years of coordinating the Shirron's strategic intelligence had drawn wrinkles around his still-young eyes, though just now they blinked with excitement. "No, Mistress Thulann, no news from Logos. But I did get a message from Crevasse this morning."

"The levitant mines? I was not aware we had eyes there."

"One of our contacts in Logos found an excuse to go. You will be pleased at what he discovered."

She saw excitement in his features. Her eyes widened. "The schematics for Braun's Needle?"

The spymaster grinned. "Locked away in a secret room, like eggs in a nest, waiting for a hungry serpent to take them."

She unfolded from the pedestal and dropped to the ground. "Great Mother, that polishes the black from this dreary morning! I shall gather my things at once. Turlogan, will you please inform Venduss of this news after he has exhausted his indignation?"

The tall Juka crossed his arms. "Of course! Seeing as the Shirron does not have any more important matters to attend. But wait, I have a serious request to make concerning my son."

"I know what you are going to say, but I must insist that Venduss comes with me. You can plan the wedding without him. It has not stopped you yet. Venduss is a valuable partner to me, and very anxious to recover what Bahrok stole from us."

Turlogan shook his head. "I do not want you to leave Venduss behind. I want you to leave Toria behind."

She swallowed and looked out at the arena. "I cannot. Her skills are as useful to me as his."

"Dhayin will go in her place. The time has come to separate those two, Thulann. You know that. Warlord Savan would be insulted if Venduss kept a mistress after the wedding, and a human one at that."

Thulann turned her face up to the drizzle. The cold splashes cleared her eyes. "I know. But this has been very abrupt for Venduss. We cannot command his heart like a soldier. We must give him time to cope."

"We do him no service to prolong this dalliance. He must accept that it is over."

She grimaced. "Hypocrisy does not become you, my love. In twenty years you have never accepted my refusals, have you?"

Dhayin coughed and scrutinized the sparring in the center of the arena.

Turlogan snorted, then stroked the Way Master's back. "Well, my stiletto-tongued dearest, what is your counterproposal?"

She leaned closer and thought for a moment. "Both of them shall accompany me to Crevasse. That will give them an opportunity to resolve their affair. When we return, that will be the end of it."

"And the girl? What will happen to her?"

Thulann gazed at the cloudy sky. "I do not know, Turlogan. I do not know."

The pace of the rain began to increase. The walls of the arena faded to grey horizons. Venduss did not abandon his training in the rainshower; rather the hissing downpour seemed to renew his energy. In short order his opponents sprawled in the mud, catching their breaths, while Venduss cursed them for idleness.

Thulann gently squeezed Turlogan's muscular arm. Then

she walked in the direction of the Hall of the Shirron, where her traveling gear was stored. She had much to prepare for. The journey to Crevasse might be very long indeed.

Like a mechanical island the skyborne city of Logos hovered above a sea of low clouds. The spring had summoned grey weather to the desert below, suffusing it with welcome moisture. The fog tumbled and plumed underneath Logos, jolted by thermals from the crimson bedrock. Playful lightning danced in the murk.

Walking along the brink of the levitating city, Sister Raveka held onto her cowl against the bluster of wet winds. She carried herself upright as she spoke to the robed man beside her.

"Lector Gaff—Your Excellency—I request that you send me back to New Britannia immediately."

The middle-aged Technocrat angled his tattooed face toward her. His cold eyes glared from a filigree of mathematical equations. "I wondered when you would ask that. You plan to retrieve the scroll from Montenegro of Cove, do you not?"

"Precisely, Your Excellency. I believe the diagram may pertain to Lector Braun's Needle. In light of our present strategy, I think it would be wise to recover it."

"You are correct. The scroll should be recovered. That diagram might be more important than you realize." He clasped his hands behind his back and lowered his volume. "You are aware that Lector Braun has maintained absolute secrecy around the Needle. Not even Sartorius or myself have access to his factories or specifications. But I have collected a great deal of intelligence on the project. Most interesting has been the news of Braun's personal set of schematics, which were lost when Enclave fell. You already know about that, of course, but what you do not know is that the schematics reappeared a few days ago in Crevasse. They were purchased from a scavenger merchant. The man claimed to have found them on a dead Garronite soldier in the desert. The crucial point, though, is that the most important diagram is missing."

"The diagram in Montenegro's possession."

"That is very probably the case. We must recover it, for the information it contains might prove extremely dangerous. You see, the missing scroll is a plan for the Needle's primary weapon. That weapon, Sister Raveka, was designed by the Techno-Prophet himself."

She clenched her fists, but quickly subsumed her frustration. "It is distressing that I was so close to such a valuable document, and yet I did not acquire it."

"Your performance was hampered by emotional factors."

She blinked. "Yes, Your Excellency. Thulann of Garron was still pursuing me. She is a terrible enemy. Your training kept my fear at bay, but the effort was not trivial."

Lector Gaff did not respond, but continued to walk until a large wind trap blocked their path. The metal scoop collected moisture from the air. Water poured from the device into canal-shaped cisterns that honeycombed the city. Gaff paused before the massive apparatus, which rumbled a metallic sigh. "Sister Raveka, you must be aware that I have a design for your future in the Order. The time approaches when you will qualify for the title of Mother. I estimate that you can become a formidable one."

Breath caught in her throat. She lifted her chin. "I thank you, Your Excellency. As always I shall endeavor to live up to your expectations of me."

"I hope you shall. I intend to ask a great deal. We are not typical Mathematicians, you and I. Ours is a delicate profession. Espionage demands trust. Your mind must be disciplined according to the strictures of the Machine, or you will lose the confidence of your peers and superiors."

Raveka looked down. "I understand, Your Excellency."

"Then you know what it means for a spy to be distrusted. We have but one method of retirement."

A chilly gust whirled around her. "Have I disappointed you in some way, Your Excellency?"

He gazed into her porcelain-white face. "You lost the scroll. That concerns me. It is not a great error, but I am monitoring your work, Sister. Your fondness for New Britannia grows unseemly. Entropy sets upon you like rust. You must not let your emotions devour you."

"I shall intensify my rituals. I can subdue my emotions."

"Excellent. We understand one another. Then I shall assign you to retrieve the scroll from Montenegro. You must depart as soon as possible."

She met his stern eyes. "Thank you for this opportunity to prove myself."

"It's not a boon, Sister. It is simply a formula in which you are a factor. We shall see what answer it produces. Now, you must recover the scroll undamaged, if possible. I want to examine it. And no one must know of your mission. There are traitors in Logos who would kill for a glimpse of that diagram."

"Understood."

"You say Montenegro has studied the schematic?"

"It appeared so, Your Excellency."

"Then you must find out what he has learned and with whom he has shared it. When you have this information, murder the knight. His knowledge is dangerous."

Raveka shuddered. Her response came perhaps too quickly. "I am not an assassin, Your Excellency."

"You are the sum of your training. You have Montenegro in your confidence. That is a skill more deadly than knife-play."

"He is only a New Britannian warrior. He cannot glean any useful information from so sophisticated a diagram."

Lector Gaff frowned deeply. "His knowledge is dangerous. There is no debate. Do not forget our understanding, Sister Raveka. The outcome of this mission determines your future."

She fought to keep her breathing steady. "Yes, Your Excellency."

The tattooed Lector bowed. "I shall arrange the fastest carriole for you. As usual you may equip yourself to your own specifications, on my authority. Arm yourself well, Sister. Montenegro is deadly. I would not want you to meet an unbecoming demise."

When he left her without a chant of departure, Raveka knew that Gaff was gravely upset. She also knew that he was not bluffing. In thirteen years Gaff had never lied to her. He did not make threats; he offered choices.

Lector Gaff presented her with a test. At that moment Raveka did not know if she could pass it.

She peered down from the steel-framed precipice at the frolicking clouds far below. The boiling patterns were hypnotic. Watching them she could almost ignore the emptiness in her belly. When she realized that the tumult had entranced her, she turned away from the edge and stalked past the gaping wind trap. Its maw whispered a throaty sigh. Condensation poured from its spout in a clean, orderly flow.

*　　*　　*

Several narrow, parallel grooves etched the amber sand of the desert. Dhayin of Garron knelt beside them, comparing the width to his finger. He nodded.

"Definitely Tech drones. Probably a scouting patrol. These tracks are a few hours old, but they might still be around."

Thulann stood close by. She scanned the rocky terrain unfolding in every direction. "I prefer to meet drones to juggernauts, but I would rather not encounter anything with metal innards. They are less likely to accept our disguise at face value."

As they tramped across the northern wastes of Logosia, the Jukan party wore the drab clothing of the native scavenger merchants. Thulann's ruddy leathers fitted tightly against her tall, slender frame. Over them she wore a Logosian long coat, derived from the Britannian nautical style. Dhayin's garb was a montage of muted leathers and tarnished buckles, powdered by windblown dust. His eyes were hidden behind mirrorlike lenses strapped to his face, which the Technocrats used to ward off the blinding sun. As he stood, the glass winked in the afternoon glare. "I would not worry. If we have to run from trouble, Clan Varang has scouts in the area as well. I can probably track them down in a matter of hours."

She squinted. "Bahrok is this far west?"

Dhayin brushed sand from his knees. "His troops have been moving this way ever since Enclave. He is preparing to attack Akar."

"Akar! I did not know about this. Why was I not told?"

"With all possible respect, Mistress Thulann, it was not your concern. You are a spy in this war, not a general."

She crossed her arms. "Your point is taken, though it is

strange that I did not hear. Akar was Turlogan's personal target. It is unlike him not to keep me abreast of such changes."

"You must forgive him. The Shirron has been very occupied negotiating the alliance with Clan Eryem."

"So he has! So much so that he neglects his own plans. Well, Bahrok hunts quite a meal this time. Akar is defended by airships. Dangerous prey indeed."

Dhayin raised a finger. "Ah, but Bahrok's informants say that Logos is mustering airships for some manner of large-scale exercise. Akar's vessels should be gone for a few weeks. That will leave the town vulnerable."

"Where is this muster occurring?"

He smiled. "At Crevasse. And now you know why I insisted upon coming. If I can confirm that the airships are indeed traveling to Crevasse, that will be the signal for Warlord Bahrok to move in."

The Way Master massaged her brow. "I must remember to keep more informed of the latest gossip. Yes, we must certainly see what is happening at Crevasse. Perhaps this airship muster has something to do with the Needle itself? If that is the case—if the weapon has been completed—then an attack might be forthcoming. We may have to change our entire strategy."

Dhayin nodded. "That is why we must not fail on this journey."

"I shall inform Venduss. He must keep abreast of these matters. He wants to begin leading troops into battle. I suspect the invasion of Akar might be just what he is looking for."

She found the youth not far from the ridgebacks that carried them across the wastes. He wore Logosian leathers as well, festooned with metal buttons and buckles. He was practicing his weaponless exercises with the same vigor he had gained after learning of his betrothal. His mood seemed dire.

She did not see him make a single mistake. She decided not to interrupt.

Nearby Toria perched atop her ridgeback, leaning against the animal's tall, bony crest. She had chosen less modest Logosian garments, the short skirt, jacket and leather bodice revealing more of her freckled skin than it covered. With her legs crossed and her fiery hair drawn back by a scarf, she reminded Thulann of the innocent little thief who had stowed aboard the Way Master's longboat two years before. Toria and Venduss had immediately bonded. More hardship than joy had transpired since then.

The girl faced away from the Jukan youth. Her expression was wistful. Thulann made out her silky voice as she sang just above a murmur:

> *My song is sung by laughing waters,*
> *Willows weeping nigh,*
> *Where once we lay in barley troves*
> *With mayflies marching by.*
>
> *The river's touch would not expel*
> *Our hearts' immortal flame.*
> *You called me from the water's swell*
> *And to your arms I came.*

The Way Master remarked, "It is not wise to dwell upon hardship, child. If you stare at the sun, your eyesight will dim."

Toria ignored her and continued in darker tones:

Far along the river's ribbon
Where the whitecaps roam,
The floods of Beltaine called me down
Beneath the lacy foam.

My bed lies deep in laughing waters,
Willows weeping o'er,
Where once we lay in barley troves,
But mayflies march no more.

Toria wrapped her arms around her knees and gazed at the rocky horizon. Thulann battled the urge to comfort the young human. These days were necessarily difficult. Toria must face them in her own way. So Thulann instead moved closer to Venduss, then assumed a disapproving countenance and prepared to criticize any error he made in his exercises. The calm of exhaustion would help the boy now, and the challenge of stern instruction would release her own tension. Over the years that pattern of behavior had grown comforting to the Way Master, like a masqueraded display of affection. She imagined that Venduss felt likewise.

Whether that behavior was echoed in his relationship with Toria was not something Thulann cared to ponder. More important affairs demanded her attention. The future was a perilous road. The only way to travel it was one step at a time.

Bolts of sunlight stabbed through the ashy clouds that vaulted the sky above Logos. In the streaming warmth Sister Raveka gathered her bags atop the roof of a blocky building. A single-seated carriole hovered next to her. Carefully she buckled each sack to the vehicle, then secured them with a weatherproof tarp.

The lilt of music touched her from a passing breeze. She followed the sound until she spotted a group of children at play in a courtyard below. The youngsters chanted the basic axioms of the Machine as they danced around a tall pole. They held colorful ribbons that attached to the top. As they moved through an intricate choreography, the ribbons braided around the pole to form symbols that illustrated the verses they sang. A teacher from the Order of Theorists looked on with dour approval.

She indulged in a faint smile. Though her own upbringing among the Mathematicians had afforded little opportunity for games, she would never forget the wonder she felt as a child when Gaff revealed to her the miracles of the Machine. For her the world had transformed into an astonishing place where numbers and formulae and vectors of force danced to an unending song. The vision of the Machine enchanted her instantly and thoroughly. As a teenager she felt sorrow for the rest of Logosia, who could not see the wonders surrounding them. But Gaff also taught that emotions feed inaccuracy. He trained her how to quell such distractions. Feelings were just a symptom of mental habits. She could tame them.

Her most profound enlightenment came when she understood that she herself, mind and body, was also a dance of numbers. She was a process defined by quantifiable equations. She was as miraculous as the world around her.

She was a component of the Machine. Sometimes she forgot what life was like without that knowledge.

The final box she secured to the carriole was also the heaviest. It contained an array of technological weapons, ammunition and replacement parts. Raveka had gathered the fiercest personal arms that Logos had created. She was well prepared for the mission at hand.

She harmonized with the children's verses as she threw a tarp over the box. The droning verses soothed her in an odd way.

Logos sprawled gloriously below the carriole as it soared between pillars of sunlight. From this vantage the hovering city resembled a mosaic of steel-plated tiles, rivets glittering like jewels in the errant sun. Rooftops textured the view like a garden of geometric sculptures, threaded together by clusters of pipes. Smokestacks forested the cityscape, their foliage the sooty clouds that swelled from their cement trunks. Wind engines sliced the air with twirling blades. Moisture traps gaped like hatchlings.

Blackthorn's floating citadel presided over the solemn metropolis like a sceptre in the clouds.

As she steered the carriole north and west, she observed darker weather creeping over the horizon. The storms of spring were almost here. This was the time of year when her father used to travel to Junction for supplies and the rains would flood the dry lake bed where she spent her childhood. When she was a young girl, this time was very magical.

Right now she felt that way again. But New Britannia was a long journey distant. Raveka was confident she could subdue those feelings before she arrived. The Machine, after all, supplied all the miracles she desired.

A gloomy cloudburst drenched the midnight air. Under the cover of a rock overhang, Toria nestled into Venduss's arms. She was alone with him. Thulann and Dhayin had sheltered under another outcropping not far away. Around them loomed the jagged bluffs of the mountains of western Logosia.

The Juka's embrace felt wonderful. Toria focused on the physical sensation of his touch, which drove away her glum thoughts.

His voice was a hush in the rainshower's din. "Sing it for me, my love. I want to hear."

"I've barely started working on it."

"I do not care. Tomorrow we reach Crevasse. I want to share tonight with you."

She grumbled and flinched from his caress, then leaned into him again. She brought his hand to her lips. His smell was comforting. She kissed his palm.

On a surge of breath she sang:

> *Zephyr spirit, sing my song*
> *Above the lands you roam,*
> *For one who loves me travels on*
> *While I am going home.*

> *From high, the mountains are a brae,*
> *The ocean is a pond.*
> *Zephyr spirit, fly away*
> *And sing my song beyond.*

He combed his fingers through her russet hair. "Toria, you will not go. You will stay with me."

Her throat welled up. "You're getting married, hey? That's that. Let's make an end of it."

"I am not frightened by either Warlord Savan or his daughter. You shall be my mistress, despite them."

She pushed away from him. "No! Damn you! I told you I'd never do that."

"You must. It is all we can have, my love. I will not accept your refusal." He cupped her shoulder firmly.

She twisted away. "Quit! That's not what I want."

His grip tightened. "It is not a request, Toria! I am the Shirron's son. I will keep who I want to keep!"

Her hand flew on a crest of rage. She slapped him as hard as she could.

Venduss plucked her wrist from the air and wrenched it, flinging her to the ground. Loose rocks grated against her face. With a snarl she jerked her arm free and scrambled to the edge of the overhang. When she wiped her flowing tears, she noticed they were smeared with blood.

Behind her Venduss was stammering an apology, but the words did not register. She shrank from his hesitant touch. She took a step forward and the rain hit her brow. A thousand droplets tapped her with tiny, cold fingers.

Thunder careened through the mountain crags, drowning out Venduss's voice. It was a moment of relief she wished could last forever.

Soaked by the downpour, Thulann crouched in the darkness and observed Toria and Venduss. At this distance she could not make out their words, but she did not need to. They would say and do irrational things tonight. That was the way of endings. It was arduous work, but necessary.

She leaned back and scanned the area. In the distance, among black mountaintops just a few miles away, flickered the many lights of Crevasse. The town was built around a levitant mine and refinery, which produced the fuel that powered Technocrat flying machines. But Crevasse also served as an aerie for many of Blackthorn's airships. Like ornaments the tall vessels hung from the lofty cliffs, their huge lamps shining through the darkness and rain, swaying gently in the wind.

Thulann found beauty in the pattern of luminant globes. The Way instructed a Juka to seek beauty wherever it may be. The task was not always easy, especially with Logosian designs. In the daylight the airships were not so appealing, tangled with iron and blackened by smoke, and yet she still looked forward to walking among them tomorrow. The military power of so many war engines could not fail to engage a warrior's fascination. If the Technocrats had any aesthetic sense at all, it was expressed in the fearsomeness of their machines.

She wondered if they regarded the Jukan Clans with a comparable sentiment.

A scuttling sound met her pointed ears. She daubed the rain from the knee joints of her armor, then crept through the shadows in the direction of the noise.

Her patience tonight had just borne fruit.

Someone was lurking around the camp. She had first detected them half an hour earlier. She had readied herself to ply the disguise of a scavenger merchant, but the intruder did not reveal himself. So she donned her armor and took to the shadows as well, waiting for the lurker to reappear. She lingered near Venduss to satisfy a twinge of maternal protectiveness.

She had silent reasons for not waking Dhayin.

The hillside was littered with tall, sharp-edged boulders, strewn about by rockslides. In the sheeting rain they provided countless locations for an eavesdropper to hide. They also allowed Thulann to move about with near invisibility.

Now she climbed over a slippery boulder that concealed the furtive intruder. She was surprised to find no one on the other side. Then she sensed a metallic quality to the thump of raindrops. In a flash she darted around another rocky upthrust.

A shape leapt out of view. Rain clattered on his armor. Thulann flung herself over a low crag and tumbled in front of the fleeing intruder. The man snatched a long weapon from his back and jabbed it at her. She pirouetted aside. The stranger's weapon spat steam as a forked tip shot past her, smashing into a wall of bare stone.

Pneumatic trident, she warned herself as she drew her own sword. *Cumbersome but lethal.* She struck back with her sword. The intruder parried her blows with astounding deftness, considering the bulk of his weapon. When she landed a strike on his hip, her blade rebounded with a familiar clatter. *Kinetic armor, as well. He is either very rich or works for someone who is.*

The haft of the trident connected with her face. Rain spattered from the recoil. She somersaulted backward to roll with the follow-through, landing on the low, rocky wall. Her boots were uneasy on the slippery stone.

A bright moon peeked through a rift in the rain clouds. The light revealed a Juka wearing kinetic armor, a Technocrat invention that employed spring-mounted plates. His pneumatic trident retracted with a *click,* ready for another steam-driven thrust.

Thulann met his tiny eyes. "Janissars do not patrol alone. Are you a deserter or merely lost?"

"Janissars are nothing but well-trained dogs. They lack the skill to hunt alone."

She touched her swelling cheek. "Your skills are exceptional, I do confess. You must be the pride of your village. But I hope you are not offended if I say I do not recognize you."

He smirked. "But I know you, disguise or not. The legendary Thulann of Garron. I have dreamt of a second chance to face you."

"Second chance?"

"Never mind. I'm finally going to get my satisfaction. Defend yourself, old woman, if your rickety joints are up to it."

"No!" cried a third voice from the murky drizzle. A shape resolved into Dhayin, running into the moonlight. He inserted himself between the combatants. "Stop it! I brought Thulann here to talk, not to fight!"

The Logosian fighter sneered. "I was hired to fight. You could have talked to her in Garron. Don't steal this chance from me!"

"Remember what we are here for!" Dhayin turned to look at Thulann. "Please accept my apologies. There is more afoot than I told you. Allow me to introduce—"

The Logosian jutted a finger at him. "No names. Not yet."

The Way Master grimaced. Her temperature rose, but she fought the anger. She slapped her blade into its scabbard and growled, "Do not delude yourself that I am your fool, Dhayin. I know that you are in Bahrok's employ. You betrayed yourself by telling me about the attack on Akar. The Shirron did not inform me because he does not know, does he? You heard it directly from Bahrok's mouth, unless I am mistaken."

Dhayin paused for a moment, then bowed his head. "I have insulted you with my deception. Forgive me, Way Master."

The Logosian snorted a laugh. "Garronites! Interminably polite. I bet the pteranxes in Jukaran say 'excuse me' before they eat you."

Thulann ignored the comment. "Your friend makes an interesting point, Dhayin. You could have talked to me in Garron. Why have you lured us all this way? I wager it is not because the scrolls are here."

"I shall tell you why, but let us wake Venduss and Toria. It is their concern, as well."

The two teenagers stood with swords drawn, mostly dry under their stony outcropping. Before them was a robed human. He was bearded and heavyset, with a satchel on his shoulder and a wide-brimmed hat deflecting the rain from his face. A black horse's tail dangled from his hatband. The walking staff in his hand emitted a subtle glow.

The Way Master had not expected to meet a New Britannian sorcerer in the mountains of Logosia, but this had evolved into a surprising evening.

The wizard lifted his staff in greeting when Thulann, Dhayin and the Logosian warrior arrived. "The boy is about to cause problems. Dhayin, how about telling him that's not a good idea?"

Venduss stared at Dhayin with shock. "This is your doing? What is this about?"

The Way Master muttered, "Sheathe your blades, please. Dhayin is going to tell us presently."

The youths complied, reluctantly. The corpulent wizard rewarded them with a smug grin.

Dhayin motioned to the bearded human. "First, allow me to introduce Grynholt of Yew, an associate of mine in this endeavor."

Thulann bowed her head. "I greet you with respect and

honor, Grynholt of Yew. Tell me, is Brother Rictor with you as well?"

Dhayin shook his head. "Rictor is not here, but you are correct. He works for the same employers as we do."

"You mean Warlord Bahrok."

"And others. Their identities are not important. What matters is that we are all on the same side here. We are working toward a victory for Garron."

The Way Master swallowed and lifted her chin. "Is the Shirron a part of this deception? Before we left Garron he requested that I leave Toria behind. I wonder if he did not mean to protect her."

"No, he does not suspect. He only wanted to separate Toria and Venduss because of the wedding."

Thulann felt relieved, though she saw a look of despair on Toria's freckled face.

Dhayin continued, "I shall try to be brief. Our Technocrat sources have confirmed that the construction of Braun's Needle is complete. It is my employers' intention to disable the machine, lest it turn the momentum of the war. That is why Brother Rictor took the schematics from Enclave."

The Way Master frowned. "There was no need for such a plot. I would have allowed Bahrok to study them. He needed only to ask."

"To what end? He cannot discern any useful information from them. Neither can you or I or any other clansman. But certain Technocrats in our alliance can. They have analyzed the schematics. They have devised a plan to sabotage the Needle. But they had to do so in secret, because of the danger of being discovered by Logosian authorities."

Thulann grunted. "I see the logic in that."

"We have copied the diagrams and returned them to the

Engineers, to deflect suspicion from us. Unfortunately, as you know, one of the scrolls was missing from the cache at Enclave. It is the most important one, pertaining to the Needle's primary weapon. No one knows what it does, which gives us great concern. That is why we must obtain the missing scroll at all costs."

The Way Master rolled her eyes. "Dhayin, I have already belabored this with Brother Rictor. None of us took that scroll. I give you my word as a Way Master."

"Rictor is convinced otherwise. I fear he has convinced some of my employers, as well. That is why I have brought you here."

Thulann glanced at Grynholt and the Logosian. Neither man had a weapon drawn, though both were clearly alert for action. She marked their positions and replied, "Do not be obtuse. You brought us here to tactically isolate us. The desert and the mountains will make our escape difficult. Now please, enlighten me. How does capturing us help you when I do not have the scroll in the first place?"

Dhayin rubbed his eyes and sighed. "I protested this action vigorously. My associates will confirm that. But I have pledged to carry it through. The plan is simple. We are going to keep Venduss as a hostage until you bring us the scroll."

She furrowed her brow and grumbled, "That is a very bold plan, and a very dangerous one."

The Logosian stared at her. "We are bold and dangerous men."

Under the shelter of the outcropping, Venduss's face darkened with rage. "By the Great Mother, I cannot believe I am hearing this! Dhayin, you have served my father for many years. He has trusted you. *I* have trusted you! What could possible lure you to this disgrace?"

"I am committed to a secret pact. It is a careful balance of parties with very different codes of behavior. My participation defends the Jukan Way. I cannot and shall not withdraw. Venduss, you know that I would not do this without an honorable motive! And I shall remain here to ensure that no harsh treatment befalls you."

The youth bared his teeth. "I shall see to my own well-being, if it is all the same!" He reached for his sword, until a frightened Toria clutched his arm.

The burly Logosian warrior had not moved, but locked a chilling stare on him.

Dhayin waved his hands. "Please! This need not turn to violence. Mistress Thulann, listen to me. Braun's Needle is coming to Crevasse in a week or less. From here it travels to the coast, where it will be deployed over the ocean. At that point it will be very difficult to reach. That is why I lured you to this place, because it holds our best opportunity for sabotage. But our time draws short. You must send for the scroll with all haste."

Thulann felt her anger beginning to boil. "For the final time, neither I nor my companions have the scroll. Never have I endured such a relentless assault upon my honor! I begin to think I may be required to defend it with steel, if words alone do not satisfy you!"

The Logosian smiled very wide and broadened his stance. "Now we get to the meat of the transaction."

Toria murmured, "Mistress . . ."

The girl's voice sounded meek. Her face was pale with apprehension. She could not meet the Way Master's eyes.

Thulann steadied her own breathing. "What is it, Toria?"

"I took that scroll from Enclave."

Thulann felt herself flinch.

152

Dhayin clutched the air. "Thank the Great Mother! Please, Toria, what did you do with it?"

The girl mashed shut her eyes. "I gave it to Montenegro when he was leaving Garron."

Grynholt licked his lips, twitching his braided beard. "I'll be damned. The knight does have it. Rictor was right all along."

The Way Master worked to quell a rising heat. Her voice quavered with suppressed fury. "I gave my word of honor about this, Toria. On many occasions."

"I know that! I didn't tell you at first because I was angry at you. Then when you gave your word to Bahrok, I knew you'd just hand it over to him. So I did what I thought you might've done in the first place. I'm sorry, Mistress!"

Thulann's gaze seethed. "What I might have done? Never would I break my word of honor, child. Never." She looked away to the distant baubles of Crevasse.

Venduss, however, regarded the small human with an expression of unrestrained contempt. Toria buried her face in her hands, cradling her sword to her chest.

Dhayin grew more animated. "Very well! At last we uncovered the truth. There will be no need for hostages. We must send word to Logos. Rictor and the Meer Hunter should still be in Britain, so they can fetch the scroll from Montenegro. Surely he will see the sense in cooperating."

The Logosian rubbed his palms together briskly in the rain. "But our work here is finished, correct, Dhayin? We've got no more need for Thulann?"

Dhayin smiled. "Yes, thank the Great Mother."

He shrugged. "Good." He flipped his wrist in a blur.

Thulann felt her skull snap. Her face roared with pain. Her head smashed backward against the rock wall. She thought she saw the hilt of a dagger protruding from her cheek, though only one of her eyes seemed to work.

The world reeled as she sank to the ground. Her limbs felt feathery, unresponsive, though she tried to command them to move.

Dhayin screamed, "No!"

"Dammit, Pikas," muttered Grynholt, "you need to learn to control yourself."

Pikas of Enclave, thought the Way Master, *the assassin whom Montenegro is hunting. The man who nearly murdered Venduss two years ago. He was wise to withhold his name. I was unwise not to pry.*

The Logosian assassin whisked out a scimitar. With a stroke he parried Venduss and clipped off a spray of Toria's hair. The minstrel tucked her head and rolled deeper beneath the overhang.

Thulann struggled to reach for a healing potion at her belt. It felt as if she were trying to manipulate another person's arm.

Venduss and Pikas smashed their blades together, though the assassin leered wildly as he did. When Dhayin barked, "That's enough!" and drew his own steel, Venduss let loose a howl and spun at the Garronite. Thulann counted four cuts, beautifully aligned, crisscrossing Dhayin's kill points.

Venduss's fifth stroke removed Dhayin's head.

Pikas whooped with mad excitement.

When Toria charged, her sword popping with static electricity, the wizard Grynholt flung a ball of flame at her. Using a maneuver Thulann had taught her, she tumbled underneath the fireball and leapt to her feet without breaking pace. The ground shook when the fireball hammered the rock wall. The Way Master imagined the damp stone had cracked and ejected steam.

Toria hacked the wizard's arm. The jolt rocked the heavy man to his knees. The minstrel sprang back under the outcropping as Grynholt cast another spell at her. This time a blinding pillar of fire bellowed from his hands. Again Toria dodged the blaze. It struck the hillside with a thunderous noise.

Thulann was not imagining the cracking sound. The ground lurched. Fissures streaked across the wall. Slabs of rock sloughed free.

The massive overhang was collapsing and Thulann could not move.

Venduss staggered back from the gleeful Pikas of Enclave. The boy's face was striped with cuts. He bled from several stab wounds. He looked up to see the hillside begin to fracture and fall.

Both Toria and Thulann were beneath the collapsing overhang. Venduss grabbed Thulann's arm and jerked her to safety.

Toria screamed as the jagged rocks smashed down, though her cry was clipped short. The thunderous din rolled across the black, sharp-toothed mountains.

Grynholt pointed toward Crevasse and snapped, "Pikas! Will you stop now, you brutal bastard? Dreadnoughts are coming! We have to go!"

The Jukan assassin kicked Venduss on the side of the head, toppling the warrior onto the mound of rubble that buried Toria. In several strokes Pikas's scimitar chopped a gory fissure into Venduss's side. The youth stopped moving.

Then the assassin knelt in front of Thulann. His teeth gleamed in a mocking smile. "See, that was much more satisfying than our first meeting in Britain! You almost killed me then, but as of now I forgive you."

As he grabbed the knife jutting from her face and slowly rotated it, Thulann had a quick thought: *Of course. That is what he meant by a "second chance."* Then pain stole the world from her, nor did she mourn the loss.

CHAPTER
7

Cove

A tickle of dust leapt down from the lintel as the tall door creaked open. A fresh night breeze stirred the little cloud. Montenegro blinked at the twirling particles as he stepped inside the front entrance of his manor house. In his off hand gleamed a brass lantern. With a cough he said, "I apologize for the state of the place, but I haven't been here in eight months. The caretaker only comes every other week."

Behind him followed two strapping figures. Jatha of Ishpur wore clothes of tailored leather under a light cloak, drenched in the red dust of the road. The Meer carried a scroll tube in his hand and strode with brisk purpose.

At the rear came the ranger, Fairfax, who examined the split shaft of an arrow. He looked incredulous. "Orcs! On the road to Cove! To what dismal sickness has this kingdom succumbed when travelers not two days from Britain are attacked by those flesh-hungry brutes? The natural order calls for goblins to devour us this far south, not orcs."

Montenegro dropped a pair of saddlebags onto a carved chair. "It must be the troll king's doing. His war against the world is driving the orcs south. The orcs are driving the goblins into Britain. Which leads one to wonder, where will the Britannians go?"

"A'hunting," said the ranger, examining a broken fletching, "as long as their arrows hold out, anyway. But this is embarrassing! I can't salvage any of these. It'll take me days to make new ones."

The knight rummaged through his belongings. "Then stay here while you do. I can at least offer you my hospitality, such as it is, in return for accompanying me on the road. I am almost disappointed that Rictor didn't follow us. It would have been interesting to see what those orcs might have done with him."

Jatha commented, "I can see why he and Shavade are so interested in this scroll. This diagram is . . . unprecedented." The wizard had unfurled the document on a table in the nearest parlor. The chandelier above him glowed with the unearthly light of a spell. "I'm sure of it now. These are alchemical symbols. The rendering is strange but I could never mistake the rune forms. Not these runes. In some abominable way, this machine invokes air magic."

"Indeed? That is peculiar. Can you tell what it does?"

His ears lowered. He grimaced with concentration. "It's far more complicated than anything I've seen. There is only a single person I know who might pluck some order out of this diagram. Montenegro, you've got to let me take this scroll to Mistress Aurora."

The knight jangled a ring of iron keys from the bottom of a saddlebag. He shook his head as he sorted through them. "Sorry, Jatha. I won't do that. Rictor and Shavade are out there somewhere. I dare not let that scroll from my sight."

"Then come back to Britain with us. We'll deliver it together."

"I don't want to seem ungrateful for your help, but I have work to do here. In ten days I'm hosting a dinner for Lord Gideon. It will be my best chance to request a command, and you know I won't let anything jeopardize that. So I have ten days in which to dig this manor out from under the dust." From the ring he unhooked a very large key, which he tossed to Fairfax. "There you are! The key to happiness. That is to say, the wine cellar. Enjoy what you may, my parched friend."

The blond warrior flipped the key between his fingers, sighed and lobbed it back to Montenegro. "A hundred thanks for the lubricious offer, but I fear I have abandoned the sweet sin of the droplet. My thirst has vanished. You won't see another swallow pass these poor lips, which now so tormentedly long for something more deserving of my worship than the supple milk of the grape and the grain-seed."

Montenegro wrinkled his brow. "Are you saying you've stopped drinking because you're heartsick over Shavade? You take me for quite a fool, don't you? I'm tempted to call you out for it."

"Nay, it is your very example that inspires me! You surrendered the goblet's kiss so that you might become a better knight. Now I have murdered that same part of myself, so that I may become a worthier suitor. And to a woman who will surely try to murder the remaining parts of me! Can there be any doubt that Love is the most hateful of the Principles? And the heart is the deadliest organ."

The knight chuckled. "The day you dry up, Fairfax, I shall walk to Jukaran." He turned back to the Meer. "Jatha, you haven't lost your thirst, at least?"

He flinched an ear. "Since I chant my spells, I consider my tongue to be my blade. It does require oiling from time to time."

"I'm glad someone's going to drink from my stock. There shall be another Cataclysm before it's ever emptied." He retrieved his lamp and walked toward the cellar door.

Abruptly he stopped. A small object on the ground caught his attention.

It was an eagle's feather, brown and sleek, of the sort that he had once stolen from Captain Bawdewyn's hat.

The tip of the feather pointed to the cellar door. Jotted on the dusty surface he saw a familiar geometric symbol.

Beza rhem.

He wiped the mark from the grainy wood. Jatha was captivated by the scroll and Fairfax by his arrows; neither had seen the symbol. Montenegro unlatched the heavy lock and descended into the spidery gloom.

The wine cellar unrolled in circular, woodwork vaults. The pillars supporting the roof teemed with wooden monsters either chastising or cheering him, depending on the angle of the light. The lantern revealed a maze of racks, filled with bottles so dusty they looked like stone. Cobwebs tapestried the dark.

When he stilled himself, Montenegro heard the cadence of deep breathing. He followed the murmur around a blind corner to a small, round alcove. A figure in a grey robe curled up within. A lock of rich, black hair lolled from her shadowy cowl.

The sight of the sleeping Raveka flushed him with warmth.

He chose a bottle of wine without examining the label. Quickly he returned upstairs, locked the cellar door behind him and slipped the key into a pouch at his belt.

"Jatha, I've reconsidered," he announced as he offered the grimy bottle to the Meer. "You're right. Someone should have a look at the scroll who can make sense out of it. Take it to Mistress Aurora and see what she can discern."

The wizard nodded as he wiped the label with his thumb. "Excellent. She has been extremely busy of late, preparing war spells with the Order of the Magus. But I know she will make time to read this schematic. If she cannot fathom it, I wonder if even the Matriarchs themselves could?"

"There shall be no time to find out. You may take the scroll to Britain, but I must have it back before Lord Gideon arrives. That's ten days from now, my friend. Take that bottle as payment for your services."

"Ten days? Four of them shall encompass the journey itself!"

The knight crossed his arms. "Then you had best not delay. If memory serves, you have a trick in your sorcerer's bag to make the road pass by more quickly?"

Jatha wrenched the scroll into a tight cylinder and slipped it into the tube. "So I do! But every moment counts, nonetheless. Fairfax! Forget about your arrows. We're heading back to Britain. If we leave now, we may reach the Black Goat by this time tomorrow."

The ranger brushed a shower of unruly hair from his eyes. "What's that? We're leaving without a meal and a bath to tame the road?"

"The former we can hunt. The latter has never been a priority of yours, anyway. And our friend has supplied our skins with some of the finest water ever squeezed from a grapevine." He pointed the label at Fairfax. "Yewic Crimson. Pre-Cataclysm, of course. Montenegro, this bottle is a treasure. Either that scroll is very important to you, or you really want us to leave."

Sir Gabriel smirked. "Watch for Rictor. Don't let anything happen to that schematic. I need it to help me gain Lord Gideon's support. If it is not returned in ten days, I shall have sharp words for both of you."

Fairfax examined the antique bottle of wine with growing dismay. "You are a fiend, Montenegro, blacker than any monster felled by your grandfather's blade! I have vowed sobriety and you send this liquid heaven to accompany us on the road. I would rather you had called me out for insulting you."

Montenegro smacked the ranger's arm. "Life is a herd of temptations. Try not to let them trample you."

The advice did not seem to comfort Fairfax. His posture slumped as the two men took their leave.

The knight watched them ride their horses toward the front gate of his lands. When he was satisfied that they were gone, he trotted upstairs with the saddlebags draped over one shoulder. Though he was weary from the road, his strides were long and energetic. Many years had passed since he had faced housework without servants, but with compelling motivation, Montenegro knew he was the equal to the task. Time was his only shortcoming.

Sister Raveka felt a tender breeze cooling her face. She blinked open her eyes to see an unshuttered window, through which the spring night whispered. The world outside was a rustle of tiny leaves, millions of them, a distinctive chorus only sung in New Britannia. The smell of the forest was organic and glorious.

In her mind she conjured a mathematical verse to steady her thoughts.

A shielded candle burned low beside her bed. By its light she scanned the large bedroom in which she was lying. The place was heavy with carved wood paneling, sturdy chairs and thickly framed portraits. The bed itself was a monument in oak. The giant headboard displayed, in deep relief, the crest of the Montenegro family. Raveka wondered if the dragon's claw, gripping a heart, matched the size of the actual beast's talons. The scale appeared to be correct. The thought gave her a shiver.

Raveka was still dressed in her traveling robe of the Order. Apparently Montenegro was not as indelicate tonight as he had been on board the *Menagerie* at Ruhn. But the long, windy trip from Logos had sensitized her skin and stiffened the fabric of her raiment. She decided to return to her hidden carriole and fetch something more comfortable.

A small door stood ajar. When she rose from the bed she noticed golden light pulsing beyond. Firewood snapped as she approached.

A billow of steam tumbled over her when she entered the next chamber. But it was not the hot, harsh steam of Technocrat machinery, to which she was accustomed. She had entered a warm bath chamber. A broad hearth roused hot tufts from many pitchers of water. A claw-footed tub emitted its own wisps of heat.

Next to the tub were a New Britannian dressing gown and robe. In the soft glow they sparkled with lace. Apparently Montenegro had been prepared for her.

Sister Raveka felt herself smile. Despite her stoic instincts, she did not chase away the expression. Lector Gaff had said that the confidence of Montenegro was her greatest weapon, and to that end she must take advantage of every emotional nuance her features could generate. Sir Gabriel was not going to generously hand her the schematic for Braun's Needle. This mission would require a great deal of work.

The Technocrat anticipated it almost as much as she had coming to New Britannia for the first time. The feeling was dreamlike, magical; a forgotten childhood sensation, risen up from a buried place. She began to unbuckle her Mathematician's robe. More than ever the garment felt out of place here.

Montenegro let the pleasant fumes curl across his face. A pot of mulled wine dangled over the embers of a fireplace. The sharp fragrance always comforted him with memories of seasons past. He stirred the spices with a wooden spoon.

The knight had changed into a soft tunic and hosen. Now he sat in the parlor adjacent to his bedchamber, waiting.

Gentle footfalls made him twitch. The bedroom door had made no sound when it opened. He rotated in his chair to witness a phantom in white.

Raveka glided into the parlor within a cloud of silk. The voluminous dressing robe danced around her on a draft from the bedroom window. The fabric was stark white, against which her pale skin was almost invisible. Only her dark, shoulder-length hair broke the milky spell, and the black of her feather-shaped eyes.

She furrowed her brow and smiled, clasping the garment near the hollow of her throat. Its folds settled when she shut the door. "You can't be that surprised, hey? You must have seen this robe before."

"It has never been worn in quite that way."

She tilted her head. "It's beautiful. Did you have it made for my visit?"

"Would that I could say so, but the truth is it once belonged to my cousin, Lady Aria of Coventine. Damario's half-sister."

"Does she stay with you often?"

Montenegro shook his head. "Never. She lived every moment by her father's side, at his estate near Chantry. She died of a fever two winters ago. Lord Coventine sent her belongings here, for Damario to dispense. He didn't know that his son was also gone."

The Technocrat glanced over the frilly robe with a somber expression. Then she spotted the kettle in the fireplace. "You mulled wine, too? You are a mystery to me, Gabriel. I thought knights were educated in tactics and swordplay, not the less manly arts. And here I took you for nothing but a well-dressed barbarian."

He motioned her to a plush chair, then leaned over to stir the pot. "Don't confuse a knight with an ordinary soldier. You might be astonished by my upbringing. I studied literature, philosophy, the arts, everything for a young gentleman to impress his rich elders. You can't imagine me with a calligraphy brush in my hand, can you? But I was damned good with one. Ask the other knights. They will tell you."

She laughed as she curled up in the high-backed chair. "I wouldn't say you have an honest face, but I shall take you at your word."

"You have no choice, because you know I have never lied to you, Raveka." He filled a cup with swirling wine and handed it to her. "Not even when I used to think you wanted to kill me."

The Mathematician stared into the drink, lost in the liquid movement. Her eyes glinted when she looked up again. "No wine for the educated savage?"

"You know I don't drink. How did Fairfax put it? I have 'surrendered the goblet's kiss.' "

She sipped the spiced wine and moaned with genuine pleasure. "But no one will know if you taste just a sip. We're all alone on your estate, Gabriel. I promise not to tell anyone what goes on here, if you promise to treat me nicely."

"I shall treat you how you deserve, little burglar." He chuckled and leaned against the back of his chair. "And I shall not drink."

She stretched her shoulders and uncurled one leg. It emerged from the folds of white silk. "But I've come a long way to visit you. I expected to find you in . . . an indulgent condition."

She had not worn the gown under her robe. Her leg was bare to the thigh. Her skin played with the firelight like porcelain.

He broke away his gaze and forced a smile. "I see now why you came so far."

"You invited me, Gabriel. On board the *Menagerie* you weren't afraid to look. You always say you miss Riona, hey? Well, she's come to help you lick your wounds."

Montenegro was powerless to keep his eyes from her. Raveka's eyelashes flicked nervously as she drew up her bare knee and reclined into the soft, velvet seat.

He saw his hand reaching for her. She trembled just once, strongly enough to drip wine over her fingers. His palm brushed her thigh. Then he gently tugged on a fold of silk to cover her exposed leg.

"You are not Riona Lynch," he murmured as he walked across the parlor. For some time he said nothing as he fought the blush inside his body. Raveka remained silent, as well.

He closed his eyes. "What are you here for? Tell me."

Behind him she muttered, "I cannot."

He stared over his shoulder. "Yes, you can, because in return I'm going to tell you whatever you came to find out. I want no part of your manipulations. If you want information, I'll give it to you freely."

She straightened her neck and frowned. "Why would you do that?"

"I did not invite Blackthorn or the Lectors to visit me. I invited you. This isn't about the war. If espionage is part of your agenda, then let's get it over with right now."

"You must think I'm very trusting. Even a knight can lie."

"The Virtues are not a game. You know I am trustworthy, even though your Technocrat taskmasters might not allow you to admit it." He glanced at the fire. "No more pretenses. I only want you to stay for your own sake. If you aren't prepared to do that, then leave."

Her eyes fell across the wine again. She hugged her knees. "All right. I have come about the scroll."

A bleak chuckle escaped his lips. He felt relief from some unnamed doubt. "I thought as much. Very well. For you alone, I shall confess." He returned to his chair and stretched out his long legs. Then he told her everything about the schematic, from the incident in Enclave until he sent the scroll to Mistress Aurora. To honor his vow to General Nathaniel he omitted any mention of the Pact of Four, though he would have enjoyed exposing Bahrok, Rictor and Shavade.

She listened with quiet concentration. "So Mistress Aurora has the scroll right now?"

"I apologize if that makes your job difficult. Perhaps you can sneak into the House of the Griffin and steal it? I have always been curious to know what would happen to someone who tried that." He met her eyes and smiled. "But Jatha shall return it to me no later than ten days from now. You can kill me and take it then, if you like."

"Perhaps I shall," she smirked, then drank an impressive gulp of wine.

"Is that everything you came for?"

Her eyes eased shut. For an instant her smile faltered. "Mmmm."

Montenegro crossed his ankles, his feet resting inches from the fire. "Good. You see, the Virtue of Honesty serves us well. We've concluded your business here. Now we can turn our energies to pleasure."

Raveka lifted an eyebrow. "I thought you weren't interested in my pleasures."

"Riona Lynch was appealing, but she was a disguise. I don't traffic with fantasies. The woman in front of me is flesh and blood. You are not half as confident as Riona, but positively more intriguing."

Her white skin reddened. She smiled at the flames. "And what pleasures do you want to share with Sister Raveka of Logos?"

"Tell me about yourself. Your voice is pleasing enough for me."

Her brown eyes gleamed with honest delight. Her fingers entwined around the cup. For a moment she deepened her breath, then to the knight's surprise, she began to sing an undulating chant. The notes came soft and unerring. Montenegro was reminded of the haunting murmur of Enclave's windy streets. The words were sibilant and esoteric.

He watched her dark eyes. With each note her hesitation diminished. She ended with a hint of a smile.

He sat up in his chair. "That was . . . enthralling. What was it?"

"It was me. That mathematical proof is my identity in the Order. It is a portrayal of the events in my life."

"Ah, like the Life Words of the Juka?"

She let out a breathy chuckle. "Something like that."

He opened a subtle grin. "Was there a verse that recounted your dealings with a knight from Cove?"

"It doesn't work that way. The Chant is introspective of the Order. It represents my unity with the Machine."

"I see. Then the Machine is more beautiful than I suspected. But I want to know about you, not your Order. Who is Raveka? How does she express her own desires?"

The Technocrat laughed. "By coming to New Britannia."

Montenegro spread out his hands. "Then I shall do my best to make you at home. I've always said that you belong here."

She swallowed a tongue of wine. "Perhaps so. But are you perceptive, Gabriel, or are you merely persuasive?"

He laughed. "Persistent. In my experience, no other trait yields half as much reward."

The hour grew very late as they sat in the parlor and talked. In time Raveka recounted the events of her flight from Garron, with Thulann on her trail. Montenegro was captivated by the fear in her eyes. He answered with tales of his Logosian exploits, then wondered aloud why she had never contacted him in that land. With a sigh she explained, "I'm afraid my mentor, Lector Gaff, learned of my methods to track down Pikas. He disapproves of personal business with an enemy knight. Especially not one as dangerous as you are."

Montenegro did not realize he had earned such a fearsome reputation among the Technocrats. The revelation gave him quiet satisfaction.

He grinned. "Nor should I consort with so dangerous an enemy spy. Yet some priorities transcend the vagaries of war, right?"

She blushed and nodded, then glanced away.

After the mention of Lector Gaff, Raveka's animation faded. Several cups of wine lustered her eyes. He spoke to her until the soft glow of sleep enveloped her moon-white body. Then he lifted her from the chair, carried her into his bedchamber and laid her down. Gently he removed her robe. She curled into the embrace of the lush blankets.

He locked the windows. An old rune twinkled on the latch, put there by Master Gregorio himself in his youth. The shutters trembled from a breeze outside.

When Montenegro closed the room behind him, he paused to blink away his own fatigue. Work remained for him yet. He had to prepare another bedchamber for himself. He did not relish the idea, but afterward he could finally indulge in deep slumber. For the first time in weeks, he felt satisfied with the day.

Raveka's own Chant tumbled through her mind, battling the torpor of sleep. The verses came loud and assertive.

I am the sum of my training. I am a component of the Machine.

She was standing in a smaller bedroom, wrapped in the languid haze of predawn. The white robe enfolded her in layers of fine silk. She kept one hand inside it, against her breast.

Hidden in her grip was a long dagger, with an edge polished keen by the finest craftsmen in Logos.

Montenegro slept on a large bed in front of her.

Her plan was direct and therefore carried minimal risk of

error. Montenegro had surrendered as much information about the scroll as she had hoped to gain. Jatha was going to bring the schematic here in ten days. So she had feigned sleep to lower Montenegro's guard. By murdering him now, she would secure ample time to prepare an ambush for the Meer wizard. The weapons strapped to her carriole were more than sufficient for the task.

Yet she could not seem to remove her hand from the robe. The dagger trembled from the banging of her heart.

"If you are here for something in particular, Raveka, I should be happy to help you get it."

She flinched wildly at his voice. Her feet nearly left the ground.

The knight propped up on his muscular arms. "You might want your rest. Tomorrow I shall take you to watch the eagles. You'll need to ride a horse, and if memory serves, you have never done so."

Raveka recaptured her breath. "No, I haven't. I have always wanted to learn."

He watched her carefully. "Then tomorrow is your day. For now, off to bed."

She coughed a nervous laugh, then nodded and turned toward the door. Behind her Montenegro murmured, "By my Valor, you must be a dream tarrying in my eyes."

As she returned to her room, a part of her felt like a fool. Her lips twisted into a frown. But in her mind the Chant resumed and quashed self-reproach. The event had been simple. Montenegro had not been asleep. The murder would have failed, and so her inaction was fortuitous and desirable. And many days remained before Jatha would arrive; time enough for another attempt. Her mission proceeded within acceptable tolerances.

In the luxury of Montenegro's bed she drifted away to the sound of stomping hooves, metering the rhythm of her dreams.

The morning softened the rolling hills with a coat of mist. The dew lay so thick on the grass that with every stride, their horses dashed a spray of water into the air. The droplets ignited in errant sunbeams, glittering cascades of fire.

Montenegro's ebony stallion, Humbolt, lunged with excitement over the glens and hillocks. The knight shared his mount's joy at the sensations of home. Despite the power of its gait, however, the heavy warhorse could not keep pace with the dapple-grey mare that carried Raveka. The elegant horse, named Hoshaba, was bred for fleetness. The return of her master had put wind in her strides. Hoshaba did not even mind bearing an inexperienced rider, though Montenegro had to credit Raveka for natural grace. The Technocrat's poise was impeccable. He attributed it to her experience with flying machines.

In a dress and billowy cloak from Aria of Coventine's wardrobe, Raveka portrayed a New Britannian lady with skillful self-command. But no, thought the knight, it was not a portrayal. Her gracefulness came from a deeper place, from beneath the mask of a sober Mathematician. Sister Raveka concealed many layers. After her strange visit to his room last night, he admitted to himself that she would require careful handling. Through the sleepless dawn he devised a strategy.

He could see the passionate woman inside her. She was smothered by logic and deception. He resolved to crack through the Technocrat shell, no matter the effort required. The person within deserved to breathe.

The Virtue of Honesty demanded it, as did his own, rising curiosity.

They crested a grassy hilltop and the ocean unfurled below. Pearly waves danced beside a curtain of rocky cliffs. The town of Cove lay in the distance, a picturesque tableau of thatched roofs and meandering stone walls. The forest huddled around it with rippling leaves and gnarled limbs.

Raveka perched atop the hill astride her proud, marbled mare. The ocean wind roiled inside her cloak. She caught her breath and laughed, "This is more difficult than it looks!"

Montenegro trotted beside her. "Riding is a battle between mount and man. But when their spirits join together, time and distance are just sod underfoot."

She looked out at the sun rising beyond the cove. "It's a masterpiece."

He smiled. "It is, isn't it? This is home. Surprisingly difficult to return to, alas. But look down."

She peered over the edge. He looked alongside her. In the dizzy air next to the cliff wheeled several dark shapes on broad, feathered wings. The cries of the eagles sliced through the rasp of the sea.

Raveka leaned against Hoshaba's arched neck. "They're beautiful. I've never seen so many in one place before. You know, they are a true enigma. The Engineers cannot duplicate their flight. Eagles transcend technology."

Montenegro chuckled. "So do you, Lady Aria."

She squinted. "Why call me that?"

"Because that is who you are this morning. I've got business in Cove. I want you to come with me. You'll need a name and I'm afraid 'Sister Raveka' won't do." He reached out to take her hand before she could pull away. Her fingers wrapped around his.

She smirked. "You're awfully familiar for a cousin."

"Aria and I were related only by marriage, which means we are free to pursue whatever affections we choose." He grinned and touched a kiss to her knuckle.

She smiled and glanced across the ocean. "I am no lady."

"Aria never had your grace. You are the lady she wished she could be. Enough of this hesitation. There's work to do. On the way to town I'll tell you about my late cousin, so the ruse will be convincing. Though there wasn't much to her, I fear. She was a tragic hint of a woman, a reflection in her mad father's eye."

The Technocrat shrugged. "That's more than Riona ever was. Come on, then. I want to test Hoshaba some more. No levitant engine ever fought back like this!" The horse lifted its slender legs and leapt down the hillside. Raveka tottered in the saddle for an instant, but quickly sat tall and composed.

Montenegro nudged Humbolt to follow. He could not match Raveka's pace, but that did not concern him. Now that she had taken the bait, he wanted only to keep her in view.

The population of Cove flooded the dirt streets to welcome the return of their local hero. On horseback Montenegro led Raveka through the attentive crowd. The townsfolk cheered the knight and greeted his cousin with friendly respect.

Montenegro was pleased to watch Raveka handle the attention with the aplomb of a noble-born lady. He sensed that her actions were very nearly genuine. It was a gratifying sight.

Though the people of Cove clamored for tales of Blackthorn, Montenegro somehow managed to undertake the day's business. He engaged workmen to clean up the grounds of his estate, grooms to ready the stables and carriage house, chambermaids to make the manor livable. The cook at the local inn agreed to stock the kitchen and prepare meals for them. He contracted dogs from a local huntsman in preparation for an afternoon's sport with Lord Gideon.

Throughout the day Raveka stayed at his side, no more nor less quiet than was proper for Lady Aria. He had been holding her hand for an hour before it occurred to him that the townsfolk would gossip. The thought made him chuckle.

Raveka moved closer and whispered, "You seem very cheerful for a man who's being followed."

He smirked. "It happens in Britain, too. You grow accustomed to it."

"Not to deflate your ego, but I mean something entirely different."

With a subtle nod she motioned to the corner of a nearby building. A nondescript man leaned against the wall. His eyes flicked away when Montenegro looked.

The knight glanced at his companion. "Let's have a word with him, shall we, Aria?"

She draped her arm through his. "Unless you think he might be dangerous, dearest cousin."

Montenegro laughed aloud. They convinced their entourage to grant them a moment's privacy, during which they made their way down a blind alley. He leaned against a rain barrel as Raveka vanished around a corner.

Moments later a figure appeared from the direction of the street. The man stepped into the alley with a stiff posture. Behind him walked Raveka. Her dagger urged him forward.

Montenegro steepled his fingers and shook his head. "Lady Aria has a way of appearing from nowhere like that. Take it from me, you must have a sharp eye to keep her in your sight."

The man fell to his knees. "Sir Gabriel, forgive me! I am a poor man. I could not refuse the money!"

"Money for what?"

"I was paid to watch you, sir, and to ride ahead when you leave town. He wanted to be warned before you returned home. He is at your estate now, sir!"

Montenegro grimaced. "Let me guess. 'He' is a bald man who makes a corpse look robust."

The fellow lowered his head. From a pouch he spilled several coins into the dust. "Here is the money he gave me, sir. I am ashamed of taking it."

The knight stood and massaged his eyes. "You demonstrate Honesty and Humility. In return I'll show Compassion. Keep the money. Use it to do a kind deed. The Virtue of Sacrifice is one of the noblest, after all. But if you try to warn the bald man, you shall make another kind of sacrifice. Your head would be appropriate, though I might be content with your hands."

To the dismay of the townsfolk they rode quickly out of Cove. Raveka trotted her horse beside him. "Who is the bald man?"

"Someone else looking for the schematic of Braun's Needle. He is very dangerous."

"Who is he? An agent of Logos? Of Garron?"

"He is . . . an independent operator. I cannot tell you more."

She narrowed her eyes. "I brought weapons, Gabriel. Let's fetch them before we go to the house."

"No. Whatever happens, maintain the guise of Lady Aria. You do not want this man to know where you came from. Trust me."

The landscape opened up in front of them. He jabbed Humbolt into a gallop. His mood grew more sour with the passing hills. He had important matters to handle now and these petty intrigues were a solvable nuisance. The time had come to settle them. General Nathaniel would simply have to understand.

They arrived to find the house in shambles. Every room had been roughly searched, overturning furniture and cloth-covered decorations. When they convinced themselves that the intruder had gone, Montenegro punched an oak panel. "Damn him! Does he think I'm naive enough to leave the scroll lying around for the taking?"

Raveka leaned on his shoulder, hugging his arm. "He does not know what a challenge you are."

The knight sneered. "Yes, it takes a lot more work to steal something from me, doesn't it, Sister Raveka?"

She pulled away and looked out a window. "I am going to check my carriole. It will be disastrous if he has located it."

He cursed his temper and regained his composure. "I'll join you. The bald man is a poisoner. If he catches you by surprise, you'll be dead before you know he's there."

At her hidden vehicle she retrieved some equipment from a startling collection of weaponry. They returned to the house in silence and began to right the disheveled furniture. By late afternoon they had readied the manor for the work-men to commence the next day.

The cook from Cove arrived to prepare them dinner and left before sunset.

When they were alone in the echoing manor house, Montenegro sat before a small fire and watched Raveka work with her devices. The Technocrat laid a hand-held machine on a table. From the gearbox she unrolled a long chain, the length of which was barbed with steel fangs. She began to oil the razor chain with a stylus and a small, metal bottle.

He shook his head. "If that is a weapon, it must be more ungainly than a Jukan apology. I would slice open my own throat if I flailed that at an enemy."

She did not look up. "It is exceedingly difficult to use. I have trained with it for many years. Only recently have I been proficient enough to bring it to the field."

He frowned at her cold demeanor. "I hope you don't still consider this the 'field'? I thought we were past that."

For a long moment the Technocrat made no response. Then she muttered, "You said you'd told me everything about the scroll. Yet there is a dangerous man trying to take it whom you did not mention. That does not improve my confidence in you."

"I do have other obligations besides yourself, cruel as that may sound. I have vows of discretion to uphold. Though admittedly my obligation to the bald man is close to being voided. One more incident like today and I'll mount his head in my parlor. I've been meaning to indulge in a hunt ever since I returned to New Britannia."

Raveka pulled taut a segment of the chain. The barbs snapped upward, ready to bite. "Whoever he is, he will not steal that scroll. I'll help you dispose of him, if you wish me to. He cannot be as elusive as Pikas."

He stared at her with amazement. Dressed in a lady's expensive gown, she could have been a dainty gentlewoman in any parlor in Britain. The spines of her chain whip reflected needles of light across her cheek. "Raveka, sometimes you are sublime to me. Tell me, how does one become a Mathematician? The Order must be very selective, if they are all like you."

"We are the elite among Technocrats. Few are worthy to join us."

"I do not doubt that, but I'm curious about you specifically. How did you join the Order? Were you born into it? Did you enter as a young woman?"

She paused in her work. "I was taken as a child."

"Taken? You mean conscripted?"

With a sigh she laid down her weapon. "If I'm going to talk, let me at least fix a drink to dampen my tongue. Water for you, of course?"

"You spoil me, Aria."

She returned with two cups and sat in the chair across from him. Then she told him about her childhood in a machine she called a "wind pump." For a long while he listened to the tale of her abduction into the Order of Mathematicians and the wonders she discovered there. Then the creeping weight of nighttime made his eyelids heavy. With peculiar speed darkness overtook him, echoing with her sonorous voice.

When Montenegro drifted to sleep, Raveka watched him for many minutes. In the firelight he resembled a handsome, heroic painting. The sight was captivating.

She checked his cup. It was half full. The sedation powder had been more potent than she expected. He did not react when she jostled his shoulder.

Calmly she walked upstairs and into the master bedroom. In the bath chamber she lit a fire, then stripped off the fine dress she wore. She missed its touch from the moment she laid it across the vanity. But that very emotion was the reason she came here. She enjoyed Lady Aria far too much.

The wooden floor warmed. Unclothed, she knelt beside the hearth and lifted a small pot. The paint within was inky black. She dipped a stylus into it and began to inscribe symbols on her arm.

With each new mark she recalled a lifetime of studious training. The discipline of the Machine would overcome her present mental crisis. For instance, at this moment, when she glanced at the bolt-thrower beside her, a rush of horror shot through her body. The machine looked like a deadly nightmare. But soon the equations would enfold her flesh. When she had reasserted her training, the weapon would become a simple instrument of mathematics. It would define the next step in her mission, the next verse of a formula.

Once Montenegro was murdered, she could arrange an ambush for Jatha the Meer and take the scroll from him. She would have to be cautious for the return of the mysterious "bald man." After obtaining the scroll she would return home to the metal streets of Logos and walk the path toward becoming Mother Raveka. The Order would chase away the emotions that now buffeted her. The Machine would codify her thoughts.

Gentle footfalls made her twitch. She whirled to see Gabriel entering the bath chamber. His dour gaze scanned across her.

She covered herself with her hands. Mathematical symbols shawled her arms and shoulders. "You're awake."

He nodded. "I told you the bald man was a poisoner, didn't I? So I am alert for anything in my drink. Perhaps that is paranoid of me. I apologize if my play-acting threw you off." He knelt at her side. She shrank back.

He picked up the bolt-thrower. "Is this for me?"

Her eyes turned away.

"I see. Drug me, stick an arrow in my head, get the scroll and fly home. That was your plan?"

She choked down a swell in her throat. "So it was all along."

"Raveka, look at me. Look at me!"

She did. He was pointing the bolt-thrower at her heart. His eyes blazed. "You're forgetting a very important factor in our relationship, my dear. I have never forgiven you for the assassination of Lord Valente. The day will come when you must pay for that crime, just like Pikas of Enclave must pay. But I have been patient with you, because you seem to want to make amends for it. At least I have wanted to believe that. I even thought to offer you a most generous leniency."

Raveka's flesh felt cold, despite the glowing hearth. "Gabriel, you know it's true. Of course I want to make amends."

"Do you? How? With this?" He shook the bolt-thrower. She flinched. "I don't think you understand the danger you're in at this moment, Raveka! Listen to me. Two years ago I had my entire life ripped out from under me, due in no small measure to your espionage. Since that time I've worked as hard as I can to rebuild it. I have devoted myself to the Virtues and to the honor of my family name. But in the last few weeks, the earth has started shaking again. In Logosia, in Jukaran, in Britain, even in Cove, I find the world conspiring against me! But there has always been one person I thought I could trust. One person who seemed to be working as hard to redeem herself as I am to redeem myself. One person with whom I connected." He grimaced as he fingered the firing lever on the spring-powered weapon. "Now

I find you like this. Despite everything I've done, despite everything we may be, here you are. And I wonder what I should do."

She blinked tears from her eyes. The ebon-haired knight blurred in her vision. She held her hands over her mouth and murmured, "Gabriel, we're at war. They'll kill me if I don't."

He grumbled, "I'll kill you if you try."

She saw the anguish scarring his face, the tears brimming in her eyes. With shaking hands she reached for the mechanical weapon. "Gabriel, please . . ."

Roughly he jammed the bolt-thrower against her chest. The tip of the quarrel pricked her. "Touch it and I'll pierce you!"

Her voice cracked. "Then shoot, damn you! I know you're stronger than I! I couldn't kill you last night and I couldn't have done it tonight! I'm dead now if I return to Logos, so shoot me yourself and put an end to this mess I've made!"

His tears turned icy. "Forgive me," he growled, then flipped the lever. The bolt-thrower fired with a *clack*.

The hearth spat orange cinders as the bolt smashed through the flames. Montenegro threw the spent weapon across the floor. He did not meet her eyes. "I can't kill you, either. That was the first lie I have ever told you."

Raveka's body felt limp. She dropped into his arms and buried her face into his chest. The symbols on her arms smeared across his shirt. "What are we doing, Gabriel? What am *I* doing? I didn't come here to kill you, but I don't know what else to do."

His embrace was strong and unflinching. He spoke with staggered breaths. "There is only one thing you can do. Stay with me."

"Why? So you can punish me for Valente's death?"

"Don't go back to Logos. We'll call it a step toward atonement. Stay with me and show me you're sincere about making amends."

"You're mad. I can't stay here."

"You have no choice! You said it yourself, they'll kill you if you go back. Here I can give you everything you need—a home, a life. I can give you Aria. She is my gift to you."

"No! I belong to the Order. I am a Mathematician."

Gently he stroked her hair. With one knuckle he tilted up her chin. His grey eyes gazed at her, powerful and honest. "They don't want you anymore. I do."

The flood of warmth through her body proved what she did not want to believe. He was right. She had no choice but to stay. She *wanted* to stay. Her reservations started to crumble away. "I want you, too, Gabriel," she whispered, clinging to him tightly.

After a long, silent embrace, a ticklish sensation danced over her calf. She looked down. Montenegro had taken up the stylus and was writing on her leg. In a lavish hand he penned his name: *Sir Gabriel Montenegro*. The feel of it made her flesh tremble. He continued his skilled calligraphy, inscribing the names *Cove* and *Britain* and *Lady Aria Coventine, Humbolt* and *Hoshaba,* the symbols for the Principles and the Virtues, verses of antique poetry; they swirled over her foot and up her leg, each word unfocusing her thoughts, each letter releasing emotions which she had battled to suppress. By slow increments her body rebelled. Her head swam. She turned her lips to meet Montenegro's and the pot of ink jostled over, spilling its contents in wild, rolling streaks.

Hours later, they stood on the balcony of the master bedchamber. Arm in arm they gazed at the sky above the southern ocean. Flashes of lightning bloomed in faraway clouds.

Montenegro was softly tracing her spine with a fingertip. "I keep thinking about this Lector Gaff of yours. He must be a soulless creature. What kind of monster steals a little girl from her home and coerces her into some completely alien life? A crime like that ought to be answered."

He smirked at her. His glance twinkled.

Raveka smiled. "The Virtue of Justice always prevails, right? And truth cannot be shackled."

She lay her head on his shoulder and watched the distant storm. Somewhere beyond, the Logosian armada was preparing to sail to these shores. Braun's Needle itself might be at the heart of those clouds. A nightmare mustered to attack.

She drove the thought from her mind. There would be time enough to decide what to do about the war. For now she reveled in the soft, sublime contours of Gabriel's embrace. The turmoil in Logosia was so remote that the sound of thunder did not even reach her ears.

CHAPTER
8

Braun's Needle

At that moment, under those distant storm clouds, heavy raindrops pelted an old woman's face.

Her mouth tingled with warmth. Her blood surged. Her veins quivered.

She recognized the signature of a healing potion.

Thulann could only open one eye. The midnight tempest still showered the hillside. She was lying beside the pile of fractured rock that had been an outcropping not long before. Toria was buried somewhere underneath.

Pikas and Grynholt were gone.

Venduss balanced atop the mound. Frantically he tore at the jumble of sharp stones, hurling them aside with desperate grunts. Though he must have drunk a healing potion at the same time he administered hers, his wounds still robbed him of strength. His leather garb was a tattered, gory mess.

The heap of rocks was taller than he was. Thulann knew there was no hope of burrowing through it.

She wrestled to her feet, climbed next to him and began to dig anyway.

Crevasse glittered in the distance. Lights separated from

the mining town and headed toward them. Quick spouts of flame burst from the flying entities, illuminating the nearby crags.

Thulann threw down the large rock in her hands. "Dreadnoughts. It is time to leave now, Venduss."

The youth ignored her.

She laid a hand on his shoulder. "Getting caught solves nothing. Please."

He roared a curse and spun, jamming his foot into her gut. She spilled down the rugged pile of stones and splashed into a puddle. Above her, backlit by the approaching flames, Venduss clutched his head and screamed with rage.

Then he darted to Thulann's side, helped her find her feet and led her away from the scene of the battle. The Way Master wiped rain from her injured face.

Her hand found a gap where her right eye had been.

A twinge of horror blinked through her, but she disregarded it. She tore a strip from her black shirt and wrapped it around her head to cover the empty socket. Then she scanned the terrain with her remaining eye. Escape would not be easy. Dreadnoughts moved swiftly and hounds bayed not far off. Neither she nor Venduss were in good shape to flee.

There was no remedy except perseverance. They had to put aside what had happened and take the future one step at a time.

Toria could not breathe. Her arms and legs were pinned by a crushing weight. Cold water slithered over the length of her body. Everything was blackness.

Panic seized her. She squirmed and tried in vain to cry out. The rocks around her shifted, jabbed into her ribs with a crackling sound. But her bones did not make the noise. The ground below her did.

An instant later it gave way. She plummeted into darkness and hard stones. When she thudded onto a solid surface she scrabbled away by instinct.

The rockslide crashed atop the place she had been.

She pressed against a cold wall and screamed for help, but no reply came. She could not hear any sounds of battle above.

In pitch blackness she knelt with a cool stream swirling around her ankles. The air was lively with the splash of water. It sounded like a wet cave. She pulled her only healing potion from her boot and gulped it. Her aches vanished. Then she huddled against the damp chill and waited for her eyes to adjust.

A faint light caught her attention. It pulsed a soft blue. She followed it to where the rockslide had settled. A stream of dirt from the collapsed ceiling was spattering onto the tip of her static sword, which protruded from the rocks. The metal flickered with tiny sparks. She dug the weapon loose, then took off her short-waisted jacket. Though she felt weak, she was able to cut off a scrap of sleeve. The static sword cascaded sparks as she raked it across the stone wall. The sleeve caught fire. She wrapped it around her blade to fashion a makeshift torch.

In the firelight, the little cave glimmered with rainwater drizzling down the walls. A shallow stream flowed away into the darkness. Toria examined the collapsed ceiling that had brought her here. It was clear she could not get back to the surface that way.

The cave was shorter than herself. She ducked her head and sloshed along the path of the stream.

In her mind lingered the horrific image of the fallen Thulann, a dagger buried to the hilt in her face. But the minstrel tried to concentrate on the present, as her mistress would instruct her. A hollow pang quickened her steps.

She was unsure how far she walked. The jacket sleeve burned to cinders and she had to ignite the second one. Along the way she noticed that the tunnel was tube-shaped. The rock walls were scored with spiraling grooves and what looked like acid corrosion. This place must have been carved as part of the levitant mines. Though to all appearances no one had been here in years, she felt a glint of hope. If this was a mine, it had to have an exit.

A long while later, when the rainwater ceased trickling down the walls, she heard skittering sounds in the distant gloom. She clutched her sword more tightly and proceeded.

A shaft of moonlight leapt across the tunnel ahead of her. She doused her torch in the little stream and splashed to the hole in the wall. Large, split rocks littered the ground beneath it. Doubtless this was another spot weakened by a landslide.

The hole was big enough to squeeze through. She decided to have a look first, though, and was glad she did.

The mountainside swarmed with Technocrat spark lanterns. Logosian soldiers tracked the hills, led by teams of grotesque Jukan hounds. Flying machines crept through the air.

She pulled away from the opening and leaned against the wall. Her breaths were thin. Her heart sank when she realized that she could not get back to the site of the battle, back to Venduss and Thulann. Even if she could avoid detection by the search parties, she doubted she could find the camp in the dark. With a soft moan she slid to the ground, pressing her face into her hand.

Perhaps she should not even bother to find them. Not much was left for her now.

In a matter of weeks, the world had crumbled beneath her. She had lost what little hope remained of staying with Venduss. Even the Shirron had rejected her. Nor could she continue to serve Thulann, because Venduss would always be nearby. Not that it mattered anymore, since Thulann was dead now. Almost certainly dead, and disgraced by Toria's theft of the scroll.

In a daze she sat by the hole in the wall, listening to the sounds outside. After an hour the search parties diminished. When a group of soldiers passed close to her, she heard one of them explain why.

"It was just a bunch of scavenger merchants," said the man. "They found a camp over there with some dead Juka. I guess the dreadnoughts finished them."

Toria rolled herself into a ball and lay against the curved wall. Emptiness overtook her. She dared not weep, but gazed into the soggy gloom. The little stream trickled past, mumbling of deep, hollow places.

She woke to a stinging sensation. Sunlight bolted through the hole. In the dusty glow of morning she saw metallic bodies gleaming around her. Logosians called the creatures "gutterbots," though they resembled cat-size, clockwork rodents. Five or six crowded against her.

They were chewing on her legs.

She squealed and bashed one with her sword. The blade pounded a cleft in its back while the static charge sizzled its mechanics. She sprang to her feet and hammered at the swarm. The automatons grew agitated, lunging with metal teeth. But Toria employed Thulann's teachings and after a fury of swordstrokes and electric bursts, the gutterbots lay smoking in the shallow stream.

She caught her breath. Blood streaked her arms and legs. She cupped a handful of water and sniffed it, then washed her injuries. Rainwater on her face was brisk and sobering.

Something else clicked in the shadows. Toria froze and squinted. A steel figure crawled closer on many long, pointed legs. Its rusty joints squeaked. When it crossed the sunbeam Toria saw that the automaton was shaped like a huge spider. She crouched in guard position and tensed for combat.

The creature rose up and extended a nozzle from between its fangs. A steaming fluid squirted at her. With a gasp she leapt above the spray, but it splashed her Logosian boots. Instantly the black leather crackled and smoked, dissolving under the effects of powerful acid. She stomped in the shallow water, then kicked off the boots before the acid reached her feet.

When the clockwork spider charged, she leapt over it and plunged through the sunlit hole. Daylight blinded her and sharp rocks bit her bare feet. She backpedaled with her sword at the ready. The spider did not emerge from the mine.

The rains had ceased. She was alone on the windy mountainside. Several hundred yards away she saw the muddy place they had camped the night before. She shivered at the mound of rubble that had pushed her down into the cave.

When she reached the camp, no sign remained of any of her companions. The ridgebacks and all the provisions were gone. The corpses were removed. The rain had even washed away the blood. She huddled beside the pile of fallen rocks and tried not to weep, as the morning sun grew warmer and chased away the clouds.

Venduss and Thulann stopped to rest an hour after sunrise. The mountains were a lavender ribbon behind them, miles to the west. Rocky desert stretched ahead. The air began to heat, drawing a gossamer miasma from the rain pools that strewed the flat, sandy earth.

Thulann knelt beside their lone ridgeback. Its high, bony crest blanketed her with shade. As the riding beast lapped at a puddle of water, the Way Master scooped handfuls of wet silt and caked it on the animal's hide. The mud would cool the ridgeback and lend it a camouflaged appearance. The Way Master stopped short of suggesting that she and Venduss should do likewise.

The sullen youth paced among the rubble and scrub of the desert terrain. He rarely glanced at Thulann. Not once had he spoken since dawn.

She adjusted the bandage over her eye socket, then splashed water on her face. Her cheek still throbbed. She winced and frowned.

Not far away, Venduss silently covered his eyes. Then he lifted into guard position and began a vigorous procession of unarmed martial forms. The snap of his kicks echoed from distant boulders. His mood looked fierce.

Thulann called out, "We shall see less water as we put the mountains behind us. I suggest you wash now, rather than sweat."

He made no response, but continued his exercises.

"Venduss, we have a difficult journey ahead. Exhausting yourself is not the most prudent way to begin it."

Without stopping he answered, "Thulann—teacher—please do not talk to me. Not now."

A barb leapt to her tongue, but she did not speak it. He was correct, after all. She was only talking to comfort herself. And though it pained her to consider, perhaps she resented him for saving her instead of Toria. The sentiment was unfair, but she could not exorcise it.

Venduss did not deserve her pique. He required his own course of sorrow. She turned away from him and dipped her waterskin into the rippling pool.

"Why bother?" His voice strained from anger and exertion. Thulann perked up, but did not look at him.

In a breathy grumble he continued, "We do not have enough provisions for one of us to reach Jukaran, much less two people and a ridgeback. One waterskin more will make no difference."

She corked the leather sack. "You would be correct, except that we are not going to Jukaran."

He halted in mid-kick. His face grew anxious. "You agree we should go back and settle this?"

"Do not be a fool. If it were not for some opportune healing, Pikas would have killed each of us twice over. He is a dangerous predator who must be stopped, but now is not the time. We cannot settle this grievance with him or with Grynholt of Yew, any more than you settled it with Dhayin last night. They are hawks, as the New Britannians say, and we must find the falconer."

"You mean Bahrok." Venduss threw a flurry of punches into the air, each one popping crisply. "Great Mother, he will pay for this!"

She caught his eye. "Yes he shall, but remember that it is payment we pursue. Not revenge."

"I want to be paid in blood!"

"Perhaps you shall be, nursling. It depends upon how accommodating he is. We shall find out in two days. By then we ought to have reached the territory of his patrols. They will take us straight to our prey."

The young warrior threw off his tattered shirt and snatched the sword from his scabbard. With flawless precision he carved the strokes of an advanced blade form. He finished with a long, powerful thrust.

"I shall extract payment for Toria," he growled, though the comment made him somber again. He stood, sheathed his weapon and started over, this time with more distraction. His eyes sparkled wetly.

Thulann observed him, strangely anxious to catch a flaw. But for the first time, she felt she had no right. Somehow, his flaws were his own now. She touched the bandage on her face and said nothing more.

Toria felt like a child again. She had grown up as a street urchin in the pirate haven of Buccaneer's Den. Now she found herself once again slinking barefoot through muddy lanes, stealing food from townsfolk, with a fleet of warships moored nearby. Of course the Technocrat settlement of Crevasse was scattered down a high mountain slope, and the airships hung like giant bats from the cliffs below; but the unbidden nostalgia gave her a fleeting smile.

She squatted behind a cluster of metal crates and unwrapped her tattered jacket, which she had folded into a makeshift sack. Inside were bread and jerky she had pilfered from a miners' barracks. She devoured them without stopping. It was the first meal she had eaten in a day. She slurped rainbarrel water from her cupped hands, then watched the streets as she rested.

Crevasse teemed with armored Logosian soldiers, both human and Juka, far more than the settlement could reasonably support. Toria remembered Dhayin saying that airships were going to muster here. That would explain the abundance of troops. But their presence forced her to move carefully. Civilians were outnumbered on these streets, and therefore conspicuous. And though her clothes were native, she was covered with fresh bruises and bandages. Someone was sure to ask questions. Besides, her scant bodice and skirt were likely to attract a different kind of attention, and with Venduss dead she could not bear to fight that battle. So she opted to remain in the shadows.

A face blinked past in the crowd. Toria startled. Tucking the jacket into her waistband, she scrambled down an alley-way and peeked along the other side of the building. The man walked past again, unaware of her.

They had called him Pikas last night. He had murdered Thulann and probably Venduss. That made him as deadly as any person she knew.

She shadowed him without hesitation.

Pikas still wore his kinetic armor from the night before, though it was scrubbed clean. He was a lean, broad-shouldered giant even among the other Juka. His bearing asserted calm, dangerous arrogance. The crowds on the street made a path for him.

They also allowed Toria to trail him more easily. She fol-lowed the assassin up the slope of the mountain, where shops and forges gave way to mining facilities. Freight wag-ons clattered about on crisscrossing iron tracks, providing her generous opportunities to hide. The clamor of mining equipment concealed her footsteps. She was thankful for the presence of miners rather than Logosian troops.

Pikas headed for a lift carriage. The cagelike platform was hooked to a series of large chains, designed to hoist passengers to the clifftop mines a hundred feet overhead. Toria cursed. If he rode the carriage up, she would lose him.

She slunk to a fold in the cliffside a few yards from the lift.

Pikas entered the carriage and clanged shut the iron-frame door. He nodded to a miner who was already inside. Then he pulled a lever. The thick chains lurched and began to rattle with increasing volume.

When the two passengers faced away from her, Toria sprinted to the carriage and grabbed one of the chains. It jerked her upward, level with the plate roof. She sprawled out on the metal surface and clung tightly.

The lift soared high into the air. Toria's palms grew slippery. The mountain wind chilled her bare legs.

Then the carriage shuddered and stopped, halfway up the cliff wall.

Her gut tightened like a fist. If she had been spotted, she was a dead woman.

She heard talking inside the carriage. She strained her ears. The voice of the human "miner" was familiar. It belonged to the New Britannian wizard, Grynholt of Yew, who had dropped a hillside on top of her last night. She had not recognized him in Logosian clothes.

He was muttering, "Relax, Pikas. He'll come. Give him some time. Sorcery doesn't work at the snap of a finger."

"I don't like long waits," grumbled the assassin.

A hard breeze whistled as it nudged the carriage. The chains creaked and jangled. Toria took advantage of the noise to shift her position. A bolt hole pierced the roof a few feet away. She made sure her grip was secure, then peeked down inside.

A bright light stabbed her eye. She blinked and looked again. Pikas and Grynholt were standing on either side of the cage. A third man occupied the space between them. He had not been there before.

Toria first noticed the Meer's tall ears. He wore a gown of

filmy layers as rich and flowing as any Ishpurian ambassador in Britain or Garron. He was stouter than other Meer she had seen. He held a rod of black crystal in his hand.

"A most creative meeting place, gentlemen," he commented in a satiny voice.

Grynholt bowed his head. "Chamberlain Kavah, thank you for coming. We have news both good and dire."

"Dhayin has been killed? I can sense it from your tone, and from his uncharacteristic absence."

The wizard nodded. "The plan fell apart. Thulann and her people arrived, but it turned violent. Dhayin was slain."

"And the Way Master?"

"Pikas killed her, and Venduss as well. That's going to stir up the Garronites, and no mistake."

"You're certain they're both dead?"

The Jukan assassin grinned. "As dead as I want them to be."

The Meer named Kavah grunted. "A pity. She was proving to be a very useful resource, as was Dhayin, of course. But what's done is done. I shall tend to this situation with the Shirron's son. Perhaps we can point the blame to another Garronite clan and make it work in our favor. And what is your good news? Did you learn anything about the missing scroll?"

Grynholt shrugged and chuckled. "Montenegro."

"Interesting!"

"The thief girl stole it from Enclave and didn't tell Thulann. She gave it to Montenegro when he returned to New Britannia. You'd better contact Rictor and tell him he was right. He's going to be insufferably smug, though."

"So he shall," murmured the Meer, "but this is madly inconvenient. The Needle is almost here. You can probably see it on the horizon already."

Toria glanced up. From this lofty vantage she could peer across the foothills for many miles and into the dry plains beyond. She squinted and thought she could place a dark shape in the distant sky. But no, she was viewing a small rain cloud, far away. No airship was that large.

Kavah flattened his overtall ears. "We have a day before the Needle docks, and perhaps another two before it departs again for the coast. That is our window for infiltrating the craft. I wonder if Rictor and Shavade can get the scroll in that time?"

The human wizard crossed his arms. "We have the designs for sabotaging the levitant engines. Isn't that enough?"

"Lector Sartorius prefers to disable the primary weapon but keep the airship intact. The Needle is a potent war engine. Sartorius wants it to remain in his arsenal, nor can I blame him. Besides, I believe my dampening crystal will shut down the weapon with minimal damage, if we know where to employ it. But if we cannot obtain the schematic from Montenegro, we'll have to sink the whole vessel into the ocean."

Toria squinted. Lector Sartorius? That was the name of Blackthorn's Chosen, the most senior Technocrat in Logos. Why would he sabotage his own weapon?

The Meer sighed and straightened his posture. "Very well, gentlemen. Continue to follow the existing plan. Infiltrate the Needle when it arrives. If Rictor succeeds, I'll have Sartorius determine a method to disable the weapon. But if you have not heard from me by the time the Needle passes Buccaneer's Den, scuttle it." He held up the black crystal rod. "I'll contact you when something changes. Good luck."

A dazzling glow burst from the rod. Chamberlain Kavah vanished. Toria winked at the afterimage.

Her mind raced with thoughts. If Braun's Needle was traveling past Buccaneer's Den, its destination could only be the New Britannian mainland. Blackthorn was going to attack Britain. She could hardly comprehend the idea. Thulann had never mentioned such an attack, which meant she probably did not know. Neither, Toria presumed, did the New Britannians.

She tightened her grip and peered out at the eastern horizon, where the black shape hovered in the air.

In the lift carriage Grynholt muttered, "All right, Pikas, out with it. What's wrong?"

The assassin paused. "I think someone's on the roof."

Toria blanched.

The wizard laughed. "You're kidding! No, you're not kidding. I'll heat the metal, then. If anyone's up there, they'll either roast like a duck or fly like one."

"No. We need to catch him. We can kill him slowly while he answers some questions." His volume raised. "I hope you're feeling talkative, up there!"

The carriage bucked and began to descend noisily. They would reach the ground in a matter of seconds. Toria looked around in desperation.

A nearby chain was attached to a counterweight. It rattled upward. Toria grabbed it and held on with panicked strength. She lunged skyward. Her body swayed in the high, open air. She wrapped her ankles around the cold links.

As the carriage reached the bottom Toria arrived at the summit, where a crane juggled the intricate chains. Startled miners helped her to firm ground. Her legs felt unsteady as she darted down one of the many workmen's paths. Behind her the lift clattered upward again, but the sound faded as she hurried away, ducking behind walls and freight wagons.

She did not stop until she had raced down the steep foot-paths to the busy streets below. As she huddled in a narrow alley, she watched the armed soldiers who crowded the muddy lanes. Just then, their presence gave her a small measure of comfort.

Early the next morning, the entire population of Crevasse stood and gawked as Braun's Needle approached. Toria joined them, staring from a rooftop garden of chimney pipes. She felt as if she were in a dream.

The gigantic war machine hovered in the open air beside the cliffs. It was larger than Castle Britannia and infinitely more complex. A skeleton of steel beams defined the horizontal bulk of its body. Filling the open spaces was a vast tangle of huge gears and pistons and churning axles. The mechanics powered a forest of giant propellers along the edges of the vessel, and narrow, pivoting vanes that thrust down from the underside. Smokestacks and flame vents spat waste into the air. Enormous levitant tanks peeked out from the hull.

Mounted across the airship's exterior were a battery of massive flame belchers and lightning cannons and pneumatic trebuchets. Toria guessed that the ship's firepower exceeded the sum of all the other vessels at Crevasse.

On top of the Needle, in the center, was the structure that inspired its name. An impossibly high pillar thrust toward the sky. Compared to the volume of the central bulk, the pillar seemed thin and fragile. But Toria saw that it was plated with heavy steel and secured with chains that could hoist ship anchors. A flock of birds surged around it, gnat-size by comparison.

Braun's Needle eclipsed the rising sun as it hovered near the town, momentarily creating its own, artificial dawn.

Toria leaned forward on her hands and knees, as if the action would gain her a clearer view. She gripped a nearby chimney pipe. Nervous energy clamored through her body.

Pikas was going to infiltrate that steel monstrosity. Toria intended to follow him. She was unsure how to handle the deadly assassin, but she would not allow the murderer of Venduss and Thulann to escape.

What she might do about the attack on Britain, she could not even begin to fathom.

While growing up, Toria had perfected a hundred methods for stowing aboard pirate ships. A dozen of the largest galleons could fit in the volume of Braun's Needle. For the last two days she had coped with overwhelming uncertainty, but this morning she had no doubt of one fact: she could hide inside that gigantic machine without any fear of detection. Compared to the hold of a pirate sloop, she would travel in absolute luxury.

As the war craft unfurled articulated anchors, Toria gathered her provisions, strapped them into a bag across her back and crawled to the edge of the roof. Dangling her bare feet, she plotted a course down the rocky mountainside.

CHAPTER
9

The Black Duel

On the outskirts of a sprawling military encampment, Warlord Bahrok's scouts provided Thulann and Venduss a place to sleep. In deference to the venerable Way Master, who protested her exhaustion, the soldiers of Clan Varang agreed to wait until morning to send word to their chieftain.

The walls of the tent glowed from the fires outside. Through the woven fabric came the sounds of soldiers bedding down for the night. The low, steady cacophony was soothing to Thulann's ears, after the quiet trip through the barrens.

Her companion, however, was not so calm. Venduss growled in a strained whisper, "You cannot be serious, teacher! Bahrok tried to abduct me. His agents are murderers! I shall have satisfaction from him!"

Thulann sighed. "Yes, you shall, but it is I who will force him to give it."

"Not this time! I must do it myself. You know that."

"Do not seek his wrath. If he is belligerent, let me be the one who faces the consequences."

"No! Thulann, my entire life I have hidden behind your skirt, allowed you to protect me. No more! I have to do this myself."

The Way Master softened her volume. "I think you misunderstand me, Venduss. I am tired. I am hungry. I am injured. I am old. But I shall obtain satisfaction from Bahrok at any cost. As you well know, there is but one method for me to do that."

The young warrior stared at her. His eyes twitched nervously. "I think you mean that."

"It is all I have left."

She watched his composure begin to wane, then just as quickly recover. He narrowed his eyes and lifted his chin. "This is the last time you shall have to champion me, teacher. Great Mother grant you the strength to succeed."

Thulann collected the boy in her arms and held him fiercely. Under the bandage her empty eye socket flared with throbbing agony, but she did not acknowledge the pain. Venduss clung to her; his face buried into her shoulder. She stroked his muscular back.

"Venduss, tell your father that I have a thousand regrets, and two great joys. The latter outweigh them all."

She squeezed his torso, smelled his hair and listened to the flutter of his breath. These things were all that she needed to take with her.

Warlord Bahrok's pavilion was stark in its decor. Where other chieftains embellished their campaigns with the luxuries of home, Bahrok traveled with utilitarian restraint. The belongings in his voluminous tent amounted to nothing more than what he required as a general and what he deemed necessary for the dignity of a clan leader. Even his bed was no different from those his soldiers enjoyed. For that, at least, Thulann admired him.

When she crept past his guards, she found she was the only one inside. The shadows of night lay silent. Often Bahrok stayed late in his lieutenants' pavilions, attending the details of the campaign. She was glad. It would give her time to rest and meditate. Her seasoned body could make use of the opportunity.

She selected a place in the tent where Bahrok's eyes would not be drawn, then sat in the shadows and willed herself into a trance.

When the warlord entered, he moved directly to a wooden table. Across its surface he unrolled a chart and scanned the details, under the beams of a glass lantern. He massaged his brow around the base of his stout horns.

"If that is a map to Akar, Warlord, I suggest you find a new cartographer. Your current one keeps placing you at the battlefield half a day late."

Bahrok closed his eyes with a sigh. "You need not worry about Akar, Thulann. I shall take it easily and without the help of another clan. That jewel goes on my crown."

She did not move. As yet he did not see her. She spoke toward a shield on a nearby pole, which deflected her voice. "I only recently learned of your plan to capture Akar. It is most uncharacteristic of you not to trumpet your glory well in advance."

He glanced around the room. "And where have you been, that you received word of my plan?"

"Crevasse. But of course you know that."

"Should I?"

"Bahrok, the last few days have been very taxing for me. I should be most grateful if you were to forgo the deception and speak plainly. You have always been known for your diehard candor."

He eased himself into a sturdy chair. The wood squeaked under his immense weight. "Where is Venduss? Has he come to pay me a visit, as well?"

"Yes, he has."

"I see. Then things went well for you in Crevasse."

"Dhayin is dead. So is Toria. I have had better days, but I have also had worse."

Bahrok grumbled, "You may not believe me, but I mourn both of them. These are difficult times for us all."

"More than you suspect."

She rose from her meditative position and stepped into the light. Though she had bathed when she arrived, her armor was still a mess of dried blood and desert grit. Her clothes were near rags. Her face was decorated by a torn, black bandage. Fatigue weighed her countenance.

The warlord regarded her with surprise. "You must allow my healers to tend to you. I had not thought it possible for you to look any more weathered, yet you stand before me aged a decade."

She brushed back a strand of grey hair. Her finger looped under the bandage, which she removed and tossed on the table before him. "I have come to show you this."

"Great Mother! Your eye! Who did that to you?"

"Pikas of Enclave. But you mistake my meaning."

He wrinkled his brow, then plucked the black bandage off the tabletop. His expression turned to disbelief. "You must be joking."

"When it comes to the Black Duel, you know I do not joke."

"Thulann, look at the state of you. I wonder if you could live long enough for me to put on my armor?"

A smile crossed her lips, deformed by her sour mood. "Do you want to know what is most distressing about losing my eye? Not the lack of sight. Not the disfigurement. What most concerns me is the fact that it still hurts. I have drunk two healing potions and the pain has not gone away. It is a confirmation of something I have monitored for many years. I am very old, Bahrok. My body always hurts. The pain increases daily. Once I sought retirement, but that is never to be. So what must an old warrior do?"

The warlord sniffed. "Marry Turlogan, if he will still have you in this condition."

"He would bless you for saying that, yet he knows it will not happen. I have the curse of being a good woman and a terrible wife. But I am content with what I have been to Turlogan, and what he has been to me. I have no ambitions."

"I know. That has always been a failing of yours, which baffles me. I marvel at what you could have done with your life, Thulann, had you possessed the courage to fight for your own glory instead of others'."

She cocked her head. "I have fought for the glory of Shirron Narah, and for Shirron Turlogan and for Venduss, but tonight I come to satisfy myself. Do not act surprised. This is according to your own design. You pushed me to see at what point I might break. Warlord, I stand before you broken. Let us put an end to it now."

He glanced over the chart in front of him. "That was very moving, but I have no time for this. I am winning a war for your Shirron, in case you have forgotten."

"You do not want to refuse me."

"Yes, I do, and do you want to know why? Because it will gall you beyond any other scheme I could invent. Now leave me, before I have you escorted back to Garron."

"It is interesting that you should react this way, after threatening me so many times. I thought you would have enjoyed the chance for closure. I know many of your allied chieftains are keenly anxious to see what happens when you and I cross swords again. They sit around drinking wine and speculating which of us might win. When I am escorted to Garron, I shall make it a point to exercise my right to tell them that you refused. I am certain they will admire your pragmatism."

The warlord jerked his face toward her. "Are you accusing me of cowardice?"

"It is yours to disprove, Bahrok."

He bashed his fist on the table and stood. "Dammit, let it be said that I gave you the chance to avoid this! Name your conditions, old woman."

"If I win the duel, you will answer my questions about this secret pact you have with General Nathaniel and the others. And you will make reparations to Venduss for the death of Toria. I leave it for him to decide what that entails."

"Done! And if I am victorious you will return to Turlogan, where you will remain by his side and out of my business."

She blinked, then sighed. "Agreed."

He stormed across the tent and snatched his armor from the stand that supported it. "There is a canyon less than a mile from here that will give us privacy. You had best hope you do not leave your other eye out there!"

The trip across the brushy desert was choked with bitter silence. The canyon formed an ugly crack in the plains, with serrated walls reaching sixty feet deep. Funnels of dust swirled within. A treacherous footpath led to the rocky floor, which was littered with giant slabs. The thick, flat rocks had separated from the cliffs and piled at all angles, creating a surreal labyrinth in the moonlight. Spiky plants wafted in the canyon's erratic gusts.

They climbed to the bottom and prepared themselves.

Warlord Bahrok was a titan in his chieftain's armor. The steel plates and crimson designs exaggerated his already mountainous proportions. He was no taller than Thulann, but easily twice her weight. When he donned his helmet, which was capped with long spars like stylized horns, he cast a moonshadow on the canyon wall that could frighten seasoned veterans.

From his pack he selected a pair of ceramic vials. He set them on a boulder by the path.

Thulann donned her own helmet and commented, "There are no healing potions in a Black Duel."

"These are for afterward. I do not want to carry you all the way back to camp."

"I can spare you that burden, if you will accept a proposition."

He looked at her askance. "What is this?"

"A simple bargain of honor, if you will agree to it."

"I am listening, old woman."

"I want you to give me your word that you will no longer interfere with Venduss's affairs."

"You are deluded! I will do what I please."

"In exchange, I shall agree not to yield in this duel."

Bahrok squinted. "You mean you will fight to the death?"

"If need be. Unless you are the one to yield."

His massive arms crossed. "Why should I want to kill you?"

"Who is deluded? Do not lie to yourself. You have wanted to kill me since your son's death in New Britannia, if not before. This is your opportunity to do so in an honorable way. It will be a highlight in your career. You can mount my sword in your dining hall, if you like, and brag about it to your grandchildren."

He sneered. "You tempt me, but I am no fool. This is some kind of trick."

"Bahrok, I am beyond tricks with you. I am offering you the chance to put this to rest. Pit your legend against my own. Let history record which of us survives." She adjusted the fresh bandage over her eye socket. Her stomach quivered, despite her efforts against it. "And if that is not enough for you, then do it for my sake. You heard me, Warlord. By the Great Mother, I am an old soldier now. I have few years left to me, and they will be nothing but a chronicle of slow disintegration. But if you agree to this bargain, I shall have won the only thing for which I truly fight. Venduss will be safe. And I will be spared the humility of fading away."

The warlord huffed with disdain and turned away from her.

"Bahrok, please. Despite everything, you and I are both Jukan warriors. In that spirit we are the same. Let me die fighting while I can still do it well. There is no blade but yours worthy of the task. You know that, damn you."

Over his shoulder he muttered, "Venduss must not cross me, or the bargain is nullified. And it only lasts until he becomes chieftain. Then he shall be my equal and no longer immune."

Thulann's heart beat faster. She concealed her excitement. "Of course."

"Then I give you my word."

"And I give you mine. I shall not yield."

He faced her again and saluted with a staff, at the end of

which was mounted a swordlike blade. The warlord's expression looked almost solemn. "Neither do I intend to yield. Great Mother, you astound me, Thulann of Garron."

She smiled and raised her own staff, also gleaming with a bladed tip. "Thank you. Begin."

The clash was as swift as lightning. Thulann had swept her blade at him but a sudden blast of force flung her backward. Her spine rammed against a boulder and she rolled to the ground. When she moved to stand, her chest and arm seized with pain.

Bahrok had connected with the butt of his staff. Her shoulder was dislocated.

She winced and looked up at her opponent. He had staggered off a few paces and held one hand tightly with the other. Then he turned and roared, "Damn you! My fingers!"

Two of them were missing from his right hand.

Thulann swiveled her arm until the shoulder plunked back into place. The sensation was not pleasant. "You may yield, if you wish. The healing potions might stitch them back on."

Bahrok howled as he snatched up his staff and charged. The blade sliced down with a hurricane sound as Thulann tumbled to the side. The steel slashed across a boulder, which showered sparks. She readied a counterthrust but had to move again when Bahrok pressed his attack. The Way Master dodged a whirlwind of blows. When he forced her against an upright slab she twirled her own staff in the way, smashing back his furious attacks. At the same time she retreated up the steep rock face. Near the top she jumped, somersaulting over his head and ramming the butt of her haft into his armored neck. The force shoved him face-first into the vertical surface.

She trotted backward and said, "By the Hand of Honor, go and bind your stumps. This is undignified."

He spat and threw down his weapon, then stalked beside his pack and yanked out a bandage.

Thulann assumed a one-legged stance and indulged in a brief meditation. Her shoulder screamed in torment. Her knees grated from the sharp landing. She subsumed the pain into the organic currents of her body.

Bahrok returned with a thick wrapping over his hand. He stroked the air with his bladed staff. "I have eight more fingers to give. You have but one neck. If you desired a quick death, thank me now."

She knew he was just barking. A Black Duel was as much a mental contest as a physical one. He would try to goad her to distraction, as she had already done to him.

They cracked their staves together again. Now the combat assumed a more strategic pace, with slow circling and conservative attacks. Thulann evaluated the effect of Bahrok's missing fingers. He was beyond the pain now, but certain maneuvers were no longer available to him. She exploited the limitation. Her weapon smashed against his armor on several occasions, though she inflicted more bruises than cuts.

He took advantage of her injury, as well, using the blind spot of her missing eye as a stage from which to strike. After several parries he hammered a brutal cut to her waist, drawing a rush of blood. She sprang atop a boulder and caught her breath.

She frowned. This duel could last for hours or longer. Fatigue was her worst enemy. The warlord knew that, and drove her to use more strenuous defensive techniques like jumping and tumbling.

But the Way Master practiced schools of combat of which Bahrok was little aware. One of them asserted somber dignity as its core principle. The art was taught only among elder masters. Thulann employed it now, under a bright moon, assuming a haughty, upright stance as Bahrok climbed atop the boulder. When he thrust his spear she twisted at the waist, then tangled her weapon in his legs and knocked him off the slab with an easy kick. He snarled and clambered up again. She cracked his jaw with her haft, warded off his blows with slippery curls of her staff, and kicked him from the boulder once more.

The technique involved more sleight of hand than quickness or strength. It created the illusion of stillness where there was actually movement. Used judiciously, it could make an enemy either despondent or furious.

Bahrok's face darkened with frustration. When he scrambled up the rock a third time he burst into a powerful lunge. She twitched a parry. His spear sailed past her hip and bashed into another stone slab. It stuck there. She cracked her elbow against his spine while the warlord yanked at his weapon.

Then something huge made a grinding sound behind her. A shadow swooped down. She dove from her perch to avoid a falling slab, which shook the ground as it shattered to pieces and split the rock where she had stood.

Bahrok had levered the stone atop her. She cursed herself for inattention. The warlord leapt in front of her and hurled a barrage of spiraling thrusts. She barely deflected them as she backpedaled. Then a jab connected with her chestplate. Breath pounded from her lungs.

Bahrok's blade had punctured something.

She braced her staff atop his and threw a high kick, snapping his weapon in half.

His hands jutted forward and grabbed her.

She sailed through the air. Her rib cracked against the cruel edge of a slab. Bahrok's foot smashed into her abdomen, wedging her between two boulders. Her arms were pinned. Her legs went numb. She groped for handholds. He landed a savage punch on her wounded chest, then a high kick shoved her farther between the stones.

Despite her efforts she could not squirm free.

He plucked her bladed staff from the ground. "I trust Venduss will sing you to the Blessed Halls of Honor." He thrust quickly. The steel tip plunged at her gut.

Thulann gritted her teeth and popped her shoulders from their sockets, loosening her from the narrow fissure. She kicked up her legs to avoid the blow. The weapon jammed underneath her, clanking between the boulders. Her arms were limp but her legs had recovered, so she broke the haft with one heel and pummeled Bahrok's face with the other. Something in his mouth cracked. He staggered backward.

She leapt from the fissure and danced a combination of whirling kicks, allowing her arms to wrench into place. With each kick the warlord's face emitted a wet thump. He reeled back. She dropped to the ground and knocked his legs out from under him, then pounded his face with her boot, again and again. Blood darkened his features in the silvery moonlight. He tried to drag himself away. Thulann did not relent.

She saw Toria's face in her mind with each blow.

He was barely moving when she collapsed onto her back. Her chest wound seeped. Her abdomen shrieked with pain. Her strength was slipping away. She crawled toward their provisions and fished out several bandages, which she applied to the gory punctures.

She found her feet, struggled up the slope of a boulder

and perched at the top. Below her Bahrok had regained his senses. He clutched his head and choked down several breaths. Then he sat on a stone to rest.

Thulann folded her legs and began to meditate, applying every method she knew to control her physical decay.

Some time later their eyes met. Each of them struggled for balanced footing. They moved to their equipment, unsheathed their swords and resumed the duel.

Hours passed with no victor. Darkness thinned to twilight. Weariness slowed their pace. Thulann's flesh was a bramble of slashes and punctures, cold from the loss of blood. Her single eye blurred. Though her vision was indistinct, she could see that Bahrok was in little better shape. Both of them continued on sheer will power. They rested more and more frequently.

Another respite ended. She finished her meditation. From atop a vertical slab she nodded at him. He returned the gesture and rose from the flat stone where he lay. She jumped down from her high perch.

Her leg buckled. She slammed hard against the ground.

She closed her eyes and assessed the damage. The small bone of her calf was broken. Bahrok had not struck her there. The bone had simply failed.

This is the way it ends, she thought.

Bahrok gazed at her with swollen eyes. His mouth was a ruin that forced him to mumble. "If you wish to yield, I shall forget our arrangement."

Thulann disregarded him. She limped to their bags and began to fashion a splint. When it was complete, she climbed to her perch and resumed her meditation.

★   ★   ★

Her leg had gone numb. The splint allowed her to maintain her footing, though her repertoire of maneuvers was cut in half. Through another bout they battled to exhaustion, then collapsed again. This rest was longer than before. At the end of it Bahrok grunted to his feet, retrieved his notched blade and stretched his blood-streaked arms.

His voice was mangled, but stronger than it had been in several hours. He smiled amid the bruises that covered his face. "Thank the Great Mother! My second wind has come. Do you feel it, you broken old pteranx?"

The elder Juka sighed. She did not feel refreshed at all. Her body craved the succor of sleep. With every pulsing heartbeat, her single eye wanted to close. When she tried to uncoil from her meditation, her legs refused to move. She pushed them apart with her hands.

The Way Masters, venerated keepers of Jukan lore, possessed ancient techniques for use by the elderly in their last days. These methods blanked out pain and compensated for bodily ruin. They were destructive and temporary, but they afforded power to the dying. Thulann wished to employ those techniques at this moment.

She could not, of course. She had been in the field, in the service of Turlogan, for too many years. She never had the opportunity to learn them.

Perhaps it did not matter. Even with them she would not make it to the next respite.

She stumbled before her opponent. The fiery rays of sunlight had not yet crested the canyon walls, but the morning was in full bloom. Warlord Bahrok raised his bloody chin with pride. She studied his huge form. He was a tattered giant, dangling bandages from every limb, his exquisite armor hacked and bloodied, his face unrecognizable. She knew he did not possess her skills at overcoming pain, yet he endured on the strength of passion and arrogance and legendary mettle. In so many ways, he could have been called heroic.

She marveled at what he might have been, if he had fought for something besides his own glory.

Thulann looked him over again. "So this is the man who is going to kill me. Such a grand specimen."

"History will recall that I am grander than you."

She smiled. "I can accept that."

Their swords clanged together furiously. Metallic cries leapt about the high cliffs of the canyon. Thulann retreated more than she would normally find comfortable, but she no longer worried. The end was near. When she smacked her broken leg into an unexpected rock, the agony overcame her for an instant. She collapsed back onto her elbows. As she looked up, Bahrok's sword cracked through her chestplate and snapped across a series of ribs.

A scarlet mist sprayed from her chest. Her lung was nicked open. Her body began to fade.

Serenity overcame her. Nothing remained but action.

Her boot slammed underneath Bahrok's jaw, staggering the warrior. She sprang to a one-footed stance and jabbed her blade into his abdomen. It was one of many punctures, but he was already in torment. He snarled as he parried her next blow, then slashed his sword across her broken leg. The splint fell away.

The warlord grabbed her foot and twisted it, shattering what remained of her calf and ankle bones.

Using her unbroken leg, she jumped up high. Her arm wrapped around his neck. His sword strokes were awkward as she sliced off his chinstrap and flung away the ornate helmet. She prepared to cleave his unarmored skull.

He lunged with the horns that jutted from his brow. They bashed her face. She felt herself topple from his shoulders.

Thulann could no longer sense her body. She moved by instinct. Her shoulders lay against a large stone. Bahrok charged her. She kicked away his thrust and stuck her blade under his exposed jaw.

The tip drew blood.

The warlord froze before he impaled himself, battling his own momentum. His eyes grew frantic in his pulverized face.

The Way Master forced out a word, though it was agonizing: "Yield?"

His eyes blazed defiance.

Then in the inferno of the morning sun, someone appeared on the canyon peak. Thulann spotted him over Bahrok's shoulder, a tiny figure, difficult to see with her muddy vision. But she could not mistake his proud, youthful bearing.

His arrival was a breach of propriety, but she was glad Venduss had come. This was her final gift to him.

In her moment of distraction, Warlord Bahrok plunged his sword into her gaping chest.

Venduss cried out in horror.

The shock nearly finished her, but she flicked her wrist with absolute precision, laying open the warlord's throat. He clutched at the flow that issued forth, mouthing soundless words. She grabbed his hand.

Her voice was bloody: "Yield! Healing!"

He clutched her fingers tightly.

"Venduss?"

He clutched again, more weakly.

"Accept," she coughed, then scrabbled for the boulder

AUSTEN ANDREWS

that held the healing potions. She flailed her ruined leg to gain any manner of footing. Her body was a shadow, a spirit, something disconnected from her. Something that was vanishing.

She grabbed a vial from the rock and hurled it at the warlord. He plucked it from the dust and shoved it into his mouth.

Her hand refused to reach for the second potion. Her body was gone. She sagged to the ground, listening to the sigh of air that pressed from her open lung.

Her body tingled. The potion was tangy on her lips.

She woke to Venduss's face. A smile crept across hers.

"This is . . . becoming a habit, nursling."

The canyon walls towered above them. She was still in agony, but her worst injuries seemed to be healed. Her chest was no longer peeled open. Her leg appeared straight. An empty vial lay next to her, in a pond of fresh blood.

Venduss grinned. "This time you got a better bargain for your death. Judging from Bahrok's demeanor, I would say he is chastised. He gave me a look that would make a dune gazer blink."

He pointed to the steep path that led out of the canyon. Bahrok was stumbling up toward the sunlight. The warlord's expression was as hard as the cliffs.

The old warrior closed her eye and chuckled. "Please, child. Laughter is no balm for the aches in this poor body. Take me back to the camp healers. Tell them I shall pay for their services, if necessary. And feel free to speak with Bahrok while I am recovering. I suspect he might have something for you."

"I shall wait for you to be present, teacher. This is your

217

victory. And your redemption for the defeat he gave you four years ago."

"We do not tally Black Duels like a score, Venduss, and thank the Great Mother for that! I would rather lose my remaining eye than face Bahrok in a tie-breaker. Swords on the anvil take less of a beating than I just did."

As he helped her to stand, he tried not to chuckle. He was not altogether successful, but the aching Way Master appreciated the effort.

That evening the three of them sat around a table in Bahrok's pavilion. Though the warlord's mood was bitter, aggravated by a thickly bandaged hand, he addressed his obligation without pause. He told them about the Pact of Four, comprising himself, General Nathaniel, an unnamed but high-ranking Technocrat and the Meer diplomat who organized them, also anonymous. "Each of us in the Pact seeks the same thing. We are working together to orchestrate a war that will be favorable to all concerned. You must see the reason in it, Thulann, and the need for secrecy."

The Way Master frowned. "I do not understand. There is only one way I can see to benefit both the Technocrats and the Clans. We could negotiate over the disputed territories. Every other course leads simply to more bloodshed."

"Bloodshed is the path to glory. That is a fundamental truth. I am amazed that one of the deadliest swords in Jukaran does not understand that. My motivation should be no surprise to you. If Garron and Logos negotiate peace, Turlogan becomes a hero. If I win this war, I am the hero. I need that advantage. I intend to secure my place as the next Shirron of the Clans."

She muttered, "How many lives will your ambitions cost our people?"

"If the Pact of Four succeeds, not so many as you might think. I do intend to have living followers when I move into the Hall of the Shirron."

"You assume that my father will die," growled Venduss, "and that you will win the Great Tournament."

"Your father is old, boy, and I shall win that tournament. Trust in that. Thulann, why is Venduss here? My business is not with him."

The Way Master nodded. "But it is. You must make payment to him for the death of Toria."

He grumbled. "So I shall. And I will hold Pikas of Enclave accountable for his behavior, as well. I do not abide madmen in my employ. Now, tell me your price, Venduss. I do not want to spend a lot of time on this."

The young warrior assumed a proud stance. "Stand down your army. Clan Kumar will lead the attack on the town of Akar, not Clan Varang."

Thulann lifted an eyebrow.

Bahrok widened his eyes. "What extravagance is this? You think you can make that kind of demand?"

"That is what I ask, in payment for the death of Toria."

"Great Mother, we happen to be in the thick of a war, boy! I shall not jeopardize the course of our nation over the memory of a thieving human. Her life was worth less than a single Jukan warrior."

Venduss bolted to his feet and met the warlord eye-to-eye. "You may not judge her! That privilege rests in my hands alone. You have hurt me and I have named the cost. Clan Varang will not attack Akar. Clan Kumar will. That is as plain as I can state it!"

Bahrok shot him a hot glower. "Be careful how you phrase yourself. You might offend me."

"Save your threats! We are not children in a nursery. You are a chieftain and I am the heir to one. Our two clans are the greatest in Jukaran. Our transactions drive the course of history. Do not shrink from that burden!"

The giant warrior sneered at Thulann. "Tell your student he pushes too hard. I am liable to push back."

The Way Master narrowed her eye. "I have left this matter to Venduss's discretion. If that is his price, by the Black Duel you must pay it. And I do not need to remind you of our other agreement. When our business is concluded today, you must stay out of his affairs. Which means, Warlord, that you will not 'push back.'"

He spat a growl and quickly stood. The motion of his huge body rocked Venduss back a step. Bahrok's teeth glinted. "By the crows of Garron, Venduss, the time will come when you do not have the trickery of this old witch to protect you! I hope you are just as bold that day. We shall see what course history takes then."

Venduss blinked slowly. "You did not answer my demand."

After a furious pause, Bahrok stormed to the door of his pavilion. He wheeled around with an angry glare. "Clan Varang will stand down for three weeks! You have that much time to march on Akar. If Clan Kumar is not victorious by then, I am conquering the town myself. Is that clear?" He threw open the tent flap. "Now get out of my home, you spitting viper!"

Venduss smiled grimly as he walked past the warlord. In the words of an old farewell he uttered, "I leave this place happier than when I came." Then he vanished into the falling dark.

Though it brought pain to her wounds, Thulann let out a chuckle.

Bahrok growled, "You should have taught him restraint!"

"He follows your own example. Normally I would chastise him for it. At this moment, though, I could scarcely be prouder."

"Enjoy this day, then, for when he becomes chieftain we shall address these offenses again." He glanced at the open tent flap. "Now you leave my presence, as well, Way Master. Your half-face churns my bile."

"I am sorry about your bile, Warlord, but I shall not leave. You have much yet to tell me."

"I have explained the Pact of Four. I met my obligation."

"You have named the pact. You have not explained it. I want to know how you and your cohorts are perpetrating this scheme. Tell me about the muster of airships that will conveniently leave Akar undefended. And most of all, tell me about Braun's Needle. I have won the knowledge through honorable means, unlike yourself. I shall not depart from this chair until you have explained everything I require of you."

The warlord ground his teeth as he tied the door flap to a ring on a post. "Ask your questions, then. I give you one hour of my time and no more. You seem to have forgotten that there is an army outside that requires my attention, and three more weeks in the desert shall not come without extra work!"

For the entire hour she interrogated him. Afterward, Bahrok showed her to the door. His demeanor was weary but not resigned. His glance was grave. "Thulann, you should know something very important. This has not changed anything between you and me. Our differences have not been settled."

She tilted her head. "I never thought they would be, Bahrok. It was not a miracle. It was only a Black Duel."

Venduss awaited her not far from the tent. He matched her tired pace. "You are still limping, teacher."

"So I shall for the rest of my days, I expect. Healing restores health, not youth. Time is a tireless enemy. Think nothing more of it, Venduss. There are pressing matters that demand our attention."

He appeared reluctant to disregard her injury, but sighed and looked up. "Indeed. We have to get to Jamark quickly. I hope my father is still there. The army has to move out soon. Three weeks is scant time to crack open a shell like Akar."

"True, we must set those wheels in motion. But neither can we tarry in Jamark. The port shelters a handful of New Britannian ships. We must engage the fastest of them and sail for Britain."

"Britain! What business is there?"

"Just this: Blackthorn has dispatched a naval force to destroy the New Britannian fleet. Braun's Needle is at the center of the attack. Bahrok confirms that the Pact of Four has a plan in motion to stop it, as Dhayin mentioned, but naturally I do not trust him. So we must go ourselves and do what we can."

Venduss pursed his lips. "The two of us, you mean? Facing Braun's Needle? Your head must still be ringing from the blows, teacher."

She sniffed. "Suckling, it is not wise to disparage your elders. The old are proven survivors. The young, by definition, are not." A twinge stung her calf. She leaned against her student's arm. "No, our goal is simply to make sure that the Royal Senate knows of the danger. We shall leave it to the senators' discretion whether or not to engage our services as warriors. Personally, after another sea voyage, I will prefer to trade my weapons for a cup of spring water and my armor for a hot bath. I have a limited number of such opportunities left to me. I do not have the luxury of refusing them."

The lanky warrior rolled his eyes. "Now I know the duel rattled your skull. You are not decrepit, Thulann. You are craftier than death. Mark my words, you shall outlive me."

Brusquely she snapped, "Never say that to me again, child! Now find me a ridgeback to sit on, or I shall sit on your shoulders instead. This leg of mine aches like a block of ice. I mean to take out my frustration on a beast or a Juka, depending upon how quickly you act."

Venduss rushed away into the bustle of the camp. Over the din she heard an echo of his laughter. His voice was that of a proud, powerful man. Though she was saddened to lose the boy she had raised, he sounded so much like his father that she could not hide her smile.

CHAPTER
10

Old Bonds

Toria scrambled through a jungle of copper pipes. The interior of Braun's Needle was a nightmare world of steam and metal and endless scaffolds, thrumming and huffing with the animation of vast machinery. Huge gears and pulleys grumbled and clanked. Corridors and catwalks blasted with sultry heat. Smoke turned the air a bitter grey.

The red-braided minstrel was a dark streak amid the loud, mechanical chaos. To become less conspicuous she had donned the sturdy leathers of a crewman, though she was confident the Logosians would not catch her. The human and Jukan workers on board were engaged in tasks so brutally demanding that they paid no attention to the plentiful shadows. Toria could have walked around in full view and hardly a soul would have paid her notice.

One man took particular interest, however. Presently he was a sleek spectre chasing her through the hissing, clanging pipework. As she fled, Toria's body quaked with terror.

For four days she had stalked Pikas of Enclave and Grynholt of Yew inside this steam-gorged world. They were disguised as crewmen, as well, though they had a more difficult time concealing themselves than she did. But Toria did not underestimate the skills of Pikas. The assassin was as deft with stealth as Thulann had been. Toria took particular care to avoid his detection.

She failed. Today her safety ended. She had not held her breath in proper rhythm with the throb of the Needle's steam pumps. Pikas had heard her. A wound now burned in her leg where he had thrown his dagger. The pain slowed her down, though she was not sure she could have evaded him even if she was unhurt.

He was a dozen yards behind her and closing. She could hear the deep rasping of his breath, the clank of his hands and feet as he climbed through the tangled machinery.

She dreaded this day, though she had planned for it.

A large chamber opened before her. A thousand rattling pipes converged in the center, forming a central mass of junctions, venting tanks, gauges and valve wheels. Toria leapt onto an iron staircase that wound through the intricate pipework. She reached for a particular lever, just as Pikas slithered into view. His face was twisted into a sadistic leer.

Toria pulled the lever. A bolt of steam smashed over the Juka, ejected from a nozzle beside him. The steam swallowed him, its touch so hot that nearby metal began to groan. He shrieked and fell backward.

She had seen a Technocrat use the emergency vent while the Needle was still moored at Crevasse. The jet would probably continue for a minute or more. Crewmen would not arrive before then. Crouched in the thicket of pipes, Toria dared to watch for a few moments more.

A shadow moved inside the searing cloud. Pikas roared

with pain and stumbled forward. His kelp-hued flesh was bloody and ragged. His eyes blazed with fury.

Toria bolted away.

She had wanted to slit his throat as he slept, but the opportunity never presented itself. The assassin had been too careful; either he or Grynholt was always alert. Revenge would have to come while Pikas was awake. She knew she could lure him into a chase and away from the wizard, but beyond that her plan was very limited. The steam nozzle was the only trap she had been able to set under these conditions.

But the trap did not kill him. Escape was her only option now. She jumped down a ladder shaft. Years as a street urchin in a pirate haven had taught her the importance of a well-tested escape route.

As she fled, her anger rose. Once again she had failed Thulann. Her revenge was a travesty. The frustration joined a tempest of self-chastisement that had grown every day since the battle outside Crevasse. Sometimes her head ached from it.

She tugged on a red braid. The pain restored her concentration.

Much of the lower levels of Braun's Needle encompassed cranes and storage space for munitions and supplies. In one such cargo bay she crept between mountains of steel crates. Ahead was a steam-powered winch, hoisting chains through an opening in the floor. High winds whistled from below. A few Jukan laborers were loading boxes onto a broad lift platform. A black-hooded Technocrat supervised them.

Toria moaned. These workers blocked her exit from the cargo bay. She knew that Pikas was mad enough to reveal himself if he caught her here; he could simply kill these

Logosians after he slew her. That meant she had only one course open to her.

As the laborers converged around a hefty, steel crate, she darted from the shadows and into a gap between boxes. They did not see her as she nestled into a cramped, hidden space among the cargo.

A net was strapped over the hillock of large boxes. The steam engine chugged faster as the crane engaged, hoisting the platform over the trap door and lowering it down. Wind smacked Toria like a hand. She crawled to the edge of the platform and surveyed the lofty vista.

Braun's Needle had reached the mountainous coast of Logosia. The titanic war machine hovered hundreds of feet above the green, furrowed sea. Its shadow was monstrous upon the white-flecked waves. The water itself was spotted with a small flotilla of Technocrat seacraft, while the space around the Needle teemed with hovering airships like vertical smudges in the sky.

The platform lowered toward the surface of the water. Underneath it waited a slender, seafaring ship, plated with metal and bristling with mechanical accoutrements. Toria guessed it was a scout vessel, built for speed and quick combat. She withdrew into hiding as the cargo platform thumped onto the iron deck. Logosian sailors unfastened the netting.

She made her break moments later. The crew did not spot her. The scout ship was crowded with chains and gears, providing her no shortage of concealment. When the empty platform hoisted up once more, Toria remained as a stowaway on a far less spacious and far less dangerous vessel.

Soon the ship's steam engine coughed and spat. It wakened the windmill fans that propelled the craft. Slowly they gained speed atop the low, nervous waves.

Great horns bellowed from the sky just as the scout ship set off. The sailors clustered on deck and watched the Needle with excitement. Toria peeked out from her hiding place. Her eyes widened.

Braun's Needle was erupting to life. Every smokestack vomited its full capacity. Furnaces roared inside.

Then streams of white energy danced up and down the height of the central pillar, collecting at the summit into a knot of bright light. The light burst open. Streaks of impossible lightning radiated horizontally in every direction.

Toria saw flocks of clouds gathering around each shaft of energy, as though drawn to it. Within minutes the Needle was the hub of a great wheel whose spokes were made from clouds. When the wheel began to turn, Toria understood what she was seeing. She suddenly felt tiny and weak.

The clouds thickened and swirled, darkening as they did, tumbling together into the beginnings of a gigantic storm. Braun's Needle was creating a hurricane around itself. The scope was unfathomable. Toria had seen hurricanes before. She guessed that this storm, when it matured, could destroy half the fleet of New Britannia simply by approaching within a mile of it, if the navy was caught unprepared.

Toria had been on board the Needle, and perhaps could have done something to stop it. But instead she ran away. The thought made her grind her teeth.

A memory of Thulann waxed into her thoughts. If the old Way Master were alive at this moment, she would comfort Toria by reminding her that these events were greater than a single person. Thulann could find solace in being powerless. But as the scout ship built speed Toria could only curse her own impotence, while Braun's Needle and the man who murdered Thulann vanished behind a wall of roiling, screaming winds. Then the waves from the storm pushed the vessel forward. Toria crawled back into the darkness and watched no more.

Turlogan's hand was warm in Thulann's grip. Above all others, that sensation meant happiness to her. Not even the foul weather mustering in the south could darken such a moment of contentment.

She walked with the Shirron through the bustle of Jamark. The large seaside town currently housed much of the army of Clan Kumar. The granite buildings and flagstone avenues were noisy with preparation. Wagons and ridgebacks were loaded with supplies. Soldiers readied to march.

Thulann felt at ease while Turlogan spoke. "I calculate five days for the advance troops to reach Akar. Then we shall see if this fabled airship muster actually leaves the town vulnerable. If so, the bulk of our forces will arrive two days later. Without airships, Akar will not stand against us for more than three or four days."

She nodded. "Beware of Warlord Bahrok, though. He will try to gain some benefit out of this. Make sure to leave enough forces in Jamark to meet any action he might take here. I would not be surprised if he tried to occupy the town."

The tall Juka chuckled. "Thank you, my dear. I believe I have that situation in hand. I welcome any attempt on his part to take advantage of me. My patience with him has ended."

"That is a shred of reassurance, at least." Thulann sighed and stroked her thumb over his palm. Her gaze drifted toward the ocean. "And what of this damaged old woman? Have you had your fill of me, as well?"

"Great Mother, what makes you say that?"

She smirked, though it was cursory. "You gaze at my face with only half as much longing now."

"What is this? You think my feelings are dictated by the number of eyes you have?" With a swift motion he lifted her in his powerful arms, as he might hold a child above him. "I shall pluck one of the moons from the sky! Nature does not dare seek to outshine your beauty."

Thulann grunted and wrinkled her brow. "Please, love, my injuries."

He laughed and set her down. "My apologies. But you must never doubt me, Thulann. The day I stop adoring you is the day I am ashes."

She stared beyond the outskirts of town, to the rocky shoreline. "Or perhaps the day that I am."

A figure stood near the waterline, gazing northwest across the gruff sea. Venduss wore the white, ceremonial robe of a Follower of the Way. He did not acknowledge them as they neared.

Turlogan gave her hand a squeeze and murmured, "Venduss will never stop loving you, either. You are the world to him."

The ocean breeze shoved her with cold hands. Deeply she inhaled the salt-tinged mist. "Yet sometimes we must move on to different worlds."

The Shirron nodded. "You have taught him well, but to be a chieftain he must be an officer. It is my time to teach him, now."

He wrapped his arm over her shoulder. Thulann enjoyed the old soldier's warmth as she listened to Venduss. The young warrior was announcing poor Toria to the Blessed Halls of Honor:

Zephyr spirit, sing my song
Above the lands you roam,
For one who loves me travels on
While I am going home.

The Way Master closed her single eye and indulged a bleak melancholy. Her thoughts soared away, nor did she fight them. She had no fear. Turlogan's warm hand was anchor enough. She realized now, on this rocky edge of the world, that it had always been enough.

A Jukan sailor jammed his knife at Toria. She twirled around his blow and kicked. The weapon flew from his hand.

Toria's static sword crackled as she plunged it into the man's abdomen. He dropped into the bilge water at her feet.

In the blackness of a cloudy midnight, the Technocrat scout ship rocked with bloody pandemonium. Another vessel was attacking. Toria had not yet seen the intruders or their ship, but the Logosian sailors were so frightened that they sought out the same hiding places that had sheltered her for three days. When they discovered her, Toria was not greeted warmly.

More Logosians clambered into the cargo bay that had served as her home. Toria decided to take her chances on deck. She reached open air with halfhearted resistance. What she found made her heart soar.

A tall barquentine of New Britannian design had clamped its hooks alongside. Golden torches lit the ship like a festival. A mob of rowdy warriors flooded aboard the scout vessel. Toria could never mistake the countenance or demeanor of pirates from Buccaneer's Den.

The night air flashed when the Logosians employed scourges and flame belchers. The pirates responded with glittering magic from a small group of spellcasters. In skill and in numbers, the buccaneers overmatched their prey. This battle would end quickly.

Toria knelt in the gloom and calculated where she might stow aboard the tall ship. Just the smell of its tarry wood brought her a thrill. Then a noise startled her. Something was growling, not three feet away. At her side she discovered a short, tawny dog, its ears flattened and its teeth bared.

A tingle shot through her. In a whisper she said, "Kiye?"

The canine perked its ears. She scratched the coyote's head and let a smile overwhelm her.

In minutes the melee was over. As the New Britannian troops herded the Logosians into the scout ship's hold, Toria stepped into the torch light and leaned against an ironclad mast. Crossing her arms she started a loud chant:

Now pull, bully boys, and I'll tell you a fable
'Bout Ramshackle Jack and a lassie named Mabel!
He loved her the most though he liked her the least,
But he never had nothin' on Bawdewyn the Beast!

Without hesitation the pirates joined in:

So hey-holly-hoy-o, now pull, bully boy-os!
'Twas never another like Bawdewyn the Beast!

They gathered around the strange Logosian girl with oversize work clothes, fiery red braids and pale features masked by soot. She recognized many of them, but said nothing more until the tallest appeared.

The captain wore an overwide hat that shaded his dark, rugged face. He barked commands to his distracted men as he pushed through them. When he met eyes with Toria, his mouth flopped open.

She giggled. "Who told you there was anything valuable on this ship, hey?"

Captain Bawdewyn bared a rampant grin. "They say the sea hides untold treasures and here's the proof of it, lads! Is this really Tiny Tori standing before me? By the lost shrines, I think it must be, or else someone put liquor in my grog!"

The minstrel wrinkled her nose. "You drink grog now, Bawdewyn? Privateering has beggared you! You had better taste when you were a pirate. Sink this iron tub, then, and I'll stay on board. Maybe the pirosohmoi will offer me something worth drinking."

He lunged forward and wrapped her in a sturdy embrace. "Get your little stern down to my cabin, sweet filly! I'll cook you a bath and get you some decent clothes. You can't parade around looking like a greasy Technocrat. It ain't becoming." He released her from his long arms and patted her dirty cheek. "Then you've got some tales to tell me, hey?"

She blew out a long, heavy breath. The sensation of unburdening was almost cathartic. "Don't even bother to guess. My tales will numb your bones and put a stiff wind in your sails."

"It's the times we live in, lass. Now onto the *Menagerie* with you! There's nothing left but swabwork here."

The feel of Vesper wood rolling under her feet gave Toria more joy than she could have imagined. As she stepped below the main deck, she heard Bawdewyn singing to his men:

Now pull, bully boys, and I'll tell you a story
'Bout the wee little minstrel they call Tiny Tori!
Though her shape was a nibble, her mouth was a feast!
But she never had nothin' on Bawdewyn the Beast!
So hey-holly-hoy-o, now pull, bully boy-os!
'Twas never another like Bawdewyn the Beast!

An hour later they had plundered the scout ship and set it adrift. Toria bathed and donned an exquisite dress of green velvet brocade. The gown was made for a much taller woman, but the minstrel did not protest. The feel was luxurious. As a pirate, Bawdewyn had only plied the most discriminating clientele.

They sat in his cabin sharing spiced rum. The ocelot Annis lolled in her lap, rumbling at her touch. The privateer's clove incense smelled like home.

Bawdewyn's face was anything but peaceful, however. "Let me make sure I understand what you're saying. That hurricane blowing up from the south is a weapon? A machine?"

"If you don't believe me, sail through to the eye and tell me what you find. But bring along a change of trousers if you do."

He set down his cup. "So it's finally happened. Blackthorn drew his sword."

"It's five hundred feet long and pointed at Britain. That's why we have to hurry and tell the Royal Senate."

"I could outrun that storm with half a crew, but we'll fly full sail on this journey. There ain't much time for the Senate to prepare for the attack. I'd better get topside, roust those dogs. They'll be fat and lazy after tonight's milk run." He stood and splashed her mug with a refill. "You drink up, now. It'll help you sleep. I'll stay in the mate's quarters if you need me for anything."

"Bawdewyn? Thanks. You were always a gentleman."

He shook his head. "I ain't half as polite as those Juka of yours. After two years in their company you must think I'm a barbarian."

"Nah. I never did fit in there." She shook her head and sighed. "I never should have gone with them."

Amid the sumptuous textures of fur blankets and the warmth of Annis in her arms, Toria faded quickly. A curious thought followed into her dreams. She hoped that Pikas and Grynholt would succeed in sinking Braun's Needle. In some indefensible way it might justify the murder of Venduss and Thulann.

Then sleep overcame her with a clove-scented kiss.

The stone docks of Jamark busied with a strange, nervous quiet. The morning sky was blackening as a hurricane approached. Both Jukan and New Britannian ships moved away from the wharf, preparing to weather the storm in the harbor, a safe distance from the rocks of the shore.

But the Britannian clipper on which Thulann stood was ready to embark on a longer trip. The Way Master balanced on the pitching deck. She held the hands of two men whose faces comprised her only joy.

Haltingly, she bade them farewell.

Turlogan smiled. "Stop worrying. This is the fastest

ship in Jukaran. You will arrive in Britain with plenty of time. Give my regards to Regent Salvatore when you see him."

She nodded. "I shall. And you, Shirron, must vow not to grant this young suckling a moment's respite. He was too often distracted while I taught him the Way. Now that he must be an officer, there is far more at stake than an old woman's wrath."

Venduss blinked at the mist in his eyes. "Teacher, I wish—"

With three fingers she popped the underside of his chin. "None of that. Listen to your father, and watch him, and you will learn how to become a leader of men."

The young warrior swallowed. "I will make you proud, Thulann."

"Just look in a mirror, child. My pride is chiseled into your body and your face. It is the sun that shines from your eyes. You are my worthiest victory."

Venduss knelt and squeezed her hand, then let go and turned away. He walked down the gangplank with his face averted.

Turlogan took both of her hands and pressed them between his own. His eyes twinkled with irony. From the look she knew his exact thought: *Bad poetry.* She giggled. Then he kissed her and departed, without another word.

It was precisely what she needed.

The clipper opened sail and hastened northward. She leaned on a new walking staff, which was clapped in steel, and observed the coast of Jukaran as it shrank away. Her body complained of the tossing waves and the chilly, oncoming storm. But though her many old wounds smarted, age did not concern her. She did not feel decrepit. Rather she felt something unexpected: a deep sense of *completion.*

The sensation was foreign to her, hollow and empty. She took no pleasure in it.

After several hours a cry rose among the sailors. Another ship had been spotted. The human captain sought out Thulann. "It's the *Menagerie*, mistress, a privateer warship. She looks half-laden. Normally I would flag her down, but privateers can be a rough-edged lot. I leave it to your judgment."

The Way Master grimaced. She recognized the vessel that Montenegro had once used to spirit away a Technocrat spy. "Sail on. Our mission is urgent. There is nothing on board that ship to warrant a distraction."

Thulann put the incident out of her mind. The *Menagerie* dwindled behind them, a dark spot outracing the vast, grey bulk of the looming hurricane.

CHAPTER
11

Downfall

Through the trees the sky purpled, blackening the dusky forest. Evening birds took flight at the snap of a whip. An open-top carriage rattled away behind a team of horses, leaving two figures on the porch of Montenegro's manor house. Golden light from the open doorway threw their shadows long across the front drive.

Raveka waved to the departing guests. Her taffeta dress rustled gently. "It's a shame they have to leave so early."

Montenegro shrugged. "The orcs come out at sunset. Perhaps we should have invited them to dinner as well, eh? Their manners are probably better than half those councilmen." He nudged her toward the door. "The true pity is that your performance was cut short. Another hour and they would have elected you to the Royal Senate."

She laughed. "It wasn't a performance. I had a wonderful time. *Beza rhem.*"

"You are disarmingly elegant. You shall be more than ready for Lord Gideon's visit. If his lordship tells the Britain socialites about you, I daresay some invitations are liable to flutter to our doorstep." The knight cupped her shoulder. "But see here, my dear, the time has come for you to explain something. I know the symbol and I know the name, but I'm not sure what *beza rhem* actually means. Pray enlighten an ignorant soldier."

"It's part of the syntax of a geometric proof. *Beza rhem* translates as, 'It shall be continued.' When a proof must be halted, we use *beza rhem* as an assurance that more verses will be forthcoming."

"Ah, I see. I always took it to mean that you would visit me again."

She grinned. *"Raveka beza rhem."*

"And what do you say when a proof is finished?"

"Beza ilthem."

Montenegro spread out his hands. *"Aria beza ilthem.* Almost. When we go to the city you'll need to commission new clothes. I've never cared for the garish fashions of Britain, but I'll be damned if my lady will not outshine all those preening pigeons who strut through the court."

Raveka laid a palm on his chest. "I require no special plumage. I prefer to understate myself, as you do."

"But you'll need some way to distinguish yourself from your old Riona identity. Someone in Britain might recognize you."

"Riona and Aria travel very different circles. Riona spent her time with courtesans and Jukan warriors. As Aria I shall confine myself to courts and parlors. If I happen to encounter someone who's met Riona, I have techniques to deflect suspicion. Acting is most of what I do, after all." She wrinkled her nose with mock disdain. "Besides, the Lady Aria you've described to me would never dress extravagantly. It's not her idiom. Really, Gabriel, you must become acquainted with the subtleties of disguise. Consistency dictates success."

He shrugged as he closed the front doors. "My mind is not filled with slots and compartments like yours. I work by instinct and training. Life is much simpler that way."

He paused. Hoofbeats echoed outside. He opened the door to see a light jogging up the road, as though carried on horseback. The color was unearthly blue.

"We have another visitor. A spellcaster, it looks like. Perhaps that's the scroll coming home at last." Two riders approached the house. As they passed into the light of the windows Montenegro said, "It's Fairfax and Jatha both. I was beginning to think they wouldn't make it in time. I'll feel better with the schematic in my own hands again." He glanced at her. "You're not going to kill me and take it, are you? I would hate to end a wonderful evening on a sour note."

She shook her head. "I'll let you live, if you stay true to me. It is a harsher sentence than death for such a hated enemy."

He smirked. "Well, it's time to put your acting skills to the test. These two were admirers of Riona. If they recognize you, we'll have to rethink your entry into Britain society."

The dark-haired Raveka narrowed her eyes. "They will not recognize me."

Fairfax nearly ran Montenegro down as they converged on the drive. The ranger sprang from his horse and clutched the knight's arms. "Quickly, man! It is most grievously urgent that you tell me if you know anything!"

The knight raised an eyebrow. "About what?"

Fairfax clawed the air. "Shavade of Arjun, of course! By all the stars, what else am I capable of thinking about? In the space of more than a week I have not enjoyed a single restful night. Not one! My eyes burn red and dry, yet when I close them I am haunted by the memory of her miraculous beauty. She is a hex upon me! I shall die of wanting! Can you see how haggard my face has become?"

"I see that you've stopped shaving."

"That part is intentional. I may not be a Meer, but I can grow my fur, can I not? Jatha disapproves. He calls me a yeti cub. But I must take some action, however trifling, toward the goal of wooing my silken-coated angel, lest my heart break open like a goblin's tender skull!" He raked fingers through his wind-knotted hair. "Even this business of invasion is only a trivial annoyance. My world has contracted to the dimensions of a single girl. I am trapped in the hollow of her absence!"

Montenegro lifted a finger to silence the dusty traveler. "Did you just say 'invasion?'"

Jatha approached, panting as wearily as the horses. Like his companion, the Meer was battered by the hard ride. "Fairfax is so mad with longing that he's forgotten our task here. The city is in a panic, my friend! Blackthorn has deployed an attack force that's sailing for Britain as we speak! It may arrive in as little as a few days. We're on our way to notify the ranger brigade on the other side of Cove. I thought you might want to hear the news yourself, as you have some interest in fighting the Logosians."

"Are you sure about this? Where did the information come from? Scrying?"

"No, the seers know nothing. I was with Mistress Aurora when the word came, three days ago. General Nathaniel learned of it through his own spies."

The knight grumbled. "And his sources are damnably

credible, as you well know. By the Virtues, I should have been told sooner!"

"We could not have ridden any faster if we shoed our horses with lightning."

Taffeta whispered behind Montenegro. Slender fingers wrapped around his arm. "Gabriel, is something wrong? From the tone of your voice I might think there was another Cataclysm."

The knight subdued his rising irritation. He almost shrugged off Raveka's touch, but patted her hand instead. "Yes, my dear, there is a great deal wrong. We can discuss it later. Jatha, Fairfax, let me introduce Lady Aria of Coventine, a distant cousin of mine. She is . . . staying here with me."

The Meer flattened his ears as he bowed. "It is a thousand-fold pleasure to meet you, my lady. My name is Jatha of Ishpur and this is my cohort, Fairfax the Ranger. Montenegro has mentioned you in the past, though quite selfishly he never disclosed Your Ladyship's resplendent beauty! Yet you are no lady. You must be a queen in hiding, for I'm certain I have seen such radiance before, painted by an antique brush or sculpted in marble at the hands of an ancient master. Your Majesty flatters me with such an exalted smile!"

Montenegro gave her a glance, but Raveka would not compromise the ruse. She blushed. "I am queen of nothing, I'm afraid. If it weren't for Gabriel inviting me here I would never have seen our own kingdom, much less another."

Jatha chuckled. "And here I stand with half the dirt from Britain to Cove strewn across my clothes. What a shabby welcome I offer you! Please forgive my abominable appearance and even more so, that of my distractible companion." He punched the ranger in the arm. "Fairfax! Be a gentleman and introduce yourself to her ladyship, or I'll feed you to the dire wolves for breakfast."

The blond warrior presented half a bow. "I am honored, my lady. Please accept my apologies if I am quiet and woebegone. I am a wan ghost of myself, a tattered shroud enclosing a famished heart."

Montenegro grunted. "Enough of this! Aria, please go back inside. I shall follow you in a moment."

She pinched her brow. "Will our road-weary guests not be staying?"

"I doubt it. They've got important business to attend. Go on, now, my dear. You have nothing to offer this conversation, except privacy." He urged her toward the house.

Raveka flashed him a glimpse of a scowl, but complied.

When the front doors closed, Montenegro grew more animated. "What is the nature of the attack? What response are we taking?"

Jatha explained, "The Logosian armada is both naval and airborne. General Nathaniel says it's a strike force designed to cripple the New Britannian fleet. He intends to stop them before they reach the capital. Admiral Duarte has ordered every warship to ready sails. Of course the House of the Griffin has been formulating spells for the war, but this has taken them by surprise. I do not know how prepared they are."

"Valor and Sacrifice must serve us now. I'll leave for Britain at once. Did you bring my scroll?"

The wizard pulled a tube from his saddlebag and handed it to the knight. "Mistress Aurora made her own copy for further study, so you may offer this one to Lord Gideon. Though I daresay the present emergency dampens your plans for a dinner party."

"I'll seek out Gideon in the city. If the war has begun, then I can't delay my command any longer. Did you learn anything from the diagram?"

Jatha frowned. His neck fur bristled. "Mistress Aurora cracked the enigma. That device makes storms. Enormous ones. It conjures them like a giant, iron sorcerer. By my ancestors, Blackthorn's corruption of alchemy is profound! If that machine is ever built, it would be an heroic affront to the disciplines of sorcery. It's repellent to even consider raising such energies and then placing them inside that cold, clockwork shell! Blackthorn is a contemptible madman. No outrage is beneath his pursuit of power."

A strong wind buffeted the trio. The forest rasped in a million whispers. The knight's frown hardened. "I believe that now, my friend. Will you come inside and rest?"

The ranger Fairfax sighed. "We cannot. We must make Cove before the inn closes, to spread the black tidings. The road ahead of us is difficult, and yet not enough so to weary the dragon in my soul. I beg you, Montenegro, have you heard anything of Shavade? Is there some way for you to contact her?"

Montenegro's eyes narrowed. "No, but I can offer you hope. When your mission is complete, meet me in Britain. I have a suspicion she will try to reach me very soon. Braun's Needle must be part of the Logosian armada, which would explain why she and Rictor want this scroll so urgently. Well, their goal may be a worthy one, but I swear by my grandfather's bones I will die before I give them this schematic. Dishonor plagues me like an insect and it is past time that I swatted it!"

*   *   *

The front door slammed closed. In the ornate foyer, Raveka cocked her head to one side. "I told you they would not recognize me."

Montenegro glowered at her. "Blackthorn is attacking."

"I heard. I only pretended not to."

"But you knew. All along you knew that this attack was coming."

She glanced away, for only an instant. "Yes, I did."

He felt his heat rising. "Was that one of the goals of your mission? To distract me until the armada arrives?"

"No! Gabriel, I'm here because I want to stay with you."

"Indeed? You care for me, do you? Then how could you hide something like this from me?" He shoved past her and mounted the white staircase.

She called after him, "I wanted to keep you from danger."

"An honest battlefield would be paradise right now! We could have had a week's more preparation to defend ourselves. Thanks to your deceit, we barely have time to gather our ships! How do you justify that kind of betrayal?"

"Because it was the right thing for me to do."

"The right thing?" He whirled and looked back at her. She seemed tiny at the foot of the stairs. "Blackthorn wants to sink our fleet. Whose purpose does that serve except his own? Whose purpose do *you* serve, Raveka?"

"Do you think it was an easy decision? I don't want the war to come to Britannia. I don't want the war at all! I've been working against it all these years, if you haven't been paying attention."

"I am unmoved by your sacrifice."

"You're a soldier! You know the appalling choices we have to make. Look, without those ships, the Royal Senate can't aid the Juka Clans. That means Garron cannot conquer

Logos. Gabriel, do you know how Warlord Bahrok treats his captives when he conquers a town? Like apprehended criminals. I'm talking about families. Children. They would rather flee to the desert than face his custody. He has terrorized them for over a year. Those are my people!"

He growled, "Not anymore. You told me you weren't going back."

She climbed after him. "And I shall keep that promise. But I cannot forget them. What would you do in my position?"

"I would never forsake New Britannia. I am a knight of the Silver Serpent."

Her brown eyes searched his gaze. "And I am a Mathematician. But I gave it up for you."

"Then that is the difference between us."

His glare was as sharp as steel.

A powerful breeze moaned outside. Raveka herself seemed jostled by it.

In the bedchamber he collected his traveling clothes. He made no acknowledgment when her slender shape filled the doorway.

Her voice sounded controlled. "What action will you take?"

"I'm going to Britain to defend my homeland. I'm a soldier, if you recall."

"This war will not drive us apart. I will not leave your side."

"Of course you won't." He snatched a hooded cloak from her wardrobe and flung it at her feet. "Get your flying machine ready. It's the fastest way to the city. One less day on the road could save a hundred lives."

"So you still trust me, despite everything."

Something churned in his breast. He paused, waiting for

the feeling to diminish. When it did not, he let out a grumble. "Don't mock me, damn you! You're fortunate I don't run you through. Now go prepare the machine!"

"Give me half an hour. I will bring it to the balcony." She clasped her hands together and peered over them. "I am devoted to you, Gabriel."

The words stabbed like a knife. He squeezed his eyes shut. "Then do something for me."

"I promise."

"Teach me to drive that carriole. If I can ride Humbolt I can master that machine. From now on I intend to hold the reins instead of the damnable bit!"

The journey to Britain was long and windy. Throughout the night they soared hundreds of feet above the water, tracing the jagged coastline. In the beginning, Montenegro did not trust the flying machine. An hour's passage acquainted him with its disposition. To his surprise the carriole's operation was relatively simple in the open air. As dawn approached his growing confidence allowed for greater speeds. The sensation of flight was transcendent.

Raveka spoke very little. She embraced him from behind. Her perch was quite stable without holding on, yet never for a moment did she let go. From that gesture he took a peculiar comfort. Streaking among the clouds Montenegro could almost imagine that they were very different people, with no barriers between them. Fantasy was not one of his vices, yet he understood how Raveka indulged them. The freedom of the sky conjured dreams unbidden.

He resisted the urge to reverie.

When daylight came they veered inland, letting the forest canopy hide their passage. Every hour lashed their windblown bodies and strained their tired muscles. The following nightfall greeted them with the glow of the city's warm lights.

Near Britain he relinquished the carriole to Raveka. She landed the machine and concealed it in the thick woods. Afterward she commented, "The levitant is three-quarters spent. Unless you are hiding a supply somewhere, in a month this machine will be very exquisite scrap metal."

He struggled to waken his heavy limbs. An errant pain caused him to wince. His eyes were swollen from the cruelty of the wind. "It is just as well. Flying is intoxicating but I still prefer a horse. They may be slower and more willful than a carriole, but I like a mount to wear out before I do. Now let's keep moving. We'll reach my townhouse in less than two hours. That will give us plenty of time to bathe and rest before we pay Lord Gideon a visit."

"We? You want Lady Aria to join you?"

He regarded her with a heavy look. "I have no choice. I don't want you out of my sight. You may take that in whatever sense gives you the most pleasure, because I am too tired to argue about it."

They leaned on one another and trudged toward the sparkling lights of Britain. The wind still roared in Montenegro's ears. He resigned himself to its presence.

Late the next morning the sky mellowed with clouds. Humidity glazed the cobbled streets of Britain, waking familiar smells and sounds from the trees and mud and buildings. Townsfolk hurried about their business before the onset of rain. The air crackled with electric anticipation.

Raveka held Montenegro's arm as they stepped out of the ebony carriage. She was playing Lady Aria as somewhat meek, reasoning that the noblewoman would be intimidated by a visit to Lord Gideon. Nor did she truly have to pretend. As they entered the spike-crowned gates to the lord's townhouse, she walked so closely to Montenegro that their hips bumped together.

The knight acted just as eager to keep her near. He pinned her arm to his side. Over the last week they had established an unabashed intimacy, rarely coming out of physical contact; yet Raveka knew he was equally motivated by the fact that she was carrying the schematic for Braun's Needle in a hidden pocket of her skirt. Montenegro was taking no chances with the bald man, nor with her.

A butler welcomed them inside the lavish house. They were led to a large sitting room with a fresco painted on the ceiling, depicting a radiant sunrise. Montenegro ignited a smile as the two occupants of the parlor rose to greet them.

"Aziz! Evanthe! By the lost shrines, I did not know you had already arrived! Why didn't you send word to me?"

He clasped the forearms of the two knights. The pair looked strong and alert. Aziz was an olive-skinned man, well muscled in his simple tunic and hosen. Evanthe kept her sandy hair short and wore a utilitarian dress over long, athletic limbs. Each of the warriors dangled a blade at the hip.

Raveka did not like the hesitation in their eyes. Both of them avoided her glance. Something was very wrong.

She considered the bolt-thrower strapped to her thigh.

Evanthe tried to smile. "You're looking contented, Montenegro."

Aziz added, "Sorry for the surprise. We wanted to see the shock on your face."

Both of them had a somber demeanor. Montenegro furrowed his brow and chuckled. "Come now, Bahrok and Jukaran are long behind us. Home is no place to bring such dour faces. This time we'll meet Blackthorn with all of New Britannia behind us!"

Another voice boomed, "I'm afraid it isn't that easy. There are some matters to settle first." From an open door emerged an oak of a man, with a bull neck and large hands. His doublet was wrought in satin and velvet, while gold adorned his fingers. Lord Gideon was neither old nor young, but possessed an ageless dignity that demanded attention. His strong, clean-shaven jaw thrust forward in a grimace.

Raveka had not expected him to be so strikingly handsome.

Montenegro bowed at the waist. "Your Lordship, I appreciate your receiving me today. Allow me to introduce my cousin, Lady Aria of Coventine."

The nobleman's jewelry flashed as he bowed. "What a delightful surprise to meet you, my lady. I thought Sir Gabriel was coming alone."

She curtsied with a demure smile. "My cousin shows me around so much that I feel like a shiny, new sword." When Lord Gideon met her gaze she did not allow him to turn away. In his expression she detected sad anxiety. He was not comfortable looking into her eyes, though not once did he flinch.

Montenegro continued, "Aria, this is Lord Gideon, head of the House of the Lion. He oversees all military affairs for the government. And these two are my fellow conquerors of Logosia, Sir Aziz and Dame Evanthe."

Raveka worked her face into an innocent greeting as she evaluated the situation. Aziz and Evanthe feigned calm. Their spacing, however, was tactical in nature. Gideon was likewise prepared for physical action. They expected trouble.

Montenegro recognized the situation, as well. Raveka felt

his body stiffen. To Lord Gideon he said, "Well, Your Lordship, what matters must we settle? They must be grave indeed to warrant this cold reception."

Gideon grumbled a sigh. "They are. Perhaps Lady Aria had best wait in the next room while we discuss our business. My lady, I shall send a servant to bring you tea."

She wrinkled her nose and held Montenegro's arm. "I do not mind. I'll stay, please."

Gabriel rubbed her half-bare shoulder. "It's all right, my dear. Go."

"No." She flung him a sharp glance. "I won't leave your side, cousin."

He blinked and nodded. With his elbow he drew her closer. "Aria is not as fragile as she looks, my lord. What is this about?"

"Very well. My lady, I apologize for placing you in this uncomfortable situation, but time is short. Sir Gabriel, of late I have been engaged in a disheartening conversation with General Nathaniel. He has informed me of your recent actions."

Raveka felt Montenegro squeeze his fist. "What actions would those be, Your Lordship?"

"You know very well what I'm talking about! There is an important diagram, is there not, a Technocrat document that you have been concealing from us?"

Gabriel's eyes mashed shut. "I have concealed nothing, Your Lordship. It was my intention to present it to you personally, as a gift."

"A gift? For what purpose? Nathaniel tells me it's to garner my favor so I'll give you a command again. Is that true?"

Montenegro sighed, "Yes, my lord. The scroll—"

"The scroll should have been in my hands the moment

you set foot on Britannian soil! Blackthorn's armada is halfway to our doorstep and you're hoarding intelligence as political coinage? That is not like you, Sir Gabriel. Did your time with the Juka rearrange your priorities?"

"Your Lordship, listen to me! I only just learned that the Logosian fleet is on its way. I came here immediately. You know I would never jeopardize our security! My record as a defender of New Britannia is sound."

The lord grunted. "But not unblemished. The black marks you put there two years ago have not been forgotten. And General Nathaniel alleges that your transgressions are increasing. He claims that his agents requested the document from you and that you not only refused to surrender it, but that you drew steel on them. Again I ask, is this a true account?"

"Those are the facts," muttered the knight, "but not the entirety of them." His face and his tone became icy. "In my defense, Your Lordship, I have a tale to relate that shall place these events in their proper context. General Nathaniel's accusations release me from my vow of discretion. When I returned to Britain weeks ago, my first action was to seek out the general. I intended to hand over to him the spoils of my Logosian victories, including the diagram you mention. But when I visited his estate, I learned something that made me reconsider the wisdom of it."

Lord Gideon cast a glance at Aziz and Evanthe. Raveka imagined that they anticipated Montenegro's words. "Go on," said the nobleman.

The room stilled as Gabriel explained about the Pact of Four. Raveka was startled to learn of the existence of the secret alliance against Logos, and especially the participation of a high-ranking Technocrat. But when Montenegro named the bald man, the Logosian poisoner who served as the Pact's agent, a chill assaulted her bones. She had heard of Brother Rictor of Logos. He belonged to the Order of Theorists. His recipes for poison knew no equal. Pikas of Enclave had been his frequent customer. He was a disciple of Lector Sartorius and infamous for his cruel efficiency.

Montenegro was correct to be worried when Rictor appeared in Cove. The poisoner trusted no one and his enemies rarely grew old. Raveka had no wish to meet him in person.

She was very interested, however, in the mysterious Technocrat member of the Pact of Four. His treachery explained Warlord Bahrok's unusual victories in Logosia. By Raveka's quick calculations, if this unidentified traitor was removed, Logos would have no cause to fear the Juka Clans. Lector Gaff could make tremendous use of this information. But no, she reminded herself, that leg of her life's journey was ended. She and Logos had rejected one another. There would be no return trip.

She caught herself chanting in her thoughts, to calm the tension.

Montenegro continued, "And that, Lord Gideon, is why I believe that General Nathaniel wants to use the war to overtake your position in the House of the Lion. The true nature of the Pact of Four is revealed by the motives of its members and the behavior of its agents. The Pact does not serve Britain or the Virtues. It is a sinister, selfish enterprise."

The nobleman's hands rested on his belt. His knuckles brushed the hilt of his longsword. His stare was as hard and black as onyx. "Thank you for delivering that tale, Sir Gabriel. Allow me to pay for it with some advice. Intrigue is not in your nature. Don't try to employ it when you deal with me."

Gabriel's eyes flashed. "Do you accuse me of lying, Lord Gideon?"

"Your facts are true enough, but you shine a wicked light upon them. Nathaniel warned me that you would cast him as the perpetrator of some insidious plot. But let us take away your unflattering interpretation and look at the facts. The general coordinates with the Juka against the Logosians. He employs Meer and Technocrat spies. He restricts knowledge of this arrangement to those few who must act upon it. Nathaniel himself freely told me the same information just this morning, because he knew you would come. Now, Sir Gabriel, can you explain to me why I should be concerned? Which of these facts constitutes evidence of treachery?"

"It is the spirit behind the Pact that is evil. They are exploiting the war for selfish goals. Greed, Pride—the Pact of Four serves the Anti-Virtues. And victory without Virtue is false. Your Lordship knows that."

Gideon bared his teeth. "Do not lecture me about the Virtues! You have no right to do so. Sir Gabriel, I used to believe Lord Valente's praise of you. I thought you truly wanted to honor your grandfather's name. I might even have investigated these accusations against General Nathaniel, fantastic though they are. However, I received a certain letter just a few days after our last meeting." From his pocket he withdrew a fold of brown parchment. He pointed it at Montenegro. "Do you recognize this?"

The knight creased his brow. "It's Jukan parchment. A message from Garron?"

"Precisely! And do you know what it says? That you are a traitor. That as you departed Jukaran, you interfered with the apprehension of a Technocrat spy. That because of your assistance, this spy escaped with extremely damaging information. That you acted with full knowledge of whom you were aiding. Do you know who wrote this letter?"

Raveka tightened her grip around Montenegro's elbow, but he did not react to her. His every muscle seemed clenched. Through gritted teeth he answered, "Thulann of Garron."

"I thought you might know that answer! Did you also know that I met Thulann when she visited us two years ago? That I participated in her negotiations with Regent Salvatore? In my estimation you will find no more honorable person, human or Jukan, anywhere in this world. If she points these charges at you, then I believe her. But I want you to tell me your side of the story. Do you deny these accusations, Sir Gabriel?"

Montenegro's eyes seethed hot. "Your Lordship, with all respect, I've had enough of this damned piece of theater. Plainly you're not here to listen to what I have to say. Please make your point."

Lord Gideon narrowed his eyes, then slammed the fold of parchment on a side table. "Very well! My point is this: You are an arrogant, deceitful hypocrite and far worse, a traitor who may well be responsible for the biggest tragedy in New Britannia since the Cataclysm itself! You look shocked? Listen to the evidence. It's my belief that the spy whom you assisted returned to Logos with information about our impending invasion of Logosia. Furthermore, this information prompted Blackthorn to launch his armada against us. Furthermore, your concealment of that scroll might well have hindered the defense of our shores, were it not for the good fortune that the House of the Griffin obtained its own

copy. The sum of these circumstances leads me to one conclusion. Every death caused by the Logosian armada puts
more blood on your hands. It is truly that simple." The
nobleman's face purpled. "In the name of Justice and Honesty! Did Blackthorn hook you with marionette strings while
you were in Logosia? Have you become his clockwork slave?
Through what irresistible mechanism does he direct your
treachery?"

Raveka's heart froze when Montenegro pulled his arm
out of her grasp. His palm flattened against her chest. "Get
away from me, Aria." The room whirled as he shoved her
off. She stumbled against a paneled wall.

Lord Gideon barked, "Enough! Leave the lady be! Surrender yourself, Montenegro. There is a cell waiting for you at
the palace. Once we repel Blackthorn's armada, the Senate
will rule on your guilt."

Raveka tried to catch Montenegro's glance, but he glowered at the three knights before him. His knees bent and his
fingers spread. The black sword Starfell hung loosely against
his left thigh. He answered simply, "No."

She held up a hand. "Gabriel—"

"Don't come near me."

"Perhaps we can—"

"Stay away, Aria!"

Sir Aziz spread open his arms. "This doesn't help anything. Come on, Montenegro! We're your friends."

"Would friends call me a traitor?"

Aziz shook his head. "Lord Gideon's evidence is strong.
But Evanthe and I are here to make sure it goes well for you.
Montenegro, hand over your sword. I give you my word of
honor, I'll attend to your case personally."

"I shall not be imprisoned. Rictor and Shavade would kill

me in my cell. I might as well slit my own throat and lie down on General Nathaniel's doorstep."

Gideon snapped, "This is not a negotiation! Surrender, sir. You will be safe in my custody."

"I don't believe you. So I'm going to leave. Before you stand in my way, I advise you to consider that I've hardly drawn Starfell since I left Jukaran. Sometimes it gets thirsty after so long at rest."

Evanthe sighed, "Please, Montenegro. Let's settle this lawfully. You know we can't let you go."

He nodded. "I know."

Abruptly the room broke into a flurry. Gabriel's hand swept toward the hilt of his blade as Aziz and Evanthe dove at him. They each seized an arm, preventing him from unsheathing. Lord Gideon followed behind as the two knights slammed Montenegro against the wall. The impact jostled a vase from a shelf, crashing it against the marble floor. A mirror split in its baroque frame.

Montenegro's boot thrust from the fray and kicked Lord Gideon backward. The combatants grunted as they wrestled, smacking knees and elbows against the wood paneling. Then Montenegro locked an arm around Aziz. The shorter knight upended and toppled into a small settee, the curved legs of which cracked outward. Montenegro landed a punch on Evanthe's jaw. She staggered off, but Gideon replaced her while Aziz jumped his opponent from behind.

Raveka crouched. With a Mathematician's speed she inventoried her options. Montenegro could well lose this fight. He would then be imprisoned. She could not accept that. In combat she was no match for any of these knights, but she did possess one advantage.

From under her gown she retrieved her bolt-thrower. Palming it, she leapt among the red-faced warriors.

Sir Aziz was pinning Montenegro's hands. Raveka hurtled atop the olive-skinned knight with a terrified wail. She pounded his head as Lady Aria might, with wild, feeble blows, while a false accident jammed her heel into the back of his knee. The joint gave way. Aziz collapsed.

Powerful arms clamped around Raveka's body. Lord Gideon plucked her from Aziz's back as though she were made of straw. He squeezed her chest to his side. She knew she could not resist his strength.

Nor did she want to. Instead she maneuvered the concealed bolt-thrower until it was nestled between them. One shove would poke the weapon under his jaw, at which time he would be forced to surrender. She and Montenegro could escape with their hostage.

The plan was murky, but at this moment Raveka knew one thing with absolute clarity: She would not leave Gabriel's side, no matter how vehemently he might reject her. She would not let it end this way.

A shriek pierced the room. Raveka saw that Aziz and Evanthe had fallen away from Montenegro. Evanthe's dress was soaked with blood from her abdomen. She sagged against the wall. Aziz knelt and clutched his right arm, which was now barely attached.

Montenegro stood between them with the black fang Starfell steady in his grasp. His glare held back a hurricane. "I have no more business here," he growled, then lunged for the nearest window.

Lord Gideon let go of Raveka and snatched out his own sword. But when he charged forward Montenegro brandished Starfell, smacking the nobleman's weapon from his hand. Unarmed, Gideon stared at the point of Sir Gabriel's blade, inches from his rib cage. The nobleman froze in place.

"I am no traitor!" panted the knight.

The lord muttered, "You insult both the memory of Lord Valente and your grandfather's good name."

"Judge me as you will! But I have been faithful to the Virtues."

"Lies are most egregious when directed at oneself."

Gideon's back was turned to Raveka. The two injured knights crawled to the nobleman's aid. They were oblivious to her actions. Only Gabriel could see her.

Raveka's anger swelled. She aimed the bolt-thrower at Lord Gideon's skull.

Montenegro caught her eye with a fierce glance, then shook his head. "I am sorry, Aria. *Beza rhem.*" He pushed open the window and leapt out.

Swiftly Raveka pocketed the bolt-thrower. No one had seen the device.

Lord Gideon bellowed for guards and healers as he climbed after the escaping Sir Gabriel. Raveka knew the heavy-boned lord could not give effective pursuit, nor could Aziz or Evanthe. For the moment, Montenegro was safe.

The tension eased in her chest, though her heart began to ache. Her body started to tremble. She fell to her knees, pressed her hands to her face and broke into sobs.

Crying, of course, was one of the simplest actions to counterfeit.

Near the window Sir Aziz rasped, in defiance of his personal agony, "Have courage, Lady Aria! You bear no responsibility for Montenegro's misdeeds."

His further comments did not reach her ears. Montenegro's career might just have ended. All that he strived to become had unraveled. Despite Aziz's reassurances, the largest factor in Gabriel's downfall was his relationship with Raveka herself. Yet in the midst of feigned weeping, her thoughts focused on a series of calculations. No transgression was unredeemable. In time Raveka could manipulate this affair to a favorable outcome. Lady Aria was the perfect tool to do so.

Lord Gideon had spoken the truth. Montenegro had no gift for intrigue. But Raveka had once snared nations in her webs. The time had come to start spinning again.

CHAPTER
12

Meeting in the Dark

Britannia Bay was crowded with warships. Along the busy wharf Thulann walked past the oaken behemoths, teeming with sailors who readied for war. The stamp of hammers and the scent of hot tar described the character of the afternoon. The sky was brushed steel overhead.

The Way Master leaned on the heavy staff she carried. The ocean voyage had tortured her leg. Her damaged face ached less now, though the empty socket often jabbed with pain. The rest of her body entertained its usual banquet of torments. She was stiff, dirty and for the moment unstable on the motionless ground. She could see pity in the eyes of the humans who beheld her.

Yet the verdant trees of New Britannia offered a more pleasant greeting. The capital city was laced with vines and greenery. Britain itself was a sea of buildings large and small, fashioned of brick and slate and timbers, cresting with thousands of lamps and chimney pots. The Cathedral of the Virtues raised its spires in the distant center of town, while the bulk of Castle Britannia lurked farther in the west.

Britain had always reminded Thulann of a colony of swallows' nests, built of mud and sticks and pebbles with little regard for order or symmetry. The city's charm derived from its primitive chaos.

In less than a week Blackthorn's iron armada would arrive. The Techno-Prophet's steam-blooded war machines would cloud the sea and sky. She wondered how these Britannian nests might fare under a hailstorm of acid and flame. *Not as well as granite Garron,* she was saddened to admit to herself.

The bustle of warships revealed that the Royal Senate knew of the coming danger. Doubtless the Pact of Four had alerted General Nathaniel. But she was unwilling to trust Bahrok's partners. She would deliver her own knowledge to the Senate. They must act according to the truth, not the agenda of a band of ambitious schemers.

What she might do after imparting her message, she could not guess. She was in neither the health nor the mood to join the impending fray. New Britannia held no other business for her. Though a fast ship could skirt the Logosian fleet and return her to Jukaran, her body decried the proposition of another ocean voyage so soon. And in truth she had little desire to return home right now. She had determined to leave Venduss alone in Turlogan's care. Nothing else waited for her there.

She felt relentlessly empty.

Her mind conjured the words of the philosopher Darhim, who had codified so much of the Way: *The future is a road. To walk it you must move your feet. When you stand still, time ends.* And so she limped achefully into the pandemonium of Britain, searching more than anything for a carriage or hansom to ride. In this case a horse's hooves would proceed into the future more steadily than her own, exhausted feet. *Old Darhim*, she thought, *would understand.*

Twilight choked the silent parlor. A single lantern burned very low on a table. Beside it sat Montenegro in a high-backed chair, his fingers steepled before his face. He wore his traveling plate armor. A Technocrat bolt-thrower rested in his lap.

His patience smoldered in the dark.

When the front door of the manor house squeaked open, Montenegro used both hands to cock the mechanical weapon. He aimed it toward an entryway across from his seat. A figure appeared there moments later.

Montenegro turned up the flame on the lantern as he murmured, "There was a time, you recall, when I was invincible."

General Nathaniel whisked his blade from its scabbard. When he spotted the bolt-thrower, his face pinched into an angry frown. "By my Honor, what crime is this? How did you get into my house?"

"Back then, I never lost on the battlefield," continued the knight, "and only rarely in tournament. I was ruthless, you see. Some even called me cruel. I admit that on occasion the Virtues suffered for my success, but I believed that winning was the only path to reclaiming the glory of my grandfather's name. I used to have a motto: 'Victory is a necessary evil.' "

The long-braided officer stood motionless, gazing at the point of the quarrel. "What did you do with Sergeant Matthias?"

The knight raised a finger. "Then something happened two years ago. This would be around the time of Lord

Valente's murder. I was stripped of my command, ostensibly because of my ruthlessness. It forced me to reexamine my ethics. I decided that Virtue was in itself the greatest triumph of all. I could only honor my grandfather's legend by honoring the Virtues to which he devoted himself."

"Sir Gabriel! Time is too precious for frivolity. I heard what happened between you and Lord Gideon. You must understand, I had no choice but to break our agreement. This invasion changes everything. War supersedes these personal affairs. I need that scroll and I shall force it from you if I must. You should have told me about it to begin with."

Montenegro's eyes wandered through a memory. "When that epiphany came to me, I distilled a new philosophy for myself. It was quite elegant. You see, the purpose of great skill is not to win more victories, but to win better victories. So I let the Virtues guide my path. For the first time, I felt Humility in the face of success." He kept one hand on the firing lever of the bolt-thrower. His other hand reached for a faceted bottle of brandy, which he poured into a glass. "And do you know the culmination of my enlightenment? I have begun to lose. In the name of Honesty I have succumbed to intrigues. In the name of Honor I have ruined my career. In the name of Compassion I have invited Blackthorn's armada to our shores. These are not, of course, the rewards I expected."

General Nathaniel lowered his blade. "Enough! I have important matters to handle. If you seek an apology from me, then take it. I never wished misfortune upon you, but through my agents you refused to help me. Like you, I do not brook refusal. I feel sadness but not regret." He slitted his eyes and regarded the bolt-thrower. "If you go now and fetch me the schematic for Braun's Needle, I shall not hand you over to Lord Gideon. But whatever action you choose to take, I can give you no more of my time." He took a step through the doorway.

Montenegro lifted the brandy glass. "Don't turn away from me, General."

The officer snorted. "You would not shoot me in the back." He faced away.

Montenegro swallowed a gulp of liquor and fired.

The bolt punctured Nathaniel in the spine. He collapsed facedown with a *thump*. He drooled blood and pawed without strength at the hilt of his sword. "B-by the Virtues!"

The glass was now empty. The brandy sizzled in Montenegro's throat. "I'll be damned. After two years, it still tastes like heaven." He rose from the chair and moved beside the gasping general. "You summoned this upon yourself, of course. I was a beast on a chain and you tormented me. Sooner or later a link was bound to give."

The officer gurgled, "I must . . . send my agents to stop the armada. Your revenge will cost hundreds of lives!"

"I don't want revenge. I want victory." He grabbed the general's tunic and lifted him so that their eyes were level. "Maybe Gideon is correct. Maybe I am a dupe of Blackthorn. But you have stolen from me every lawful means to set things right. By the Lost King, I cannot even fight alongside my fellow knights for fear of imprisonment! Command is only a dream now. The Virtues have abandoned me, but by the souls of Stonegate I shall not surrender. I shall defend Britannia with ruthlessness again. Only once before did it fail me."

Nathaniel was weakening from loss of blood. "Only I . . . can help you now."

"I know. That's why I came. If I cannot fight beside my

fellow knights, I will fight beside your barbaric agents. All I want is to stop Blackthorn. All I want from you is to tell me how."

"Give me the schematic."

"You have already consulted Mistress Aurora's copy. Mine will tell you nothing new. Admit it, you only want my scroll because your Technocrat counterpart needs it for his own political purposes."

The officer nodded. "Nevertheless, you must give it to me. Exchanges of intelligence . . . hold the Pact of Four together. That is the price of success."

Montenegro growled, "I have lost a great deal more than one scroll! Do not forget that. You have cost me everything, General. This invasion is the only reason I am not seeking vengeance tonight." He let go of Nathaniel's tunic. The general smacked onto the floor and groaned.

A vial of healing potion dropped next to the dying man's fingers. Nathaniel suckled it like a baby. The steel bolt clanked out of his back. When he recaptured his breath the general grumbled, "Sir Gabriel, this war gives me power. You have not yet seen the brunt of my anger."

"Nor you of mine, Nathaniel. But that is for another day. Tonight let us make plans. Whatever your agents are doing to stop the Logosian armada, Starfell will be in the thick of it. You ought to be glad. The Technocrats fear me. I am perhaps the closest thing to an honorable opponent that they have ever known."

"You insult Starfell. You have no more honor."

Montenegro ground his teeth. "Then I have nothing left to lose. Which means, General, that I am the most dangerous man in New Britannia. Sharpen your tongue on that." He walked away from the sprawled officer. "Now let's make our plans before Sergeant Matthias wakes up. He is sleeping in the next room. You're surprised? I would not visit harm on a decent man, but of course that does not concern you in the slightest."

Darkness fell quickly under the charcoal grey of an imminent storm. Not even the leering moons could pierce the blinding, boiling murk. The shadowy clouds flashed, as if stars battled within.

Lord Gideon's office was a jumble of papers and maps. Tables were strewn with charts. Flat drawers yawned open. In the glow of many lamps the chamber resembled the aftermath of a hurricane. Thulann wondered how the New Britannians could locate a particular document in such a flurry of papers, much less conduct a war according to it. Yet Lord Gideon wrote down every number she related to him, adding her information to the chaotic heap.

She proceeded, "I saw twenty-six airships moored at Crevasse. The most recent figure from Akar is thirty. I do not know how many more were deployed from Logos or elsewhere, but it is reasonable to assume that Blackthorn's armada comprises between sixty and seventy airborne vessels. He has fewer naval ships, perhaps thirty that might pose a danger. And of course there is Braun's Needle itself."

Lord Gideon used a quill to scratch her figures into a book. "Thank you, Way Master Thulann. These numbers corroborate General Nathaniel's. It is reassuring to know that our intelligence is accurate."

She paused before asking, "And did the general explain whence his information came?"

"He employs spies, naturally. I do not know the details,

except that he has an arrangement with parties in Logos and with your own Warlord Bahrok."

"So he does. Though I find it interesting that you know of their pact. I won the same information from Bahrok at considerable cost." She winced at a sting in her leg.

The nobleman grunted, "I am sorry to hear that, though I cannot feign surprise. I have not forgotten Warlord Bahrok's schemes when he visited here. He is a devious man. But I assure you that while General Nathaniel is a crafty soldier, he is also an honorable one."

She resolved to make no accusations until she interviewed Nathaniel personally. "I see. Then I should like to speak with him. I feel sure we can enlighten one another a great deal. Tell me, if I may ask, what is he planning for the defense of the city?"

"We have no intention of allowing the armada to get this far. Our fleet is gathering to intercept them. The House of the Griffin is preparing spells that we hope will sink the Technocrat machines. I only pray that they do not arrive before we are ready to deploy."

"And what of Braun's Needle? Have you an answer for it?"

"For that we must rely upon our wizards. If they cannot guide our warships through the Needle's storm, then all will be lost. Though General Nathaniel mentioned to me that his agents will attempt to sabotage the device, using the schematics we have received."

"Schematics! Everyone except myself has obtained them, though I have worked the hardest at it." She remembered Toria's confession at Crevasse. "Did Montenegro bring the schematic from Jukaran?"

"Quite so, though he attempted to conceal it from us. But Mistress Aurora obtained a copy."

Thulann felt an odd relief, as though somehow Toria's actions were obtusely vindicated. She indulged a sigh while Gideon continued, "Montenegro's story is a sad one. Dishonor lures him like a siren. He is in a great deal of trouble. He attempted to interfere with the general's plans."

Her ears perked. "Did he indeed?"

"Perhaps his prejudice against Warlord Bahrok tainted his judgment of General Nathaniel. He assaulted the general's agents. In any case, it was your own testimony about the Logosian spy that convinced me he must be locked up."

"He is incarcerated, then?"

"Alas, no. He nearly killed his own friends while escaping this morning."

"But you are following his trail."

"So far he has left none. We expect he may try to contact his cousin, Lady Aria of Coventine, though. She visits me again in an hour or so. If he's appeared this afternoon, she will tell me then."

"He once mentioned his cousin to me. He told me that she was wasting away from poor health. How glad that she did not." Abruptly an old spark of resentment kindled in the Juka's chest. Thoughts of the knight stirred from her memory. She was not surprised that his temper had once again brought him to ruin. He had always lacked restraint.

Then the Way Master recalled poor Toria, who had never lost faith in the knight. Perhaps minstrels were naturally attracted to people in need. Thulann certainly was. She nibbled her lip. "I myself have matters to discuss with Montenegro. I shall lend you my aid in locating him. Please introduce me to his cousin tonight."

Lord Gideon sighed. "Respectfully, Way Master Thulann, I must decline. Lady Aria is in a fragile state. She was present when Montenegro sliced up two good knights. He nearly injured her as well. I have pledged her my personal care. Please understand, your presence would not put her at ease."

Thulann almost chuckled, though it was a dry sound. "I confess, I am not at the moment an attractive sight. Very well, then. But please, Your Lordship, keep me apprised of any developments. I am at your service in this affair."

"I welcome your aid. And I shall notify General Nathaniel that you would like to meet with him. Have you arranged accommodations for your visit? I can prepare a room at the palace for you. It is late and you look weary."

Her flesh tingled at the thought of a steeping bath. "Lord Gideon, you have my eternal gratitude. Though I warn you, for a woman this old and broken, eternity is measured one hour at a time. And that is a merciful thing."

The nobleman laughed. "If I am as hale and intact at your age, I shall consider my life to have been a great success."

The comment gave her little succor, but she smiled for the sake of the compliment. Honor and good will were all that remained for her. She must learn to accept them for their own merits.

The night's downpour scrubbed the roofs and cobbles of Britain. Moon-grey clouds lit the splashing rain, lending the city a ghostly cast. The springtime air gained a brisk snap.

The heavy shower roared in Thulann's pointed ears. She huddled under a cloak, in the shadow of a wall around Lord Gideon's townhouse. She fought back an ache in her joints.

The hot bath at the palace called to her, but she was determined to ignore its summons. There would be time later to tend to her own needs. If Montenegro knew something about the Pact of Four, then Thulann intended to ask him about it. He was a brash man, and sometimes inscrutable, but in his heart he was Virtuous. She imagined a meeting might be fruitful for them both.

As she watched, a carriage rattled from the coach house and the driver unfurled an awning. A door opened in the house. Two people emerged. One of them was the stout Lord Gideon, proud and handsome. On his arm was a long, slender Britannian lady, with dark hair and very pale skin. When Thulann first saw Lady Aria of Coventine, two impressions leapt into the Way Master's thoughts. The first was that the noblewoman appeared healthier than Montenegro had portrayed her, though certainly her white complexion admitted to years of indoor seclusion.

Her second impression was that Aria and Gideon behaved with more than casual intimacy. Thulann could not pinpoint why, but she could sense a chemistry expressed in the couple's mannerisms. It explained the nobleman's protectiveness.

Lady Aria squeezed Gideon's hands and then stepped inside the coach. A mailed guard climbed onto the back. The driver whipped the horses and eight hooves struck a beat on the rain-slick flagstones.

Thulann separated from the shadows and dashed after them. Through the empty streets she kept pace in the gloom. Mental disciplines allowed her to disregard fatigue, though she did not want to consider how long they might be effective. She simply kept moving her feet.

After a short trip the carriage halted in front of a more modest townhouse. The drenched soldier helped Lady Aria inside. Thulann watched through slatted shutters as the noblewoman left her escort downstairs. She locked the door to her second-floor bedroom. While she undressed, the Way Master secured a high perch outside the window.

The lady did not put on a sleeping gown. Instead she wrapped herself in a darker, less voluminous dress. From a wardrobe she retrieved a cowled cloak. This one was blacker than the stormy night.

Thunder pealed as Lady Aria moved to the window under which Thulann was hanging. The Way Master scrambled to one side. The noblewoman threw open the shutters, behind which the old Juka hid.

Thulann observed as a weak, pampered New Britannian lady climbed into the hissing rain and slipped down the side of the building. So practiced was her execution that when she nudged the shutters on her way out, they closed with perfect silence.

Lady Aria did not see Thulann as the human slipped away into the storm.

Though she found it strange, the Way Master did not question the smile that worked onto her jade lips. Instead she slithered to the ground and resumed her pursuit. This time she used greater care with her stealth. The increased exertion seemed to heighten her energy rather than to sap it.

Aria of Coventine made her way to a tiny, arched building in an alleyway. Inside the structure was a stone staircase that dropped below street level. Thulann recognized the sewer entrance. Though a thunderstorm was not the ideal time to travel underground, she followed the noblewoman into the wet, rushing clamor of the subterranean canals.

A blue light ignited in the darkness. Thulann knew the tenor of a Logosian spark lantern. It was doubtless one of the spoils of Montenegro's campaign. The pale light gleamed furtively across millions of damp bricks, lending the tunnel the complexion of a dragon's black scales. Endless stone vaults and archways created an abundance of shadows. Thulann moved easily among them. Her footfalls were likewise concealed by the din of rushing water. Rain flooded the mildewed sewers, sloshing over the walkways on either side of the swift channels. The cacophony was almost painful.

The Way Master receded into a corner. Her instincts tickled. Lady Aria was rounding a bend ahead, but someone else was nearby.

A thick, filthy smell assaulted her. In a single motion she lunged forward and thrust her metal-clad staff behind a pillar. It cracked against bones. Something small and humanoid toppled into the greedy current and vanished. Thulann had not glimpsed enough to make out what it was.

Footsteps slapped across the half-flooded walkway. More stooped figures charged her. Animal grunts leapt through the darkness. Eyes and teeth glinted.

Then Lady Aria's spark light disappeared.

Loud darkness swallowed Thulann. She wheeled her staff in violent patterns until the first creature entered her space. She cascaded a hail of blows atop the thing. Its body snapped and bent. She leapt over its slumping mass and kicked at the space where the next one ought to have been. Her foot struck empty air. The things were hunched over like apes, presenting shorter targets. A claw latched around her waist. She swatted the creature aside, which barked and gurgled as the water carried it off.

She had taken the measure of her opponents. They were less of a threat than a human warrior. With welcome relaxation she unleashed a sequence of kicks and parries and staff thrusts. A few stray claws raked her legs, but in less than a minute she had dispatched the loathsome band. She stretched her throbbing limbs and caught her breath.

She was alone in the torrential sewers. Lady Aria was gone. Thulann had little hope of tracking the noblewoman now. Her energy ebbed. She knelt and leaned hard on the bloody staff.

Perhaps the time had come to admit her own age. Her endurance was not what it used to be, and that steaming tub beckoned to her from the palace. Still she paused for several minutes longer. Her heart paced its rapid beat.

The stormy current thundered past in the canal and the old woman squatted beside it, wondering if she had the courage to surrender. For all of her life's adventures, she truly did not know. Time kept the only answer, though she had very little of that left.

In the roar of the flooding sewers, two figures in black met around a burning lantern. The glow illuminated a thousand bricks that formed the low barrel vault. Like a snare the little niche captured the clamorous sounds of water. The pair spoke with voices slightly raised.

"Did you bring it with you?" Montenegro held a faceted bottle in his fingers. The brandy within twinkled by the lamplight.

Raveka produced the scroll from the folds of her dress. "As I said I would. A pack of goblins wanted to take it as a toll, but I lost them easily enough."

"Give it to me."

"Have it. But I'm doing this because I do not believe it will change the outcome of the battle. And because I know it will appease General Nathaniel."

"I'm through with your schemes. Do not try to help me. You have accomplished nothing but bringing me disgrace!"

She seemed to ignore him. "With Nathaniel on your side, you'll be safe in prison. Then I shall convince Gideon to forgo his accusations."

Montenegro squinted. "You mean to seduce Lord Gideon, don't you?"

"It's the fastest way. I've already begun. His interest was present from the moment he saw me."

"Do not waste your time."

She grimaced. "What else do you propose I should do?"

"Leave the city before the armada arrives. Go back to Cove. Be the Britannian lady you always dreamed of."

"I shall not quit you, Gabriel."

The knight clutched at the damp air. "By the lost shrines, how do you think I arrived here in the first place? My faith in you blinded me to my own dishonor! And doomed this city to invasion. I dare not trust you, Raveka. Leave me alone."

Her expression soured. "The brandy puts venom on your tongue. Don't do this to yourself."

"Go home, woman! I won't be following behind. My peerage is finished. Cove is my last gift to you, on the condition that you forget Montenegro. We were . . . a poor match."

When he drank another mouthful, she pursed her lips in disdain. "Let me know how General Nathaniel reacts. Good night, my love."

She vanished into the shadows. Montenegro swallowed the liquor and tried to dispel her face from his mind. Her disdain was staged, of course. Underneath he had seen compassion. It stung him like a bright ember.

He beat back an urge to pursue her. It would solve nothing. She was a distraction. That was all she had ever been.

He had succumbed to her and lost everything, except his love for New Britannia. Even as an outlaw, though, he could still defend his homeland. And as an outlaw, he had no further need of the Virtues.

The admission was as liberating as it was terrible. He drove it quickly from his thoughts.

The brandy danced in his skull. He lay atop a small slab in the rear of the niche, glad for the coolness on his scalp. Time spun around him. The rain diminished and the roar of the sewers mellowed to a watery chorus.

"That lantern of yours is liable to attract unwanted attention," said an elderly woman nearby.

Montenegro leapt to his feet, plucked Starfell loose and aimed it at the voice. A willowy figure sat cross-legged in the corner.

The knight turned up the lantern's flame. The coppery glow fell upon a one-eyed Jukan warrior. She looked somehow familiar.

"I thought you had given up drink," she said, "but then I once thought I had given up espionage. Such is the tenacity of addiction. We are kites battling the wind, you and I, Montenegro."

His stomach knotted. He let out a grumble. "Thulann of Garron. I must be dreaming."

"Then dream me twenty years younger. My joints will stop bickering and I can look you in both eyes at once. Presently, I confess, I feel outnumbered."

"I ought to kill you right now! What in the name of Mondain's gem are you doing here? Have you come to drag me to prison? I very much want you to try!"

"Lock up the famous Sir Gabriel of Cove? I could never do that. Troll children might stop fearing the daylight."

"You've lost none of your charm, I see. You're still as warm as your granite city." He dropped the tip of his sword. His voice turned grim. "I hope it gives you pleasure to see me like this. It was your word that brought me down."

"I know. I take no satisfaction from your suffering, but you stole a spy from me. I am tired of people stealing from me."

"You're tired? Dammit, you've ruined me, without even asking for an explanation!"

"Neither did you ask why I was chasing that Technocrat."

"You turned your back on me at Garron! It was your boot that kicked my knights out of Jukaran. Forgive me if I felt no urgent duty to help you after that."

"Nevertheless I wanted that spy. I earned her. She stuck nine bolts into my gut."

"Her missiles bury deep," he muttered. "On that, we can agree." Then he snorted and drank from the bottle of brandy. The fiery taste upset his balance. He leaned on the stone slab and rubbed his eyes. "It doesn't matter. She escaped me just as she would have escaped you. She is elusive as an eagle."

"The eagle fears a persistent crow. I am very persistent."

"It is a curse upon everyone in your acquaintance. Venduss will agree with me there." He sniffed and shook his head. "Where is the noble boy? Trapped in the palace like a penned up dog?"

Thulann glanced away. "He is in Jukaran, with his father. They are marching on Akar, since Blackthorn's airships have so obligingly left it to come here."

"I knew he would leave your service soon."

"It was inevitable, of course." Her voice bittered slightly.

"What about Toria? Did she stay with Venduss or has she finally come home?"

The old woman tightened her lips. "Toria is dead. She was killed outside of Crevasse."

He shut his eyes. His fists closed. "And so dies our innocence. Damn it all! How did it happen?"

She stared at the rushing water. "Agents of the Pact of Four."

He glanced up quickly. "You know about them?"

"All too well. They are the last thing I saw with both of my eyes."

"Tell me what you have learned!"

"I rather thought you would be better informed than I."

"I know damn little about anything. That is a brutal fact."

"Perhaps, but do not be coy, Montenegro. You are in an excellent position to learn. After all, you serve them now."

"I, serve the Pact of Four? I should cut you down for that!"

"Stay your sword until the truth sees light! We shall observe what shadow it casts." She pointed a leather-gloved finger into the deeps of the niche. "In that corner is a cloak wrapped around a scroll. I know because I looked. That scroll is my property. Toria stole it from me and gave it to you. And I cannot expunge this suspicion of mine that you intend to give it to General Nathaniel tonight."

"You were always suspicious to a fault."

"Yes, and attentive as well. I overheard the last of the conversation with your cousin. She is, might I say, a remarkable lady."

"Keep out of my business, Thulann, or I'll expunge you myself!"

"Pact agents are trying to sabotage Braun's Needle. Bahrok told me everything. You are helping them, are you not?"

He slapped Starfell back into its scabbard, then grabbed his cloak from the darkness. He shoved the scroll into his belt. Without meeting her gaze he rumbled, "I shall defend New Britannia by whatever means are available to me. Thanks to you, I have only one option left." He turned away, retrieved the lantern and began to walk along the path that skirted the teeming canal.

From behind she called out, "The Pact of Four employs criminals! To serve with them makes you no better than Bahrok himself. Do not dishonor your name this way."

"What name? Honor has abandoned me! But I can be ruthless again, if it serves my needs."

"You are better than this. Trust your Virtues. Find another way."

He sneered and gave no answer. Instead, he slogged through the water that brimmed over the sewer walkway. When a dark shape appeared before him, he grabbed the hilt of his sword.

Thulann had somehow moved past him. She blocked his path. "You have the scroll. It must contain useful information. Let us employ it, not Bahrok's men."

"Get out of my way!"

"You do not need the Pact of Four. I have seen good men destroyed by them. Stronger men than you."

"I'll show you how strong I am."

In a lightning motion he struck with Starfell. But his thrust found no target, pricking the space where her rib cage had been. She bent her torso aside and shoved her staff to parry. He slashed again. His blade skidded from her staff's metal sheath. He threw a stampede of cuts and jabs and yet somehow nothing connected. His attacks veered gently astray, guided by the slippery twists of her weapon. Her stance was upright and haughty. He swore that her feet never moved.

Then her pole jammed between his ankles. She tripped him back onto the flooded walkway. He jutted out his legs, twirled his feet beneath himself and spun into a crouching lunge.

Her weapon was out of position to parry. She resorted to a backward cartwheel to evade his thrust. The ancient warrior seemed less nimble than she had been two years earlier, and yet she remained far more agile than Montenegro would ever be. Her prowess dazzled him anew.

After his own spin, his head reeled. The alcohol robbed him of balance. He did not press his advantage.

Thulann resumed her arrogant pose, as tall and straight as the pole in her hand. "You have improved since I last watched you fight. The brandy demeans you, though. It is undignified. Liquor is a coward's armor."

"By the lost shrines! You don't know how to stop meddling, do you?"

"No, I do not! It is a flaw in my character. I collect lost souls and nag them until they are skilled enough to escape me. But I have always acted with honor. At the end of the day, that is all we really have. Believe me, I know. My day is quickly drawing to a close."

"You hasten it by provoking me!"

"Then I shall die as I have lived! Can you say the same if you die tonight? We are two of a kind, Montenegro. We are both stranded. Let us work together, and not call despair our master."

"Despair!" The accusation struck like a hammer. "Despair requires inaction, which has never been among my weaknesses!"

He rushed at her and tossed a series of feints. For an instant she parried in sequence, which gave him an opening. He slashed his enchanted sword down the length of her staff. The steel plating creased. Rivets sheared. The metal casing peeled into tatters that hindered her grip. She tumbled past him and tried to strike his knees, but he arced his blade in the path of her weapon and cleaved the haft in two. The broken staff plunked into the surging torrent.

Thulann rose with a sword in her hand. Montenegro slashed before she could gain her bearings, missing her wounded face by inches. She kicked high on his chest and jarred him, but his blade tip landed on the inside of her thigh. He felt the pressure of the contact. As another kick approached he plunged Starfell into the Way Master's hip, as deeply as his weight could push it. The blade split the hard wall of her pelvis. Then her kick landed, bashing his nose and reeling him against the wall.

The old Juka shrieked. The gruff noise sobered Montenegro. She toppled hard on the brickwork path, contorting her long limbs and flexible torso. Her Jukan sword clattered, unused, across the shallow current that swept the walkway.

Montenegro rubbed his face, which was bloody and swelling. He stumbled beside the fallen woman and drew Starfell from her body. "I am my own master, Thulann. I do what I believe is right. That is how I live and that is how I shall die."

Her groans and spasms ceased. Her breaths came deep. The knight assumed she was employing some technique of the Way to relieve her pain, though only a healer could keep her from dying soon. Blood streamed from her wounded leg. Her emerald color grew ashen in the lamplight.

He tore a strip from the hem of his cloak and fashioned a

bandage into place. Then he lifted her from the cold, dirty water. She was much lighter than he had expected. Her slender body draped easily around the back of his neck.

If she remained conscious he saw no signs. Her skin was cool and pliant. Her muscles were relaxed.

Unexpectedly, he felt relaxed himself. A hint of fatigue brought calm to his body. The brandy no longer whirled in his head, but faded to a tranquil murmur.

His thoughts were clear enough now to make his plans. He knew what he must do. With sure steps he sloshed through the rising stormwaters. The vaults and tunnels rasped with wet voices that echoed in the dark. The glow of his lantern threw webs of light across the dragon scale brickwork of Britain's fabled sewers. The patterns danced around him like ghosts.

A constellation of candles lit the marble-tiled bath chamber. The water was marvelously scalding. Thulann lay back until only her face touched the air. Tendrils of fragrant steam wafted around her like strands of ethereal grass.

The Way Master inhaled the robust air. It felt cool as it entered her steeping chest. Her heart thumped strongly. The coursing of her blood felt like a massage. The sensations were so cathartic that she could almost ignore the aches in her body. The relaxation provided an opportunity to review the night's events with welcome detachment.

Montenegro had surprised her after their battle. Through no little effort in the sheeting rain, he had hauled her carcass, paralyzed by trance, across the city to the Cathedral of the Virtues. The brothers and sisters of the Order of the Shepherd were glad to heal her injury. Diligently neutral, they asked no questions and offered no judgments, though they seemed happy to accept Montenegro's donation of gold. In fact, he had given them every coin in his purse, as well as the jewelry he wore.

But most curious was something she witnessed as the Shepherds were pouring water magic into her wound. Half hidden from her view by an inconvenient pillar, Montenegro had knelt before the Shrine of the Lost King and whispered a very long prayer. His face shone with sincerity. His Spirituality bloomed. Thulann should have celebrated the knight's reassertion of his beliefs, but a certain quality of Sir Gabriel's demeanor tempered the gladness she felt. She recognized his mannerisms, for she herself had exhibited them before her duel with Bahrok and perhaps when she left Jamark.

Montenegro was praying at the shrine for the last time. His body language and the timbre of his chant suggested a measure of finality. He was completing his affairs. He had conveyed to her one last glance before departing, a look of rich, sad honesty, as if he had no more need of psychological defenses. Brisk thoughts had animated his dark grey eyes.

Then he had walked out of the cathedral. Thulann doubted she would ever see him again.

She blinked and glanced at the petal-flecked bath. Under the surface floated the image of her weary, wizened body. The water blurred her jade skin. Thick steam entwined with wafts of grey hair. She flexed her arms and legs, evoking a tingle that remembered a major healing.

In that gentle moment she pondered a lingering emotion. Of course she was disappointed that she had failed to help Montenegro, but the feeling was simply appeased. He had always been an unreceptive man. Rarely had he ever listened to her. However, in the knight's features she had read a different conclusion altogether. Now that he had beaten her in combat, he was finished with her. He had nothing more to learn.

She had grown to esteem the man. His departure was painful. Again she endured a cold feeling of completion, or worse, rejection.

She closed her eyes and sighed. *My day is quickly drawing to its close.*

A knock rattled the chamber door. A maidservant entered. When the woman laid a note on the vanity, Thulann asked her to hand it over.

After the human departed, the Way Master examined the message. It was sealed with a nondescript imprint. She broke the wax and read: *Meet me at the Shrine of Compassion before dawn. Come armed and ready to travel.—M*

A smile captured her lips.

Shirron Turlogan always took glee in reminding her that she was a profound fool. At that moment she had to agree with him. Why did old women insist on inventing their own obsolescence? In that insecurity, Thulann felt a connection to doddering old crones everywhere. It was as joyous a sensation as she could have wanted.

Many candles were doused with spray as she leapt from the tub, cloaked herself with a towel and considered her traveling equipment. She would need a new staff, of course. She had a great deal of walking yet to do.

The Shrine of Compassion was a tall stone ankh looming in the sleek night rain. The pine forest that surrounded the monument hissed with a wet, needly voice, but the trees provided some shelter from the tempering downpour. In these furtive shadows materialized a black apparition in a cloak and hood, to greet the armored Thulann. Montenegro held out his hand. Within it rested the schematic for Braun's Needle.

She regarded the scroll with trepidation. "Are you surrendering it to me?"

The knight answered, "Indeed I am. Do not feel flattered. The Virtue of Justice requires it."

She bowed and accepted the scroll tube. "Thank you for this, and also for bringing me to the Shepherds tonight. I should prefer not to die in a sewer, if I have any choice about it. Yet unless I am mistaken, you saved my life because you have some enterprise in mind that involves me. Or so your message implied."

"That's not why I saved you. Compassion gave me no choice. I am aligned with the Virtues again." He brushed a handful of rain across his face and sighed. "I have admitted something to myself that I never imagined I would tell you. Yet here it is, to judge as you may. Way Master Thulann, despite your manipulative, patronizing behavior, I know that your intentions are true. I have seen it in the past. I saw you risk your life for it tonight. And in a faithless world I can think of no other quality that might earn my trust. So I tender my apology for every unkind thought and action I have taken against you."

She resisted the urge to smile. "We dwell in dark times, Montenegro. Hardship tries us all. I do not need an apology."

"Take it anyway, dammit. I carried it all the way out here."

She cocked her head. "Quite so. Thank you, then. You are as honorable as I judged you at our first meeting, when I was one eye sharper and you were a proud knight on a Vesper beach. And so we stand together now as we did then, heavily armed and sopping wet. Pray inform an arthritic old woman where we are going from here."

He pointed into the forest. "There's an old house down the path. The mendicants have abandoned it because of the goblins. We can make our plans there."

Thulann held up the scroll tube. "Plans to strike against the Needle?"

"You did offer to help me."

"So I did. I hope you have secured a ship, though. It is a long swim to intercept the Logosian armada, with an ugly storm in between."

"I have transportation that is more than suitable. We must focus on what to do once we get there. To say the least, the odds are stacked against us."

She smirked. "What enemy can repel the two of us together?"

The knight shrugged his cloak tighter and began to walk. "You and I are always losing, Thulann, but at least we're persistent."

The Way Master grimaced. "You have always been candid to a fault. How comforting that you are still reliable."

She followed his phantom shape through the trees until the starless gloom devoured them both. The Shrine of Compassion looked on with its single, blind eye, dampened by the midnight showers.

CHAPTER
13

The Pit and the Eye

Rain brushed the docks of Britain with curtains of steely grey. Though the downpour was cumbersome, still workmen labored in the night to prepare dozens of warships for battle. When Toria saw the urgency in their work, she knew that the Royal Senate had already been warned of Blackthorn's armada. She did not slow her pace.

Under a hooded cloak she wore a bodice and colorful skirt from among the chest of women's clothes Bawdewyn carried on the *Menagerie*. None of the shoes had fit her and so she was barefoot once more. She did not mind. Even in these dire circumstances, the New Britannian mud felt like paradise to her homesick feet. The buildings created familiar, glorious silhouettes in the hissing shower. The clop of horses was magical.

Captain Bawdewyn walked beside her. An oiled overcoat kept the rain from his tall, lean body. Annis the wildcat snaked around his neck, sheltering under the wide brim of his hat. The privateer glanced around the docks and shrugged. "I think we're a little late, Tori. Either these ships are going to meet the Technocrats or they're evacuating the town by sea. I've never seen the fleet all together like this before."

She tightened her cloak against a sweep of wind. "I told you Chamberlain Kavah has allies here, a man named Rictor and a Meer Hunter named Shavade. He was going to contact them with a magic spell. I bet they broke the news to the Senate before I even left Crevasse. That's a relief, hey? I was afraid we'd be caught unprepared."

"It's excellent news. That means we ain't got to rush off to the Senate right now. And across the street I see the Golden Cork, which I've been dying to visit ever since I finished my cask of Vesper Crimson off the coast of Jamark. Come on, let's go pop a bottle worthy of our tongues."

Toria shook her head. "Our tongues can wait. The Senate might know about the armada, but they probably have no idea that Lector Sartorius and Chamberlain Kavah are their allies. It might make a difference."

The sailor wiped rain from his dark face and flicked a drop onto Annis's ear. The ocelot winced. Bawdewyn sighed. "Yeah, I guess you're right. Well, we'll get there quicker in a coach than on foot. I'll see if I can track one down. You get yourself out of this rain, lass." From his pocket he fished a handful of gold coins, which he slapped into her palm. Then he pointed to the wineshop across the lane. "Do me a favor and pick up a bottle of Ravenmoor and a pair of cups. We'll toast the Royal Senate on our way to meet them. We'll look like hell to the senators, so at least we should feel like heaven."

The Golden Cork was crowded with patrons escaping the gloom of the rain. Shorter than most, the minstrel nudged her way inside the packed room and made her way to the counter. Damp body heat enveloped her. As she awaited her turn, a slice of conversation caught her attention.

"You are a heartless glacier of a friend," said one man to another, a few yards away. "I have gallantly divorced myself from the sweet succor of wine, and yet you torment me by obliging vintages more exquisite than we ever partook before! And after so brutal a ride back to the city. I say you are a changed man and I defy you to prove otherwise."

His companion replied, "Every morning I conclude that your histrionics cannot grow worse, and every evening I am made a liar. Your heart has swollen like a goiter. It pushes all reason out of you. Fairfax, I am no different from a month ago. You are the one who has changed. Your thirst vexes you. And presently you are a victim of simple economics. Since one person drinks half the quantity of two, I can afford to purchase wine of twice the quality. Or have you forgotten that it is the stipend from my family that keeps us in this opulent condition?"

"You see? Where is the Jatha of old? He would never have degraded himself by using gold as a weapon against me. Just as I would not dream of questioning his debt to me by pointing out that my skills in the forest have kept us alive on occasions too numerous to number."

"My bellicose friend, I preferred you as a drunkard. You were more rational then. Nor shall I quench your thirst for an argument. For that you must woo your Huntress lover. Judging from her disposition, you and she will loose more quarrels than a broadside of Yewic crossbowmen."

Toria thrust her head between the two men and tossed

back her rain-soaked cowl. Her russet curls tumbled free. "They say rangers are experts at starting fights and Meer are experts at avoiding them. I'd love to see who wins, but the contest might suffocate the room."

Fairfax and Jatha startled for an instant, then laughed and gathered her between them. Their embrace felt almost like family.

The flaxen-haired ranger tapped a kiss on her forehead. "By the cruel Virtues, I thought never to see your freckled splendor again! Have you come home at last from the noseless barrens of Jukaran, or are you simply dazzling the city with a brief yet pulchritudinous visit?"

She giggled and wrinkled her brow. "You're as unintelligible as ever! And all the more appealing for it. No, I'm home to stay this time, my friends. Destiny must favor my return if it's led me to the two of you."

Jatha grinned and wrapped his arm around her shoulders. "Destiny has a powerful call, but the love of good wine is more compelling still. Which is why we have this shop to thank for our paths crossing again."

She snuggled into the Meer. "Indeed we do. But what's this I overheard about Fairfax giving up drink? I would have thought a Skara Brae merchant would sooner give up slug weights."

Jatha chuckled. "These days my moss-bearded companion derives his stupor from a woman's lips rather than his own. He abstains on the assumption that it makes him more charming. In my estimation his appeal has fallen like a meteor, implausible as that may sound."

Fairfax countered, "Wizards shutter themselves from the storms of the heart and so do not understand the dips and swells of unfettered passion. Blocks of ice with hats and wands, that's all they really are. But we know where real magic comes from, eh, Toria? So tell me, what has become of mighty Venduss and his hold on your tempestuous heart?"

She glanced at the bottle of wine in Jatha's hand. "I left all the Juka behind in Jukaran. I'm exhausted from that place. Let's talk about New Britannia instead. I have an errand to run at the Royal Senate and after that, I've got two years of news to catch up on. Not the least of which is this business of Fairfax's beloved! Many a heart will be broken by that news."

"None more so than my own," said the ranger, then glanced at the doorway. A small commotion stirred outside. "Strange," he shrugged.

Jatha muttered, "What is it?"

"Perhaps I am drunk from the air in this place. I swore I just heard a wildcat scream."

"What?" Toria jolted from the two men's arms and cleaved through the crowd in the wineshop. On the rainy street outside she discovered a group of townspeople clustered around a lamppost. Atop the tall structure was a small, sinewy shape. In the glow of the lamp Annis the ocelot looked ragged from her limp, drenched fur. She flashed long fangs at her pursuers.

Toria whirled around to scan the area, but saw no sign of Bawdewyn. She tried to push through the townsfolk under the lamppost, but rough elbows jabbed her off.

One of the men bellowed, "That beast will fetch a month's wage in the court!"

"Someone find a net!" shouted another.

Toria cried out, "No! It belongs to Captain Bawdewyn!" When the group ignored her, she threw her cloak over one shoulder, unsheathed her static sword and carved a swath through the air. The electrified blade crackled brightly with every raindrop that struck it. The townsfolk turned to face her.

"Back away!" she growled, stepping closer. "I'm taking the cat myself."

Several of the men crossed their arms. One of them smirked, "Look at the toy this little girl has! That may fetch a decent price as well, don't you think?"

She lunged forward and barked, "You'll need the money to pay a healer!" Most of the men fell back from the whirling of her sword, but two of them rushed her. She dove between them, tumbled on cobblestones and swatted at them. A burst of static charge flattened one of the men. The other one grabbed her arm. She twisted from his grasp and boxed his nose, then slashed her blade toward his head. At the last instant she changed her stroke to slice apart the man's high-crowned hat. It fell into two smoking pieces.

He yelped and scrambled away.

Fairfax and Jatha burst out of the Golden Cork. The ranger drew his sword and yelled, "Anyone who attacks that girl shall regret it!"

Jatha held him back and motioned to the crowd. "I think the point is already made."

The townsfolk gave Toria a wide berth as she tossed her blade into its scabbard and sprang onto the lamppost. With ease she scaled to the top. Annis was relieved to see her and used fierce claws to grip the minstrel's bodice.

Toria held the animal close as she dropped to the ground. She scowled at the bystanders. "This cat belongs to a tall man with an overcoat and a buccaneer's hat! Where did he go? What happened to Captain Bawdewyn?"

A woman pointed toward the docks. "A bunch of sailors jumped him! Musta been fifteen of them. He killed two before he went down. They dragged him off that way."

"Dammit!" Toria dropped the ocelot into the bowl of her doffed hood, then ran toward Jatha and Fairfax. Her voice cracked as she begged, "Please help me! My friend has dangerous enemies!"

Jatha flattened his ears. "For you we'll strike down Blackthorn himself!"

They dashed toward the boardwalks, where endless masts swayed against the drizzling sky. Workmen pointed out where the gang had taken their captive.

They were too late. The small ship headed for the mouth of the bay at full sail. Toria screamed, "No!"

She recognized the vessel. It belonged to Mister Chase, the right hand of Anzo, the Pirate King. Bawdewyn had mentioned that Anzo wanted his head. Toria could not shake the feeling that she had led the privateer to this fate, because she had demanded to be taken to Britain.

Jatha peered out at the ship. "Do you want me to stop it?"

Her heart pounded. "Yes!"

The Meer magician swirled his arms in a dance-like gesture. A crack of silence split the air, as if the raindrops stuttered in their descent.

The clouds roiled. A pillar of lightning lashed down from the sky and slammed the two-masted vessel. On every warship along the docks, sailors and workers looked up in amazement. A roar of thunder shook the harbor.

The deafening sound echoed all the way to the center of

the city, where knights and lords kept their lavish townhouses.

A film of smoke drifted away from Chase's ship. When they could see the craft again, they knew it was undamaged. It picked up speed away from the shore.

Jatha grunted. "That ship has magical defenses. Your friend's enemy has impressive resources." He glanced at Toria, though the girl had dashed farther down a pier to get a closer look.

Fairfax gaped at his companion as they jogged to catch up. "No more impressive than yourself, you rabbit-eared fleas' nest! When did you learn to call lightning that potent?"

"If you had bothered to look up from your bootless womanizing, you would realize that I've been studying with Mistress Aurora quite heavily for several months. We've been preparing for the war."

The ranger narrowed his eyebrows. "War? You? I did not realize your allegiance to this land extended so deeply. Your kind is supposed to remain neutral. I thought you helped me in my duties out of simple friendship."

The wizard's eye sparkled. "So I do, but crusades are contagious whether we admit it or not. I have seen too much suffering on our travels to turn away from this war. And Logosian technology insults every precept of sorcery. However, until a few weeks ago I was committed only to supporting the House of the Griffin, not to joining the battle myself. Do you know what decided me to become an active participant?"

Fairfax opened an irreverently joyful smile. "Shavade of Arjun and her forbidden magic crystal."

"The very beguiler herself! If other Meer are nosing into this conflict, ones powerful enough to obtain those ancient secrets, then I feel no shame in my own involvement. There is wickedness afoot and I cannot root it out as a bystander."

The blond human shook his head. "We have a nobler crusade at this moment. Our friend is in distress. Toria! What can we do to help you?"

Gazing out at Chase's fleeing ship, the girl was rocked by a shudder of despair. The sensation had become familiar. She had felt it when Thulann and Venduss died, and again when she failed to kill Pikas. She almost let it pass unresisted.

Then her fists clenched atop a weather-cracked post, her face twisted into a scowl.

"Let's gather the crew of the *Menagerie* before they're lost to the taverns. We're going to rescue Captain Bawdewyn!"

Fairfax remarked, "I thought you had an urgent appointment with the Royal Senate."

"I'll write them a note! I'm tired of losing. This is an enemy I know. If I learned anything among the Juka, it's that your worst enemies come from home, not abroad. Let's show Anzo who his worst enemies are!"

Jatha smacked the girl's shoulder. "Say what you will about the Juka, but I like the fighter they've turned you into! Tell us your plan, Toria. We're with you to the end. Your best allies come from home, as well, and you've returned home to us at last."

The ocean was a field of pearlescent waves a thousand feet below Thulann. High winds thundered against her body. A cloak protected her from the sting of the rushing air, but the constant pressure thumped her like fists. She squinted her one eye protectively.

The carriole was a dark streak in the morning sky. Montenegro controlled the flying machine. The Way Master rode behind him. She clung to the saddle with her legs and studied the mood of the weather. Though the clouds overhead looked dark and angry, the rain had finally broken apart. They had several dry hours ahead. Unfortunately, the hurricane on the southern horizon looked fiercer than anything she had witnessed in her long lifetime, but that was a danger they anticipated. Braun's Needle was the greatest weapon Blackthorn had ever devised. They intended to destroy it, even at the cost of their lives.

The black wall of the storm front suggested that the latter outcome was not unlikely.

What now concerned the old Juka, however, was something more immediate. Their altitude made her stomach wring. She could not shake the memories of her flight over Garron. With white knuckles she grabbed Montenegro's shoulders and shouted into his ear, "Did your Technocrat spy mention how we can tell if the levitant is almost gone?"

The knight called back, "No! The machine is supposed to drop slowly, though, and it will float. Then we use these." He patted the wooden oars lashed to the side of the carriole.

"Have you ever landed one of these contraptions?"

"Not really."

"Take it from me, it is neither slow nor painless. Perhaps your spy meant for you to fall out of the sky? I know it would be a relief to the Logosians if you were to vanish into the ocean."

"You would make a very good point, except that the spy doesn't know I took the carriole. I don't want her schemes to interfere with this mission. No one knows what we're doing except the two of us."

"You risk your life without glory? It is a testament to the Virtue of Humility."

"Watch carefully. I am a creature of Virtue now. That is why I returned the scroll to you."

She squeezed the leather tube strapped to her belt. "That is a feeble sacrifice, since we go together to face the Needle. If you truly want to serve Justice, you will deliver that spy to me when we are finished."

Montenegro waved a hand dismissively. "I have other plans for her, Thulann. Do not fear. She shall receive her lawful reward. I promise you that."

Thulann sighed as she ducked her face behind him, to dodge the wind again. "Laws count for little in the midst of a war. The honor of soldiers is all that matters. Thank the Great Mother for knights and noble warriors." Of course, he could not hear her in the bellowing wind, nor did she want to continue the conversation. Her stomach had not yet settled. The time had come to focus on her body. She summoned a Way Master's trance and lost herself in the mysticism of the flesh.

Sand and scrub grass whispered around Toria's ankles. The spring air was cool and wet. The sun threw a bolt of afternoon warmth across the island of Buccaneer's Den. Farther south the sky blackened. Pine trees capered in the rising winds.

Toria peeked over the jags of a cliff and observed the quiet port below. The Den was a vast junkyard of flotsam collected into the shape of a town. The carcasses of ships were overturned to form buildings. Shanties were fashioned of driftwood and stones. Sometimes it appeared that a lake of shallow mud was all that held the settlement together.

The sight of the Den conjured ghosts from Toria's memory. This was her only real home until two years ago. In the intervening time she did not long to come back, but rather she listened with fascination to its subtle echoes. The Den lived inside her.

Strange, then, that it seemed so small and decrepit now. Perhaps it had lost some of its ego over the course of two long years.

The filthy streets were nearly empty. The few visible townsfolk busied themselves preparing for the hurricane. Only five ships rested in the harbor, and of these Chase's alone showed signs of activity.

Jatha pressed flat his ears as he drew beside her. "I thought this place was a haven for pirates. Where are all the ships?"

"Fled around the cape to New Jhelom. The size of that fleet in Britannia Bay must have scared the chocolate out of them. Pirates hate a standup fight."

"Then who do those ships down there belong to?"

"Privateers, like Bawdewyn. Enemies of Anzo. Their crews are probably dead and their captains . . ." She swallowed. "Well, they're chained up inside that rocky hill on the east side of town. Anzo's fortress is a bunch of caves down there. I don't want to think about what those poor captains have been through."

He patted her shoulder. "We'll get Bawdewyn out of there. I can see now why we couldn't sail into the harbor. That's a lot of artillery around the entrance." He pointed to a barrage of catapults, trebuchets, ballistas and other heavy weapons that guarded the narrow mouth of the bay. From a distance some of them appeared Logosian in origin. "It will be gratifying to see what happens when they're turned on that hovel of a city. The *Menagerie*'s crew must be closing in on them by now. We need to hurry into town. If we're not under cover by the time they start firing, we're liable to find out how much chocolate we've got in us!"

A day had passed by the time Thulann and Montenegro reached the edge of the hurricane. The sun was a patch of lighter clouds overhead. The levitant had endured longer than they expected, perhaps because they had maintained a steady altitude, but the faltering pitch of the flying machine portended the boundary of their flight.

So far they had spotted no Technocrat scout vessels. They had hoped to overpower a small crew and hijack the craft to take them to the Needle. But the sputtering demise of their levitant extinguished that possibility. And so with dour faces they used their remaining moments of altitude to pursue their next plan of action.

When the carriole crossed inside the storm, a hammer of wind smashed them senseless. Thulann clung to the flying machine as it rolled and careened in the torrent. The hurricane sucked away her hearing and her balance. She could not tell if Montenegro was conscious. She did not know if they were rising or falling. All of her will focused upon cleaving to the saddle of the carriole, though she had little reason to think that it mattered.

So violently did they tumble that Thulann's bones began to protest. Her limbs jarred against the metal vehicle. Her head snapped back and forth until she jammed it against Montenegro's body.

She realized the knight was moving. She peered through the howling rain and spotted his hand on a lever. Gently he eased it forward.

He was lowering the carriole to the surface.

Giant wave crests rolled beneath them, like ponderous hillsides marching across a nightmare landscape. As the carriole dropped lower, the wave peaks sheltered them from the wind. The respite would be brief. Montenegro sat up quickly and slapped a vial into her hand. "Drink!" he bellowed.

She nearly bit the vial in half. The potion tingled through her chest as an enormous bluff of seawater leapt overhead. With inches to spare she dove into the water. The mad ocean gulped down Thulann and Montenegro and the carriole and all sense of direction and every remaining glimmer of light.

The black, cold throat of the sea pressed against her from all sides. Its titanic maw growled and huffed. She held tightly to the rope around her waist. With a flinch she opened her mouth and let the salty water pour into her windpipe. Her lungs screamed. Her body convulsed. With a quick trance she resisted the rising panic.

The swimming potion coursed through her and the panic subsided. She could breathe the seawater, though her mind could barely comprehend it.

She tugged on the rope. From the other end Montenegro tugged back. Hand-over-hand they reeled themselves together. The touch of another person in that black abyss chased away some of Thulann's animal terror. She sensed the same reaction from the knight.

A blue light appeared. Montenegro held a sealed spark lantern next to a glass compass. They agreed on its reading and then swam due south, toward the eye of the storm that cradled Blackthorn's armada. Thulann guessed that the wind had blown them two or three miles inside the hurricane's perimeter. That gave them at least ten miles to traverse. Though the two warriors had donned the lightest possible armor, and the swimming potions imparted great strength and stamina, the weight of their weapons posed a constant threat of sinking. The likelihood of losing their bearing forced them to be vigilant. And neither Thulann nor Montenegro was certain how long the potions would last.

Ever since her first trip to New Britannia, Thulann had hated the sea. With each subsequent journey it became a crueler enemy. This afternoon, engulfed by its gurgling maw, Thulann kicked it with relentless vigor as she would any other opponent.

For more than sixty years she had held time itself at bay. By comparison the ocean was a childish bully. She could beat it for one mile more. Just for one mile more.

The thump of a bowstring kissed the gloomy air. An arrow whispered down the length of a dim stone corridor. Dust spiraled at the passing of the missile. It struck a man at the far end.

The guard fell with a soft clatter. Fairfax motioned down the hallway. "After you, Captain Toria."

The minstrel grinned as she darted through the bowels of Anzo's fortress. The caves were hewn from the sandstone of a broad hillside. Small grates pierced the ceiling, admitting shafts of glittering sunlight. She avoided the beams by instinct.

The guard was unconscious but not quite dead. Toria left him to Fairfax and Jatha, who followed close behind her. She turned her attention on the wooden door that terminated the corridor. An embedded iron lock secured the heavy latch. With a pick she probed the mechanism. She smirked. Compared to Technocrat locks, this rusty contraption was barely a nibble. In seconds it clanked open.

Jatha stared at the hallway behind them. His ears perked high on his head. "This makes me nervous. Shouldn't there be more resistance?"

Toria tested the hinges of the door. They squeaked a bit. She paused. "Not really. I told you, I came in here lots of times when I was a kid. That collapsed side tunnel got us past most of the guards. Besides, half of Anzo's thugs have left the island, and half of the ones who stayed are trying to recapture the artillery from Bawdewyn's crew. There's not many ears left to hear us. If we're careful, we can pull this off."

"Careful and fast," added Fairfax. "What's beyond that door?"

"An antechamber to the prison cell. There's probably three or four guards in there. Once we're past them we can free Bawdewyn and whoever else is inside. Getting out will be easier. There'll be a lot more of us. The guards won't be able to hold us back."

After a brief regrouping, Toria shoved open the door and tumbled inside. A pair of men in studded leathers leapt from their chairs in shock. Each of them flashed a loaded crossbow. Toria dropped one with a thrown dagger. The other yowled in horror when the rock wall thrust out tentacles. Jatha commanded the spell to entwine the guard and squeeze. The man passed out seconds later.

The minstrel pulled stray curls back into her ponytail. When her breath returned she glanced at the wizard. "No matter how many times I see that, it always sends a chill through me."

The Meer covered his nose with both hands. "It's far less disturbing than the condition of this prison. Do they ever clean this place?"

Fairfax examined an iron-banded door on the far side of the guard chamber. The latch was fixed with a padlock. "It's not supposed to be pleasant, Jatha. And I suspect it's worse yet behind here. Toria, would you care to perform your own magic?"

"Stand back," she answered as she approached the cell door. "Fairfax, search those guards for the key to the outer door. Lock it and watch it close, hey? Jatha, can you get ready to heal some prisoners? They're probably in a nasty state. Let me do this lock." She popped it open with ease. "Hold your noses," she warned as she shoved on the heavy door.

It opened with a woody croak. The prison exhaled a ghastly, cloying breath. Toria's eyes and throat stung. She peered through a damp murk, trying to resolve an image by the light of a single pillar of sunlight. The sight was appalling. The cell was a vast, recessed pit of mud and filth. Carpets of vermin scurried away from the entrance. Less animated were the silhouettes of the prisoners, who stirred with sluggish dread. Innumerable chains shifted and clinked. As her vision adjusted Toria picked out details. Over a hundred men and women lay on a bed of moldy sewage. All of them were shackled to the ground. Some of them were bound by the neck, their faces barely above the surface of the muck. Others were encased in sadistic contrivances of wood and iron. None of them seemed to possess the strength or the will to even moan.

Her stomach reeled. Two years ago she might have run away. But her experiences with Thulann rendered that notion unthinkable. Instead she conjured a hearty breath and sang:

Now pull, bully boys, and I'll tell you a story
'Bout the wee little minstrel they call Tiny Tori!
Though her shape was a nibble, her mouth was a feast!
But she never had nothin' on Bawdewyn the Beast!

From the shadows of the pit came a lone, feeble answer:

So hey-holly-hoy-o, now pull, bully boy-os!
'Twas never another like Bawdewyn the Beast!

"By the Virtues," rasped Bawdewyn from somewhere below, "tell me they haven't got you, too, lass."

She ground her teeth and forced a smile. "This time we've got them! I'm here to turn you out. If anyone down there has the strength to pick a lock, call out your name. You can help me free the others. Your ships are in the harbor and there's no one barring the way. Let's spit in Anzo's face and laugh as we leave!"

The cheer that rose from the dismal cell was pathetic and uplifting at the same time. She snatched Jatha's wrist and bounded down the steps, anxious to get started.

Thulann considered drawing her sword, but opted for a knife instead. She saw no sense in losing the larger blade to the deep. The heavy bowels of the ocean surged around her. She and Montenegro held fast to the rope, with only a yard of slack between them. A curtain of greenish illumination tumbled overhead, the glow of the surface, showing them vague hints of the creature that stalked the chilling abyss.

The Technocrats called the mechanical monster a clockwork leviathan, though it bore little resemblance to that legendary sea serpent. Its shape reminded Thulann of a carriage-size crustacean with a thick, riveted shell. A pair of giant claws dangled from its body. Propellers chugged through the viscous sea. When the automaton's shadow vanished in the inky depths, its metal components squeaked through liquid distortion, hinting at its location below.

Thulann and Montenegro treaded water underneath the moaning hurricane. In silence they waited for the creature to make its move. Then a mountainous form heaved up from below and a huge claw lunged at them. They slackened the rope and pushed away from each other. The pincer clamped between them.

The rope did not sever, but stayed taut. Thulann gripped the knife in her teeth and pulled herself back toward her companion. When she could almost discern the knight's shape, the entire ocean lurched.

The clockwork leviathan was building speed while holding the rope that connected them. The two warriors dragged behind it like snared fish. Montenegro paralleled Thulann on the opposite side of the mechanical claw. She glimpsed a flicker of light. He was checking his compass. She fumbled through the gloom until she located his hand. He squeezed her palm three times. Three was the pre-arranged code for *all is well*.

The monster was taking them in the direction of the hurricane's eye. Did it think they were captives? Corpses? Flotsam? She could not know the creature's thoughts. She only prayed that they arrived at their destination before the swimming potions expired. She did not want them to drown. In the open air she might have a chance to announce Montenegro to the Blessed Halls of Honor; under the ocean she could not sing. She wondered if anyone else knew the man he had become in the last few days. Though he claimed glory meant little to him now, Thulann did not want him to die unheralded. History deserved better than that, and so did Montenegro.

"My my, this is an unpleasant find. Someone has broken into my jail. I would chastise my guards, but I believe they're all dead."

The words came from a man at the door and sprang across the murky air of the prison cell. In a flash Toria dove through the muddy filth, hiding against the pit wall where she was invisible from the doorway. She was confident she had not been seen. Quietly she unsheathed her static sword.

The voice had belonged to Mister Chase. The immaculate man was not much older than herself, but occupied a coveted position in Anzo's organization. The deadliest henchmen answered to him. A large band of those cutthroats now crowded into the cell, forming ranks around the doorway. Toria made out spears and crossbows from their long, looming shadows.

So far she had unshackled half of the prisoners. Some of them started forward, but halted in the face of the well-armed ambush.

A body careened over Toria's head and splashed into the mud. Jatha leapt from the shadows and gathered up the bloody form. "Fairfax!" he shouted, jostling the limp ranger. When no answer came, the wizard conjured a ball of white light and cascaded it over his companion's wounds. Fairfax sputtered and sat up.

"Damn, it stinks in here," he grumbled.

Mister Chase called out, "We haven't seen many wizards down here! Mostly we kill them outright, because they're nothing but work for us. So I propose, my Meer friend, that you not cast any more spells. It would be a shame to puncture you before we get a chance to talk."

A tall figure rose from the pit floor. Captain Bawdewyn had been stripped to his breeches. His dark skin glistened with muck. Jatha's healing had erased his wounds, but the pain of his capture was evident in his scowl. "Don't kill them, Chase! Shoot me if you're hungry for it. They're here on my account."

"Yes, I know that. Your crew has seized the harbor artillery and turned it against us. A quarter of the town is in flames. We'll drive them off in good time, of course, but it is you who must pay for the damage."

Bawdewyn snapped, "You can tell Anzo to talk to my ghost, 'cause I'll die before he sees another copper from me!"

"Whatever suits you, Captain. Though I assure you it will be a long, long time before you perish. Did you know it is possible to torture a man for years before his body gives out? But it's only worthwhile if the victim offers no alternative."

Fairfax wagged the mud from his hands as he stood. "Jatha, who is this officious prinker?"

Bawdewyn grumbled, "Watch him careful, friend. He's Anzo's favorite pet."

Jatha flattened his ears. "He's a dead man if he threatens us again."

Chase's henchmen growled their displeasure. Tension swelled in the room. Toria knew it would break apart in seconds. The time to act was now. She extended her arm and hurled her static sword out of the pit. When it struck the side wall, a burst of sparks pierced the darkness.

In that moment of alarm she leapt up and rolled over the lip of the pit. Like a bolt she vaulted behind Chase and pressed a knife to his throat. "Back off or he's skewered!" she wailed at the startled thugs.

The henchmen whirled their crossbows toward her, but hesitated to take aim. She pinned Chase's arm behind his back with a powerful Jukan hold. His right hand was missing, she noticed with surprise. A knot of bandages capped his sundered wrist.

She held him more tightly. Her knife drew a welt from the man's skin.

"Be wary of tricks!" shouted Bawdewyn.

"Marry me, Toria!" laughed Fairfax.

"Everyone shut up!" she commanded, "except you, Chase. Tell your men to throw down their weapons. All these prisoners are leaving with me."

Mister Chase lifted his chin to ease the pressure on his neck. In his spotless white silk he sustained unflinching dignity. "That won't do. If that is my only choice then you may as well slit my throat, because Anzo will do much worse to me if I release these people. Oh, and Toria, might I add that it is a pleasure to see you again."

"I'm not joking, Chase!"

"Of course you aren't. You have succeeded in getting my attention. Now you must decide what you will do with it."

Toria cursed under her breath. She realized he was not bluffing. Anzo was a businessman and Chase's reason for living was to protect the Pirate King's interests.

Thulann's voice rang in her head: *Creativity is the foundation of victory.*

Her thoughts raced. She steadied her tone and said, "Here is my proposition. There's going to be a naval battle. Put these prisoners on as many ships as they can crew. Send them to help the New Britannian fleet."

"What good does that afford me?"

"The Senate will be indebted to Anzo. That's bound to be worth a few months of relief from Admiral Duarte, and you risk nothing for it. If these prisoners die in battle, it's no great loss, hey?"

Mister Chase sniffed. "It is an intriguing proposal. But Anzo will want more."

"What more?"

"Salvage rights to any Technocrat ships these prisoners defeat."

"I can only ask. Admiral Duarte may listen to me. He was very taken with my old mistress, Thulann of Garron."

"I know. That is why I mentioned it. And yet there is still something missing from your offer, Toria. I am not quite convinced."

In the dark of the pit Captain Bawdewyn stepped forward. Chase's henchmen bore their crossbows at him. He sneered back. "Lass, tell him about the assassin who's hidden on board that Logosian warship."

Toria squinted. "You mean Pikas? He's riding Braun's Needle with a sorcerer from Yew."

She felt Chase stiffen. "Are you referring to Pikas of Enclave?"

"I saw him myself. I almost ended up on the point of his sword. You know him?"

"We have broken bread, and other things."

Bawdewyn crossed his arms. "Turn us loose and I'll bring you the assassin's head. I give you my word."

Chase snorted. "You have many debts you do not intend to pay."

"Those were extortion! This is an honest trade. You know I'm good for it, damn you!"

Toria nudged her blade against Chase's neck. "Do we have a bargain or is your blood going to be the first to spill?"

The silk-clad businessman smiled. "Pikas will kill you, but the attempt shall be worthwhile. Very well. We have a bargain. Break it and you will never know peace." He glanced at his henchmen. "Gentlemen, remove the quarrels from your crossbows. Help these prisoners outside. I'll have munitions delivered for two ships. Do not tarry. The storm is almost upon us." He swallowed. "Toria, the contract is struck. Kindly take the knife from my throat. Have a look at my right hand while you're back there."

She broke the nervous tension in her limbs, then stepped away. Chase lifted the stump of his right forearm. Something metallic glinted in the bandages.

The minstrel looked closer. The tip of a steel arrow protruded from the wrappings, of the sort launched from Technocrat bolt-throwers. Chase unwound a portion of the bandage to reveal just such a weapon strapped to his cleaved arm.

Toria blanched. He could have killed her at any moment, but had held out for a better profit.

He held the barbed missile close to his face and opened a cold grin. "Do give my fondest regards to Pikas when you see him. If I am going to mount his head for a trophy, he may as well be smiling."

She exited the filthy prison in silence, clutching her chest without realizing it.

*　　*　　*

As the clockwork leviathan hauled her through the ocean at brutal, churning speeds, Thulann found herself starting to gag and cough. Her lungs felt swollen. The murky water seemed to press against her skull.

The swimming potion had nearly run its course. Unless she reached the surface in a few minutes, she would drown.

She fought the current to grab hold of Montenegro, then tugged his belt twice, the signal to surface. The knight did not move, except to sway limply in the salty, rushing water. He had already fallen unconscious.

Thulann focused on her body once more. Her chest stilled. The action conserved air. Breathing techniques were fundamental to the Way, but never had she expected to use them in such a novel fashion.

She worked a solid grip onto Montenegro's wrist. With her other hand she drew her dagger and cut the rope in half.

The ocean hammered them to a stop. The clockwork monster streaked off into the gloom. Thulann could not determine which direction was up, so she drew a healing potion from her shoulder sack and thumbed off the cork. The little stopper wriggled away. She gulped the dark cloud that issued from the vial and then swam after the cork. Montenegro was a lifeless weight dragging behind.

For an eternity she chased the cork until it outpaced her. She continued on what she presumed was the proper course. Her torso began to hurt. Even the techniques of the Way could not maintain her once that last breath was gone.

Then a giant roared up from the depths. The mechanical leviathan had returned. When it bashed against her Montenegro wrenched from her grasp. She battled the creature's roiling wake and plunged after the knight's fading silhouette.

She caught him as the monster rumbled close again. Her vision started to sparkle and dim. She only had seconds left.

Her gloved hand found Starfell and whisked it from the scabbard. As the leviathan charged she slashed at its steel claw. To her surprise the blade passed easily through the viscous water. The sword clanged against the creature's arm, which threw up a cascade of sparks and bubbles.

Thulann swam after the bubbles and sucked a few into her mouth. Her lungs devoured the hot, welcome air. When the monster lurched up again she kicked its riveted armor to propel herself into a spin. A deafening propeller chopped the sea less than a foot away. She jammed Starfell into the mechanism, which shredded itself against the enchanted blade.

The leviathan emitted an eerie, metallic squeal and listed aside for an instant. Thulann did not waste the moment. She pumped her legs frantically, hauling her limp companion toward a cluster of lights above.

They broke the surface. She chewed a deep breath from the air. The wounded leviathan did not give immediate pursuit, and so she paused to survey their surroundings. The ocean waves rolled but not in mountainous peaks. The darkening sky had a pale green cast. No wind swept the sea. The calm was almost unnatural.

They had reached the eye of the hurricane.

Dozens of armored boats tossed in the waves around them. The clouds were dotted with Logosian airships. A colossal black shape loomed overhead, throwing bolts of lightning in all directions like the spokes of an impossible wheel. The sound of it rattled her old bones.

So that's Braun's Needle, she thought. For such an ugly monstrosity, it had an awesome, even majestic presence. She imagined the Technocrats must be very proud of the accomplishment. It surely meant devastation to both Jukaran and New Britannia. And so the thought of destroying it kindled a new fire inside her. Her fatigue receded. She pressed the water from Montenegro's lungs until the knight hacked and flailed. Then she emptied another healing potion into his mouth, collected him under one arm and swam for the nearest Technocrat vessel.

There had to be a way to get up to the Needle. She intended to find it or perish in the attempt.

CHAPTER
14

Black Sword, Black Heart

The flying carriage soared upward from the tossing sea. The vehicle resembled the horse-drawn variety except for a levitant tank bolted to the roof and movable vanes where the wheels ought to be. Suited mainly for vertical travel, the air carriage was one of many that transported Technocrat officers between the surface vessels and the airships high above. Only their arc lamps were visible in the night sky. The activity was routine and drew little attention from the other Logosians. It was an ideal arrangement for surreptitious travel.

The interior of the carriage was designed to accommodate officers, with a small writing desk and a collection of drafting tools. A spark lantern buzzed overhead. Thulann disregarded these amenities. Nervously she monitored the control levers. Though Braun's Needle was a giant target above them, they had to reach it without drawing attention to themselves. That required a steady course. The slain pilot in the corner gave them no assistance.

Across the desk Montenegro unfurled the schematic for the Needle's primary weapon. "You can see where Mistress

Aurora made notes on the diagram. Here's the main pole, which she's labeled as the 'sowing tower.' These three tanks are 'reagent urns.' And this big contraption in the center is the 'storm engine.' If I read this diagram correctly, that's where we can shut the whole thing down."

"Does she explain how we might accomplish that? Do not let my flying experience fool you. I am probably less conversant than you in Logosian technology. I doubt Braun's Needle has a lever marked 'off.'"

The knight formed a half-smirk. "I have never met a Technocrat machine that could resist Starfell's attentions. I prefer to kill it like we would any other beast, by stabbing it in a tender spot."

"I see the simple elegance of your plan. Except, of course, that Technocrat machines enjoy rather explosive deaths."

"Then so shall we." He chuckled. "Your passing will be a sad day for Clan Kumar. Venduss will long for you when he becomes chieftain. In my own case, I believe poor little Toria was the only person who would have missed me. Maybe she'll sing me a song in the next world."

The cabin listed slightly. The Way Master nudged a control stem. The carriage righted itself and continued to rise toward the looming, black Needle. "Toria awaits us in the Great Hall of Honor. I have no doubt she is a popular attraction. But you do yourself an injustice, Montenegro. I believe your cousin, Lady Aria, may shed a tear for your demise."

He winced. "She has no love. She gives poison in its place."

"You are wrong. Before you scowl at me, listen to an old woman whose hours are numbered. I heard your conversation with Aria in the sewers. I know real affection when I see it. She is true. This scroll proves it." She tapped the diagram.

Montenegro sat up. "Why do you say that?"

"Because this scroll could make the difference between victory and defeat. She may have ensured the downfall of the Technocrats. And she is a Technocrat herself, is she not? The very spy you stole from me at Ruhn? To strike down her own armada for the sake of devotion to you—I call that the act of a true heart."

He growled a sigh and rubbed his face. "Little point in denying it now. Yes, she is that spy, or once was, at least. She claims to have forsaken Blackthorn for me, though it's difficult to believe. And this"—he thumbed the scroll—"is but a thimble of water against an inferno that I inadvertently set."

The old Juka kept her eyes on the controls. "You once asked me how the Way advises a man who has been stabbed in the back. Here is the best answer. The Way instructs us to find beauty in all things. There is nothing under the sky more beautiful than one person's devotion to another. It grants honor through forgiveness. It plucks glory from defeat. In the past month I have learned these things anew. Remember them when you think of your faux cousin, Riona."

Montenegro stared out the window. The storm was a misty grey wall surrounding them. He murmured, "Her name is Raveka. And you presume far too much."

The Way Master bowed her head. "You are correct. I am old and maudlin. Please forgive me."

The carriage soared close to the massive bulk of the Needle. Both of them attended the vehicle's levers. Cautiously they maneuvered away from the landing bays where soldiers and crewmen greeted newcomers. Instead they angled underneath the huge airship. The levitant tank on the roof bumped a giant steering vane that hung from the bottom of the vessel. Montenegro held fast the controls to keep them steady.

Thulann kicked open the carriage door and climbed out. The drop to the ocean was high enough to bring sweat even to her callused palms. She found handholds between the slatted planks of wood that formed the surface of the vane. Quickly she climbed. The wind endeavored to dislodge her, but after a few minutes she reached the top. The mast-length vane protruded from a cluster of immense gears inside an iron cage. She secured a perch among the sturdy beams and tugged on the rope around her waist.

Moments later the rope tugged back. She braced herself. Twenty feet below, Montenegro appeared in the door of the wobbling air carriage. He reached inside the cabin, sabotaged the controls, then leapt out. The flying carriage toppled down, shrinking to a tiny mote before vanishing in a speck of white water.

Montenegro dangled on the other end of Thulann's rope. He braced his feet against the wooden vane and pulled himself up, walking on the vertical surface. By the time he clasped her hand he seemed eager to stand on the solid iron beams. They hurried away from the whistling breeze, deeper into the mechanical bowels of Braun's Needle.

The warship comprised its own hurricane of steam and smoke and thundering metal. They headed for the center, navigating a tight, sweltering labyrinth whose walls were made of heaving gears and clanging pipes and chains that hammered a staccato rhythm. Their gloves smoked from the heat of the beams they gripped. Choking steam penetrated their armor and squeezed their tired bodies. Each warrior could see the other as little more than a stir of motion in the dense, clutching air. Thulann found the ocean itself to be less oppressive. But she willed herself to press on, side-by-side with the New Britannian knight.

From the sultry murk appeared several more shapes: a crew of workmen, startled from their chores. The Way Master loosed her new, oaken staff from the strap across her back. The butt of the pole smacked a Juka in the face and another in his leather-clad stomach. The men dropped. Montenegro's response was less humane, as Starfell cut through the two remaining workers in a flurry of blood and screams. He examined the fallen men as Thulann scouted ahead.

When she was convinced no others had escaped, she returned to find Montenegro with his ear pressed against a vertical conduit. He pulled back and thumped the copper pipe with his finger. "Listen."

She raked a handful of drenched, grey hair from her face and laid a pointed ear on the metal. Crackling noises stirred the liquid inside. She turned to her companion and squinted.

"Lightning," he explained, "and magical in origin, not mechanical. I know the difference." He motioned upward, where the conduit ascended through a smoke-black scaffolding. "There's a battle somewhere above us. At the other end of this pipe is a sorcerer. I intend to bet my life on it."

Abruptly Thulann felt a sting in her scalp. An arc of electricity sprang from the copper and bit her. The pipe rattled in its mounts. She scratched her singed head. "It must be the Pact of Four. Their agents seek the same destination as we do. How courteous of them to show us the way."

The knight grumbled, "When this hellish contraption is

disabled, perhaps we can return the favor and show them the way out. I know several graveyards that would welcome them." He sheathed his enchanted sword and began to climb. Though her bad leg had begun to ache, Thulann followed close behind.

They emerged onto a wide catwalk. The corpses of armored Logosian soldiers were draped all around them. "The trail is fresh," noted Montenegro.

The catwalk led into a riveted wall. Brilliant flashes danced within. Montenegro started forward, but Thulann grabbed his shoulder. "We have more insistent business in the other direction."

She pointed out the five more Logosian soldiers who jogged toward them on the catwalk. They wore kinetic plate armor and steel kite shields. In their hands were short spears for close fighting. The tips of the weapons sparkled with static charge, in the same fashion as Toria's looted sword.

Thulann readied her staff again. Montenegro gripped Starfell with both hands. The Logosians saw the threat and charged in a tight formation.

With only yards separating the intruders and the soldiers, the two soldiers in the lead jumped high into the air. Thulann recognized the offensive tactic as distinctive of the elite Janissars. The leaping assault gave them a tactical and psychological edge.

She also knew how to counter it. Despite her game leg she hurled herself up to meet them. They sailed on a course for collision. Just before they clashed she threw down the staff, granting herself extra momentum to maneuver. Her body contorted to dodge one spear. The other weapon she scissored with her legs, wrenching it from her opponent's grip. She landed holding the static spear, which was much better than a staff against spring-plated kinetic armor.

Three more Janissars lunged at her. She fell into a tumble, using the cover of their shields to her own advantage. She thrust her spear through a joint of one soldier's armor. A dazzle of sparks erupted from his abdomen. The Janissar roared and brought down the keen edge of his shield. It snapped the haft of her weapon. She kicked his gut, shoving him against the catwalk railing. He scrambled to keep from falling.

A boot smashed into her side. She flipped with the momentum of the blow and landed on her feet, batting away speartips with her gauntleted hands. She found herself retreating. Though not as skilled as a Way Master, Janissars were expert melee fighters. If this battle did not end quickly, she and Montenegro would lose. With a lunge she dropped inside the reach of one spear. She stunned the soldier with her elbow. She pushed his shield to block an incoming attack, then elbowed the man again. He staggered. She crouched and hurled him over her shoulders, into the path of the next Janissar.

Thulann used the stunned man's spear to puncture him, then jabbed the next soldier's throat. As her last opponent circled she dared to glance at Montenegro. The knight's magic sword had sheared corners from his two enemies' shields. One of the Janissars stumbled, clutching a savage chest wound. The other had his hands full parrying a barrage of furious blows. Thulann recognized that Montenegro was using her own techniques, though he interpreted them with his own Britannian idiom. If somehow they survived this mission, she resolved to analyze his style.

Her opponent closed. They swatted each other's spears again and again, until it was unclear who was attacking and who was defending. In the middle of this energetic exchange Thulann seized an opening. She jammed her spear into the Janissar's chest. He yowled and cracked his weapon under her jaw. She reeled. He kicked her chest. She flew back against the catwalk railing. When he charged her she ducked, forcing him to brace against the railing to stop his own inertia.

At that moment a metallic *clang* split the air. Montenegro had chopped through the metal rail. It gave way, hurling the Janissar fifty feet down the hard iron scaffolding. The knight's own opponents lay dead on the catwalk. He patted the Way Master's back. "Come on. They were going in there as reinforcements." He pointed to the door in the riveted wall, from which the flash and thunder of battle emerged.

Thulann felt her chest. Her Jukan armor had held against the static-charged spear, but just barely. Then she caught her breath and chased after her much younger companion. "Montenegro! Stop. Let me go have a look. We do not know what is happening in there. I do not want to rush into a fight if it does not serve our goal here. I am bleeding enough already."

"Hurry! In three minutes I'm coming after you."

She dashed through the entrance. On the other side she lurched into the depths of a steamy shadow. The chamber was larger and more open than most of Braun's Needle. In the glare of lightning and venting flames she immediately recognized the machinery here. There were three large, coppery tanks connected to a huge central bulk of gears and wheels and clicking levers, which was clad in heavy steel armor. Bursts of light sprang from within. This was the storm engine. This was their destination.

It was guarded by three dreadnoughts. A small band engaged the half-mechanical monsters in a hopeless attempt to sabotage the Needle. Thulann spotted Grynholt of Yew strewing lightning and fire around the chamber with terrible, floor-shaking power. The bolts bounced without effect from the armor that encased the storm engine. Pikas of Enclave, wearing his kinetic armor, and a small Meer warrior danced about one dreadnought and peppered it with weapons blows. A Technocrat in a Theorist's robe fired a two-handed static scourge at a human enemy who was shrouded in a wall of steam.

The Way Master was startled by the sheer futility of this action. These agents of the Pact of Four stood no chance against a single dreadnought, much less three of them. Then she looked again and realized why the agents were not dead already. The dreadnoughts could not fight back. When one of the creatures struck, its huge drill-arm rebounded in a cascade of white embers. The agents were unharmed. A pendant around each of their necks pulsed brightly for a few seconds afterward.

Powerful sorcery shielded them. No doubt this was the contribution of the high-ranking Meer contingent of the Pact. Thulann marveled as the agents hammered the dreadnoughts with attack after attack and ignored counterstrikes that would mangle an unprotected warrior. She was still unsure if they could defeat the creatures, but they seemed to be in no real danger themselves. Only the mobility and bulk of the floating dreadnoughts prevented the Pact agents from approaching the storm engine unhindered, as well as the intervention of the lone human defender, who presently emerged from a curtain of steam and drew a heavy, curved sword.

The man was dressed in pneumatic armor. The mechanical suit used cushions of steam to render far more protection than any other mail. Pistons augmented several key joints, granting the wearer enhanced strength. The only drawback was that unless such a suit was meticulously maintained, it was very prone to malfunctioning. And of course, the steam engine that powered it scorched the wearer to such an uncomfortable degree that only a madman might bear the torture.

As it happened, the human who wore the pneumatic armor appeared to be a madman. From the open face of his helmet thrust a wild, wiry beard of silver and black. His leathery skin was a webwork of wrinkles and scars. His bared teeth glinted metallic. His eyes were half-white and terrible. "Gaff figured you'd have sorcery on your side, damn your lubbing bones! You think them baubles will protect you from me? Shanty Lynch ain't no machine! Bring yourselves up here and I'll show you how Whalesfang bites!" He stroked the air with his heavy cutlass. A shimmering glow trailed behind the blade.

Thulann considered the wisdom of lending aid, but that fray would be suicide without a magic pendant. So she watched the surreal scene as the agents charged the strange human, whose accent recalled Buccaneer's Den more than any Logosian region. Lunging dreadnoughts blocked their path but Shavade made it through. She pelted Shanty Lynch with a hail of blows from her crystal sword. He struck back with a single swipe. His curved blade sang as it moved. Shavade cartwheeled out of the way. When she readied herself to counterstrike, she emitted a sudden cry.

Her protective pendant lay at Shanty Lynch's feet. The bearded human cackled as he smashed it with his cutlass. A dreadnought swooped at her and the Meer darted away for her life.

Two bolts of lightning thrust at him, from Rictor and from Grynholt. One of them he blocked with the blade he called Whalesfang. The other bolt crashed against his pneumatic armor. He toppled backward, then sat up and howled with laughter. "Try me again, hey? I've brawled harlots with more punch than that!"

From nowhere Pikas of Enclave appeared. He clattered hit after hit upon the human's armor, but three glowing cuts from Whalesfang drove the assassin back. Lynch barked fiercely, "Bring me some more of that, you murderous viper! I've wanted a slice of your hide since you tried to kill my Raveka! You ain't nothing but a slithering coward!" With an animal roar he smashed his boot atop the second pendant at his feet. Pikas patted his chest, then crouched. A dreadnought flew at him. The unprotected assassin somersaulted away from the storm engine. Shanty Lynch screamed, "Come back, you tender-bellied snake! I'm gonna decorate this place with your innards!"

Thulann grimaced. She had seen enough. When the battle grew noisier she crept back out the door, hoping the mechanical senses of the dreadnoughts would not detect her movement.

On the catwalk, Montenegro had donned one of the Janissar's kite shields. His face burned with impatience. "What's happening in there?"

"The agents of the Pact of Four are inside. They have concocted an interesting strategy. It is failing. They will be dead in a few minutes. Unless you imagine that we will fare better against three dreadnoughts, you and I must concoct a new strategy of our own."

"Are there any other entrances?"

"None through which we might travel without the notice of the dreadnoughts."

He grumbled. "How about the floor? Can we sneak in underneath the storm engine? If we're quick we can destroy it by surprise before the dreadnoughts see us."

"If we were ghosts we might pass through the steel and come up directly beside it. But I saw no grates or ducts in the floor and the panels are riveted into place."

"Starfell can slice rivets. If we work slowly, we might not be heard."

"Perhaps. It would take a day to cut through."

He snorted. "You have some urgent appointment before then? Listen, at the soonest it will be two days before we meet the New Britannian fleet. Let's use that time. Impatience has always been my nemesis. By the Virtues, if this is the end of my life, I'm not going to let it foil me again!"

The prow of the nimble *Menagerie* sliced through the choppy ocean waves. A few rays of dawnlight nudged through the cloud cover. Captain Bawdewyn stood on the deck and faced the pounding wind, the plumage of his hat fluttering. His eyes fixed on the savage tempest that darkened the southern horizon. With narrowed eyelids he mumbled, "You're sure Jatha can get us through that mess?"

Toria joined him at the stem of the ship. Much of her hair was bound under a colorful scarf. The rest frolicked in the breeze. She clutched her shoulders against the wet chill and answered, "He says he can. He's got spells ready to block the worst. He trained in Air Magic under Mistress Aurora herself. There's no one better at it, except maybe some Meer Mystics in Avenosh."

The privateer glanced starboard. "And how about the *Gavrielle* and the *Trinsic Lass*? If he can't protect them, they're dead already. A seasoned crew would have trouble surviving that hurricane. Healed or not, those freed prisoners ain't used to working together."

"We'll all get through," said a purring voice from behind them. Jatha of Ishpur bowed a greeting. "Mistress Aurora created a spell that will let one spellcaster escort as many as four vessels through any kind of storm. I happen to have learned that spell myself."

Bawdewyn pinched his jaw. "Oh, yeah? How many other people know it?"

"There are ten of us in all. Others tried to learn it, but were unable." He grinned. "My humility fails me. I am an excellent student."

The captain muttered, "Uh-huh. But we've got a problem. Ten wizards times four warships means no more than forty of us will get inside to reach the Logosian armada. That ain't even half our fleet. We ain't going to beat Blackthorn that way."

The Meer nodded. "The plan is for those forty to cripple Braun's Needle. Remember, our best sorcerers will be part of that vanguard. Once the Needle is destroyed, the hurricane will dissipate. Then the rest of the fleet can join the battle."

Bawdewyn spat a whistle. "This is more desperate than I thought."

Toria boxed his arm. "You had backbone when I was growing up. What happened?"

"I've still got it," said the captain, "I'm just more protective of it now."

Jatha laughed. "Don't fret about the storm, my friend. Put your faith in the Order of the Magus. Target your arrow at the heart of the hurricane and prepare your men for battle."

"If it's all the same, I'll wait to rendezvous with the fleet."

"They will be here in a few hours," said the wizard.

Toria shook her head. "A day or two, you mean. They hadn't even set sail when we left Britain."

Bawdewyn added, "Unless they've got another spell up their sleeve."

The tall Meer flattened his ears and grinned. In a burst of motion he flung his arms into the air and bellowed a measured incantation. The mainsail snapped taut at the head of a blast of wind. The *Menagerie* pitched forward and groaned.

Captain Bawdewyn's hat lifted from his shaven head. He snatched it from the air and howled, "Stop it, you crazy bastard!"

Jatha bowed again and the wind ceased. The ship tottered back into place. The sailors lobbed unkind words as they regained their positions in the riggings. Their captain reflected the sentiment in his glower. "You trying to sink us before we even get there?"

But Toria's freckled features drew into a smile. "Think of what that will do to a Technocrat airship!"

The Meer gave her a nod. "Blackthorn perverts alchemy with his execrable machines, but he's about to learn what wholesome sorcery can achieve. My caste elders will condemn me for it, but I confess this victory will be worth the chastisement! You've never seen rain like the iron that will fall from the sky. We can fill our barrels and take it all back to Anzo. May it serve him as well as it serves Blackthorn!"

The voice muttered behind Thulann, from a shroud of roiling steam: "I could have killed you and the boy in Crevasse, but I didn't."

The Way Master recognized Pikas's voice. She knew the assassin must be prepared to murder her quickly. He would not have revealed himself otherwise. She remained still, though her body calculated many pathways of reaction. "You are alive. How splendid."

"I let both of you live. You owe me."

"What do I owe you?"

"I need your help. You need mine. You owe me a truce."

She furrowed her brow. "I confess, on board this giant war machine you do seem less of a threat. Very well, I shall listen to your proposition, on one condition. Tell me why you let us live."

"It was too easy. It didn't feel right. I need to beat you fairly and it seemed too . . . professional."

"Fairly? I daresay you are maturing from an assassin to a warrior."

"Assassins are peacetime warriors, when there's little glory in honorable defeat."

"You live in a sad world, Pikas, but we have no time to debate. You are correct. We can both use assistance. Tell me your plan. Perhaps I can shackle my vengeance long enough for us to accomplish our goal."

The atmosphere was an acidic haze of foul, ashy smoke. Montenegro took thin breaths to assuage his nose and throat, which the polluted air had chafed over the course of many hours. His eyes were swollen and red. His flesh was soaked with perspiration so heavy that he wondered if his smell might alert passing enemies, though he knew the ambient reek of soot and grease overpowered all other sensory impressions.

He knelt at the crux of several iron beams. A few feet above him was a steel ceiling, the underside of the floor around the storm engine. In the murk he could barely see each rivet as he gently sawed through it. After an eternity of work, he was finishing the last bolt. The metal panel overhead was nearly ready to move aside. He would rest for a few minutes. Then he and Thulann would sneak into the chamber above. They were going to die there, of course, but he was confident they could do plenty of damage beforehand.

A finger tapped his wrist. At the Way Master's signal he crawled down from his perch and onto a platform below. Thulann leaned close to his ear and said, "Someone is here to assist us. Promise me you will not be rash."

He grimaced. "I told you, I am beyond that."

From the smoke emerged a large Juka in kinetic armor. Four severed Janissar heads dangled from his hand. He tossed them onto the platform, then lifted the face plate of his helmet. Montenegro immediately recognized the kelp-hued features of Pikas of Enclave.

The knight whisked Starfell from its scabbard and plunged it at the assassin's heart. The blade stopped short of penetrating. Pikas clung fast to the end of the sword and struggled to hold the weapon off. Blood squeezed between his fingers, despite his Logosian gauntlets.

Thulann growled, "You agreed not to be rash."

The knight retorted, "This is an action I have thoughtfully

considered for two years. Have you forgotten that you once had a second eye? He is an animal!"

From tight lips Pikas rasped, "If I wanted to kill you, I would have done it when Thulann was relieving herself."

Montenegro sneered. "That was at least two hours ago. You've been watching us that long, but you waited until we were finished cutting the rivets before you showed yourself? You're still a contemptible coward!"

"I'm alive because I'm a survivor. That's how one succeeds in my profession. Knights are never satisfied until they're honorably dead."

Thulann interjected, "Silence! Montenegro, lower your blade and listen to him. Then you may take your revenge, if that is what you wish."

The knight cast her a frown. "Listen to this filth? What about dishonoring my name? Where did your lofty arguments go, old woman?"

"Listen, then judge."

A heavy tension lay between them. Then Montenegro jerked back his weapon. Pikas released the enchanted blade in time to keep his fingers attached.

The assassin flexed his hand and spoke quickly. "These four Janissars were poking around close to here. I bring you their heads as a truce flag. Look, Grynholt is dead. Rictor and Shavade are captured and as good as dead. I don't plan on letting that damned Shanty Lynch keep me from doing what I came here to do! That means we have to work together."

"We don't need you," said the knight.

"The hell you don't! I don't know about you two, but we came here prepared. In Rictor's bag is an Ishpurian crystal that will shut down the hurricane generator. All we have to do is put it inside the machine. What was your plan? Bash the generator until it stops working? You're liable to blow the whole damn Needle apart!"

Montenegro snorted. "It will be an honorable death. Something you're not interested in."

Thulann raised a hand. "You and I act honorably, Montenegro, unbeholden to the Pact of Four. There is no question of honor here. I am only interested in Pikas's sabotage device. The three of us may settle our debts after we undo this mechanical horror. Pikas, tell him your plan."

As the assassin explained his proposal, Montenegro wrestled his growing ire. The plan was viable, though the company was odious. He could not articulate his trepidation beyond a general loathing of Pikas and his deeds. And so he slammed Starfell back into its sheath. "When this is done, Pikas, our blades will reconcile. No more tricks. No more running away. The time has come."

The assassin replied, "On my honor," and followed the comment with a grin that exasperated the knight. Montenegro kept his hand from drawing Starfell again, but only by the narrowest margin.

The hurricane screamed all around them, but the *Menagerie*, the *Gavrielle* and the *Trinsic Lass* pushed through the giant waves without a single crest pounding their decks. Not even the black rain touched the vessels. Aboard Bawdewyn's ship, at a hub of cyclone of light, stood Jatha of Ishpur, commanding the air and sea by means of a strenuous spell. The wizard's blousy shirt and trousers whipped about in a sorcerous fury. His spotted fur and chestnut hair whorled in strange patterns. His voice was lost in the clamorous din.

Not far from him waited Fairfax, gripping a ratline to brace against the lumbering motion of the vessel. His blue eyes did not stray from his friend, who appeared to exert every ounce of strength to maintain the storm-quelling enchantment.

A small figure drew beside him. Toria had strapped herself into an oversize leather hauberk. Her hair was knotted into braids. She took Fairfax's arm, looked out at Jatha and said, "He's brilliant. If he'd had this much power two years ago, the troll king wouldn't have dared to show his face aboveground!"

"Perhaps so, but I am concerned nonetheless. I don't know how long he can hold this pace. When are we going to stop circling the eye of the hurricane and get this battle started?"

"We've lost sight of the Britannian vanguard. Bawdewyn wants to find them again before we attack. We're safe from the Logosian submarines because they can't surface in these waves, but once we hit calm waters we're going to have our hands full. So we have to wait for the other ships."

The ranger furrowed his tanned brow. "The point will be moot if Jatha exhausts himself. Without this spell, the storm alone is all the weapon Blackthorn needs."

"Jatha will hold up. Look at him. He's got fire in his belly. This cause is important to him, strange as that may be. He's a changed man."

Fairfax sighed. "I told him that, but he is wary of my judgment. He is a stubborn oaf."

Toria nodded. "That's why I know he won't fail us. Keep watch over him, anyway. We'll need his magic inside the storm's eye." She stood on her toes and kissed the ranger's cheek. "Watch over yourself, too, hey? I don't want to lose you halfwits."

He grinned and tugged on a braid. "A thousand airships couldn't separate us, little sister. I swear it on the last drop of wine that ever passed through my lips."

It was the sort of casual lie that was inevitable before a battle. Toria was happily thankful for it.

CHAPTER
15

Battle in the Hurricane

By no more than an inch every minute, Thulann and Montenegro nudged the ceiling panel aside. A space slowly opened. When it was large enough to pass through, the two Juka crept into the room above while Montenegro kept silent and waited. Given their prowess at stealth, the knight was unsure if he would ever see them again.

The plan was straightforward. Pikas would make his way to Rictor's bag, which Shanty Lynch had dropped beside the storm engine. From it he would retrieve the magic crystal that was designed to sabotage the machine. Thulann would attempt to administer healing potions to the fallen Shavade and Rictor, so that they might distract the dreadnoughts when the creatures realized what was happening. At the appointed time Montenegro himself would climb onto the storm engine, employ Starfell to cut through the armor and then wait for Pikas to deliver the sabotage crystal.

He did not bother to contemplate what would happen once they succeeded. In Logosia his company of knights was a match for a single dreadnought. Surviving a battle with three of the monsters was not worth the effort of considering. He simply resolved to serve the Virtues during these last remaining minutes.

When he gauged that enough time had passed, he drew a vial from his belt. The potion within was bitter and syrupy. As its magic tingled through him, he watched his body vanish from sight. Invisibility was an outrageously expensive effect, but he had no use for money now.

An old proverb questioned whether all of a man's riches would be worth trading for a few more moments of life. This was Montenegro's answer.

He climbed through the narrow hole formed by the shifted floor panel. The chamber above was a theater of steam and pipes and strobing lights from the mechanics of the giant storm engine. He knelt just a few yards from the thrumming machine. Several yards farther squatted one of the large, copper reagent urns. In its shadow lay three shackled figures. Montenegro recognized Rictor, Shavade and Grynholt. The portly wizard gaped with lifeless features. The Meer Huntress looked unconscious. Brother Rictor's white face was twisted into a scowl as he tried to ignore his brassy-voiced captor.

Shanty Lynch was a stocky man in pneumatic armor. The mechanical mail hissed with every movement. With a boot Lynch nudged his Technocrat captive and said, "Still awake? You want to tell me who your master is in Logos? Ahh, keep it clenched, then. Damn stubborn Theorists. Lector Gaff will make you talk. He's the one who put me here to greet you, hey? He's gonna crack your scheme and no mistake. He's the wiliest man in Logos and ol' Shanty is close behind him." He patted his chestplate. "You killed my Janissars and got past them dreadnoughts, but you ain't no match for me! A lot of folks more dangerous than you have learned that same lesson. Even Anzo is gonna learn. On the way home we'll steer over to the Den and the 'king' will wish he never crossed me!"

Brother Rictor made no response, except to wince when the grizzled man kicked him.

Montenegro observed the old sailor with interest. Raveka had told him about Captain Shanty Lynch, the pirate lord who had feuded with Anzo more than a decade ago. For his trouble he had been shipwrecked on a desolate shore far to the south. The land turned out to be Logosia. The boisterous pirate was welcomed as a curiosity among the Technocrats. Lynch had been Raveka's instructor for much of her life, training her in both the finer and coarser lessons of New Britannian civilization. He was, of course, the ostensible father of Raveka's courtesan identity, Riona Lynch. And he was a trusted advisor of Lector Gaff. Captain Lynch was an anomaly in Technocrat society, a New Britannian outlaw who had won respect through wit and skill and unbound audacity.

Something about him haunted Montenegro. Seeing him in person gave the knight a singular chill.

Of course, the real danger here was not Shanty Lynch but the three dreadnoughts that attended him. The hovering, steel-plated creatures were dispersed around the chamber. One of them nursed the cracks it had received during the battle with Pikas and his cohorts. The other two looked undamaged.

Montenegro knew the monsters would detect him soon. He intended to be in his designated position when that happened. He took a deep breath and started to climb a ladder mounted to the storm engine. Not far above was a small panel that had appeared on the schematic, which he had judged to be the likeliest place to cut through the machine's heavy armor. He calculated how best to make the attack.

When he had almost climbed beside the panel, a loud rumble filled the air. The huge beams of the Needle's skeleton shuddered and croaked. Montenegro held on tightly.

Shanty Lynch glanced up from his captives. "What's this? The battle's already started? Damn your treacherous heart!" He kicked Brother Rictor again. The Technocrat bounced across the floor and groaned. "You warned the Senate, didn't you? Well, it ain't gonna matter! They ain't no match for us. The Needle by itself will be the death of Admiral Duarte!" When the room shook again, the old pirate frowned. He pointed at the nearest dreadnought. "You! Take your metal carcass outside and see if they need any help. The House of the Griffin must be out there. I don't trust them wizards."

The dreadnought complied, floating out through a large doorway. When the creature was gone Montenegro felt incrementally safer. He knew it was an illusion, though, and took care to be quiet as he unsheathed Starfell. He hoped the roar of the battle outside would mask what little noise he made.

The eye of the hurricane quaked with thunderous noise. The vanguard from New Britannia, thirty-three ships in all, clashed with the Technocrat armada in a cataclysm of magic and machines. Giant pillars of flame and water and lightning hurled from the tall British vessels, smashing Logosian craft in the air and on the sea. The Technocrats answered with clouds of acid, curtains of steel missiles and titanic strokes of blinding electricity. Propeller-driven warships raced through the Britannian formations, only to be trapped by sheets of magical ice. When enemy ships converged, the hand-to-hand battles were swift and brutal in favor of the larger British vessels. Husks from both forces blazed atop the waters.

On board the *Menagerie,* Toria clutched the bulwark and observed a particular segment of the combat. Jatha had pointed out a galleon named the *Akalabeth* that carried Mistress Aurora herself. Since the death of Master Gregorio two years earlier, the ancient sorceress was regarded as the most powerful human spellcaster alive. Her magic created a scintillating glow around the four-masted ship. Her sorcery devastated the Technocrat sky fleet. Serpentine whirlwinds swatted the airships like insects, flinging them out of the hurricane's eye and into the raging fury of the storm. The Logosian counterattacks were useless against her sparkling, radiant defenses.

But a nightmarish iron cloud descended from above. Even while it generated the unnatural hurricane, Braun's Needle lowered nearer the surface to bring its own weapons into range. Toria wondered if Mistress Aurora's spells were potent enough to damage the gigantic machine. She was not heartened by the other sorcerers' lightning bolts, which deflected from the Needle's structure and left no discernible scars.

A sudden pitch of the *Menagerie* reminded the minstrel of her own situation. She noted the crew's progress. With the help of the *Trinsic Lass,* Captain Bawdewyn had snared several long chains around a Technocrat submarine that had surfaced to attack. The ironclad craft tried to submerge, but with each attempt Bawdewyn and the *Lass* hoisted it up again.

To his men the tall captain bellowed, "Tack into her, lads! We're closing fast! Heave to those windlasses and we'll land us a steel-bellied fish!"

Toria dashed to a crowd of sailors. They manned three large winches, the chains of which were keeping the submarine above the water. Annis the ocelot watched them from a high ratline. Toria climbed beside the wildcat and shouted down to the privateers:

Heave, me bullies!
Heave ho, me mates!
Blood's in our cups
And bones on our plates!
The cap'n's a lush,
The mate's a sinner!
Let's drink from the vein
And have Blackthorn for dinner!

The sailors cheered her song and shoved the windlasses with renewed energy. Slowly the Technocrat submarine ratcheted toward the *Menagerie*. Armed privateers prepared to board, as well as Fairfax the Ranger, whose bow glinted with multiple fangs.

Annis twitched her striped tail in approval. Hungrily she licked her lips and sniffed the oncoming carnage.

From a cloak of steam Thulann reached out and laid a finger on Brother Rictor's lips. The chained Technocrat startled and looked at her, but kept silent. Recognition passed between them. The Way Master offered him an unsympathetic frown.

Then she worked a lockpick into his shackles. Just as the manacles loosened, a gravelly voice lifted above the rumble of battle and the clang of the storm engine. Shanty Lynch cried out, "Hey, you there!"

Thulann looked up to see the human facing another direction. He drew his enchanted cutlass and charged at a shadow. Pikas of Enclave tumbled into view, parrying the human's strokes. Something gleamed in the assassin's hand.

The two dreadnoughts moved forward, their metal joints clanking and squeaking.

Pikas dodged Shanty Lynch's attacks and kicked the human in the face. The pirate sailed backward. The assassin raised his hand, which held the magic crystal. He scanned the tall storm engine and snarled, "Montenegro!"

A flicker brightened a waft of steam ten feet up the height of the machine. The knight's shape appeared on a ladder. He drew back Starfell and smashed the ebony blade against the machine's armor plating. Sparks blossomed where his blow fell.

Brother Rictor stumbled to his knees a yard from Thulann. She pressed a healing potion into his hands and examined the Huntress named Shavade. The slender Meer was bent at painful angles. The dreadnoughts had nearly killed her. The Way Master knew these potions would not suffice to restore the woman. In her remaining moments Thulann decided to focus on the dreadnoughts that harried her companions.

Before Pikas could throw the sabotage crystal to Montenegro, one of the mechanical giants barreled atop him. The Logosian cursed and sprang away, by inches avoiding the swipe of a steel arm with the girth of a tree trunk. A clockwork longsword buzzed in the assassin's grasp, yet the spinning blades of the weapon barely nicked the dreadnought's iron shell. Pikas broke into a run to escape the steam-breathed monster.

The second dreadnought, wounded from its previous battle, rushed in the direction of Montenegro.

Thulann drew her own blade and searched for a way to distract the creatures. A copper reagent urn was riveted to the floor nearby. With a shriek she rammed her sword against the polished metal. The sound resonated through the pipes in the chamber, but the copper showed only a marginal scratch.

A fierce bellow met her ears. Captain Lynch rushed at her. She parried his glinting cutlass and struck him multiple times, but his pneumatic armor repelled each impact with a loud, searing hiss. She grunted. There was no time for this. Through the haze of steam she carved a sequence of arcs to distract the mad human. When his eyes followed her blade, she kicked his armored wrist. The blow did no real damage, but it loosened his grip on the cutlass. A curl of her sword plucked the weapon from his gauntlet.

She snatched Whalesfang from the sultry air and pirouetted. The enchanted blade crashed against the reagent urn and rent through with a howl of metal. A viscous, boiling liquid oozed out. Thulann leapt away as the substance engulfed Shanty Lynch below the chest. He burst into a gurgling scream. The heavy pneumatic armor prevented him from escaping.

Thulann grimaced. She turned back to face the old pirate. Pushing her game leg, she jumped over the boiling reagent and landed on the ruined copper tank. A powerful stroke from Whalesfang knocked Captain Lynch unconscious. His screams halted. Then he collapsed under the scorching sludge, which pooled thickly around the broken urn.

The dreadnought turned away from Pikas and soared at her instead. She flipped from atop the reagent urn and bounded across the chamber, hoping Montenegro would have an answer for the steel devil that attended him.

*   *   *

Clinging to the ladder, the knight bashed the metal access panel. Starfell chewed enough of a cleft to insert Pikas's sabotage crystal. But Montenegro did not have the crystal. The assassin had been chased away by an angry dreadnought. The second dreadnought now roared atop Montenegro himself. The creature's mechanical arm jutted forward. At the tip was a long drill that smoked and whined.

Montenegro slammed his kite shield against the drill bit and pushed himself out of the way. The maneuver came from his jousting skills. It would only be effective once. He felt the rush of air from the dreadnought's attack and the heat of its churning motor. The drill stank of burning grease. The dense bulk of the monster muffled the ambient din of the room. Its arm drew back for a second attack.

The knight ground his teeth. He could not wait any longer. With a gruff cry he rammed the tip of Starfell through the cleft in the panel.

The storm engine rattled and squealed. Chains and gears destroyed themselves as they grazed Starfell's edge. Something within cracked. Then heavy, loose pieces clamored inside, bashed out the armor plates and blew apart the giant machine. Montenegro felt pain and a sense of flying, but the rest of the world had gone.

From the decks of their tall ships, the sorcerers of New Britannia commanded a host of elements to attack Braun's Needle. In the flurry of spells the sea glowed with unearthly illumination. Lightning and fire and crystal rain and spouts of water and meteors from the sky, all converged on the black machine in a violent, thundering chaos. The wild sorcery obscured the giant iron hulk. Yet the Needle showed no ill effects. Its spire continued to radiate bolts of light, churning the hurricane around the battle. The undaunted war engine drifted downward until it hovered a hundred feet above the white-toothed waves. Then it unloaded gouts of fire and acid and steel missiles on the Britannian ships below. Several of them crumpled like toys under the attack. The Logosian surface ships retreated underneath the shadow of the devastating Needle.

Toria watched in horror as Mistress Aurora and the *Akala-beth* disappeared in the inferno that drooled from the mountainous craft. She could almost make out the glitter of the sorceress's defenses, but the blinding light played tricks on her eyes. She would have asked Jatha's opinion but the Meer was presently engaging an airship that ventured close to their own vessel. The wizard's lightningstrokes battered the floating craft and his wind unbalanced its vanes. Yet the airship did not relent. Jatha battled the will of its crew. If the craft maneuvered overhead, where its weapons could strike, the *Menagerie* would be in immediate danger.

Abruptly the ocean let loose a sigh. Toria could find no other way to characterize the odd, overwhelming change. The hurricane itself seemed to soften and pale.

She realized what had happened. The streams of light had ceased to flow from the spire of Braun's Needle. The horrifying tempest stumbled and weakened. Toria almost spat a cry of joy, except that the Needle's more familiar weapons continued to rain destruction on the New Britannian fleet. At this pace she could see that the end would come soon. Blackthorn's armada would wipe out the vanguard.

The northern horizon revealed signs of the rest of the Britannian fleet. A ribbon of sails approached like a distant cloudbank. Toria could only pray that they would arrive soon enough, though Braun's Needle darkened what little hope she had.

*   *   *

Thulann looked up from the cover of a large iron conduit. Fragments of giant gears littered the sizable chamber. A billow of smoke engulfed the storm engine, or whatever remained of it. The dreadnought that had attacked Montenegro lay shattered on the floor. The knight himself was surely gone, nor could she see Pikas or Rictor. Shavade still lay unconscious on the ground.

By contrast the monster that had pursued Thulann was blackened and dented, and apparently confused for the moment, but had survived the potent explosion. It righted itself and searched for a target again. Thulann kept still, though it was difficult. The creature had grazed her in a few places, leaving deep, throbbing bruises. The force of the explosion made the rest of her body feel as if she had been pummeled. She dared a quick trance to still the insistent pain.

The plume of smoke around the storm engine began to dissipate. Arcs of white light dashed through the murk. Thulann could discern that the machine was not destroyed. Rather an outer layer of mechanics had flown apart. The core of the device was a bundle of pillars or long rods, stretching up through the ceiling, that pulsed with subtle, elusive color. A more modest arrangement of gears was mounted in a filigree around them. Several of the rods looked cracked. They skittered with cascades of energy.

The destroyed machinery must have rotated the beams that had stirred up the hurricane. These rods more resembled a power source. She could not shake the impression that they were not only damaged, but on the verge of causing a second eruption.

Abruptly a small shape darted across the room. The Way

Master recognized Pikas, running with fleet steps despite a nasty limp. The assassin found the hole where Montenegro had cut away the floor panel. He dove through frantically.

The dreadnought whirled around with a clatter and soared after him. Its giant claws tore a larger plate from the floor. The creature chased Pikas out of the room and left behind an eerie quiet.

"Thulann," said a raspy voice.

"Montenegro? You are alive?"

"Take Shavade and go. There isn't much time."

She knelt down and hoisted the unconscious Meer over her shoulder. "Thank the Great Mother! How did you survive?"

"You can thank my last four healing potions and a lucky armored panel. I was thrown clear. The dreadnought wasn't so fortunate."

"Fortune has its favorites. Of that there is no doubt." She arranged Shavade across her shoulders. "I have the Huntress now. Let us hurry before those rods crack apart."

"I have to stay."

"What do you mean?" She stepped closer to the sound of the voice and saw the knight standing beside the storm engine. In his hand was the magic crystal, which he held against the glowing rods. "What purpose does that serve? The machine is not functioning, if you have not noticed."

"The crystal keeps the rods from exploding. It dampens the alchemy, or something like that. Pikas explained it. He saved our lives by doing this."

"You mean he saved his own life!"

"Naturally. And I relieved him. I want this war machine destroyed and I don't trust him to do it. So I advise you to exit the Needle quickly, Thulann, because I'm going to remove the crystal before any more Logosians arrive. I caused this invasion and I shall end it."

The Way Master held her breath and said, "Let me do it. I am old. You are young. It is the natural order."

"Don't argue with me! Venduss still needs you, old woman, no matter what you might think! You have a life in Jukaran. I have nothing left."

"You have Raveka."

"Enough!" bellowed Montenegro. "The dreadnought might come back soon. Go! Live for Venduss!"

Thulann blinked her one eye. "Your grandfather must be proud of you now, as he watches from beyond." Then she held tightly to the Meer and turned away, driven by thoughts of Jukaran.

Montenegro watched her rush from the chamber, hauling the limp body of Shavade. He gave her several minutes, then pulled the crystal from the shivering rods. With a shriek the metal wheels started to turn. Streams of unbound energy coursed through the rods and gearwork. Steel cracked and shuddered as uncontrolled pressures gathered inside.

Braun's Needle was doomed. He nodded with satisfaction.

Before embarking on this final assault, he and Thulann had gauged a route to the nearest launching bay. If any chance remained of evacuation, he would find it there. He charged from the room and headed along the path, down winding catwalks and shivering ladders. The gigantic war machine thumped and clanged all around him.

He burst into a windy launch bay. The Logosians in the area must have fled already, as the wide chamber was almost empty. Only a single flying carriage perched near the whistling exit. The knight hoped it was functional. He threw open its door and shoved the agitant lever, raising the carriage from the floor. Then he climbed inside. The vehicle drifted down the gentle slope of the launch bay and spilled into the gusty air beyond. From the dizzying height it fluttered downward at a slow pace, though the unchecked steering vanes caused it to twirl and rock. After a moment the knight gained control and steadied the cabin.

Then the world shook in a deafening explosion.

Montenegro stood and gazed through the window in the ceiling. Braun's Needle erupted into an inferno. The enormous, hovering nightmare of steel began to list and fragment and plummet. Giant scraps of rent metal smashed into the sea. The Logosian ships that had gathered beneath it vanished in a downpour of iron and flames.

Montenegro's air carriage drifted lazily away from the destruction, nudged by the stirring wind.

Something cold pressed against his throat. It was the blade of a small knife, held by a person behind him. He smelled a tangy whiff of poison. Montenegro thrust out his jaw and growled, "Brother Rictor."

The Technocrat answered in his familiar, icy voice. "We meant to disable the Needle, not destroy it. This is most inconvenient."

"Yet it makes a pretty flame, doesn't it? For those of us who appreciate such extravagance, anyway."

"Don't be so flippant, Montenegro. Your final words ought to carry more weight than that."

"I was never intended to survive this battle, was I? Even if I had joined you from the start."

"There's no need to be offended. You had no place in our arrangements. Honor and initiative are a dangerous combination."

"So they are," answered the knight, then moved with blinding quickness. He batted Rictor's blade hand away and elbowed the man in the nose, whirling around to face the Technocrat. Starfell rang as it kissed Rictor's throat, forcing him against the back wall of the carriage. Montenegro held up the man's captured knife. "I don't like poison, Rictor."

"Then throw it away," grumbled the Technocrat. Red streaked from his nose. His face was bruised from the day's ordeal. "Before you kill me, think about your situation. Lord Gideon wants you locked up. The House of the Lion has a price on your head. The army rejects you. The Silver Serpents reject you. You are a disgrace to your lineage. Your life in New Britannia is over."

Montenegro darkened his tone. "I have had better months, to be sure. What is your point?"

"The Pact of Four has the power to help you. You need us."

"So now you want to help me instead of murdering me? Why the sudden change?"

Rictor grimaced at the sword creasing his throat. "You make a persuasive argument."

The knight laughed sourly. "You are devious, and yet you are honest! I find you to be an engaging paradox. But your alliance trades carnage for personal gain. The Pact of Four is a blight on Sosaria. You rape the honorable arts of warfare. I would rather die than accept your help." He took a deep breath. Something shifted inside him. "In fact, that's exactly what I intend to do. And I do need you for that, Rictor."

He flung the poisoned knife at the Technocrat. It stuck in the man's lightly-armored chest. Rictor's eyes bulged in terror.

Montenegro glowered. "Try not to be offended. Remember, you are simply part of a larger Machine."

The Technocrat reached for the antidote in his pocket. Montenegro slammed a boot against his wrist and pinned it.

Then the poison seized Rictor's gaunt frame. The toxin was the same one that had nearly killed Fairfax outside of General Nathaniel's estate. Rictor's skin dried and cracked. His flesh contracted against bone. His muscles battled one another until his skeleton cracked and bent.

The bloody thing that collapsed on the floor of the carriage was hardly recognizable as human. No identity could possibly be affixed to it. Montenegro counted on that.

Outside, Braun's Needle poured smoke and orange flames into the cloudy ocean sky. Under the dazzling, deafening spectacle, the air carriage floated down to the water's surface. Turning away from the sight, Montenegro began to undress. His body was grateful to be free of armor. He felt a tremendous weight lifted. He welcomed the relief. The day had been a strenuous one and his struggles had only begun.

CHAPTER
16

Homeward

The destruction of Braun's Needle trumpeted the end of the fiery battle. Great horns yowled from the remaining Logosian vessels. The armored air- and seacraft hurried south toward their homeland. As the last wisps of the hurricane died away, the bulk of the New Britannian fleet crowded the northern horizon and hastened the retreat of the vanquished Technocrats.

Stalks of smoke lifted into the air. Cheers of victory skittered across the debris-strewn ocean.

Thulann sat on the bulwark of the tall ship that had rescued her. The unconscious Shavade was shackled belowdecks. The haggard sailors of the *Trinsic Lass* patrolled the scene of the conflict, eager to scavenge whatever Logosian scraps they could catch in their hungry nets. The air carriage in which the Way Master had escaped was already stowed in the *Lass*'s hold. A second one was being lowered through the cargo hatch.

In a pile before her lay spoils the sailors had retrieved from within.

They had described to her the corpse upon which they found the expensive armor and weapons. It was nothing more than a jumble of bones and desiccated flesh. Thulann remembered that Brother Rictor's poisons created such an effect, according to Montenegro's account.

The sailors had dumped the corpse overboard before Thulann knew what was happening. Of course she forbade them from dividing the goods among themselves. When she intervened they had been arguing over the single piece of evidence that convinced her of the identity of the dead man.

It was the black sword named Starfell. Thulann knew Montenegro would die before parting with it.

He had escaped the Needle after all, only to be murdered by the Pact of Four. His demise bore a ruthless irony, though the Way Master preferred not to dwell on it. Montenegro had truly died as he lived. It was what he wanted. She could wish revenge upon Rictor and Pikas and all of the Pact leaders, but wishing never slew an enemy or fed a hungry mouth. And if every dead soldier asked for revenge, wars would never see end.

She picked through the heap of his belongings. The armor was marginally damaged. A few potions clinked in his pouch. Little else remained of the knight's gear, however, but for the curious exception of a folded, sealed note. The name Aria was jotted upon it in hasty but ornate letters. The paper was fresh, unwrinkled. Montenegro must have written it inside the air carriage, just before Rictor had killed him.

She thought of Montenegro's false cousin, the Technocrat spy. Raveka, he had called her. Thulann imagined that *Sister* Raveka was closer to the truth.

The Way Master decided to hand over the knight's belongings to her personally.

A feeling of disquiet made her shiver. She expected some

grief for Montenegro, but the haunting sensation felt more immediate. She spotted a sailor working nearby, an emaciated man masked by a heavy beard. In coarse tones he chanted a gentle tune:

> *Zephyr spirit, sing my song*
> *Above the lands you roam,*
> *For one who loves me travels on*
> *While I am going home.*

She bolted to her feet and grabbed the sailor's wrist. When he began to struggle she locked his arm in an unbreakable hold. With a seething glare she barked at his face, "Where did you hear that song?"

The man fought back a panic. "It was the girl! The girl who rescued us from Anzo!"

"What girl?"

"They call her Tiny Tori! She's with Captain Bawdewyn on board the *Menagerie!*" With his free hand he motioned toward a familiar barquentine. The large ship danced on the waves several hundred yards away.

Thulann released the seaman's arm. "How do I get there? Find me a boat to get to the *Menagerie!*" To the gathering sailors she shouted, "The man who helps me shall keep this blade as his reward!" She unsheathed her fine Jukan sword, a gift from Turlogan, and slammed it into the bulwark. The edge stuck. A short brawl ensued as the sailors fought to reach her, but the Way Master got what she wanted. A few minutes later she was riding a small boat on a course for the battle-scarred *Menagerie*. Montenegro's possessions were bundled beside her. The unconscious Shavade was bound at her feet.

Though every inch of her sore body complained, she scrambled aboard the barquentine without waiting for a ladder. The sudden appearance of a Jukan warrior caused alarm among the privateers, but Thulann ignored them. She scanned the deck. Near the forecastle sat two humans on either side of a Meer. Jatha of Ishpur looked worn from the fight. Fairfax the Ranger was handing him a drink.

Toria held the wizard's hand and leaned against his shoulder. The old woman's heart struck like lightning. She crept behind the three companions. Her voice quavered as she called out, "You have been neglecting your duties to me, child! But I am inclined to forgive you this once."

The red-braided minstrel swiveled around in disbelief. Her sea-green eyes sparkled with tears.

Thulann opened her long arms as the girl ran into them. She squeezed Toria's body, smelled her hair and listened to the flutter of her breath. These things were all that Thulann could have wanted.

Raveka sat alone in Lord Gideon's cluttered office. The satin of her new dress whispered. She stopped herself from fidgeting. Her ears worked to follow the tap of footsteps outside the door. The person in the corridor walked past with a servant's quiet. After a moment they were gone.

When Raveka was certain she would not be interrupted, she removed a fold of paper from her pocket. It was addressed *For the Royal Senate* in a commoner's hand. It bore no seal. She had removed it from a locked drawer in the nobleman's desk.

She scanned the note with rising interest. It was written by Toria, the young thief who served Thulann of Garron. In brief, the girl explained a secret plot to sabotage the Logosian armada. Technocrat insiders had devised a plan to disable Braun's Needle.

Chief among the Technocrat conspirators was Lector Sartorius himself, aided by the Meer named Chamberlain Kavah.

Raveka returned the note and locked the desk drawer. Her mind was awhirl. If Blackthorn's Chosen was himself a traitor to Logos, and Kavah was his accomplice, then the war was truly lost. The Pact of Four would succeed in its goals. Warlord Bahrok would rampage across Logosia.

She sat down in a high-backed chair. Her fingers locked around the arms, as if she fought the urge to leave. More than anything her instincts commanded her to deliver this information to Lector Gaff. Only he could stop Sartorius. But Gaff had promised to kill her if she did not assassinate Montenegro. Raveka could never go back.

Perhaps Toria's information was wrong. She was only a thief, after all. It was outlandish to believe that Blackthorn's Chosen would sabotage his own war effort.

The door swung open. Raveka flinched. She had not heard anyone approaching. When Lord Gideon entered she rose and took his hands, hiding the conflict from her expression.

The nobleman stretched a smile across his broad jaw. "I have splendid news, my lady! The House of the Griffin has just received word from Mistress Aurora, who is still at sea. The battle is over. The Technocrats have been repelled!"

Her heart sank, though she returned a faint echo of his smile. "Then we're safe. You did it, Gideon."

"It was Admiral Duarte and the Order of the Magus who

fashioned the miracle. And I suspect General Nathaniel's agents had a hand in defeating Braun's Needle. We shall find out soon enough." When he glanced over her face, his smile faded. "Aria, I am sorry. There is still no news of your cousin. Now that the danger is over, I'll spare no resources from the search. We'll find him. I promise you he'll be treated fairly."

She squeezed his hands. "Thank you, my lord. I'm sorry to be such a burden in these dangerous hours. It's just that I have no one else to turn to."

It was almost the truth. The nobleman was her best hope to redeem Montenegro, though she suspected General Nathaniel could solve many of her problems once she persuaded him to speak candidly. Already she had calculated her best approach to the officer. Nathaniel posed a more difficult challenge, of course, being a married man. But Raveka was prepared for the challenge.

Lord Gideon kissed her knuckle and smiled. "Dispel your worries, my dear. I shall look after you now. I give you my word."

For a brief time Thulann and Toria sat on the deck of the *Menagerie*, trading accounts of the last two weeks. The girl did not hide her surprise at the weakened, disfigured condition the ordeal had imposed upon the Way Master, but neither did she shrink from assisting Thulann in every way she could. Her attention nursed a warm feeling inside the old Juka.

Toria's smile broadened when she heard of Warlord Bahrok's defeat in the Black Duel. At the news that Venduss still lived, however, the minstrel froze. She looked as if buried emotions might erupt from her freckled skin. But she offered no deliberate reaction, except finally to nod and turn away.

Thulann stroked the girl's back. "Venduss mourns you. You have stolen a part of him, but he faces the loss bravely. He meets his destiny as a stronger man."

"So he's leading the troops into Akar, hey? You must be proud of him."

"He has far to go yet. He is excellent as a warrior but not as a soldier. My time as his teacher may have ended, but as an advisor I shall not rest until he is a formidable chieftain. He will long for the days when his cruelest punishment was nothing more than the physical exhaustion I visited on him. The Technocrats and the other chieftains shall not be so kind."

Toria paused before murmuring, "And what about his marriage? Is he ready for it now that he thinks I'm dead?"

Thulann closed her eye. "There will be time for such matters after Akar. Only then can he bear that burden."

A thought brushed through the Juka's mind. She raised her hand to catch the attention of Captain Bawdewyn. The privateer stood nearby, scanning the waves for more Logosian salvage. He squinted at her and trotted closer. A sandy-furred coyote padded alongside him, licking blood-stains from its muzzle.

The old Juka said, "Captain, I need an estimate from you. How many airships do you think sailed with the Technocrat armada?"

The tall man shrugged. "Three dozen, I'd say. Mistress Aurora probably cut that number in half."

Thulann clenched her fists. "As I suspected. That is far less than my calculation. The Logosians must have changed their plans. Captain Bawdewyn, can I persuade you to transport me to Jukaran? I have urgent business there."

"I'm sorry, my lady. I gave Mister Chase my word. I've got to take this salvage back to the Den. Besides, this poor tub needs careening before she's going anywhere else but home. Blackthorn left some nasty teeth marks in her."

She pursed her lips. "Then be so kind as to help me find one of these ships that can take me to Jamark. I need to leave without delay."

The captain nodded as he stepped away. "I'll see what I can do." The coyote eyed her warily as he followed his long-legged master.

Toria touched the old woman's knee. "What's the matter? Why must you go so soon?"

"Because I am suspicious of foul play. The Technocrats were supposed to bring thirty airships from Akar. The armada was short that number. Perhaps I am easily frightened, but I suspect this might be Bahrok's doing. No treachery is beneath him. He may well have warned Lector Sartorius not to leave Akar undefended."

"Why would he do that?"

"To strike at Clan Kumar. If Turlogan requires assistance to capture Akar, then Bahrok steals the glory. It would be marvelous currency to buy the support of the other clans."

The minstrel grumbled, "You should have killed that bastard."

The Way Master lifted her chin. "It was an honorable duel, not an act of punishment. Swallow that anger, child. You must think clearly. You have an important decision to make. I want you to return to my service. Come back with me to Jukaran."

Toria looked at the water-strewn deck and did not reply.

Thulann cupped the girl's shoulder. "I shall understand if you refuse. Jukaran may be an awkward place for you. Venduss must walk his own path and we must not impede him. And I know you miss your homeland terribly. But Toria, I shall miss you if you stay here. In two years I have come to rely on you, despite your occasional mistakes."

A brightness lit Toria's face, though she remained hesitant. "I . . . don't fit in over there. I'm just a thief, remember?"

The Way Master jabbed her with a cold stare. "You are no thief. You are a skilled spy and a strong woman. And I am old, Toria. I need your service. So does Garron. You are important."

The girl tugged on a long, red braid. Her eyes searched the riggings of the *Menagerie*, as if the sails might pluck an answer from the wind.

Captain Bawdewyn's stateroom choked with the scent of cloves. Dishes of incense whispered smoke in every corner. The air was a pale haze. Dressed in a clean, white shirt, Fairfax knelt beside the bunk. A thin, green snake lolled across his shoulders. Swaddled in lush furs before him lay a small, unmoving figure.

Shavade of Arjun had not yet regained consciousness. Though she had been very close to death, healers had mended the worst of her injuries. Sleep would usher a more complete recovery. Her soft-coated features were delicate and serene.

Her wrists and ankles were bound.

Standing behind Fairfax, Jatha paid the Meer no attention. Instead he held a fist-size object up to the light of the window. The large, bulbous insect was lashed with twine to a wooden handle. The Huntress's Living Weapon looked unreservedly nasty. Its many stingers protracted when the wizard held it close, causing Jatha's gut to ache at the memory of their venom. He returned the creature to the bag that held the rest of her belongings.

"You're going to scare her if she wakes up," he commented to his rapt companion. "You should get rid of that snake."

"I can't. It is one of the captain's pets. If I turn it loose it will crawl beside her. Snakes make poor company in bed."

The magician snickered. "Do you imagine you're any better? Already you're suffocating her with this distinctly intrusive smoke."

"She shall not awake to the reek of the ocean."

"If you have some delusion that she might wake up with a cheerful disposition, I propose that you think back on the first time we met her. I have seen goblins more mannerly than that."

"I do not seek your approval."

"Nor will she seek yours."

The ranger snapped, "Why must you nettle me? You know I'm hung on a line here!"

"Because Toria says Shavade is in league with Chamberlain Kavah," answered Jatha, "so Kavah must be the one who stole forbidden spells from the Matriarchs. You don't understand the gravity of that crime, my friend. Some sorcery is too dangerous to use. Not long ago the old Lore Council tampered with the wrong powers and unleashed the Cataclysm itself. Perhaps I'm being callused, but if Shavade serves that cause I shall find it difficult to call her my chum."

"What would you have me do? Did I choose this curse of infatuation? I am a prisoner inside her!" He leaned closer to the unconscious Meer. "Just look at her. If all of your women are so excruciatingly beautiful, it is no wonder that men go mad enough to tear the world apart."

From the open door a third voice said, "You have always been a madman, Fairfax, but until now you were rarely monotonous." Toria giggled as she stepped into the room. "Besides, I can't approve of your infatuation. You gave Shavade my bed."

Jatha grinned. "At last, I have an ally! Rescue me, Toria! Take me back to Anzo's dungeon, where I shall be free of this misery."

The ranger sneered. "And I shall pay for his passage! Finally he discovered a pit that's blacker and fouler than his own heart, though only just so."

Toria stepped behind the crouching Fairfax and gave him a hug, then nuzzled the little snake's head. A doleful sigh poured from her lips. "I'm in a bad way, my friends. I need your advice."

The wizard crossed his arms. "Thulann wants you to go back, doesn't she?"

"I don't want to leave home again, but I don't want to leave her alone, either."

"And you don't want to face Venduss again," added Jatha. "That is the soul of the dilemma, unless I am blind."

She said nothing. Fairfax took a deep breath, stood and wrapped her in his arms. "Toria, listen to me. I have traveled the breadth and depth of this continent with my mangy, heartless clod of a companion. We have been nothing but drunken fools for longer than I can remember. Our skulls are thick from scars and intemperance. But despite Jatha's sometimes misguided sensibilities, there is one mistake we have never made and shall never make. We have never turned away from the call of our hearts. And if we catch you dallying with that mistake, we shall be forced to set things straight. See here, we've already got one beautiful goddess tied up in our custody. There's room beside her to squeeze you in."

Jatha laughed, "He's telling you to get your bum to Jukaran and solve this business with Venduss. Don't run away from it. You rescued Bawdewyn. Now go rescue yourself."

She nestled between them with a warm smile. "I'm going to miss the two of you. Try to get along without me, hey? If you kill each other before I come back, I'll be very upset."

"We've seen you upset," said the Meer. "We may be foolhardy, but we know our limits."

In the fog of overthick incense they laughed as the *Menagerie* rocked around them.

In the foyer of her townhouse, Raveka stared at the heap of armor on the side table. A Britannian soldier laid a black longsword across it, while another arranged several pouches nearby. The various fabrics looked slightly damp. The collection gave off a salty, ocean smell.

Lord Gideon clung to her pale hands. His face was drawn with sadness. "I am sorry, my dear. Word of his passing came less than an hour ago. I would not allow anyone but myself to deliver the news, though it devastates me to see you in pain. I never intended for him to die."

Her mouth became dry. "How did it happen?"

"Technocrat poison, the cowards. They could not defeat him honorably."

She pulled her hands free and lifted Starfell. The impossibly small weight confirmed its authenticity. Her eyes began to mist. "You're certain it was he?"

"Thulann of Garron herself found the body. She left for Jukaran without returning to Britain, else I would have brought her to meet you in person. There is no word more reliable than hers."

"I see." She returned the sword to its place on the heap. It occurred to her that Lady Aria should be weeping, but Raveka did not dare to open that floodgate. Instead she selected a sealed note from one of the pouches. Her name was written on it in Montenegro's script.

She popped open the wax seal. A single glyph perched in the center of the page.

Beza rhem.

Quickly she folded it back.

Lord Gideon peered into her brown, feather-shaped eyes. "I'm going to take care of you, Aria. You're welcome as a guest in my manor if you don't want to be alone. You must tell me if there's anything else I can do."

She looked away from him. "Please, Gideon. Leave me. I want to be by myself for a while."

"Of course." He reluctantly stepped toward the door. "The sword belongs to Lady Valente, but I'll leave it with you for now. Send for me at any time, my dear. I shall not sleep."

As he walked outside she called over her shoulder, "Gideon! Did you see the body?"

"No. I fear the poison left little behind. He was given a burial at sea."

A tear rolled down her nose. She forced herself not to smile. "Thank you. Good night."

The front door clicked shut. Raveka was alone. She snatched up Starfell and pressed the cold blade to her cheek. The smoothness of it comforted her.

From the doorway to an adjacent parlor a deep voice remarked, "I never imagined Lord Gideon could be so obsequious. It is unseemly."

She cast down the sword and ran to the dark figure in the parlor door. Montenegro embraced her tightly. For a long while they remained in each other's arms.

"You're wet," she said finally.

"I barely salvaged a carriole from a sinking gunboat. It was damaged. I spent the last few hours rowing. My dear, I shall not be sad if I never see the ocean again."

"And Braun's Needle? Was that your doing?"

"Myself and Thulann and Pikas of Enclave. I'll explain in due course. It is a long, tiring story and we haven't much time. I need you to write a note to Lord Gideon. Tell him you have to travel to Coventine to settle your affairs. You realize, of course, that you shall inherit my manor in Cove."

"That is not practical. What will happen when you come back?"

He smirked. "Gather what you need for a long journey. We're setting sail tonight."

"Setting sail! I have Lord Gideon in my hand. He has fallen for me. I cannot leave. Gideon is your only hope for redemption."

"I rely on no one but myself for redemption. But you are in a position to help me in that quest. You must come."

She creased her lips and sighed. "Then you have to trust me again."

Montenegro furrowed his fingers through the back of her hair. "I trusted you once because we pursued the same goal. When our goals conflicted, that trust could not survive. But we have a common enemy again—the Pact of Four. We both want to stop them. So let's work on trust once more, from the beginning. Shall we?"

Raveka gave him a kiss and said, "You always break my expectations."

"And you challenge mine. A few days ago you proved me a hypocrite. I intend to rectify that." He glanced away and chuckled. "Prepare yourself. We have a long journey ahead, and believe me when I say it shall be much harder for me than it shall be for you."

The morning sky was overcast in shades of mother-of-pearl. The craggy sea danced underneath. Thulann sat on the deck of a three-masted pinnace and observed the approach of a distant, undulating shore. The cliffs of Logosia lay ahead. Sawtooth mountains blackened in the grey light.

She had requested that the New Britannian ship take her to the coastline west of the Technocrat city of Akar. By her estimates Turlogan's battle must be well under way. She was proven correct by the haze of smoke that clouded the far side of the mountains. She hoped that Blackthorn's forces were the ones being burned and not the troops of Clan Kumar.

If all went well, she might be present for Turlogan's victory. The joy on his face would be paradise. Venduss, of course, would meet his glory with awkward pride. Thulann might be forced to scold him for it. He would scowl but remember the lesson.

Such moments were fleeting, and yet they comprised life's greatest rewards, more than any victory in battle. Such moments were worth living for. And they were worth dying for. Neither Bahrok nor Blackthorn nor her own weathered body would keep the Way Master from enjoying them. When her heart stopped beating, she would let go of life; but until that day she would hold it tightly in her arms. It was the sum of her wealth. She would not trade it for anything, even to be young again.

Behind her on the deck sat Toria, cross-legged, wearing an oversize shirt. The human girl was braiding Thulann's ghostly-white hair. The old Juka sensed anxiety in the motions of Toria's fingers, which increased as the shoreline drew nearer. The minstrel had her own challenges ahead. Yet when she sang her voice was as mellow and smoky as ever, and lush as the endless waters:

> Of all the winds o'er sea and foam,
> The warmest is the one blowing home.

The wind that brushed Thulann's face was quite warm. She closed her one eye and indulged the sensation, before they arrived at the shore.

Logos was a dreamscape of iron and grease. The floating city was a single machine with a million components, churning like a clock in the sky. Lanes and alleys threaded among steely, gear-driven tableaus, the works of master engineers wrought in cogs and axles and proud, ashy smokestacks. Wheels spun wildly. Oil and soot peppered the air. Venting grates exhaled sultry breath. Copper pipes sang in their work. The city murmured in the smoky language of industry, thrumming and clanking in the diligent custody of the Technocrats.

Evening swept quickly through that soot-darkened world. The pale sky yielded to the flames and lanterns of the Logosians. Fumes dangled heavily in the air. Nighttime in Logos turned like a foul mood.

Beside the roaring walls of a foundry, in a cascade of twisting, animated shadows, waited the leader of the Order of Mathematicians in black, stoic silence. His yawning cowl revealed only an expressionless mouth, bearded by tattoos. Other figures stood around him. Their silhouettes were sharpened by the armor they wore and the weapons they carried.

Lector Gaff watched a woman approach. Raveka was clad in New Britannian clothes of flimsy construction and impractical design. Gusts of steam billowed her skirt. She was an apparition in the web of shadows.

She knelt before the lector without meeting his gaze. A chant of greeting poured from her lips, though he did not return its answer. Her brown eyes fluttered closed. "Your Excellency, thank you for meeting me under such unusual conditions. You will see the need presently."

Gaff's mouth curled into a frown. "Sister Raveka, I am saddened by your return. Your mission to New Britannia was an abysmal disappointment. Lector Braun's Needle was destroyed, causing the defeat of the armada, and it is said that the knight Montenegro himself participated in the sabotage. I appreciate that you sent me the schematic, but the gesture is now moot. Montenegro still lives. You have failed." His voice grew icy. "I fear your retirement is at hand."

Raveka glanced up as the soldiers around Lector Gaff

inched closer. Then she looked down again. "With respect, Your Excellency, the New Britannians were organizing a funeral for Montenegro as I left."

The soldiers halted. Gaff grunted, "Were they indeed? And did you yourself arrange Montenegro's murder?"

"No."

"Then you have not proven your loyalty to the Order. It is a shame, Sister Raveka, to waste your talents. Yet we had an understanding, you and I. Your emotions toward Montenegro have brought your career to its close."

The Logosian soldiers lifted their weapons. Mechanical blades whirred to clockwork life. But the soldiers reacted not to the words of Lector Gaff but to the appearance of a man cloaked in New Britannian fashion. Plate armor glinted in the dark. Montenegro stood proudly as he drew forth a longsword hammered from ordinary Minoc steel.

Sister Raveka caught the lector's eyes. "I confess I have not secured my feelings in this affair. However, my work has borne fruit that Your Excellency might consider as a step toward atonement for my weakness."

The knight's face passed through a flicker of light. In an ominous tone he said, "Lector Gaff, I believe you will want to call back your men and listen to what I have to say. The alternative could prove unbecoming."

The older Technocrat stiffened his posture. "This is unexpected. I am impressed, Sister, that you were able to bring him here without my knowledge."

"Thank you, Your Excellency," murmured Raveka.

Montenegro shook his head. "Technocrats. Interminably formal. Call back your men, Gaff, or this might turn informal very quickly."

The lector waved a hand. The Logosian soldiers stepped

away into the shadows. When the knight sheathed his sword the Technocrat commented, "I am intrigued by your presence here, Montenegro. Is this a defection? Do you expect Logos to embrace you?"

The knight hardened his gaze. "Let's be clear about this meeting. You and I are enemies. I shall always fight to keep your troops from harming my people. However, according to Raveka we have a common desire: to avoid needless bloodshed. And there is another force at work that plays us against one another. The Pact of Four is our mutual enemy. I have come here to devise a plan to get rid of them. You can take care of your traitors, I can take care of mine, and then we can stop this war and go home."

Lector Gaff pursed his lips and looked down at Raveka. "You know the identity of the traitors?"

She recited a short mathematical verse, the meaning of which seemed clear to Gaff: *Lector Sartorius*. His mouth twitched. His perfect dispassion faltered for an instant.

"I see. A most compelling discovery, Sister."

"I brought it to you at once, Your Excellency."

Montenegro stepped behind Raveka, who was still kneeling. "Lector Gaff, I propose a collaboration to bring down the Pact of Four. You have my word I shall act in good trust. My only condition is that no harm comes to Raveka. If she is threatened, I shall kill you myself. Is that understood?"

The Technocrat stared at Raveka. "Your skills remain as formidable as I dared to wish. It is a dangerous game you play, and yet a potentially productive one. I desire to hear more."

The young woman remained on her knees, though her

chin lifted with growing confidence. "Then my career is not at an end?"

Lector Gaff's expression fell stoic again. *"Beza rhem."*

She rose, bowed her head and blinked slowly. It was as close to an overt smile as she might come in the presence of her mentor.

Behind her Montenegro stepped close. In her ear he softly rumbled, "You are still my lady. I shall not lose you to the Order again."

"Not now," she whispered so that only he would hear.

"Precisely now," he replied.

"You know my heart."

He sighed gruffly, then stepped forward. The Logosian soldiers tensed, but he gave them no heed. "Lector Gaff, time is a weapon against us. We must begin tonight. I know enough about the mechanisms of Britannian intelligence to gain any information we need. Let us calculate how best to use it."

The tall Technocrat nodded slowly. "So we shall. And yet, Montenegro, I am dubious of your sincerity. Are you not famously loyal to New Britannia? Do you not faithfully uphold the Virtues of the so-called 'Lost King?'"

His grey eyes narrowed, though they did not darken. Instead they lit with a starry glimmer. "I live to serve the Virtues. I shall restore them to New Britannia even if I must bring down all of General Nathaniel's army to do it."

Lector Gaff pressed his palms together and bowed. "Then let us retire to my chambers and construct our plans. They must be rigorous. The war may well turn on this moment. We must ensure that the final result benefits us all."

Sir Gabriel grumbled, "I shall not lose again. Not this time."

He followed the Technocrats into the pungent shadows. The massive, steam-choked technology that animated Logos gave him no worry at all. Wheel and gears and machinations had always churned about him. The time was long past for a few of them to spin his way.

ABOUT THE AUTHOR

A second generation writer and SF fan, Austen Andrews spends his daylight hours as a computer programmer in Austin, Texas. At night he transforms into an author, cartoonist and father. He dreams in the colors of horror, fantasy and mad, unbridled science.